I0634041

The Mage's Limits

Book Two in the Mages of Martir

by Timothy L. Cerepaka

An Annulus Publishing Book

Annulus Publishing, Cherokee, Texas, 2015

Published by Annulus Publishing

Author: Timothy L. Cerepaka

Formatting by Timothy L. Cerepaka

Contact: timothy@timothylcerepaka.com

Cover design by Elaina Lee of For the Muse Design
(http://www.forthemusedesign.com/)

ISBN-13: 978-0692437094

ISBN-10: 0692437096

Acknowledgments

I would like to thank my uncle, James Wilhite, for helping me get this manuscript into publishable shape. I'd also like to thank the rest of my family for supporting me while I wrote this novel. You guys rock.

Chapter One

When Aorja Kitano awoke in her prison cell, she did a quick check of her body to make sure that her fellow prisoners hadn't tried to rape her in her sleep. Considering her privates felt in order, she supposed she had only been paranoid, even irrational. It wasn't like the other prisoners of Rock Isle had the guts to so much as touch her. Not after what she did to that disgusting Vicrun her first week in the prison, anyway.

Sitting up on her cot, Aorja yawned widely as she looked at her cell. It wasn't much, especially in comparison to her old room back in North Academy. The walls were made of old gray rock, slightly damp thanks to the ever-present sea mist that covered Rock Isle like a veil. On the wall opposite her was a series of scratches that acted as a simple calendar that let her know how many days and months she had been here. Her cell door was open, but it almost always was, seeing as that Vicrun fellow she had killed had torn the old door off during her first week here. She had tried to repair it, but Aorja had never been very good at etimancy and had been unable to convince the guards to repair it.

Again, not like the other prisoners would think of even trying to gut me in my sleep, Aorja thought, a smile crossing her lips at the thought. *They remember Vicrun.*

1

And Tascum. And Ohmak. They all may be a bunch of the world's worst murderers, rapists, thieves, blasphemers, and general thugs, but they have enough common sense to know that they shouldn't mess with people like me, at least if they want to live a full, long life.

A scream of pain, followed by a loud *thud*, didn't even make Aorja flinch. She was used to waking up to the noise of prisoners fighting each other. Sometimes, the fight ended in a draw and both prisoners lived; other times, one of them would kill the other in cold blood.

And sometimes, Aorja would awake to the sound of the prisoners violating each other. That was always disturbing, but Aorja was of the opinion that as long as they weren't touching her or looking at her lustily, they could do what they wished to each other.

It's not like I even want to be here, Aorja thought, feeling her hair, which used to be long and beautiful, but was now short and grimy after going so long without a proper bath. *But those guards are way too good at their job. Last time someone tried to escape Rock Isle ... oh, those guards are even more merciless than me.*

For some reason, Aorja giggled. Perhaps it was because she genuinely loathed her fellow prisoners, so anytime the guards mistreated them, it was like free entertainment for her. Sometimes, she would even frame a prisoner she particularly disliked for doing something that she did just to get him or her punished. That was always fun.

But as fun as it was, Aorja was beginning to think that she would have to get out of here sooner rather than later.

When she first got here, she hadn't expected to still be in here after a year. She had thought that maybe her former master, the Ghostly God, would save her; after all, she had served him faithfully for about a year before her treachery was revealed and she was banished from North Academy, the most elite mage school in the world, forever for her crimes.

Then again, I guess that's expecting too much from those southern gods, Aorja thought. *They treat their servants like how spoiled children treat their old toys. I probably shouldn't have expected anything better from him.*

Her throat was too dry for her to be thinking such thoughts, so she called out, "Raka, get me a glass of water. I'm thirsty."

She didn't know if Raka was around or not. The old woman, who acted as Aorja's servant, was sometimes still sleeping at this time. Based on what Aorja could see of the sky outside of her cell, it was still early morning; nonetheless, she waited patiently to see if Raka would show up.

A moment later, Aorja heard the shuffling of feet just outside of her cell door. Then an old woman, with stringy, silver-gray hair, the gray uniforms that all prisoners wore, and an empty pistol holstered around her belt, shuffled into the cell. She carried, with a shaking hand, a stone cup full of water. Aorja normally didn't trust the food or liquids offered to her by the other prisoners, but over the past year she had learned that Raka could be trusted, at least as much as any of these prisoners could be trusted.

Aorja took the cup from Raka's hand and sniffed the water. She didn't smell any poison or excrement in it, so she downed it in one gulp. Letting out a relieved sigh, Aorja handed the cup back to Raka, who said not a word as she took the cup back.

"Thank you for being so prompt, Raka," said Aorja, flashing her usual brilliant smile, even though she knew Raka didn't need it. "How are the rest of the prisoners this morning? Anyone kill someone else?"

Raka shook her head. "No, Miss Kitano, no, no. Two aquarians got into a fight, but they knocked each other out. Some of the other prisoners are taking turns assaulting them, while the former thieves are rifling through their belongings for anything valuable."

"Sounds like another normal day at Rock Isle," said Aorja. She giggled, but then stopped when her stomach growled. "Raka, could you get me something to eat? Remember, I don't want any bread more than five days old and make sure that the fish is only half-rotten."

Raka bowed. "Yes, Miss Kitano, I will be back with your breakfast shortly."

Raka shuffled out of the cell. Aorja watched her go, not letting herself breathe normally until Raka was gone.

Then Aorja leaned back against the rock wall of her cell. Raka was one of the few women at Rock Isle; at least, one of the few women who had not been thoroughly abused and discarded like a torn sock. She had been here longer than most of the prisoners, at least thirty years. And according to what a handful of the older prisoners had told Aorja, Raka had been known as the Southern Killer back in her youth, a nickname she had earned by killing in the name of the southern gods, who she claimed to worship.

Nowadays, though, Raka was quieter and slower. She never killed or attacked or stole from the other prisoners. She was probably in her seventies (though Aorja didn't know her exact age) and thus too old to get into any fights with the others. Even so, nearly every other prisoner on Rock Isle gave Raka a wide berth. Some said she was a cannibal, a trait she had taken from the southern gods, who were said to eat humans, but so far Aorja thought that that was just an unfounded rumor.

Even today, Aorja didn't quite understand why Raka chose to serve her. She suspected it had to do with Raka's affiliation with the southern gods. On some nights, when Aorja couldn't sleep, she would sometimes hear Raka praying to some southern god or another. Some nights it was the Loner God, other nights it was the Leaf Goddess, but she never seemed to get an answer to her prayers.

Maybe she heard I used to serve the Ghostly God and thinks that, if I help her, I will somehow connect her to the southern gods again, Aorja thought. *Or maybe she's just a submissive old lady who thinks allying with me will keep her safe from the other prisoners.*

At that moment, a massive, deafening explosion suddenly shook her cell. It knocked her straight off her cot, sending her sprawling to the floor tangled in her old, moldy blankets as cries and yells from the prisoners and the guards crashed together in the air to create a resounding madness that made it almost impossible for Aorja to hear her own thoughts. She untangled herself from her blankets and dashed out the open doorway onto the walkway that ran along the walls and led down to the bottom.

Rock Isle's main prison area was shaped like a pit, with the cells dug out of the rock walls, dozens and dozens of cells that were currently empty of the other prisoners. Almost all of the prisoners had gathered in the bottom of the prison, near the massive rock that stood between the prison itself and the sea on the other side

Or it *used* to, anyway. A giant hole had been blasted in the wall, far larger than something the average prisoner could even hope to create. Through the hole, the crashing of the waves mingled with the shouts of the prisoners and guards, a sound so loud that Aorja wished she had known enough audimancy to silence everyone.

Chunks of debris from the wall were everywhere, with a handful of the larger chunks having fallen on some of the prisoners, likely killing them instantly. The guards—large, burly men who wore thick black armor, with the hook symbol of the Goddess Hona carved into them, and carried long swords and spears—were trying to herd the prisoners back up into their cells, but the prisoners were so disoriented by the explosion and the water that kept splashing through every now and then that the prison guards were not seeing much success. Everyone was running around everywhere, it seemed to her, and no one seemed to know what was going on.

What in the world is going on here? Aorja thought. She looked at the hole in the wall. *Did one of the prisoners somehow cast an exploding spell or something?*

That was when she noticed someone standing in the hole. From a distance, he was hard to see, but when Aorja leaned over the railing of the walkway to get a better look at him, she saw that he was undoubtedly Carnagian. His dark skin gave that away immediately, although she had never seen a Carnagian with such light hair before, almost like he was part Shikan as well.

The man stood in the wall for a moment, as still as a statue, before raising what looked like a large war hammer and then bringing it down on the ground underneath his feet.

The minute his hammer's head hit the wall, it sent a massive tremor through the entire prison. Aorja was almost thrown off the walkway and down to the floor of the prison below, but she managed to catch herself before she fell to her death.

As for the prisoners and guards below, they had been knocked off their feet and lay in a heap on the floor, confusedly yelling and untangling each other from themselves. None of them seemed to notice the Carnagian man yet until he spoke loud enough to drown out every other noise in the area, including the crashing of the waves of the sea behind him.

"Prisoners of Rock Isle," the man's voice boomed, like that of a god's. "Cease your senseless bickering and confusion. Rise from your feet and listen to your savior who has come to rescue you from your unjust treatment by the guards."

Aorja gulped. Although she still held onto the railing as tightly as she could, she felt a strong desire to obey this man, whoever he was. She stood up, just as the other prisoners below did the same. Even the guards rose, although they quickly separated themselves from the prisoners and pointed their weapons at the mystery man.

"Who the hell are you?" one of the guards shouted. "Did you make that hole in the wall?"

The Carnagian man chuckled. "Indeed. It was a simple task, but an effective one at getting your attention, don't you agree?"

"I know what's going on here!" another guard yelled. "This guy is staging a prison break!"

The Carnagian man ran a hand through his hair. "Oh, you got me, all right. You discovered my dastardly plan. I will now give up, like a good criminal, and allow you to put me in my cell, where I will no doubt be treated very kindly by the other prisoners."

Aorja smiled. She still had no idea who the man was—he sounded somewhat older based on his voice—but she liked that kind of sarcasm in men. Whoever he was and whatever he was doing here, Aorja decided then and there to support him.

The guards, however, didn't appear as infatuated with his sarcasm as she was, because they were now climbing up the wall to reach the hole. None of the prisoners dared move a muscle, even though this was probably the best opportunity they were going to get to make an escape.

Very soon, the guards reached the hole in the wall and surrounded the Carnagian man. Swords and spears blocked off every conceivable exit the man could make, but despite that, he didn't seem very bothered by it. He simply brushed his hair out of his eyes and looked around at the guards as if unimpressed.

That was when Aorja felt powerful magical energy radiating from the Carnagian man. As a mage, Aorja could sense the magical energy from other mages, but she had never quite sensed the kind of power this man had. While it wasn't as much as the kind of power that the Magical Superior had, it was far more than the average mage had, and she could tell that he wasn't even using his full power yet, if he had a limit to his power at all, because she could not sense one in him.

That was why she wasn't surprised when the Carnagian man held up one hand and an immense fire erupted around him. The fire enveloped the guards, cutting off their cries of shock as abruptly as if they had never been there at all. The flames grew so large that they completely obscured the Carnagian man and the guards and even blocked off the hole in the wall. It kept growing larger and larger, causing Aorja to think for a moment that it was going to consume all of Rock Isle and kill every guard and prisoner on it.

But then the flames rapidly died down, retreating like they were being sucked down a drain, and when they did, they revealed that the Carnagian man still stood where he had been standing before. There was no sign of the guards except for piles of midnight black ash on the ground, but those soon vanished when a wave from the ocean outside crashed through the hole and washed the ashes away. The Carnagian man did not get wet in the slightest, which was probably because of some spell he had cast on himself to repel water off his body.

"There," said the Carnagian man as smoke rose from his shoulders. "Now, does anyone else wish to fight me or will you do the wise thing and listen to what I have to say?"

None of the prisoners said a word. Indeed, none of the prisoners even seemed to be breathing. They just stared up at the Carnagian man with awe and fear. Aorja, meanwhile, leaned even further over the railing, trying to get a better look at the man.

Even from a distance, Aorja could tell that he was a fine specimen of a man. Large muscles, gold-and-red robes that accentuated his physique rather than take away from it, a strong square jaw that was to die for ... he was practically the perfect man, much better than any of the men she had known back in North Academy and infinitely superior to the walking piles of dirt known as the male prisoners of Rock Isle.

Yet there was something about his appearance that made Aorja feel déjà vu. She was sure that she had never seen this man before, yet at the same time, she thought that she must have. It wasn't just his face, but his skin color, his hair, his whole build, even the hammer in his hands. She only wished that she could remember where.

More importantly, how could I ever forget a man like

that? Aorja thought. *He looks a little older in years, but that's fine. Older men are more mature than younger men, more experienced. Definitely make better partners, anyway.*

"I see no one has the courage to talk back to me," said the Carnagian man. "That is a problem I will have to deal with later, after I train all of you to transcend your Limits and rise to new levels of magical power unknown to most mages."

Still none of the prisoners spoke. No doubt they were all afraid of the man, too afraid even to ask him what he meant by what he just said. After that massive display of power he showed earlier, Aorja didn't fault them for it. She herself felt a little fear mixed with her desire for him after all.

Nonetheless, Aorja began climbing down the stairs to the floor of the prison, wanting to get closer to the Carnagian man to see if she could jog her memory.

"But of course, I am ahead of myself," said the Carnagian man. He held up his hammer. "Do any of you know what this is? It is a symbol of the god Grinf, the God of Justice, Fire, and Metal, patron god of Carnag, and the Judge of the World. It is a symbol of justice, a sign that all who have committed terrible crimes against humanity and the gods will one day receive the punishment they so richly deserve."

The passion in his voice as he said that ... oh, Aorja *liked* that. It made him look even stronger and manlier; indeed, he appeared almost divine. That just made her walk down the stairs more quickly, listening as the Carnagian man lowered his hammer.

"But do not fear," said the Carnagian man. "I am not here to harm you or punish you for your crimes. For Grinf is a merciful god as well as judgmental, and I am no different, even though I am not a god myself. Grinf has told me that you prisoners have served your time and that soon—very soon—each and every one of you shall be free from this wretched jail for the rest of your lives."

Aorja actually stopped when she heard that, even though she hadn't reached the floor of the prison yet. The prisoners began looking around at each other, confused, as if wondering if this was some kind of trick.

"How do we know you're not just going to do to us what you did to those guards?" one of the prisoners shouted. "And you haven't even told us your name, so how can we trust your word?"

"I am not finished speaking yet," said the Carnagian man. "There is only one condition you must swear by, if you accept my offer to walk free: You must become my servants and train under me to push past the false Limits you have created in your minds, the ones that keep you from achieving your true potential as mages."

Aorja continued walking down the stairs, reaching the prison yard just as another prisoner yelled, "What, we have to give up one prison in exchange for another? That's an awful deal!"

The rest of the prisoners began shouting in agreement before the Carnagian man glared down at them all, silencing them instantly. Aorja, on the other hand, found herself drawn even more to him when she saw that. She'd serve him even if he hadn't promised to help them push past their 'false Limits,' whatever that meant.

"I don't think you understand," said the Carnagian man. He pointed behind himself with his gavel. "The outside world is dangerous and hostile towards prisoners like you. If you walk out now, you will likely be recaptured at some point and thrown back in here. If you wish to *stay* free, then follow me and I will teach you how to keep your freedom even if the whole world tries to take it away from you."

By now, Aorja stood at the back of the crowd of prisoners, ignoring their combined body odor that smelled like sweat, excrement, and dirt mixed together to make a poor perfume. She had to stand on her tiptoes to see over the heads of her fellow prisoners, staring as hard as she could at the Carnagian man looking down on them all like one of the gods.

"And I offer this for free," said the Carnagian man, holding out one hand. "You will be under no obligation to serve me once you have learned all you need to learn. Once I have taught you how to beat your Limits, you may go and do whatever you wish with your new freedom. How does that sound?"

"Too good to be true," said one of the prisoners near the front. "You still haven't told us your name, dark-skin. We'd be more likely to take your offer seriously if maybe you had properly introduced yourself first."

The Carnagian man stroked his chin, as if considering that request, and then nodded. "Very well. I should get this out of the way now so we can continue the negotiations on more personal terms. You may call me Jakuuth Grinfborn, a Limitless mage ... and the one and only son of the great god Grinf."

Chapter Two

Two months later ...

Darek Takren walked around the huge, thick block of ice that he had just conjured from the air. Its surface was smooth, without any sort of ridges or cuts to disturb it. The ice was so clear that he could almost see straight through it, aside from the thick white patches here and there. Cold air radiated from the ice, but whereas most people would step back from it to retain their warmth, Darek drew closer to it, as he found the cold air calming.

And calmness is exactly what I need in this situation, Darek thought. *I haven't been this stressed out since Uron's attack last year.*

Darek stole a quick glance over his shoulder when he passed the front of the ice block. The lobby of the Arcanium was completely full, as every student had gathered to watch him carve this ice block into the shape of Xocion, the God of Ice and the god he had pledged his life to. The teachers, all two dozen of them, stood in the back, including the Magical Superior, who sat on a stone chair in the center of the group, and Darek's mom, Jenur Takren, who stood to the Magical Superior's left.

Everyone was quiet, as Darek had asked them to be in

order that he could think more clearly. Plus, it was tradition for the teachers and students to remain silent during the graduation ceremony. It was considered respectful to keep one's mouth shut until the ceremony was over. It also allowed the graduates the space they needed to concentrate on what they were going to do.

Darek returned his attention back to the ice block, which he stopped in front of, but he wasn't really looking at the block. His eyes darted up to the Wall of Mastery behind the ice block, which featured dozens of paintings, preserved by magic, of past graduates, the best of the best who even today were still honored and revered by the other students for their mastery over magic.

None of Darek's graduating class were getting on the Wall this year, not even Darek. That didn't disappoint him much. Very few students were ever worthy of getting their own painting on the Wall. Still, seeing all of the faces on those paintings 'looking' down on him made Darek feel anxious, more so than ever before. Bifor Kamon's painting in particular made him nervous, largely due to Kamon's thick scar and haughty eyes, as if the painting was somehow judging him.

All his life, Darek had been looking forward to the day of his graduation. He had lived in North Academy for years before becoming an official student and then spent the last ten years training vigorously under the tutelage of some of the best mages in the world. During that time, Darek had seen many graduations, but until he had stepped up here in front of everyone else, he had not truly realized just how nerve-wracking the whole experience could be.

It didn't help that Darek had decided to make this time the moment when he would break through the ceiling. Not the actual, physical ceiling of the Arcanium, of course, but rather the uppermost limits of his magical power, which was called 'the ceiling' by most mages.

Darek tried not to think too much about it, however, because thinking always slowed him down. And if the teachers even caught a whiff of what he was trying to do, they would undoubtedly put a stop to this demonstration right away.

That's why I have to act quickly, Darek thought, pointing his wand at the ice block. *If I can do it fast enough, then I should be able to break through the ceiling before any of them even realize what I'm trying to do.*

Most mages considered breaking through the ceiling highly dangerous, even lethal. Darek had always been taught that every mage had certain limits to his or her own powers. Because every mage was different, this limit varied from individual to individual; nonetheless, it was a very real and very dangerous thing to attempt to break through, as mages who tried to break through the ceiling usually fell into comas or even died. It was similar to pushing the limits of your physical body; at a certain point, you could not go any further and had to stop or shut down.

Indeed, under ordinary circumstances, Darek would have never even thought about breaking through the ceiling. The Magical Superior, his mother, the other teachers, and his books had always said the same thing: Do not break through the ceiling. No matter what.

Cracks began forming in the ice block, but so slowly and subtly that Darek doubted anyone could see them except for himself. This was a delicate procedure, as ice carving always was, although using magic was still superior to carving using actual ice carving tools, such as the kind he had been told that non-magical humans used outside of North Academy.

Despite how much of his attention that this action required, Darek was still too nervous about breaking through the ceiling to concentrate as deeply as he should. He knew he should have tried this in private, but it was difficult to find privacy in North Academy, and in all honesty, if he fell into a coma as a result of his efforts, he wanted to make sure that there were as many people to save his life nearby as possible.

I just hope the teachers don't get too angry with me, Darek thought with a gulp. *Although their anger would be preferable to falling into a coma and dying in my sleep.*

More cracks began forming in the ice, looking a little bit like the forks of a lightning bolt. They were bigger, more easily seen than the smaller ones, so Darek thought the students in the front row probably saw them by now. He carefully moved his wand to the right, chipping off corners here and there, but it still looked nothing like Lord Xocion yet.

But when it does, it will be superior to every other statue I have ever made, Darek thought. *Because I will have broken through the ceiling and have upped the limits of my power. If I am going to deal with Uron, then I'll need all the extra power I can get.*

That was the whole reason Darek was doing this in the first place. Last year, a powerful and evil being known as Uron had risen from the school's graveyard, where he had clashed with Skimif, the God of Martir, before vanishing after being blasted by an airship containing some of Skimif's power. Darek had not heard anything about Uron since then, nor did he know what the gods were doing about him.

Of course, that made sense. Skimif had told Darek, point blank, that Uron was to be left to the gods and that the mortals, even the North Academy mages, were supposed to stay out of the conflict. That was because Uron was immensely powerful, far too strong for even the Magical Superior to go toe-to-toe with, and Skimif did not want any of them getting hurt or killed.

As another layer of ice fell off the block, Darek remembered obeying Skimif's orders at the time, but over the past year he had spent a lot of time studying how to increase his power in order to help defend his friends and family from Uron. Uron had said that he was going to destroy all of Martir, and with the legendary God-killer gauntlet at his side, that threat was more credible than it first appeared.

None of us can sit idly by and let him do what he wants, Darek thought, *not when our whole world is at stake. It may be the gods' duty to protect Martir from threats like Uron, but that doesn't mean we mages can't help, even if only in small ways.*

It had only been within the last month that the answer to that question—how to increase his power—had occurred to him: He would have to break through the ceiling, which, if successful, would raise his limits to new heights.

The conclusion had scared him at the time, but since then, he had made peace with it. While Darek was not usually one to disobey the orders from his teachers, he decided that saving the lives of his friends and family was more important than following any warnings—no matter how well-meaning—they had given him.

Darek checked in with his magical energy levels. So far, he was still quite full, but he could feel his power rapidly draining from his body as he poured more ice magic into the block. If any of the teachers noticed, they were probably not going to do anything about it. It was normal for graduates to expend more magical energy than normal during their graduation ceremony, so right now, at least, Darek was safe.

Time to up my usage, Darek thought. *And find out if I really can raise my limits.*

So Darek poured more energy through his wand. He could now almost see the outline of the Xocion statue in the ice block, though he doubted the others could. It would be the grandest Xocion statue anyone had ever made, grander even than the ice statues created by the great Xocionian mage Siar.

It would be grand because Darek would break through the ceiling and reach new heights of magical power. And once he did, he would be far better equipped to defend

20

Martir from Uron or anyone else who threatened his world and friends and family.

The prospect of gaining more power excited Darek so much that he increased his magical output, despite being aware that the teachers might notice. Layers and chunks of ice kept getting shaved from the block, much faster than they normally did when he carved a statue from ice.

Whether the others will notice or not, I have to keep doing it, Darek thought. *Keep going, keep pouring energy, don't let up, especially don't let up long enough for the teachers to notice and stop you.*

As Darek thought that, he could not help but remember how powerless he had felt last year, when Uron had first appeared. Yet even before he had met Uron, Darek had felt just as powerless when facing Aorja Kitano, his former best friend who had tried to kill him and his other friend, Jiku, before she was defeated and shipped off to Rock Isle to rot with the other prisoners there.

Darek had not seen Aorja in a year. He didn't even know if she was still alive or not. Nonetheless, just thinking about her made his blood boil. It slightly disturbed his concentration, causing him to accidentally move his wand to the left. That unintended movement cut through the ice's surface in a jagged way, which would have messed up Darek's attempt completely if he hadn't reasserted his control over his wand and forced it back to where it was supposed to be.

No time to wonder about Aorja, Darek thought. *She's long gone. I must focus on the present, not the past.*

He checked his energy levels again. Already, he had used up slightly more than half his energy. Granted, it was impossible to put a mage's magical energy supply into raw numbers, but Darek knew enough about his own magic levels to know that he had now gone past the halfway point.

Most mages, in his situation, would have slowed their magical usage, maybe even stopped entirely. Then they would rest so they could recharge their energy levels. That was how afraid most mages were of going beyond the ceiling, giving up after only using half their power, despite how small that usage was in the grand scheme of things.

Not Darek, though. Not today. Reaching the halfway point was good, but it was nothing worth bragging about. He would have to up his energy usage, and quickly, before the teachers noticed. He did not dare take his eyes off his ice block to see if the teachers had caught a clue yet, but sooner or later they would realize what he was trying to do, and he just couldn't allow that right now.

By now, the ice block was perhaps halfway done. He could see Xocion's muscular arms and large chest, but no legs or head just yet. There was still so much to do, and he wasn't sure if he had enough energy to do it; nonetheless, he pushed further, pouring as much of his energy as he could into the block.

His wand hand shook, but he forced it to steady. A shaky, unsteady wand hand was a clear sign to even amateur mages that another mage was reaching his or her limits. Darek was not going to let his body betray his plans, at least not until it was too late for anyone to stop him.

It wasn't easy, though. The more magical energy he used, the more tired he got. His knees were getting weaker and his arms felt like lead. His eyelids became as heavy as armor and sweat ran down his forehead. For some reason, he felt hot, rather than cold, even though he was using ice magic, not fire magic.

This must be why so many mages refuse to go beyond the halfway point, Darek thought, although his thoughts were barely coherent even to himself. *It feels like I'm dying.*

Once more, Darek checked his energy levels. By his estimations, he had only a quarter of his usual magical energy left. It occurred to him that he was losing energy after the halfway point far quicker than he had when his magic was fuller. He was close to the ceiling now, so close that he was surprised none of the teachers appeared to sense his proximity to it.

Not ... a problem, Darek thought, watching as Xocion's legs began forming in the ice block. *All ... the ... better ... for me ...*

He staggered forward involuntarily. He heard the students behind him gasp, prompting him to shout, "I'm fine! Just getting a little tired is all. No need to worry about me. Everything will be fine."

Even he could hear how awful his voice sounded. No doubt he sounded like a talking corpse to everyone else. He might even sound bad enough for the teachers to intervene, though so far, he did not hear any movement from them.

His magical energy levels were so low by now that he could barely even sense them. This frightened him more than he'd like to admit. Ever since he began his formal training as a student, Darek had always held the comfort of his magical energy levels in his own body no matter where he was or what he did.

Now, however, it felt like he was missing several of his internal organs. *Vital* internal organs, like his heart or lungs. Breathing was becoming a task suited only for a god, while standing was as difficult as pushing a three ton boulder up the tallest hill in the world.

Despite how his body was practically screaming for him to stop, Darek didn't. He had read only a handful of accounts of mages breaking through the ceiling. He had heard about what lay on the other side, for those lucky few who didn't fall into a coma. If he could just stay conscious for a little while longer, just a little while, then he would be all right.

The statue was almost complete now; he could tell that even in his half-conscious state of mind. A figure like a titan towered over him. Strong, muscular arms, lithe athletic legs, and a chest like the Walls that surrounded the school formed his statue of Lord Xocion. The only thing that wasn't yet complete was the head; however, Darek could already see its vague outline; although whether it was in his head or in the world, he could not tell.

Despite his heavy breathing and intense sweating, his robes getting drenched in the sweat, Darek couldn't help but crack a smile. *My best work ... ever. Looking at these muscles. The abs. Even the fingernails. Is this what everyone is afraid of? Afraid of exceeding their limits and doing what they could only ever dream of?*

He almost laughed. Of course, he hadn't yet reached the ceiling yet. It seemed unlikely that he would, but he kept pushing anyway. He had to. The teachers would have to be complete idiots if they hadn't noticed the immense amount of power he was expending at this point.

Just keep going, Darek thought. *Don't let up. Remember Aorja. Remember Uron. Remember how you want to keep your friends and family safe from people like—*

Darek stopped mid-thought. The tiredness in his body vanished. He stopped sweating. He no longer felt a heavy burden on his shoulders. He felt like he could jump for joy.

His senses came alive. He could hear the boots of Taci Xeon, one of his fellow graduates, scuffling across the floor, and she was on the other side of the lobby. He smelled the soap used by another student, which was scented like grapes. He saw the Xocion ice statue in far greater detail than before, noticing little cracks too miniscule for even his trained eyes to notice normally. And his wand felt *real*, more real than it had ever felt before, as though up until now he had not actually been holding it at all.

Time itself seemed to have slowed down around him. No; not slowed down. Darek was seeing time as it actually moved, rather than how his senses interpreted it. Everything around him looked slower, but in truth, his human senses had simply been blinding him to the true nature of time.

That was how Darek knew he had done it. He had achieved the impossible: He had broken through the ceiling.

And it felt *great*.

I feel so powerful, Darek thought. *Is this how the Magical Superior feels? Is this what it feels like to be strong? It feels like there are no limits to my power. I feel more alive than I have in thirty-five years, as though I spent my entire life dead up until this point.*

Darek wanted to laugh and cry at the same time. He didn't understand why he had always been warned against breaking through the ceiling. He suspected that his teachers had simply been falsely concerned over his well-being. After all, none of them had ever broken through the ceiling, so how could any of them know whether it was as bad as those old books said it was?

His face broke into an enormous grin. He wanted to compose a hymn to Xocion right there and then, even though he wasn't much of a poet. He no longer felt afraid of Uron or anything else in the world. He believed, as sincerely as he believed anything else, that there was no force in this world that could stand against him now.

"I wouldn't be so sure about that if I were you."

Darek looked to his right. A skeleton stood there, with eyes glowing bright green, its mouth etched in a perpetual, creepy grin. Unlike everyone else in the room, the skeleton moved as normally as he did.

"What?" said Darek. "Who—no, *what*—are you? Where did you come from?"

The skeleton chuckled. "Just an interested observer who has decided to see just who was dumb enough to 'break through the ceiling,' as you mortals call it."

"Dumb enough?" said Darek. Anger rose within him like a geyser. "Who are you calling dumb? I have transcended my limits. You want to fight me and prove who's the real dumb one around here?"

The skeleton stroked its chin, its bony fingers as thin as sticks. "Fighting me would be a very dumb move on your part, Darek Takren. Thank you for the offer, though. Perhaps I will take you up on it later, once your sanity has returned."

"Sanity?" said Darek. "I am already sane. I am saner than I have ever been."

"That was what the last mortal who broke through the ceiling said," said the skeleton. "Then he became a raving lunatic. Not that I care. Sane or insane, you mortals are much the same to me."

"Why are you here?" said Darek. "If all you're going to do is question my sanity and insult my intelligence—"

The skeleton held up one finger. "I apologize for that. I just wanted to let you know that your high is about to end and it will probably be very painful once it does."

Darek blinked. "Wha—"

Without warning, the Xocion ice statue before him exploded. At the same time, Darek's arms and legs became tired and heavy again, making it impossible for him to stand. His breathing became so intense that he start coughing and choking, perhaps even coughing up blood, but his eyes were screwing up so badly that he couldn't tell for sure what was coming out of his mouth.

A chunk of ice from the exploding Xocion statue

knocked him flat off his feet and onto the floor, the impact of which, combined with his sudden, extreme fatigue, forced him to black out completely.

Chapter Three

The minor spirit, more properly called a katabans, known as Durima hauled herself up over the edge of the cliff and onto solid ground. She rested there for a moment, her wet fur heavy on her shoulders, but after a few minutes, she sat up and deposited her catch—three disc-shaped fish that she didn't know the species name of, but which she had discovered over the last year were quite tasty and nutritious—onto the ground next to her.

That is the last time I am going fishing like that, Durima thought, glancing over the edge of the cliff into the ocean waters below. *I will have to ask Gujak to make a fishing pole or something. Surely he can do that, can't he?*

Shivering, Durima knew she should get inside Bleak Rock, the island that she and Gujak had called sanctuary for a year now, but it was so dark and depressing inside that she decided to sit out here for a while, even though a bitter cold wind had started and made her feel like she was sitting in the middle of a blizzard.

At least it's not raining, Durima thought, looking up at the sun in the sky. *It's not even misty today. Think this is the first time I've seen the sun in three months.*

She heard something skittering across the stone nearby, causing her head to whip to the right. A tiny, black spider was crawling along the ground near the disc-shaped fish. Without even thinking, Durima slammed her right fist down onto it, despite the fact that the spider probably hadn't even noticed her.

The spider had reminded her of the deceased Spider Goddess and Durima's own hand in the Goddess's death. Although that had been a year ago, it seemed like it had only been yesterday that Durima and Gujak had been captured by the Spider Goddess, who had tried to eat them, only for her to end up on the receiving end of the God-killer.

Durima didn't want to remember that. All her life, she had thought of herself as a loyal and devout follower of the gods. Sure, she didn't necessarily like each god equally, but she knew better than to conspire against them. It was a fool's errand and she knew that the only proper punishment for rebellious or disobedient katabans was nothing less than death.

But like all living beings, Durima and Gujak didn't want to die. It was technically what they deserved, after everything they had done, but just because they technically deserved it did not mean that they could get over their fear of being put to death that easily.

That was why they hadn't told anyone where they were going. After the fiasco at North Academy, in which some frightening being known as Uron had killed yet another goddess, the two had escaped in the confusion to Bleak Rock.

The reason for choosing Bleak Rock as their new home was simple. The island was well known for its mysterious and otherworldly nature. Most beings—mortals, katabans, and gods alike—always steered clear of it. Magic did not work on Bleak Rock exactly the same way it worked in the north or even on other southern islands, a fact Durima knew well after living here for a year and almost always being surprised by her spells acting in ways they were not supposed to.

Granted, Durima feared that the gods would get over their superstitious fear of Bleak Rock and sink the whole island into the southern seas anyway, but so far, they had not seen even a hint of the gods anywhere. As far as Durima could tell, the gods had completely abandoned her and Gujak, maybe even forgotten about them. Or maybe they associated Bleak Rock with the Spider Goddess's death and were too afraid to come for fear of their own lives.

Better than being executed for our crimes, I suppose, Durima thought. *Though it still doesn't explain what they're doing, exactly, if they're not after us.*

Another cold gust of wind blew through her fur, causing her to shiver even more violently, but she still didn't want to go back inside just yet. She wanted to enjoy the sun for as long as she could, as she had no idea when she would see it again, especially with the unpredictability of Bleak Rock's weather patterns.

Sometimes, great clouds of mist would surround Bleak Rock and cover the sky, clouds of mist that would remind Durima of her former master, the deity known as the Ghostly God, the God of Ghosts and Mist. There were none today, but she still thought about him anyway.

Like all of the other gods, Durima had not seen or heard from him in over a year. She found it strange because she assumed that the Ghostly God would want to take them in personally. After all, their accidental killing of the Spider Goddess had to have made the Ghostly God look bad in the eyes of his fellow gods, seeing as the only reason she and Gujak had been on Bleak Rock at all was because he had ordered them go to there.

Maybe that's why he's ignoring us, Durima thought. *Maybe the other gods hate him for being so easily manipulated by Uron. He probably can't show his face in public anymore and doesn't think bringing us in will redeem him in the eyes of his siblings.*

Of course, that still didn't make Durima feel better. Sooner or later, *someone* would come after her and Gujak. Who, she didn't know, but someone had to come after them. It was a miracle that they had been free for so long, despite spending an entire year in one specific location.

Anyone else would have let their guard down after so much time had passed with so little action. Not Durima, though. Having been a soldier in the Katabans War, she knew that just because everything seemed peaceful, did not mean that the enemy was not hiding somewhere nearby, waiting to take you down the minute you lowered your guard.

So far, that has not happened just yet, Durima thought. *But as soon as Gujak or I get careless, we're done. I saw it happen to too many of my fellow soldiers during the War to have any illusions about safety.*

Rising to her feet, Durima slung the disc fish over her shoulder and headed into the opening cut in the stone of Bleak Rock that led to its interior. She would take these fish to Gujak, who would then prepare them for their lunch, and then she and Gujak would spend another few hours or so sitting around in the darkness.

Because there just really wasn't much to do here. Gujak had taken to exploring Bleak Rock, which was apparently far larger than it appeared, for over the past year he had discovered a vast tunnel network that extended deep under the island, possibly even beneath the sea floor. Where it went to, neither of them knew, as most of the lowest tunnels were flooded with water or blocked off with heavy stone, but it was there nonetheless. The only hint of what lay below was a severed human hand, though who it had belonged to, they didn't know. They had left it where it was, as there was no point in taking it with them or doing anything with it.

Durima slid down the steep slide that always used to get her during their first month or two here, but after a year of living on this island, she could now slide down it as easily as if she was born to do it. She came to a graceful stop at the bottom, where she stood up, wiped off the grime her behind had collected as she went down the slide, and then looked to her left, toward the only tunncl that lcd deeper into the island's interior.

"Gujak!" Durima shouted, her voice echoing off the narrow walls of Bleak Rock's interior. "I got the fish! Get the fire going because I'm hungry!"

There was no answer, which immediately put Durima on

high alert. Gujak always answered her whenever she announced that she had returned with food. He wasn't sleeping at this time, because he didn't take his afternoon nap for another hour, at least. And she doubted he was down in the lower tunnels, as there was nothing down there that Gujak could possibly want.

Then why didn't he answer? Durima thought. *Either he's dumber than I thought ... or someone or some*thing *got him.*

Durima's hair rose on her back, a habit she had developed over the past year or so whenever she sensed danger. She had been afraid that this day would come, the day when the gods finally gathered the courage to storm Bleak Rock and kill her and Gujak for their unforgivable crime against the Pantheons. Granted, she couldn't sense any godly presences in the area, but the gods were perfectly capable of cloaking their presences if they wanted, meaning that there could be a whole Pantheon of gods underneath her feet that were just waiting for her to come down and check on Gujak.

Her body's instincts told her to run, but Durima stayed where she was. While running seemed like a logical idea, Durima had nowhere to go. If she went to any other island, she would likely open herself up to certain death from the gods. There was still a possibility, however small, that Gujak was indeed all right, that there was a perfectly innocuous reason for why he had not responded to her yet, and it was a chance worth taking.

You have no choice, Durima, she thought. *You'll have to*

go down below and find Gujak.

Bracing herself for whatever was to come, Durima began walking to the left, toward the tunnel that would take her to the staircase that would lead her down to the chamber below, where Gujak usually was at this time of day.

As Durima descended the slippery stone staircase, she stopped every two steps to listen for any sounds of enemies waiting in the dark. Her ears, although superior to mortal ears, picked up nothing except for the dripping of water somewhere in the distance. She didn't smell anything, either, except for her own wet fur that had yet to dry and the stench of the fish slung over her shoulder, which were starting to rot in the damp air.

This reminded her far too much of her and Gujak's first time going down these steps, when they discovered webbing left over by the Spider Goddess. Back then, the Spider Goddess had taken them both by surprise and almost succeeded in killing them. Durima did not expect a repeat of that event here (minus the Spider Goddess, obviously), but she nonetheless paid closer attention to her surroundings and senses in an attempt to detect any dangerous enemies lurking within.

Yet the interior of Blcak Rock seemed as dark and silent as always, aside from the slapping of her footsteps against the wet steps of the stairs. She tried to walk as stealthily as she could, but her bulk always made that a challenge, so she doubted she would have the element of surprise on whoever was hiding in wait for her below.

Finally, Durima reached the bottom of the steps. She stopped and listened once again, hoping that she would catch anything that shouldn't be here. Again, there was nothing, although she still heard that water dripping somewhere nearby.

Making sure her claws were ready, Durima stepped out of the stairwell and into the chamber where the God-killer had been prior to her and Gujak's theft of it. As always, the room was wide and circular, with a stone walkway running around its perimeter and the middle being nothing more than a pool of salty water that came from who-knows-where. The stone peninsula from before jutted out halfway over the middle, where Durima saw someone standing on it that she had never seen before.

Her first thought was that the person was a human, because he was largely hairless, aside from a purple tuft on his scalp, and he was humanoid like them. Then she noticed the large, falcon wings that sprouted from his back, saw his armor, which shone like a brilliant crystal, with a stylized depiction of the Temple of the Gods carved in it, and she immediately knew where he was from, even though she didn't know his name.

"Durima," said the being, his eyes literally shining as he looked at her. "Also known as the Devil. Veteran of the Katabans War. Fought briefly under the command of the Pseudo-Grinf before becoming a double agent and working with the Katabans Council to bring him down."

Durima snarled, "Are you just going to stand there and recite facts and trivia, like a couple of Tavian priestesses, or are you going to arrest me, Soldier of the Gods?"

"So you know what organization I belong to," said the Soldier. "I don't need to ask how you guessed. "

"Of course you don't," said Durima. "Every katabans recognizes the crystal armor that only Soldiers wear. I was offered the job myself once, after the end of the War, but I rejected it because I had no interest in becoming a dog of the Katabans Council."

"I was told you are a rebellious one," said the Soldier, "which explains why you and your friend ran, rather than face justice at the feet of the Katabans Council."

"I'm not afraid of justice," Durima replied. "I'm just ... well, it doesn't matter. How did you find us? Where is Gujak?"

The Soldier tapped his chin. "You were easy enough to find. There was nowhere else in all of Martir that you could have possibly disappeared to but this island, where no one, not even the gods, goes to. Granted, we didn't want to come here, but if justice is to be served, that sometimes means doing things we'd rather not."

"Still haven't told me where Gujak is," said Durima. "Is he alive? Did you kill him, you bastard?"

"The role of a Soldier of the Gods is not to kill criminals, but to bring them to the Katabans Council, who will give them the fair hearing and punishment that they deserve," said the Soldier.

"Avoiding the question," said Durima. "Of course you did. I never could get a straight answer out of any of you guys."

"Gujak has been detained by my brothers-in-arms," said the Soldier. "There are three dozen of us in total. If I fancied, I could order them all to attack and kill you on the spot and tell the Council that it was necessary because you had resisted arrest."

The ease and quickness with which the Soldier came up with that lie surprised Durima. Then again, knowing how scummy the Council could be, she became less surprised at this Soldier's behavior.

"But I should introduce myself," said the Soldier. He pointed at a star-shaped badge on his shoulder armor. "I am Commander Erich, Commander of the Soldiers of the Gods. I was given strict orders to bring you and Gujak in for your unspeakable crimes against the gods."

"We didn't mean it," said Durima. "It was an accident. We didn't go to this island planning to murder a goddess. We'd have been idiots to even entertain that idea."

"That will be for the Council to decide," said Erich. "You now have two options: One, drop any rebellious thoughts of fighting me and come peacefully; or two, I beat you within an inch of your life and drag you to World's End myself."

Durima considered those two options. If Erich did indeed have three dozen Soldiers with him, Durima knew that she would lose against them in a straight battle. Yet she didn't want to give up and let Erich take her and Gujak to World's End, where they would likely be executed for their crimes.

"If you are thinking of fighting me, I think it's only fair that I inform you that I also fought in the Katabans War, like you, and that I was the first place winner of the International Katabans Swordsmanship Championship for three years running," said Erich. "Though in recent years, I've retired my old blades in favor of these."

Erich held up two crystalline tiger claws that were clamped to his hands. The claws looked as thick as swords and far sharper.

"Mican crystal claws," said Erich. "Very rare, but very powerful. This particular set was said to have been created by Mica herself shortly after the Godly War. They're supposed to be unbreakable and unable to decay or break down no matter how often you use them. They are easily capable of cutting through steel ... or flesh."

Durima winced when he said that. She could just imagine what it would feel like to have those sharp crystal claws cutting through her body. It made her shiver as if she was still outside in the cold wind.

She tried to think of some way to beat Erich. Unfortunately, without knowing the full extent of his own fighting abilities, coming up with any sort of tactics against him was essentially useless. Even if he wasn't as good of a fighter as he made himself out to be, those Mican crystal claws might more than make up for his lack of fighting ability.

Then there was the fact that Gujak was already captive, according to Erich. If that was true, then Durima had even less reason to fight against him. After all, even if she managed to defeat Erich, his three dozen Soldiers were still around and could easily take her down if they wanted.

Seems like I'm screwed no matter how you look at it, Durima thought. *If I fight him, I will probably die. If I try to run, I will undoubtedly die. And if I do either, Gujak will most assuredly be killed. This is one of those un-winnable situations I always try to avoid yet always find myself stuck in.*

"I'm waiting for your answer, Durima," said Erich. "Any day now."

In an attempt to buy some more time, Durima said, "Why did you wait so long to go after me and Gujak? You knew where we were, but you didn't bother us for a whole year; why is that?"

Anger flashed in Erich's eyes. "That is none of your business, murderer. And if you keep asking those kinds of questions, I will retract my previous offer and end your miserable life right here and now."

Durima took a step back, even though she had nowhere to run to. No doubt the rest of his Soldiers were hiding in the shadows nearby, ready to strike her down the minute she tried to escape. For a moment, Durima almost considered using the ethereal to escape, but then she remembered that the ethereal could not be accessed underground.

"What if you're lying?" said Durima. "About Gujak? Maybe Gujak got away and you decided to hide down here and lie to me about your capturing him so you could trick me into going to the Katabans Council."

"If you are truly naïve enough to believe a lie as ridiculous as that, then allow me to show you undeniable proof of my claims," said Erich. "Men, bring in the other murderer."

Behind her, Durima heard two sets of footsteps dragging something between them. She looked over her shoulder, despite knowing that it left her open to an attack from Erich, and was horrified by what she saw.

Two more Soldiers stood in the entrance behind her, carrying Gujak between them. His head had been bashed in, his right arm, the one that had grown back after Uron had ripped it off a year ago, was broken at the elbow, and he was so still that she might have mistaken him for a corpse if she hadn't known better.

"Gujak," said Durima, reaching out to him.

"See? We captured him, just like I said," said Erich. "Again, you have two choices: Resist or surrender. Choose wisely."

Durima's claws dug into the palms of her hands as she stood there, looking from Erich to Gujak and back again. Seeing Gujak beaten so badly had shaken her more than she realized. He looked barely alive, like he was hanging onto his life by only a few thin threads, and he was clearly not faking it.

Because Durima knew that she couldn't win, she let out a deep sigh as her shoulders slumped. "All right, Erich. I give. Take me and Gujak to the Katabans Council, where we will accept whatever punishment they choose to give us for our crime against the gods."

Chapter Four

Darek couldn't move his body. It felt like his limbs refused to budge, no matter how much his mind told them to move. His body was like a prison, a prison he couldn't escape from, and that terrified him greatly.

It didn't help that his eyes were closed, making it impossible for him to see anything. He remembered breaking through the ceiling and the euphoria that had resulted, as well as that eerie skeleton that had spoken to him mysteriously, but his memories ended there.

I must have fallen unconscious, Darek thought. *Maybe even fell into a coma. I've never been in a coma before, though. Is this what a coma feels like?*

With great effort, Darek forced his eyes open, which was the only part of his body that he seemed to have any real control over right now. He blinked several times as he looked up at the white ceiling directly above him before realizing that he was in the medical wing of the Arcanium.

Of course I'd be put here, Darek thought. *Where else would I be taken? Outside?*

Though the sheets covering his body were comfortable enough, Darek wanted to get up and walk around. He wanted to know how long he had been out and what everyone else was doing. Part of him was nervous that the teachers and the Magical Superior were angry with him for risking his life like that, but he decided that he could take whatever rebukes they tossed at him. It couldn't be any worse than what he felt right before he broke through the ceiling, after all.

"You're awake," said a voice to his right, a voice he remembered well from his childhood.

Turning his head to the right, Darek saw his mother sitting on a chair next to his bed. Like always, she had dark, curly hair, although he was starting to notice her first gray hairs appearing here and there. She wore the gray robes of a necromancer and looked so worried that Darek felt ashamed of himself for worrying her so.

"Hey, Mom," said Darek, trying to smile, but he was so weak that even that small gesture took a lot of effort. "What are you doing?"

"Waiting to see if you were ever going to wake up again," said Mom. She leaned forward, her worried frown turning into a stern scowl. "Listen, Darek, I know you are an adult and have been for quite a while now, but do you know what I saw when you broke through the ceiling?"

Darek groaned inwardly. *Uh oh. I know what's coming.*

"I saw a cocky teenager thinking he could do what every single responsible adult in his life has ever told him not to do," said Mom. "You know, that thing we repeatedly told you would at best put you in a coma for years and at worst kill you?"

"But I didn't fall into a coma or die," said Darek. He

hated having to explain himself like this, as it made him feel like a little kid again, but he hated seeing Mom so worried and wanted to assuage her fears. "I'm alive and well. See? I'm even talking with you."

"I know," said Mom. "It's a miracle from the gods that you didn't die there and then while everyone went crazy after your statue exploded and you fell onto the floor. I think it must have been the Magical Superior's healing magic that saved you because he acted well before any of us did."

Darek winced. "Sorry for worrying you. I didn't mean to. I thought—"

"Thought what?" said Mom. "That you, a student who was supposed to graduate today, could achieve what even the most experienced mage never even dreams of doing because it is so stupid and dangerous?"

"I just wanted to see if I could up the limits of my powers," said Darek, speaking as quickly as he could so Mom couldn't interrupt him. "That's all. What's wrong with wanting to become stronger?"

Mom sat back in her chair, looking like she had been struck by thunder. "But why, Darek, would you ever want to become stronger? We already worked out your limits years ago, when you first began your formal training as a student. Why would you ever want to test them? Who do you think you need to be that powerful to fight?"

Darek hesitated for a moment, but, seeing no point in hiding his true motives from Mom, said, "Uron."

Mom looked around as if she thought someone was

eavesdropping. Then she leaned in again, like she wanted to share a secret with Darek.

"Now I have never met or seen Uron before, Darek, but from what you and the Magical Superior have told me about him, even Skimif was barely a challenge for him," said Mom. "Skimif said that the gods would deal with him. Why in the world would you ever feel the need to prepare to fight him?"

"Because Uron is a threat to Martir in general," said Darek. "I don't want to be powerless against him, even though I know we mages are no match against his power. I felt like the only choice I had was to break through the ceiling; that way, if he ever comes here again, I would have a better chance of defeating him."

"Well, did it work?" said Mom. "Do you feel more powerful or are you just the same as you've always been?"

Darek did not know the answer to that, so he felt his energy levels to see if he could spot any increase in power. Unfortunately, his energy levels were still quite low; not low enough to put him in danger of breaking through the ceiling, perhaps, but not high enough for him to determine if his limits were the same as before or not.

"I don't know," said Darek. "I'd like to think it worked, but right now I don't feel very different from how I did before I tried to break through the ceiling."

Mom threw her hands into the air in exasperation. "See? You almost killed yourself for something that didn't even work."

"Well, where is everyone else?" said Darek. He looked

around the medical wing. "Is the graduation ceremony still going on? Is it over yet?"

"The ceremony should be over by now," said Mom. "After you fell unconscious, the Magical Superior ordered me and Junaz to take you here. Eyurna was just here looking you over and casting some healing spells to help you recover, but she left when I told her I could look after you just fine."

"So I missed my own graduation ceremony, then," said Darek. "That sucks."

"And that's another bad thing about what you did," said Mom. "Your fellow graduates are probably eating at the Graduation Dinner even as we speak. I thought about leaving to grab some food for you, but I decided I'd rather stay here and chew you out for being so stupid instead of rewarding you with the no doubt delicious food that Dovor prepared for everyone tonight."

That made Darek feel even worse than he already did. He always looked forward to the Graduation Dinner every year, as all students were invited and the food served was always the best he had all year. His stomach growled as he thought about all of the goodies that Dover, the school chef, had probably made.

And I missed it, Darek thought. *Missed it because I was dumb enough to try to transcend my own limits. There probably won't even be a cup of Mican pudding leftover for me.*

"I should probably go and tell the others that you're alright now," said Mom. "Everyone was worried, especially

Jiku. He's probably at the Graduation Dinner right now, but I'm sure he'll be thrilled to hear you're going to be okay."

Darek nodded, but he still felt miserable about his utter failure. He had hoped that the inherent risks in breaking through the ceiling would have been worth it, but now, he thought it was just a useless stunt that had worried everyone and almost gotten him killed.

That was when Darek remembered the skeleton. He looked at Mom again and asked, "Mom, did you or anyone else see a skeleton talking to me after I broke through the ceiling?"

Mom frowned. "A skeleton? No, of course not."

"But it was standing right next to me," said Darek. He gestured at his shoulder. "Even touched my shoulder. You sure you didn't see it?"

"Darek, I think you must be have been hallucinating," said Mom. "I've heard that mages who break through the ceiling and survive report seeing all sorts of strange things. You were probably just imagining it."

Darek wasn't so sure about that. That skeleton had been real. He knew it. Where the skeleton had come from or what its true identity was, he didn't know, but he was still as certain of that skeleton's existence as he was of his own body.

Guess I probably shouldn't worry too much about it right now, Darek thought. *There's no way I am going to find out about the skeleton sitting here arguing about him with my mother. I should probably take it easy and let my body recover. Maybe later, I can do some more research into it, if there's time.*

Mom stood up as if her seat had caught fire. "Did you feel that?"

Snapped out of his thoughts, Darek looked at Mom in confusion. "What?"

"That pulse of energy," said Mom. She reached for her wand. "Divine energy."

Then Darek felt it, too. It was a familiar feeling, one he had not felt in quite some time. It was like a heavy mist falling on his shoulders. Just feeling the energy flow through the room was enough to bring back agonizing memories of that horrible night in the graveyard a year ago.

It can't be him, Darek thought. He tried sitting up, but his body was still too weak. *He's not supposed to be here. I mean, I knew he was going to come back sooner or later, but I thought maybe he had forgotten about our deal. If I can just—*

"Darek Takren," whispered a familiar voice in his ear. "Long time, no see."

Darek looked to the right side of his bed. A huge, hulking figure, with ghostly pale armor and equally pale skin, towered over Darek and Jenur. He didn't have legs; just a wispy, ghost-like tail that writhed like a snake. His fingers looked like they were made out of metal and his eyes glowed blue like fire.

"The Ghostly God," said Darek, though he said it in a whisper, because he was so afraid of the deity who hovered before him.

The Ghostly God nodded. "I'm glad to see you remember

me, Darek. I thought that you might have forgotten about me since I haven't spoken with you in a year, but I see your memories of me are as fresh as the morning dew. That is good."

"So you're the Ghostly God I've heard so much about," said Mom. She hadn't drawn her wand, likely because there was no way she could fight a god, but she didn't cower underneath the Ghostly God's powerful gaze, at least. "You're a lot uglier than I expected."

The Ghostly God rubbed his index and thumb together, creating an annoying screeching sound that made Darek wince. "And just why should I care about your opinions? Who are you, another useless teacher?"

"Useless?" said Mom. "My name is Jenur Takren. I am Darek's mother as well as one of his teachers."

"Ah," said the Ghostly God. He frowned. "My understanding of human biology really only extends to which parts of you are edible and which parts aren't, but you two don't look similar the way relatives are supposed to."

"I adopted him when he was five," said Mom. "Besides, you're one to talk. No two of you gods look exactly alike and yet you're all siblings."

"True, but we were not created like how you humans create each other," said the Ghostly God. He stopped rubbing his fingers together, a look of puzzlement on his face. "Exactly how *do* you humans procreate? I've heard so many conflicting rumors from my siblings and from my servants that I—"

"It doesn't matter," said Mom. She pointed at the Ghostly God's chest. "Why are you here? I thought you southern gods didn't like coming up north."

The Ghostly God looked annoyed at being interrupted; nonetheless, he said, "I am here because I require Darek Takren's service, obviously. Didn't he tell you that he swore his life and service to me for ten years in exchange for a brief power boost I gave him during the battle against Uron last year?"

In truth, Darek had made certain that only a handful of people would ever know about the deal he had made with the Ghostly God. And none of them had been his mother, although with the way she was now looking at him in sheer disbelief, Darek realized that keeping that particular fact a secret from her had probably not been the wisest decision he had made in his life.

"Is he telling the truth, Darek?" said Mom, her voice full of barely suppressed rage. "Did you really swear to serve him for *ten* years?"

Darek was very careful to avoid looking at Mom as he said, "Well, Mom, you gotta understand, it was a very tense situation and I didn't have a whole lot of choice in the matter, so—"

"As amusing as it is to watch this disrespectful mage get angry, all it does is waste precious time," said the Ghostly God. "The point is, there is no backing out of a deal you make with a god or goddess, not unless you wish to spend the rest of your life walking with your hands, anyway."

"But Darek is too weak to go anywhere at the moment,"

said Mom. "That's why he's in bed here. He tried something monumentally stupid earlier and now he's paying the price for his mistake."

Oddly enough, that made the Ghostly God grin. "Monumentally stupid? Excellent. I look for that kind of stupidity in my servants. It usually means they lack the intelligence to question my orders."

"I'm not *that* stupid," Darek said, though he wasn't sure the Ghostly God had heard him.

"Still doesn't change the fact that he's not in any condition to be moving around right now," said Mom. She pointed at the nearby window. "Maybe you can leave and come back in a couple of days ... weeks ... months ... oh, let's make it a few dozen years, which is probably about half a month for you gods, right?"

"This is not something that can wait," said the Ghostly God, glaring at him. "Even if it was, I find your obvious attempts to get me out of here quite pathetic and uninspiring."

"Mom's right," said Darek. He tried to lift his arms, but they might as well have been lead weights for all the good that did him. "Can't move a muscle. Looks like I can't do whatever you want me to do for you."

"Are you so sure?" said the Ghostly God. He leaned over slightly. "Tell me, what kind of sickness ails you?"

"It's not a sickness," said Mom. "He tried to break the ceiling and ended up falling into a coma. He just needs to recharge his magical energy and he'll be fine."

The Ghostly God tapped his chin. He was leaning over

Darek so closely that Darek could now smell the stench of corpses on his body. "If that is all, then that is an easy problem for me to fix."

The Ghostly God jabbed his hand down and clamped his fingers around Darek's right arm. The god's fingers were thick and cold, like an iceberg, and their abrupt contact with his arm made him shiver.

"What are you doing?" said Mom. She had drawn her wand now and was aiming it directly at the Ghostly God's head. "Let go of Darek. Now."

"Control yourself, woman," said the Ghostly God. "He will be fine once I am done with him; in fact, I suspect he will be better than ever. You should let me do what I am about to do, rather than allow your motherly instincts to override the rational part of your brain."

"What are you talking about?" said Mom. "How do I know you won't hurt him?"

"Because an injured servant is useless to me," said the Ghostly God. "Anyway, I don't need your permission to help him. Once I restore his strength, we can move onto the real work."

Darek found enough sense to ask what the Ghostly God was planning to do to him when the god's grip around his arm tightened considerably. As soon as it did, Darek felt a surge of energy enter his body from the Ghostly God's arm. It was like getting struck by a lightning bolt.

When the energy spread over Darek's body, he gasped. His limbs no longer felt heavy and useless, but light and easy to move. He felt like he could hop out of his bed, run three laps around the Walls surrounding the school, study for four straight hours on the most complicated magical subjects in the school library, and still have enough energy leftover to perform an entire play using only the basics of geomancer to make stone 'actors' come to life to play the parts he couldn't, all for the pleasure of his fellow students and teachers.

Now Darek didn't know if he could actually do all of that or if he just felt like ir, but he did fling the blankets off his body and jump out of the bed like a rabbit. The Ghostly God had let go of his arm, looking quite smug as Darek stretched his limbs like he was readying to participate in a race soon.

"There," said the Ghostly God. "All better, I hope."

"Much better," said Darek. He looked up at the Ghostly God. "What did you do to help me?"

"I gave you a portion of my own energy, of course," said the Ghostly God. "Your magical energy, after all, is nothing more than the divine aura that we gods continuously produce. It is similar to what I did back in the graveyard a year ago, except this time your power will last for as long as you conserve it."

"Amazing," said Darek. He looked down at his hands, which felt strong enough to crack rocks. "Utterly amazing. I feel alive."

"What's the catch?" Mom asked.

"Catch?" said the Ghostly God. "For this specifically or in general? Because if we're talking generally, the catch is that Darek must work for me. The only reason I came here, after all, is because I have a job I think he is well-suited for.

Restoring his magical levels to their normal power was not a deed I did out of charity."

"It's okay, Mom," said Darek, jumping up and down. "Whatever job the Ghostly God has for me, I can handle it. I mean, I have so much power flowing through me that I can barely contain it."

The Ghostly God rolled his eyes. "Well, it is good to see that you are confident you can complete it, at least. Then again, I suppose it's hardly accurate to say that confidence always translates to competence, now isn't it?"

Darek stopped bouncing immediately, but he still felt too jittery for his own good. But a question had occurred to him that he realized that he had forgotten to ask.

"So, Ghostly God," said Darek, "just what *is* this mission you're going to send me on, anyway? Does it happen to involve looking for another ancient object designed to kill your siblings?"

The Ghostly God glared at him for that, even though there was some truth to it. After all, it had been the Ghostly God's servants, Durima and Gujak, who had brought the legendary God-killer out into the wider world, where Uron stole and used it to murder a goddess. It probably wasn't the smartest move for Darek to make, angering the Ghostly God, but he was so bouncy and full of energy that he could hardly control himself.

"It is top secret," said the Ghostly God. His glanced at Mom. "Which means I'd rather not discuss it in the presence of someone who has nothing to do with it."

Mom scowled. "What is that supposed to mean? Am I

suddenly untrustworthy now or something?"

"It means that I will tell Darek everything he needs to know in private," said the Ghostly God. "You, on the other hand, will not know any of it until well after the mission is completed, if even then. You have nothing to do with it, so why should I tell you anything about it?"

"Because I'm Darek's mother," said Mom, jerking her thumb toward her chest. "And if you're going to be putting his life in danger on the day of his graduation, I want to know why."

"Graduation?" said the Ghostly God, staring blankly at Mom. "He is graduating from the school today?"

"Yes," said Mom. "This is something he has been working toward for ten years. Right, Darek?"

Darek nodded. "Yes. And because the graduation ceremony ended a while ago, that technically means I am officially free to leave when I want and go where I please."

"That makes things simpler," said the Ghostly God. "You will be able to focus entirely on the mission at hand without having to worry about such inane things such as homework, teachers, and studying."

"But what about Darek's future?" said Mom. She looked at Darek pleadingly. "Darek, do you really want to serve the Ghostly God for ten years? What about Xocion?"

"Xocion doesn't care," said the Ghostly God before Darek could reply. "Trust me, my icy brother, if he had any problem with this arrangement, would have made it quite clear well before today."

"I understand your concern, Mom, but you remember

what the Ghostly God said," said Darek with a shrug. "I can't back out of my deal with him now. It's too late. Besides, it's just one mission. It's not like I'll have to do a mission for him every week or whatever."

Mom lowered her wand and put it in the belt around her waist, although she continued to look as worried as ever. "Well ... you're an adult now, Darek, so I guess that means I can't tell you what to do anymore. Especially if you've made a prior arrangement with a god. Still, I don't like it."

"Don't worry, mother dearest," said the Ghostly God as he floated over to Darek. "I will make sure to bring your little boy home safe, although I cannot guarantee that he will be sane."

Darek started when the Ghostly God said that, but before he could ask for an elaboration, the Ghostly God grabbed Darek's upper arm and pulled. In a minute, everything around them went black and Darek saw Mom no more.

Chapter Five

It had been a long time since Durima had last set foot in World's End, also known as the Throne of the Gods, the very last island in Martir before one entered the Void. In fact, the last time she had been here was when she was packing up her things when she went to work for the Ghostly God shortly after the end of the Katabans War. The Ghostly God had told her that her service to him was likely to be long-term, which meant that she had had to get rid of or sell anything she couldn't take with her to Zamis, the Ghostly God's island.

That had been twenty-four years ago. As she and Gujak were walked through the streets of World's End, Durima noticed how little the city had changed since she had last been here. The streets were as white and soft as ever, with not a speck of dust to be seen anywhere. The skyscrapers, all set together to resemble a giant throne from a distance, were as huge and magnificent as always and appeared to be made out of rubies and diamonds and emeralds and other precious metals and stones. There weren't any new ones that she could see, but of course there wouldn't be. World's End had been finished by the Powers year ago and had only required minor repairs since then, though even those were rare and unusual.

Not surprising, Durima thought. *Everyone who lives here treats the city as delicately as a newborn baby. Even during the Katabans War, both sides kept World's End out of the conflict as much as they could. And I imagine that it will stay undisturbed until the end of time, if that day ever comes.*

One odd thing that Durima had noticed, when they had landed on the beach of World's End via the ethereal, were the array of battleships anchored in the harbor. None of the Soldiers had explained where the battleships had come from or what they were supposed to do, nor had Durima asked, as she didn't think they would answer the questions of a criminal like her, no matter how innocent those questions might have been.

But the fact was, World's End was never defended by a navy. As it was home to the gods, it had only the barest defenses, because it was believed that the gods themselves would defend it should the need ever arise. Last time Durima had been here, the only defense that World's End had had was the city walls, but even those were not highly fortified.

They're expecting an attack, Durima thought. *But who are they expecting to attack? You'd have to be a complete imbecile to attack World's End ... unless you are Uron, that is.*

Durima was snapped out of her thoughts when the Soldier who held her chains jerked them. She staggered forward, almost tripping over her own feet before regaining her balance and resuming her walk behind the Soldier.

Gujak walked beside her, his head hanging on his chest. He looked much better now—he had been healed by one of the Soldiers, who had said that Gujak needed to look his best if he was going to stand in the presence of the Katabans Council—but he had clearly resigned himself to their fate. She didn't say anything to him, mostly because she didn't know what she could say to cheer him up.

The two detainees were surrounded on all sides by about a dozen Soldiers, with Commander Erich in the lead. Originally, Durima and Gujak had been escorted by three dozen of them, but when they arrived on World's End, Erich had dismissed the two dozen extra, stating that he didn't think their help was going to be needed or necessary right now.

Isn't that true? Durima thought. *Neither I nor Gujak are going to be making any escape attempts any time soon. Of course we aren't. There is literally no place we can run to now.*

One dozen well-armed and well-armored Soldiers escorting the two most wanted criminals in all of Martir did not go unnoticed by World End's general populace. Most of the people they walked past would take a moment to stop and stare—and often glare—at Durima and Gujak. One such gawker even threw a stone at them, which had hit Durima in the shoulder, though she had been forced to ignore it thanks to the convoy of Soldiers forcing her to keep walking.

The citizens of World's End were katabans like Gujak and her; however, many of these katabans looked far more human than Gujak and she. For most of them, the only clue to their true nature was their strange hair color: blue, silver, golden, green, purple, and many others. Their clothing, too, looked different from what humans wore, more closely resembling a cross between the mage's robes worn by mortal mages in the Northern Isles and common worker's leather.

Despite the kinship Durima and Gujak shared with the citizens of World's End, however, Durima hardly felt welcomed among them. Every eye that followed their progression up the street was full of hate and anger. Every single person here knew why Durima and Gujak were in the city, but none of them actually approached her or Gujak, partly because of the convoy of Soldiers escorting them, partly because the katabans were trained by the Council to let the Council handle such serious matters.

On one hand, that made Durima feel relieved. She had been expecting her and Gujak to get mobbed the minute they stepped foot in the city, but the Soldiers had so far been an excellent mob deterrent. Still, she saw more than a few katabans who looked like they wouldn't mind slitting her throat if given a chance. There was even one katabans— who resembled a small child—that was not-so-discreetly following the Soldiers wherever they went, though the Soldiers themselves didn't seem to notice.

More likely, they just don't care, Durima thought. *Still, it's unnerving to be followed around by someone who obviously would like to kill me. Then again, this isn't the first time someone who wanted to kill me has stalked me. I had quite a few such stalkers during the War, especially after everyone started calling me the Demon.*

That was why Durima kept her head down as much as she could while they walked. She didn't want to look at the glaring eyes, the hateful glances, or hear the whispers and murmurs from the citizens about the crime that she and Gujak had committed. She was not normally afraid of false rumors and harsh looks, but given what her and Gujak's ultimate fate was going to be, she didn't want her last memories of her people to include the hatefulness with which they treated her. It was just too much on top of everything else.

"Here we are," Erich said, in a slightly singsong voice. "The Hall of Judgment, where the Council will hand out your final sentences for your unforgivable crime against the gods."

Although Durima had seen the Hall of Judgment several times before, she looked up at it again as they approached, as it had been many years since she had last seen it and so didn't remember it very well.

The Hall of Judgment was not as huge as the skyscrapers, perhaps being about the same size as the Temple of the Gods. Nonetheless, it was an imposing building in its own right. Titanic stone columns, made of a burning red rock, supported a shining silver roof, upon which a metal statue of the God of Justice himself, Grinf, towered over all. The Grinf statue featured the god holding his gavel aloft while treading on a criminal who appeared to be dead or at least unconscious.

Massive stone steps led up to the front doors of the Hall

of Judgment, which were made out of thick marble and had rubies and sapphires embedded along their edges. Even from their current position, Durima could see the words *JUSTICE IS FROM THE GODS* written above the door, because they were written in gold which reflected the light from the sun's rays above.

The Soldiers forced Durima and Gujak up the steps to the front doors, where they found two other Soldiers acting as guards protecting it. The two guards immediately noticed Durima and Gujak and one of them whispered quite audibly to his friend, "There they are. The god-killers."

Great, Durima thought. *We have a nickname now. I guess we've really made it.*

Erich walked up to the guards and flashed his badge in their faces. "Commander Erich, leader of the Soldiers of the Gods, here with the two god-killers who murdered the Spider Goddess on Bleak Rock last year. I am here to bring them before the Council, who will decide their ultimate fates today."

The two guards peered at Erich's badge and then stepped aside once they were certain that he was telling the truth. Erich then knocked on the doors and stood back as they opened inward; albeit, slowly, due to their massive size.

When the doors were fully open, Erich entered the Hall. The Soldiers behind and around Durima and Gujak forced them to follow—not that Durima needed the encouragement. It wasn't like she or Gujak could run away; after all, where would they run *to*?

The interior of the Hall of Judgment was, in Durima's opinion, just as magnificent as the exterior. Soaring walls, so clean that they gleamed from the light of the crystal chandeliers above, made Durima feel like she was walking in an open field, rather than inside a large building. Another statue of Grinf met them in the lobby, but whereas the outside statue had been standing on top of a captured criminal, this Grinf was sitting in a high-backed chair, his gavel on his lap, his fingers curled around the chain of a criminal who sat by his side with a long face.

This statue of Grinf was huge, towering over everyone else, yet because the interior of the Hall of Judgment was so wide open, it still didn't quite take up the entire room. Still, Durima felt like the golden eyes of that Grinf statue followed her and Gujak specifically, as if it knew what horrible crime they had committed against the gods and did not want to let them out of its sight.

Aside from the gigantic Grinf statue, the Hall's lobby had several armed guards protecting doors to various rooms. No doubt those rooms were other judgment halls, where criminals were likely being tried by katabans judges who had been carefully handpicked by Grinf himself to deliver justice.

If only the same could be said about the Council, Durima thought, scowling as she and Gujak were led past the Grinf statue. *Apparently, the only reason they're allowed to rule is because they're 'wiser' than the rest of us. I don't know how they managed to convince the gods of that, but there you go.*

Beyond the Grinf statue was another staircase leading up to yet another set of double doors. Durima, having once visited the Hall of Judgment many years ago, knew that what lay behind those double doors was the Justice Chamber. It was only where the worst of katabans criminals were tried by the Council itself. It was rarely used, since most katabans criminals rarely committed crimes great enough for the Council to try them. In fact, the last time that the Justice Chamber had been used, to Durima's knowledge, was at the end of the Katabans War, when the leader of the defeated side and his loyalists were brought before the Council and sentenced to life imprisonment.

It only makes sense that Gujak and I would be tried there, Durima thought. *After all, we've committed a crime that not even the worst criminal would ever think of committing. I am surprised that they didn't just execute us on the spot back on Bleak Rock and call it a day.*

They climbed up the tall stone stairs, each step difficult for Durima, as her legs were short and the steps were fairly tall. Gujak had no problem making the climb, but he didn't look at all excited about having to do it. The Soldiers, however, did not let her or Gujak slow down; in fact, they did quite the opposite, poking them in their backs to keep them moving up and up.

The double doors to the Justice Chamber resembled the front doors, although much smaller in stature due to being indoors. The symbol of Grinf, a golden gavel covered with fire, decorated both doors. Erich pushed the doors open, as they were small enough for him to do that, and then stepped aside as Durima and Gujak were herded directly into the Justice Chamber.

This was the first time Durima had ever been inside the Justice Chamber, so she paid more attention to her surroundings than she normally did. Unlike the lobby, the Justice Chamber was very small, more like a normal-sized room than an open field. Four benches, each equal in size and made of a fine deep brown wood, stood on the back wall, near a door that probably led to the room where the Council itself was debating their fates. The benches looked more like thrones to Durima and there was no jury, but that was normal for criminals to be tried by the Council.

Durima and Gujak stood in the slightly depressed pit in the center of the room. There was no place for them to sit, but that didn't matter because Durima doubted this trial would be very long. Once the Council came here, it would all be over quickly.

Then half of the dozen Soldiers exited the room, leaving only six to surround Durima and Gujak on all sides. Erich closed and locked the doors. Without any windows, there was truly no way for Durima and Gujak to make an escape unless they tried to fight the Soldiers first.

Which would most definitely be suicide at this point, Durima thought, eying the sharp crystalline swords of the Soldiers and their bulging biceps. *I imagine the only reason they haven't torn us to pieces yet is because they have orders from the Council not to. I wonder if these six will get the honor of executing us once the Council tells them to.*

Erich walked over to the door next to the benches and

entered without knocking. He emerged a minute later, a smirk on his human-like features.

"The Council will be here in a few minutes," Erich said, folding his arms across his chest. "In the meantime, you two keep your mouths shut. You will have plenty of opportunity to defend yourself before the Council once they appear, although I do not think anything you say will help."

Gujak gave a great, big shuddering gasp, like he was going to cry any minute. Durima jabbed him in the side with her elbow and glared at him. She didn't want Gujak losing his composure in such a delicate situation. They were in this together, so if one of them looked weak, it would make both of them look weak.

Just as Erich said, a few minutes later, the door to the Council's chambers opened and four katabans walked out of it. Although each one of them was different, they all wore the same red-and-gold robes of Grinf that all katabans judges wore. The four Council members climbed onto their benches without even bothering to look at Durima or Gujak, though Durima could sense their intense hostility toward her and Gujak just the same.

As the four Council members adjusted their seats, Durima looked at them. She had only seen the Council members from a distance, when they were making pronouncements in front of the Temple of the Gods or at the yearly Festival of the Gods that happened at the beginning of each new year, in which they were always the guests of honor. This was the first time she had seen them up close, so she took this opportunity to get a better look at them than she normally did.

The first one was Valumor, the oldest member of the Council, who had a wolfish face that looked odd with his judge robes. If Durima remembered correctly, Valumor had been a General in the Katabans War, fighting on the side of the Council, and had in fact won the final battle of the War. That was why he had been given a spot on the Council, although Durima had never fought under him, so she didn't know how good of a General he actually was.

The one on Valumor's right was Kaxu. She had a vaguely humanoid face, except her hair was as scruffy as a lion's mane. Her claws were neatly trimmed, almost too neat, which Durima thought was a pointless thing to do because it left her vulnerable to attack. Then again, Kaxu hadn't fought in the War, so it made sense she'd know nothing about using every advantage she had in order to survive.

To Valumor's left sat Huju, the most human-looking of them all. He had a very young, almost boyish face, with the only clue to his true nature being his purple eyes. He sat with slumped shoulders, like a sulky teenager, but Durima was no fool. If the rumors she had heard about him were true, he was the most devious and manipulative of all of the Council members. He only pretended to be an immature little boy, which made him someone to watch out for, in her opinion.

On Huju's left was the final member of the Council, Namusa, who in contrast to Huju resembled an aquarian more than a human. She had an eel-like face that seemed to be constantly sweating some kind of greenish liquid, which somehow did not stain her judge's robes.

Normally, Durima would not be afraid of the Council, as she believed them to be nothing more than self-important fools who thought they were better than everyone else. Today, however, she could not deny the tingle of fear creeping up her spine as she watched the Council members finish adjusting their seats.

Beside her, Gujak didn't make a sound—which was good; very good, in fact. Durima wanted to go out with dignity, and she did not think it would look very dignified if Gujak was acting like the blubbering mess he usually became when under intense pressure like this.

Durima stood straight and tall while the Council members looked down on them with utter contempt on their features. Having once been looked at by enemy soldiers who had wanted to kill her, she wasn't as bothered by the Council's contemptuous glares.

Erich walked up to the front of the Council and stood ramrod straight. He saluted the Council and said, "Sir and Madame Council Members, I present to you the divine murderers, Durima, also known as the Demon, and Gujak, the one who, according to all reports, personally murdered the Spider Goddess himself."

"The Council knows that, Commander," said Valumor, putting the tips of his fingers together, "but thank you for reiterating the facts. It is important we are all on the same page here in order to make sure that the judgment we will pass on Durima and Gujak is perfect and just."

"Yes, Sir Council Member Valumor," said Erich, bowing.

He then stepped aside, allowing the Council a better view of Durima and Gujak, who were still surrounded on every side by Erich's Soldiers.

Valumor held up a scroll and unfurled it. "Now, there is no doubt in our minds that the accused who stand here are indeed guilty of the murder of the Spider Goddess. Correct?"

He looked at his fellow Council members. None of them uttered even one word of disagreement.

"Very well," said Valumor. He then returned his attention to the scroll. "Even so, that does not mean we must execute them right away. Although Durima and Gujak are criminals of the worst order who have forfeit their right to life by taking the life of a goddess—an unspeakable crime that has never been committed by any katabans in the history of Martir—to execute them right away without giving them a fair hearing would, in my opinion, be a perversion of justice, and we Council members love justice more than anything else."

"This is a waste of time," said Kaxu, shaking her head. "Grinf gave us specific orders to capture these two and bring them to justice. We already know they did it. Why bother listening to their pitiful defenses?"

"I already said why," said Valumor. "It is a part of our justice system. Every accused person has the right to explain himself or herself to the Council. Not that it will do anything to change our minds, but I feel it is only fair that we do so."

"I'll kill 'em myself if I must," said Kaxu. "They've been

running free for a year. That is far too long for any criminal to run free, especially criminals as wicked and evil as they."

"I am the Head of the Council," said Valumor. "And I say they get a chance to speak. It won't be very long—as you said, Kaxu, they've gone unpunished for too long—but it must be done in accordance with what Grinf commanded us many years ago."

Kaxu folded her arms, while the other two Council members remained as silent as always.

"Now, who wishes to speak first?" said Valumor, addressing Durima and Gujak.

Durima held up her chained hands. "I do."

Valumor sat back in his seat, looking slightly offended, probably because Durima had not called him 'Sir Council Member.' That had been intentional on her part. She held no respect for the Council, not after what they did during the Katabans War. She would address them as she wished, not how they wanted; after all, if she was going to be killed anyway, she had little reason to be polite.

Beside her, Gujak was still quiet. She hadn't even sensed him about to speak, but that didn't matter. Durima knew better than to let Gujak get an opportunity to blubber. In his current state, if he talked to the Council, he'd likely break down completely.

"Fine," said Valumor. "Durima the Demon, wasn't it? Didn't we offer you a position as a Soldier of the Gods shortly after the end of the Katabans War for your bravery and expertise in battle?"

Durima nodded curtly. "Indeed you did. And I rejected

the offer because I did not want to obey you."

"A shame," said Valumor with a sigh. "I remember how well you fought in the War. You went to work for the Ghostly God after that, didn't you?"

Durima frowned. "I did. May I ask what our former Master is doing now?"

"That is irrelevant to our current discussion," said Valumor. "Anyway, this is not the time for conversation. It is the time for you to defend yourself and Gujak from our accusations, even though there is clearly no way for either of you to do that."

Durima drew herself up to her full height. "All right. Although the accusations thrown against us—that we killed the Spider Goddess—are correct, there are many nuances of that action that you Council members are probably unaware of."

"What is there to be aware of?" said Kaxu. She pointed at them accusingly. "You two murdered a goddess. That is proof enough that you deserve nothing more than the harshest punishment imaginable."

"You still don't understand," said Durima. She looked at all of the Council members with disgust. "None of you understand the most important thing about what we did: Context. Nothing, not even the worst crime, happens in a vacuum. By ignoring context, you are going to commit a great injustice by putting us to death."

"Tell us, then, Demon, what this 'context' is," said Kaxu. "I am interested in hearing you justify your murder of a goddess."

"It wasn't murder," said Durima. "We didn't go to Bleak Rock intending to murder the Spider Goddess. We went there because our former Master, the Ghostly God, ordered us to get the God-killer. We didn't even know what it was at the time and only used it out of self-defense, because the Spider Goddess was going to eat us if we didn't."

"A likely story," said Kaxu with a sneer. "Why would the Ghostly God ask you to get the God-killer? That makes no sense."

"Because he was being manipulated by Uron," said Durima. "You know who Uron is, right?"

The entire Council shifted uneasily in their seats at the mention of that omnicidal being's name. Durima took that as a yes.

"The Ghostly God was manipulated by Uron as part of Uron's plan to destroy the gods," said Durima. She looked around the chamber, "which as far as I can tell has not gone anywhere, considering how I have not felt the deaths of any other gods since Uron murdered the Avian Goddess a year ago."

"Uron is irrelevant to this trial," said Valumor, although he glanced at the ceiling as if he thought Uron might be hanging there, listening to their every word. "You have no proof that Uron even manipulated the Ghostly God, so how can we accept your claim?"

"The proof is in the fact that Uron has the God-killer," said Durima. "And yes, Uron actually is relevant to this 'trial,' if you want to call it that. We wouldn't even be here if it wasn't for his manipulations. Have the gods found him yet?"

"That is none of your business," said Valumor, giving her a firm look. "Now are you quite finished feeding the Council crazy, unfounded stories about Uron manipulating the Ghostly God or are you done?"

"I'm not done yet at all," said Durima, shaking her head. "Why isn't the Ghostly God here? Call him. He can back up everything I just said."

"C-Call a god?" said Valumor with a gulp. "Durima, I hope you understand that not even the Council has the right to summon any god or goddess unless it is an emergency of the highest order. Besides, Lord Grinf told us that we didn't need to summon the Ghostly God anyway."

"Why would Grinf tell you that?" said Durima. "Surely he must know about what is actually going on here, shouldn't he? By allowing you to execute us, a great injustice is being wrought in the House of Grinf, as this place is sometimes called."

"There is no injustice being wrought here," said Valumor, speaking quickly. "Lord Grinf's orders were as clear as day: Execute the criminals who dared to kill one of his sisters. It is the only just punishment for scum like you."

Durima shook her head. That didn't make any sense. Every god or goddess in Martir had to know by now the truth about what happened on that night at Bleak Rock a year ago. Grinf had had plenty of time to find out the truth. It made little sense for him to order their deaths when they didn't actually murder the Spider Goddess.

Then Durima felt someone tugging at her arm hairs. She

looked to her left and saw Gujak looking at her. His eyes were full of despair, as if he was resigned to their inevitable execution.

"What?" said Durima. "Can't you see I'm busy?"

"Durima, I just wanted to say that it's no use," said Gujak, his voice flat and hollow. "The Council's not gonna listen to us. They're just going to kill us. We might as well go with whatever they're going to do to us."

"Defeatist nonsense," Durima snapped. "I don't have time for any of it. Don't you see all of the holes in their logic that I do?"

Gujak hung his head again and sighed. "I don't know. I just don't think it matters."

Loser, Durima thought, shaking her head as she returned her attention to the Council and said aloud, "I know this is true. We are innocent. There is no reason why Grinf would tolerate, much less order, a trial unjust as this in his House. Where is Grinf right now?

"Lord Grinf is with Lord Skimif, of course," said Valumor. "They are tracking down Uron, as all of the gods have been doing for the past year."

"If you knew we were guilty right from the start, then why did you wait so long to arrest us?" said Durima. She gestured with her head toward the Chamber's exit. "And this is probably actually irrelevant to the discussion, but where did all of those battleships anchored off World's End shore come from? Are you expecting another Katabans War?"

Valumor looked flustered by Durima's questions,

although Kaxu leaned forward and said shortly, "That is none of your business. Now that you've been given a chance to defend yourself, I believe it is time to bring this trial to a close." She sat back and looked at her fellow Council members. "Is everyone in agreement?"

"Why are you avoiding my questions?" said Durima before the rest of the Council could respond. "Is it because of Uron? Are you afraid he'll attack World's End, so you set up all those battleships to stop him if he attacks from the sea?"

"No one here is afraid of Uron," Valumor snapped. "The gods assured us that Uron is no threat to World's End. He'd be a fool, even with the God-killer, to attack World's End."

"Would he?" said Durima. "I don't think so. Last time I saw Uron, he wasn't afraid of anyone, not even Skimif. There's no one else you would need to defend World's End from anyway, considering how the only other possible threat—the Sleeping Beast—was killed decades ago."

"Soldiers, kill them now," Kaxu ordered. "Then dump their bodies into the sea. It is the only fate that murderers like them deserve."

Immediately, the Soldiers turned on Durima and Gujak, holding their weapons above their heads as they prepared to strike them. Durima crouched defensively, while Gujak just stood there with his head hanging as usual, like he hadn't even noticed that they were about to get hacked into pieces by a bunch of murderous Soldiers. Seeing the looks of eagerness on the Soldiers' faces and the way that the light above gleamed off the blades of their weapons, Durima felt about as depressed as Gujak looked.

Then Valumor held up a hand and said, "Wait. Soldiers, hold your positions. Do not kill Durima and Gujak."

The Soldiers stopped where they stood, each one of them frowning like they had been told to jump off a cliff and sprout wings on the way down. Durima didn't know what Valumor was planning, but she was grateful that, for the moment at least, she and Gujak were going to live.

"Sir Council Member?" said Erich, looking up at Valumor. "May I ask why you ordered my men not to kill the murderers? I thought that that was the punishment for murder, according to the Laws of Grinf."

"He contradicted me," said Kaxu. She was glaring at Valumor. "The Council is *supposed* to stand as one united face, Valumor. Why did you order them to halt their attack? Don't you think they deserve nothing less than death?"

"Don't get me wrong, Kaxu," said Valumor, tapping the tips of his fingers together he looked down on Durima and Gujak. "I believe that death is exactly what they deserve; however, I do not believe that this is the right way to execute them."

"Why?" said Kaxu, slamming her fists on the arms of her bench. "We agreed to make this trial and execution as swift as possible. I think that having these Soldiers hack them into pieces is the swiftest way to kill them."

"Swift it may be, but it is also inappropriate," said Valumor. He glanced at the Council members on either side of him. "Fellow Council members, don't you think that Durima and Gujak deserve a special kind of execution for their crimes? They have committed a unique crime in katabans history, that of murdering a god. Executing them like ordinary murderers is not, in my opinion, appropriate. The punishment must be more severe than that."

"Oh?" said Kaxu. "Then how, Valumor, do you think we *should* kill them?"

"I am glad you asked," said Valumor. He looked at his fellow Council members again. "With the approval of the rest of the Council, I suggest that we banish Durima and Gujak beyond the Void, into that place where no katabans—or anyone else—has ever returned from."

Durima gasped. Even Gujak broke out of his depressed rut long enough to look up in shock at that suggestion.

The other Council members, on the other hand, appeared to be giving Valumor's suggestion serious thought. Huju was smiling and chuckling like he thought it was a brilliant idea, while Namusa wore a thoughtful, intrigued expression. Even Kaxu no longer looked as angry as she previously had, though she seemed annoyed at the fact that she had not been the one to come up with that idea.

"The Void," said Kaxu. "Why the Void?"

"It's simple," said Valumor. "To my knowledge, there is no crime in the law books that results in banishment beyond the Void for the criminal who committed it. The Void is not very far away from World's End; just a quick boat trip from the southern end of the island to the edge of the world."

"What's to stop Durima and Gujak from passing through the Void back into Martir?" said Kaxu, casting a quick, hateful glance at Durima and Gujak.

"They won't be able to," said Valumor. "Remember when Lord Skimif banished Hollech beyond the Void years ago? He likely sealed it from the other side, making it impossible for anyone to return to Martir. And just to make sure, we can set up an armada of ships to patrol the waters near the Void to keep Durima and Gujak from returning, should they be foolish enough to try."

"Val, that's pretty brilliant," said Huju, rubbing his hands together eagerly. "I've always wanted to use the Void as the consequence for breaking some law or another, but I didn't really know for sure which law until today. I approve."

"I approve as well," said Namusa. "I can think of no more appropriate punishment for divine murderers than to be banished where they can harm no god."

"Exactly," said Valumor. "Let's see, according to my count, that's three to one, unless you've changed your mind, Kaxu?"

Kaxu sighed reluctantly. "Fine. I approve as well. I suppose it doesn't matter how we kill them so long as they die."

"That's the whole Council," said Valumor with a wolfish grin. "That makes it official. Erich?"

Erich stood at attention. "Yes, Sir Council Member?"

Valumor leaned forward to look at the Commander better. "The Council wants you and your Soldiers to take Durima and Gujak beyond the Void. Make sure that they actually enter the Void and that they do not escape en route."

Erich saluted Valumor. "Yes, Sir Council Member. We will do as you command."

"Don't banish us beyond the Void!" Gujak cried out, his sudden outburst causing Durima to start. "That's inhumane. We don't deserve it."

"Of course you deserve it," said Valumor. He gestured at his fellow Council members. "The Council has agreed that the proper punishment for criminals who murder gods is banishment beyond the Void. And if the Council says it, then it becomes law, which means that your punishment must be carried out as the law states."

"B-But it's too cruel," said Gujak, his voice becoming harder to understand as tears flowed from his eyes. "The Void is a horrible place. Nothing lives out there. It's just death and darkness. Not even the gods have any power out there."

"That is exactly why we agreed to put you out there," said Valumor. "Now quit your whining. It won't change our minds or make us like you any better. When the Council decrees something, it is so, and we will not backpedal the punishment that you deserve."

Gujak's lips trembled, but he didn't say anything else. Durima wanted to argue about their sentence as well, but as Gujak had already said what she wanted to, she just kept her mouth shut as the Soldiers escorted her and Gujak out of the Chamber.

I've always been curious about what lies beyond the Void, Durima thought grimly, *though I doubt, once I am beyond the Void, I will live long enough to learn much about it.*

Chapter Six

One moment, Darek was standing in the medical wing of North Academy; the next moment, after the Ghostly God grabbed his arm, he found himself standing on the front porch of a mansion that he had never seen before. Now Darek had teleported before, but he had never been teleported by a god before. The experience was so abrupt that he did not know how to handle it, although considering that he seemed to be in one piece, he supposed it hadn't been all that bad.

The Ghostly God had relinquished his grip on Darek's arm now. He floated beside Darek, looking down at him with impatience.

"Are you just going to stand there and look like an idiot?" said the Ghostly God. "Or did the teleportation mush your fragile human brain?"

Darek rubbed the back of his head. "My brain is just fine, Ghostly God. I was just surprised by how abrupt that teleportation was, that's all."

"I was in a hurry," said the Ghostly God. "The mission I have for you is one of utmost importance. But first, let us go inside. We can discuss it in more detail in there. I do not trust the outside."

The Ghostly God gestured at the mansion, which they

stood in front of. Darek turned to look at it better. It was an old and creepy mansion with a couple of boarded up windows here and there. Darek had never seen this mansion before in his life; as a matter of fact, Darek could not recall ever seeing a mansion in person before. There weren't any in North Academy, after all, and Darek had never traveled beyond the Great Berg to the Northern Isles, where mansions might be found. Its presence here confused him, to say the least.

"Are we in the Northern Isles?" Darek asked, looking up at the Ghostly God. "I thought you southern gods' territories were in the south."

"Of course we're not in the north," said the Ghostly God. "Why would you ever think that? Don't tell me you already forgot that I am a southern god?"

"No," said Darek, shaking his head. He gestured at the mansion. "The mansion confused me, that's all."

"Ah, yes," said the Ghostly God, returning his gaze to the large house before them. "I can see how that could be confusing. But no, this is my mansion on my island, which is in the southern seas."

Darek frowned. "But why would you have a mansion that looks like something a human would build? I thought you southern gods looked down on our mortal creations."

"True enough," said the Ghostly God. "Mortal creations, in general, tend to be inferior to divine creations in every way. Nonetheless, when I was first told about the buildings you humans made by Diog, I decided a mansion would be an appropriate headquarters for me. Except it is far superior to any mansion built by mortals, obviously."

"How did you build it?" asked Darek, squinting at the upper floors, which were covered in mist. "Did you build it yourself?"

"No," said the Ghostly God, shaking his head. "Many years back, I had a former katabans servant of mine—who died two years ago, I think, though I rarely keep track of my former servants' lives after they have finished their years of servitude—kidnap a human architect. I forced the architect to design a mansion for me and to make it well, which I can safely say he did, as my mansion has stood for almost a century now and has shown no signs of falling apart."

"What happened to that architect you hired?" said Darek. "Did you send him back to his home?"

The Ghostly God licked his lips. "I ate him, of course. He was delicious."

Darek didn't bother to hide his grimace. The southern gods were known for eating humans; in fact, it was the whole reason that they and the northern gods had been separated in the first place. Yet Darek had almost forgotten that the Ghostly God had an appetite for mortals, probably because the Ghostly God had shown no interest in eating Darek.

But we are beyond the Dividing Line, Darek thought. *That means that there's nothing to stop the Ghostly God from eating me alive if he wanted. Maybe that's the whole reason he summoned me here. He has no mission for me. He's just hungry and wants a snack.*

Darek rested his hand on his wand, which he was

relieved to find was still attached to his belt. Even so, he knew it wouldn't do him much good. In a straight one-on-one battle, there was no way a mage like Darek could defeat a deity like the Ghostly God. Still, Darek felt safer knowing he had his wand by his side, despite the fact that it was technically nothing more than a glorified piece of wood against the Ghostly God.

"Now, then," said the Ghostly God as he pushed the front door open. "Let us go inside. I will brief you on your mission once I am sure no one is listening."

Once again, Darek frowned. He looked around, but with the mist around the mansion so thick, he couldn't see much. "Listening? Do you mean that someone might be eavesdropping on us?"

"Just come inside," said the Ghostly God, gesturing for Darek to follow as he entered his mansion. "And close the door on your way in."

Darek hesitated. He could try to run now, if he wanted. If he walked into the Ghostly God's mansion, he would be trapped in there, at the mercy of a southern god who had already admitted to eating mortals. Walking into the Ghostly God's mansion was like walking into a pit of sharks.

But then Darek remembered that he had nowhere to run to. He couldn't even teleport off the island, seeing as he did not know Zamis's exact location. All he knew for sure was that Zamis was somewhere in the southern seas, which meant that it was too far away from the Great Berg for him to attempt to teleport back to North Academy.

So Darek, making sure he could draw his wand in a

pinch, stepped into the Ghostly God's mansion and closed the door behind him as silently as he could.

The interior of the mansion was even more bleak than the exterior. The windows were curtained by shabby gray curtains that looked like they had been torn by a mad knife man. Old empty picture frames hung on the walls, although a few were partially covered by peeling wallpaper that needed to be replaced. A stone podium, covered in dust and cobwebs, stood in the center of the foyer, right in front of the wide staircase, although what, if anything, was supposed to be there, Darek didn't know.

The Ghostly God spread his arms wide. "Welcome to my mansion, Darek Takren. What do you think?"

Darek sniffed the air. It smelled like a rotting old house to him. Not to mention that the air was cold, although as Darek had felt much colder temperatures back in the Great Berg, he tolerated it well enough.

"It's ... old," said Darek. He kept his words level, knowing how volatile the southern gods could be. "And kind of creepy."

The Ghostly God turned around as fast as lightning. "Creepy? Of course. That's the point. Why would I want to make it seem homely? I am the Ghostly God. I rule the spirits of the departed. I study what lies beyond the veil of death. None of that is very *homely*, in my opinion."

A chunk of plaster from the ceiling landed near Darek's feet, its fall so sudden that Darek almost jumped. When he realized it was just plaster, he relaxed and remained where he was.

"So the decrepit appearance is intentional, then," said Darek, hugging his body to keep in the warmth.

"Exactly," said the Ghostly God. "But that is beside the point. Now that we are in my mansion, I think it is safe for me to brief you on the details of the mission I have in store for you."

Darek nodded. "All right. I'm ready to listen."

"I'm ready to listen, *Master*," the Ghostly God corrected.

Darek bit his lower lip. "So you want me to call you Master?"

"It is the title all of my servants have called me," said the Ghostly God. "Besides, you agreed to serve me for ten years. Calling me Master was perhaps not explicitly part of the original deal, but you should have known going in that I would demand that you address me in that way."

Darek wanted to ask how he was supposed to know that, seeing as he didn't know the Ghostly God very well, but he held his tongue. No doubt the Ghostly God would come up with some terrible punishment for him if he started talking back.

And he is a god, after all, Darek thought. *Maybe not the best god in the world, but that doesn't mean he isn't worthy of the respect we mages are supposed to show all gods, right?*

"Now, say it again," said the Ghostly God. "I'm ready to listen, Master."

Dark took a deep breath and said, "I'm ready to listen, Master."

"Excellent," said the Ghostly God. "You are learning quickly. I like that in servants. You are already above Durima and Gujak in my eyes, and you haven't even done anything for me yet."

"Speaking of those two, where are they?" said Darek, looking to the left and right, hoping to see them peeking out from a nearby room. "Do they still serve you?"

The Ghostly God shook his head. "I haven't seen them since that night when Uron appeared in the graveyard. I believe they ran away."

"Why?" said Darek. When he saw the look of annoyance on the Ghostly God's face, he added, "Uh, Master?"

"They ran away because they were afraid of being caught and punished for their crime of murdering my sister the Spider Goddess," said the Ghostly God. "In other words, no, Darek Takren, Durima and Gujak do not serve me any longer. I have no idea where they are or what they're currently doing and I do not care to find out."

"Oh," said Darek. "I was hoping to thank Durima for getting the Magical Superior to safety when Uron and Skimif were battling in the graveyard. But I guess I can't do that now."

"Why would you need to?" said the Ghostly God. "Those two were always idiots, anyway. Useless, bumbling fools who never did anything right. I don't even know why I allowed them to serve me for as long as they did. Good riddance, I say."

Darek thought that that was a bit harsh, but considering how cruel the Ghostly God was, he saw no reason to push the issue. It wasn't like he knew Durima or Gujak well enough to say whether the Ghostly God's judgment of them was accurate, after all.

"But Durima and Gujak are entirely irrelevant to this discussion," said the Ghostly God. "I should have briefed you several minutes ago. Let's get to the point, shall we?"

"Yes ... Master," said Darek, remembering to address the Ghostly God that way only at the last minute.

"Very good," said the Ghostly God, nodding. He turned and began heading up the stairs. "Follow me. I will explain what your mission is as we walk."

Darek, not sure he wanted to go any deeper into this creepy mansion than he already had, reluctantly followed the Ghostly God until he was walking by the deity's side. The steps creaked under Darek's footsteps as he walked, which added to the eerie atmosphere of the mansion.

"Your mission is dangerous," said the Ghostly God when they were about halfway up the stairs. "But it is one that only a mortal like yourself can complete."

Darek didn't say anything to that, as he did not know how to respond to such vague comments.

"Tell me, Darek Takren, have you ever heard of Jakuuth Grinfborn?" said the Ghostly God, glancing at Darek briefly before returning his gaze to the stairs they climbed.

"Jakuuth Grinfborn ... Grinfborn ..." Darek frowned as he searched his memory for someone with that name. "That name sounds familiar, but distant, like an old memory I haven't thought about in ages."

"No doubt it is," said the Ghostly God. "Jakuuth

Grinfborn is a name that hasn't been spoken of by mortals in twenty-five years, since the end of the Katabans War. It's a name that *should* be long-forgotten by everyone except the gods ... but sadly, it will be one that soon everyone will remember, whether they want to or not."

"But who *is* Jakuuth Grinfborn?" said Darek as they reached the top of the stairs. "You say it's an old name, but you still haven't told me whose name it is."

The Ghostly God turned to the left and went down a narrow, creaky hallway. Darek followed behind, as he could not walk by the Ghostly God's side due to the narrowness of the hallway.

"Jakuuth Grinfborn was a human mage very much like yourself," said the Ghostly God, who was now moving at a much slower pace than normal. "He even trained in North Academy ... for a brief period, anyway."

"A brief period?" said Durima. "Was he expelled or did he leave on his own?"

The Ghostly God shook his head in disgust. "Expelled, and for good reason. He made the heretical claim that he was the Son of Grinf."

Darek glanced at the narrow wooden walls, which had holes in them like someone had bashed them in. "But that's impossible. The gods can't procreate with humans. If a god tried to do that with a human, the human would die."

"Precisely," said the Ghostly God, nodding without looking over his shoulder. "Nonetheless, Jakuuth was firmly convinced that he was indeed the Son of Grinf, which was why he took on the surname Grinfborn. He knew that no one else in the school would believe him, however, which is why he kept his 'true' identity a secret for a brief period of time."

"No one ever told me that," said Darek, scratching the back of his head.

"I imagine there is a very good reason for that," said the Ghostly God. "He was conniving and manipulative. When the Katabans War started, he quickly became involved in it by pretending to be Grinf, because while he may not actually be related to Grinf, he does bear a remarkable resemblance to my older brother. In an attempt to impose his view of the world on everyone, he managed to gather a sizable katabans army under his command before his true identity was ousted by that Carnagian king named Malock and your own mother."

"My mother did that?" said Darek in surprise. "She's never mentioned that to me before."

The Ghostly God stopped. Through the Ghostly God's slightly transparent body, Darek could see a tall wooden door at the end of the hall.

"No surprise there," said the Ghostly God with a snort. "It was an embarrassing chapter for North Academy in general and your mother in particular. I am surprised that the Magical Superior still allows her to teach at the school, considering her past with Jakuuth."

"What did my mother do with Jakuuth?" said Darek. "Er, Master?"

"That is not information you need to know," said the Ghostly God, holding up one hand as if to signal that this was off-topic. "It will only distract you from your mission if I told you. And you cannot allow yourself to be distracted."

The Ghostly God's head turned around on his body, looking down at Darek with a hungry look. "Or would you rather I terminated our contract and eat you? It has been a while since I last had a tasty mortal for lunch."

Darek shook his head so wildly that he almost suffered whiplash. "Never mind. You're right. I don't need to know all that."

"Good," said the Ghostly God, although his head didn't turn back around. "After his treachery, he was expelled from North Academy. Then the Katabans Council tried Jakuuth Grinfborn and the handful of katabans dumb enough to retain loyalty to him."

"Did they execute him, Master?" Darek asked.

"They should have," said the Ghostly God. "But they didn't. The Council instead took away his wand and trapped him and his loyalists deep beneath World's End. They put him in a magic-proof cell that he couldn't escape from. I have heard that Grinf was present at the trial, but whether he was or wasn't, Jakuuth was still kept under lock and key for the past quarter century."

"If that's the case, then why are you telling me about him?" said Darek, raising an eyebrow. "If he's locked in a magic-proof cell under World's End, then I doubt he's much of a threat."

The Ghostly God swatted Darek on the head. The blow wasn't staggering, but it did confirm that the Ghostly God's fingers were actually made of metal, as they hurt as much as being hit by a metal pole.

"Ow," said Darek, rubbing the spot where the Ghostly God had hit him. "What was that for, Master?"

"Notice the tense I used, Takren," said the Ghostly God, his voice annoyed. "*Was.* Jakuuth Grinfborn, bless his crazy mortal heart, was reported missing from his jail cell two months ago. The only 'clue' he left behind was the corpse of his jailer. His loyalists were also missing from their cells."

Darek gulped. "How did he escape?"

"How should I know?" said the Ghostly God. "I wasn't there when it happened. Even Skimif doesn't know how he did it. All we know is that he did it, and he's now loose."

"Did Uron have a hand in freeing him?" Darek asked.

"Possibly, but we do not know for sure," said the Ghostly God. "All we know for sure is that he and his loyalists are now free. They have made their way to the Northern Isles, where they are currently building up a new army under Jakuuth's rule."

"What?" said Darek with a start. "But where is Jakuuth getting his new followers from? Surely everyone must remember him, right?"

"Jakuuth wasn't exactly well-known among your kind, seeing as he primarily participated in the Katabans War," said the Ghostly God. "But to answer your question, he has recently staged a prison break at Rock Isle. Have you heard of it?"

Darek shuddered. "Yes. It's supposed to be the most secure prison in the entire Northern Isles. It's where Aorja was sent after we caught her."

The Ghostly God frowned. "Who?"

"Aorja," said Darek. "You know, that woman who worked for you for a brief time? She tried to help Durima and Gujak get into North Academy by distracting all of us."

The blank look in the Ghostly God's eyes turned into a look of understanding. "Oh. Her. Yes, I remember her now. It has been a long time since I last thought about her. I never liked her all that much even while she served me."

"I don't like her much now, either," said Darek. "Not after she tried to kill me and Jiku. Anyway, you said Jakuuth staged a prison break on Rock Isle?"

"Yes," said the Ghostly God with a nod. "He killed the guards and offered the prisoners freedom if they would only serve him."

"But that's insane," said Darek. "The prisoners on Rock Isle are supposed to be the worst of the worst. The prison is where every Northern Isles nation drops off its worst criminals. Why would Jakuuth recruit them?"

"I suspect Jakuuth is planning to conquer the Northern Isles," said the Ghostly God, "and what better way to do it than to gather the most vicious criminals in the world and train them to be top class soldiers?"

"Why hasn't anyone stopped him yet?" said Darek. "Surely the other nations in the Northern Isles know about what he's trying to do, right?"

"That's just the thing," said the Ghostly God. "Jakuuth may be hopelessly mad, but he's intelligent. He has had some of the prisoners dress up as guards and greet every prison ship that comes by just like the normal guards do.

Not a single Northern Isles nation is aware that they are supplying an enemy with all of the soldiers he could ever want."

"Excuse me for my impudence, Master, but why haven't any of the gods done anything about him yet?" said Darek. "Sure, Jakuuth may be a powerful mage, but couldn't you gods smite him? Or at least tell the mortals about what he's up to so we can deal with him?"

"As if we have time to do that," said the Ghostly God. "Jakuuth is nothing more than a minor annoyance on the gods' radar at the moment. The true threat is Uron. Skimif has given orders to all gods to keep their eyes and ears open for any sign of him. Even I barely have time to speak to you as it is."

"Why are you even telling me about this, then?" said Darek, scratching the top of his head. "If Jakuuth isn't much of a threat to the world, then I don't see the point in telling me about him."

The Ghostly God rolled his eyes. "Ordinarily, I would not. Jakuuth is no immediate threat to my domain. However, we suspect that Jakuuth may be planning an assault on World's End, where he escaped from, to exact his vengeance on the Katabans Council for putting him away."

"Can't you gods protect World's End?" asked Darek.

"Of course we can," the Ghostly God snapped. "But we are worried about how Jakuuth managed to break out of his cell and leave World's End without even us gods knowing. While Jakuuth is barely a threat to us now, if he is left to grow without hindrance, he might become a bigger threat in the future."

"I see," said Darek. "But I still don't see where I am supposed to come into all of this."

"That is the point I was getting to," said the Ghostly God. He turned his head so it was facing in the right direction. "Come with me into my room."

The Ghostly God passed through the closed door at the end of the hall as though it wasn't there. Darek, not being a ghost, had to enter the room the old-fashioned way. The door felt old and wobbly as he pulled it open, but thankfully it did not fall off its hinges as he opened it.

Stepping into the Ghostly God's room, the first thing Darek noticed were the coffins all along the walls. He almost mistook them for odd-looking bookshelves, as they were packed as tightly together as a bunch of bookshelves. But he corrected that impression quickly enough when he got a better look at them and saw their closed lids.

In the center of the room, the Ghostly God floated facing Darek. His eyes darted around the room, as if he was looking around to make sure no one was hiding nearby.

"Master," said Darek, following the Ghostly God's constantly darting eyes. "You seem a little ... worried about eavesdropping."

He almost said *paranoid*, but he didn't think the Ghostly God would take kindly to being called that.

"Uron," said the Ghostly God, his eyes focusing on Darek. "I have no idea where he is, so I am always concerned that he may be hiding nearby, perhaps listening to my plans or looking for the perfect opportunity to kill me.

Being afraid of getting killed is a feeling I have not felt in eons, since the end of the Godly War. I am not sure how to take it."

Darek wasn't quite sure what to say to that, so he changed the subject. "All right, Master, you said you were going to explain to me what you wanted me to do about Jakuuth."

"Right," said the Ghostly God. "Your mission is simple: Infiltrate Jakuuth's army and kill him. Without Jakuuth's leadership, his so-called 'army' will fall apart and that will be one less threat we gods have to worry about."

Darek gulped involuntarily. He looked down at his hands, hoping the Ghostly God did not notice his fear. "You want me to kill him, Master?"

"Yes," said the Ghostly God. "Like an assassin. Why? Is that a problem?"

"It's just ... I've never killed anyone before," said Darek. "I killed that chimera last year, but that was different because it wasn't a person."

"And?" said the Ghostly God. "Killing is not that difficult. Sometimes messy, yes, but hardly what I'd call an impossible task."

"It's just that I don't know if I can even do it," said Darek. He looked back up at the Ghostly God's unsympathetic face. "Isn't there anyone else you could ask to do it? Why not just hire a professional assassin?"

"Because Jakuuth is dangerous and clever," said the Ghostly God. "Note that he hid his true identity from his followers for almost the entirety of the year in which he impersonated Grinf. Any assassin I send after him would probably be killed quickly."

"But why not someone else, then?" said Darek. "There are lots of other far more powerful mages than me out there. I only just graduated from North Academy, after all."

"Because you are the person Jakuuth is least likely to suspect of being an assassin," said the Ghostly God. "Believe me, once he hears your name, he will trust you better than most. By earning his trust, you will be able to move close enough to him to kill him when he least expects it."

"But I don't even know him," said Darek. "How will he know that he can trust me based on my name alone?"

"He knew your mother, remember?" said the Ghostly God. "I believe I mentioned that earlier, although I'm not surprised you forgot. You mortals have much shorter attention spans than we gods do."

"You still haven't explained to me the exact relationship between my mom and Jakuuth," said Darek.

"You don't need to know it," said the Ghostly God. "That's why."

Actually, I do, Darek thought, though he kept that thought to himself.

"To recap," said the Ghostly God, "Jakuuth escaped from his prison, is building a new army that could be a threat to World's End and the world in general in the future, and it is your job to infiltrate his army and kill him before he gets anywhere."

"I know," said Darek. "Though now I'm wondering why it took you so long to tell me about this if Jakuuth has been free for two months."

"Easy," said the Ghostly God. "His escape was unexpected and by the time we located him—which isn't as easy as you'd think—he had already broken into Rock Isle. Besides, we gods have been so busy searching for Uron that it has been difficult to find the time to pick out a mortal like you and explain the situation to him."

"I see," said Darek. He folded his arms across his chest. "Well, how am I supposed to infiltrate his army?"

"Using deception, obviously," said the Ghostly God. "I will teleport you to Rock Isle, where you will be caught by Jakuuth's men and brought before him. Tell him that you no longer serve North Academy and that you think they were wrong for expelling him years ago. Explain that you want to work for him and him alone and you should be easily accepted into his rapidly growing army."

"What about Aorja?" said Darek. "If she was in Rock Isle when Jakuuth attacked, then she's probably part of his army as well."

"What does it matter?" said the Ghostly God with a shrug. "She will not be able to prove that you are trying to kill Jakuuth. If she proves to be a threat to you ... well, you can deal with her just as you will deal with Jakuuth, surely."

The idea of killing Aorja, even if she did deserve it, made Darek feel sick. As angry as he was with her over her betrayal, he had too many fond memories of her to kill her in cold blood. He doubted he would have much choice, however, if he found himself in that situation later.

"Now, then," said the Ghostly God as he put his hands

together eagerly. "You understand the situation and what you need to do. And you can't back out of it, either, because this is part of the agreement you made with me. You still have nine years left in which to serve me, remember."

Darek grimaced. "I remember, Master."

"Good," said the Ghostly God. "Now I will teleport you to Rock Isle. You must introduce yourself to Jakuuth and pretend to be his friend."

"This just seems so sudden," said Darek, spreading his arms. "I mean, how do you expect me to come up with a lie convincing enough to fool Jakuuth? I don't even know what kind of magic he uses."

The Ghostly God chuckled. "I expect you to, how do you mortals put it, 'wing it,' I believe is the term."

"Wing it?" said Darek, staring at the Ghostly God.

"Exactly," said the Ghostly God. "Now, I do believe it is time for you to go. Once there, you will know what to do."

The Ghostly God waved at Darek before Darek even realized what was happening. In a minute, the Ghostly God's room completely vanished, replaced by a rocky, bleak-looking beach underneath the morning sun.

Yet Darek was alone for maybe all of five seconds before a dozen of the nastiest, meanest-looking mages Darek had ever seen in his life surrounded him on all sides. They pointed their wands directly at him, like a couple of hunters aiming guns at a deer. Based on their shabby prison clothes and dirty hair, Darek guessed that these were some of the Rock Isle prisoners.

Of course the Ghostly God would toss me right into the

middle of a dozen killers who probably serve an even crazier killer, Darek thought, trying not to panic in the face of so many obviously violent criminals. *Can't waste any time finding Jakuuth, now can we?*

Unfortunately, Darek did not see Jakuuth among these prisoners, which meant that, unless Darek thought fast, this situation would only end badly for him.

Chapter Seven

Durima had only ever seen the Void from a distance. From World's End, the Void resembled a huge black wall. The blue sky above ended where it met the Void, though it was a ragged end, like the Void was literally eating the sky piece by piece. The sea, however, seemed to go inside the Void, though to where, she did not know. There was no light or stars from within. The Void was black during the day and black during the night. No matter what time of year it was, no matter if it was summer or winter, spring or fall, the Void remained the same.

No one knew what lay beyond the Void, but if the legends were true, there were monsters in there unlike anything that dwelt in Martir, monsters so strong that even the gods dared not cross their paths. Some legends even stated that the Void itself was a god, a fallen god who had been transformed into black nothingness by the Powers at the beginning of creation for a crime he committed.

Whatever the Void's origin or true nature, Durima felt drained just staring at it. She and Gujak stood on the deck of one of the large battleships she had seen earlier, their arms and legs tied together with metal chains to prevent them from escaping. The ship, called the *Divine Arrow*, was steadily sailing toward the Void. Around them, katabans sailors worked to adjust the sails, swab the poop, and do other chores necessary to keep a ship in shape. None of them stopped to stare at the incoming Void, although Durima suspected that was because they were too afraid to do so.

The only person on the ship who wasn't working was Commander Erich, who held the ends of their chains. He stood next to them, a triumphant smirk on his face, although unless Durima's eyes were deceiving her, his smirk wasn't quite as big as it had been earlier. Most likely his fear of the Void—a fear all katabans shared—was beginning to affect him, although if it was, he would never admit to it.

"You two should write back to me once you go past the Void," said Erich, glancing at them briefly before returning his attention to the Void. "Tell me about all of the interesting things you saw there. The Void has always captured my curiosity in a morbid way, so I am curious to see if any of the stories about it are true."

Durima leaned toward him and bared her teeth. "Better yet, why don't you come with us and find out for yourself?"

Erich yanked on Durima's chain, causing her to choke as he said, "Shut up. Or would you rather I send you beyond the Void with two broken legs? I'm sure it won't make a difference. The Void will obliterate you two no matter how good or bad your health is."

Hacking, her throat still hurting from Erich's yank of her collar, Durima spat on the deck of the ship. "Keep saying that, Erich, and maybe someday all your wildest dreams will come true."

Erich said nothing to that. He just kept staring at the Void, though whether it was out of horror or curiosity, Durima couldn't tell.

She heard a sniffle beside her and looked to her right. Gujak, as usual, appeared to be on the verge of tears. That was impressive, considering he had cried all the way from the Hall of Judgment to the docks where the battleships were ported. He had only stopped crying when they got onto the ship, probably because he now knew that there was no hope for them.

For once, Durima felt sorry for Gujak. She hated seeing youth become so distraught. Gujak may have been an idiot, but he was her only real friend. She had worked alongside him for many years, and now she was going to die with him. Part of her wanted to pat Gujak on the shoulder and tell him it was going to be okay, but she knew that was a lie. Besides, she was never the kind of katabans to be encouraging in bleak circumstances anyway. That just wasn't her style.

Half an hour later, the captain of the ship ordered the *Divine Arrow* to weigh anchor. By now, they were close enough to the Void that it was almost all Durima could see whenever she looked directly at it, but not close enough that the ship was in danger of being sucked into it somehow. The tension and fear among the ship's crew was palpable and thick, like red pudding, which didn't help Durima's nerves.

Erich walked Durima and Gujak to the ship's port. On the davit hung a simple wooden boat with a power motor. It was probably meant to be an emergency boat in the event that the ship sank, but in this case, it was going to be her and Gujak's ride to death.

"Get in," said Erich, pointing at the boat. "It will take you straight into the Void. A waste of a perfectly good boat, but I guess we sometimes have to make sacrifices for the greater good, don't we?"

Durima didn't respond to that. She just climbed into the boat and sat down on the floor. Gujak followed a second later and soon both were sitting with their backs to each other in the tiny boat. There was barely any room to stretch her arms or legs, although being short, it wasn't that big of a deal to her.

"There," said Erich as he tossed the end of their chains into the boat with them. "This will probably be the last time we see each other. Do either of you have any last words to share with me? Perhaps a message you'd like me to deliver to an old friend you haven't talked to in a while?"

Durima leaned toward Erich and locked eyes with him. "Yes. Tell the Council that I think they're a bunch of—"

She was cut off when the boat abruptly fell. Gujak let out a shriek of terror, only to be cut off when they landed in the sea, splashing water into the air and onto Durima's fur. She shivered when she felt the ice-cold water on her fur, but had no time to dry off, as the boat's engine immediately started and began taking them directly to the Void.

Durima looked back over her shoulder at the *Divine Arrow*. Almost all of its crew was now assembled on the port, watching as Durima and Gujak's tiny boat motored on toward the Void. Erich stood in the middle of the watching crowd, a smug expression on his face evident even from a distance.

There's no going back now, Durima thought as she turned back to face the Void. *I wonder what dying in the Void will feel like. Will our spirits also be destroyed or will they return to Martir?*

The little boat's engine suddenly picked up speed. As they drew closer to the Void, fear rose in Durima's stomach. Her breathing became harder and she found it difficult to think straight. Her body was trying to panic, even throw her overboard, but she kept it firmly under control. Throwing herself into the sea would not be a good escape plan at this point, seeing as Durima was still bound with heavy metal chains that would simply cause her to sink to the bottom of the ocean and drown.

Gujak was shaking behind her, shaking and sobbing. She felt his back heaving against her back. It almost pained her to feel his sadness, but there was nothing she could do or say to reassure him that everything was going to be all right. She wanted to cry herself, personally, but she never cried about anything, so she didn't.

The Void was now all Durima could see. She couldn't even see the water upon which their little bow motored across. As a matter of fact, the boat seemed to be going faster and faster, as if it was being pulled in by the Void. She could feel the Void's sucking force, so powerful that she doubted she could have resisted it even if she hadn't been tied down on a small boat on the edge of the world.

As the darkness of the Void consumed them, Durima

kept her eyes wide open. Maybe she and Gujak were going to die, but if so, she was going to die with her eyes open. She would not die like a coward too afraid to face her fate.

Durima had expected them to fall through the Void. It was, after all, set on the edge of the known world. She had thought that as soon as they passed through it, they would fall and fall forever, or maybe fall into the grasp of some terrible creature that lay awaiting anyone who dared cross from Martir into the Void.

But much to her surprise, they did not fall anywhere. The boat's motor continued to push the boat through the water. Durima could not see anything at all, not even her toes, and when she looked over her shoulder, she didn't see Martir or the *Divine Arrow* or anything else. Even Gujak was invisible in the blackness of the Void, though she could feel his wooden body against hers.

She turned back to face wherever they were going. She strained to listen for anything in the darkness, but the only sound she heard was the running motor of their boat, as well as the water parting before it. Aside from that, the Void was as silent as death.

Are we still alive? Durima thought. *Or did we die instantly and it just* feels *like we're alive?*

She decided that they were still alive. After all, they were clearly still in their boat, and boats, to her knowledge, did not go to the afterlife with their owners. Still, that didn't mean she and Gujak were going to be safe forever. Any minute now, she was convinced that some type of terrible beast would leap from the shadows and kill them in one blow.

No such monster appeared, however, and it seemed increasingly unlikely that any would. The air in the Void was hard to breathe, making her feel like she was holding her head underwater. She also had the distinct feeling that they were being watched, but it was too dark for her to see if there was indeed anyone lurking in the shadows stalking them.

Minutes passed as the boat's motor rumbled. Durima kept her ears open, even though it was probably not any use. After all, if there was something hiding in the shadows, it would be able to kill them easily. She and Gujak were still bound by their thick, heavy chains. They were easy pickings for any monster that might want to eat them.

Yet no matter how long they sat there in silence, nothing appeared or showed itself. This disturbed Durima more than anything. She had always believed the stories about the Void and the creatures that were said to dwell within it, but she was now starting to believe that all of those stories were false.

What's scary about the Void is not what's inside it, Durima thought. *What's really scary is what* isn't *inside. There's no life here at all. Only endless nothingness for as far as the eye can see.*

"Durima?"

Durima almost jumped straight out of the boat when she heard Gujak say her name. But she righted herself quickly before the boat could tip over and spill them both into the water below. "What?"

"Do you think we'll see the Powers here?" Gujak asked. His voice was quieter than usual, probably because he had been crying so much. Even so, in the silent Void, it was like he was shouting in her ear. "You remember how they came from the Void when they wanted to destroy Martir all those years ago?"

Durima nodded. She hadn't actually been on World's End when that happened—like most katabans at the time, she had been running away—but she had heard the rumors from the others and knew about it. "I don't know, Gujak. The Powers may not be here anymore. They're probably far, far away, building whatever their next world is."

"Do you think we'll keep floating until we find it?" Gujak said. "That would be amazing, wouldn't it?"

"I suppose so," said Durima. "Unless the inhabitants of that world want us dead, that is."

"But if we told them we are creations of the Powers like them, they'll have to accept us," said Gujak. "I mean, why wouldn't they? Maybe they could even help us return to Martir."

"You want to go back to the place where everyone hates us?" said Durima. "There's nothing back in Martir waiting for us, Gujak. You know that."

"Nothing for you, maybe," said Gujak. "But I guess I didn't tell you about this female I like, did I?"

Durima would have looked at Gujak in disbelief, but the Void made it impossible to see him, so she didn't. "Since when did you have a crush? You've never mentioned her to me. We've worked together for how long now, two decades?"

"Because we aren't together, that's why," said Gujak. "Besides, you never struck me as being interested in my personal life anyway, so why would I ever tell you about her?"

"Good point," said Durima. "How long have you known her?"

"Since I came into being a little over a century ago," said Gujak with a sigh. "We're close in age. She lives on World's End. She works for a salvaging company there. We're friends."

"Friends, huh?" said Durima. "Tell me, where was this 'friend' of yours when the Soldiers of the Gods dragged us before the Council? I didn't see her anywhere then."

"I don't know where she was," said Gujak in an offended voice. "Maybe she was working. Maybe she didn't even know our trial was today. She could be pretty forgetful sometimes."

"Or maybe she just didn't want anyone to associate her with a god-killer," said Durima. "No surprise there. I bet every single katabans in Martir hates our guts."

"I guess it doesn't matter," said Gujak with a sniffle. "We're never going back to Martir anyway, no matter what happens to us here. I wish I could have at least said good bye to her before we left."

"'No closure for the wicked,'" said Durima. "That's a quote from Grinf, I think. Someone I once knew said that to me long ago, during the War."

"What an insightful quote," said Gujak.

At that moment, the motor on the boat spluttered, causing the boat to jerk a couple of times before the motor died completely. The boat continued to float forward from the momentum, but it was no longer being propelled through the water like it had been before.

"The motor went out," said Gujak. "Is that a good thing or a bad thing?"

Durima shrugged. "I don't know."

They lapsed into silence. After all, there was not much else to do but wait and see what happened next.

It was maybe half an hour later, although Durima couldn't be sure due to the lack of a sun to tell time by, that she heard the first sound in the Void that was not produced by her, Gujak, or the boat. Ocean waves were lapping against a beach and it sounded like it was coming from directly ahead of them.

"Waves?" said Gujak.

"Sounds like it," said Durima. "Which means there's a beach. Which means we're about to land somewhere."

"But where?" said Gujak. "What kind of islands exist in the Void?"

"No idea," said Durima. "I guess we'll just have to wait and see."

As they drew closer to the beach, the sounds of the waves lapping against the sand became louder and louder. As with Gujak, they were not the loudest sounds in the world, but in the Void, they were like thunderclaps in

Durima's ears. Still, she was glad to hear them anyway. It felt like the silence of the Void had been eating away at her sanity and she was unsure just how much of it was left by now.

Then Durima heard someone splashing through the water toward them. Whoever it was moved fast. She squinted to try to see the person, but the darkness of the Void made it impossible to tell just who was coming in after them.

"Is someone out there?" Gujak asked, raising his voice, which was colored with fear. "Who's there?"

The person splashing through the water toward them didn't answer. A moment later, Durima felt the boat under their feet being pulled along by someone very strong. They were moving much faster than the motor had propelled them and in the next minute she heard the boat ground onto some sand underneath.

Before Durima realized it, two strong hands grabbed her shoulders and threw her out of the boat. She landed hard on her back on the sand. A moment later, she heard Gujak land next to her, although unlike her, he was screaming for his life.

"Please don't kill us!" Gujak cried out over the footsteps of the person that were drawing closer to them. "We didn't do anything worthy of being killed! We—"

Gujak choked as he and Durima were lifted up by whoever had pulled them out of the boat. The hand around Durima's neck was as strong as a horse's hoof; in fact, the hand's fingers felt like horse hooves, although that made no sense to Durima whatsoever. And oddly enough, Durima thought she smelled horsehair, although she dismissed that as her imagination going wild in the darkness of the Void.

"Tell me your names," said the being holding them up. "Now."

"Gujak," said Gujak, before Durima could tell him not to tell this obviously hostile being anything about themselves. "And she's Durima. Please let us go."

"Gujak? Durima?" said the being. "Those are katabans names, aren't they? Yes, they are. I remember. I once hired a katabans named Durima, but that was ages ago. Or was it only yesterday? I don't know."

"What are you talking about?" said Durima. She wanted to sock this being in the face, but the chains around her arms and legs made that an impossibility at the moment. "I don't know you."

The being's grip around Durima's neck tightened, causing her to gasp as he said, "Have the katabans of Martir already forgotten about one of their masters? I bet Skimif made you forget, didn't he? Of course he did. That stupid upstart godling, the mistake of the Powers, as I have taken to calling him. Oh, if I still had my powers, why, I'd give him what for."

"I don't understand," said Gujak. Based on how weak his voice sounded, the being must have been holding Gujak's neck very tightly. "Who ... are ... you?"

Without warning, the being dropped both of them. Durima fell on her bottom and began massaging her throat where the being had gripped it. Making sure that she could breathe in the heavy air of the Void, Durima looked up at the being who stood before them, although it was too dark to see his face.

"Who am I?" said the being. "Allow me to show myself."

A light shone from somewhere near the being's upper body. It was not a very bright light, but having become accustomed to the deep darkness of the Void, Durima had to look away for a moment to avoid hurting her eyes.

"Why are you two looking away?" said the being in an angry voice. "I command you to look at me, you disrespectful rats!"

Durima winced at his harsh voice. Yet she also thought it was familiar, like she had been called a rat by a god before. It had been years ago, when she had been a much younger katabans first starting out as a servant of the gods. She could not recall which god it had been, however, at least until she looked back at the light before her.

Towering above Durima was a being who almost looked like a human, save for his head and face, which were the head and face of a horse. He wore a black coat that was tattered and torn in several places, while his right hand glowed with a bright light. His left eye was completely missing, as if something had clawed it out, though it must have been a while ago because it was dried and covered with flesh.

"You know who I am, or who I was, anyway," said the being. "I am Hollech, former God of Deception, Horses, and Thieves ... and current God of the Void. Welcome to my domain."

Chapter Eight

It was the stench of the prisoners that got Darek the most. He could tell right off the bat that none of them bathed. They smelled like dirt and urine, not exactly an appealing aroma, but he didn't say that out loud because he knew they would kill him if he insulted them even jokingly. The murder in their eyes was plain as day.

Darek had drawn his own wand, but when faced with a dozen or so criminals, he knew he couldn't beat them. Darek may have been an Academy-trained mage, but there were a dozen of these murderers and none of them were likely to play fair.

It's amazing I've survived this long, Darek thought. *My sudden appearance must have taken them by surprise.*

"Who are you?" said one of the prisoners. Darek noticed that this prisoner was missing a few teeth. "Where did you come from? And how did you get here? You a spy from the Northern nations?"

Darek shook his head rapidly. "No, no, no. My name is Darek Takren and I am here to see Jakuuth Grinfborn. I heard about his escape from World's End and I wanted to help him in his goals."

"Darek Takren?" said the prisoner. "Never heard of ya. Anyone else here heard of Darek Takren?"

The other prisoners shook their heads or said things like 'No' and 'Nah.'

"I'm not very famous or well-known," Darek admitted. "I just graduated from North Academy, but that doesn't mean I won't work as hard as everyone else to obey Jakuuth's orders."

"How did you hear about Jakuuth?" said the prisoner with a growl. "We've been very careful about making sure no one outside of Rock Isle even knows he's here."

Darek bit his lower lip. Why hadn't the Ghostly God given him an excuse to explain that? Had the Ghostly God not considered it, or did he think that Darek could 'wing it' like everything else?

"He's gone quiet," said another prisoner, a bulkier man who looked like he could uproot a full-grown tree if he wanted to. "Let's kill him and toss his body into the sea."

"Now hold on a minute there," said Darek, talking and thinking quickly, "let's not get ahead of ourselves here. You don't even know if I'm a threat or not."

"Jakuuth gave us orders to kill anyone who showed up on Rock Isle without explanation," said the first prisoner. "Shoulda killed you the minute we saw you. Jakuuth's gonna be angry."

"But ..." Darek came up with an idea. "Oh, I heard about it from ... the gods. Yes, I heard about it from them—from Xocion, specifically, since I am a pagomancer and have spoken with him pretty often."

That was a blatant lie. While Darek did indeed serve Xocion, he had never had even one conversation with the

God of Ice. Xocion may have been a northern god, but that didn't mean he frequently spoke with his followers or servants.

"Xocion?" said the first prisoner with a start. "You mean the gods already know about us?"

"They do," said Darek. He hated lying, but as the only other alternative was being killed by these prisoners, he decided to stomach it. "But don't worry. They're busy dealing with another threat at the moment. They don't have any time to deal with us."

"Don't go including yourself in that 'us,' stranger," the first prisoner snapped. "I don't recollect us letting you join the Limitless Army. You're trying to sneak past us."

"Sneak past you?" said Darek, putting one hand on his chest. "I swear to the gods that I would never try to sneak past you. It was a slip of the tongue, that's all."

"The gods must have sent him to kill us," said the second prisoner. "Let's kill him before he succeeds."

"Actually, you are quite mistaken," said Darek. "I came here because I wanted to help Jakuuth. I've heard so much about him and what he did during the Katabans War that I just can't help but want to serve him."

"Jakuuth's crazier than a mad donkey," said the first prisoner. "Only reason we're serving him is because we can't leave Rock Isle on our own."

"Hey, Jakuuth's not that crazy," said the second prisoner. He tapped the side of his head. "He's the Son of Grinf, remember? His ways are above ours, so of course he seems a little weird."

"Besides, I wouldn't criticize Jakuuth if I were you," said another prisoner, this one quite a bit smaller than the others, almost the size of a child. "You saw how he annihilated all those guards, didn't you? And the burns he inflicts on anyone who disagrees with him. Those are nasty."

"Poor Ruxan," said the second prisoner, shaking his head. "Can he still even see or did Jakuuth melt his eyes shut?"

"Does it matter if Jakuuth is, er, eccentric or not?" said Darek. "I will decide that for myself when I meet him."

"How are you gonna meet him?" said the first prisoner. He gestured toward a massive stone fortress several hundred yards from the beach. "He's all the way up there in the prison. A stranger like you can't just waltz up there ... well, unless you'd like to get captured and raped by the guards, that is, for trespassing."

"You guys will take me up there," said Darek, nodding at the prisoners surrounding him. "That way, you can make sure that I'm not up to no good."

"Jakuuth will be angry that we let someone onto the island without his permission," said the third prisoner in a trembling voice. He gestured at the rocky beach all around them. "That's why we were out here in the first place, to prevent anyone from sneaking onto Rock Isle. He'll kill us."

"Not unless I vouch for you guys," Darek offered. "And trust me, Jakuuth will listen to me. Once he hears my name, I imagine he will reward you guys for bringing me to him."

"Reward?" said the first prisoner. "Jakuuth doesn't

reward anybody. He tells us what to do and we do it unless we'd like to have our eyes melted shut. Just like poor Ruxan."

"Even so, don't you think Jakuuth would be angry if you killed me and it turned out I was someone important to him?" said Darek. "Just tell him my name. He will know it immediately."

"How do you already know Jakuuth?" said the first prisoner with suspicious eyes. "He's never mentioned no one by the name of Darek Takren before, at least not to us."

In truth, Darek did not know what kind of significance that his name might have held to Jakuuth. True, Jakuuth had apparently known Mom in her younger days, but that didn't necessarily mean Darek would get preferential treatment because of it.

Remember what the Ghostly God said, Darek thought. *I mean, why else would he tell me to tell Jakuuth my name if it didn't guarantee me some protection from his usual treatment of intruders?*

Then again, knowing the Ghostly God, this could all be an elaborate ruse just to get him killed. If so, then Darek wondered if he could come back as a ghost and haunt the Ghostly God.

But that was hardly relevant to Darek's current situation. He needed to come up with a valid excuse for why Jakuuth would care about his name. Something that even these prisoners, as skeptical as they were, would not dare to question without risking Jakuuth's wrath.

Then it occurred to Darek. It was a ridiculous lie, one

that might not work, but he had to try it anyway. It was his only chance.

"Jakuuth would know that name because I ..." Darek didn't want to say the words, but he did anyway, with as much charisma and sincerity as he could muster. "I'm his son."

The prisoners started in unison. Half of them stepped back, giving Darek a clear escape route if he wanted, while the other half lowered their wands and looked at each other in worry and confusion. At least one grabbed what appeared to be a Jukanian necklace, a common symbol worn by followers of Jukan, the Goddess of Protection, from around his neck and held it closer to his chest, as if he thought it would protect him from whatever he was afraid of happening.

"You're his son?" said the first prisoner in a weak, almost squeaky voice. "No way. You're lying. You don't even look Carnagian."

"That's because my mother was a Ruwan," said Darek, gesturing at his skin. "I inherited her skin color, but I can assure you that I am indeed the son of Jakuuth."

"By Tinkar's clock," said the second prisoner with a gulp. "If you're really Jakuuth's son, what does that make you? A quarter god?"

"I don't know," said Darek, shaking his head. "All I know is that I have been separated from my dad for too many years. And if you keep me separated from my dad for no good reason, what do you think Jakuuth will do to you when he finds out?"

That did the trick. By now, all of the prisoners were giving Darek a wide berth. A few of them had even fallen over onto the sand as they backed away. He had scared them good, which both sickened and excited him.

"Oh, oh," said the first prisoner with a gulp. "Well, then, uh, Mr. Takren, er, son of Jakuuth, we apologize for treating you so harshly. We didn't know that you were his son."

"Few do," said Darek as he dusted off his robes, which he didn't really need to do, but which he thought would make him look more imposing and no-nonsense. "Now, are you going to take me to my dad or not?"

Being escorted by a dozen smelly, frightened prisoners did little to lighten Darek's nerves, but he put on a show of confidence anyway so as to dispel any remaining doubts they might have had about his parentage. He felt almost like royalty, the way the prisoners treated him. They kept their eyes away from him, as if they thought that by looking at him in the wrong way, they would anger him or somehow get in trouble with Jakuuth. One prisoner even took off his shirt and laid it across a mud puddle in their path, which Darek walked over in order to keep up appearances.

The ground was rocky and uneven, even despite the rough path that had been created by the prisoners. Darek's shoes were made of a soft leather, which had not been designed to walk across the pokey, rocky path. As a result, Darek's feet quickly became sore, although he pretended not to feel it because he didn't want to show the prisoners any weakness.

The closer they drew to the prison, the better Darek saw it. It was a massive stone fortress, easily twice as large as the Arcanium, shaped somewhat like a stone block combined with a castle. Huge stone walls towered above Darek, perhaps a hundred feet tall and half as thick. On the tops of the walls, Darek saw people, probably other prisoners, patrolling the area, although they were too high up for him to make out any specific details about them. He did notice that they wore the same black armor that Rock Isle guards were said to wear, although if what the Ghostly God said was true, that was merely a ruse to prevent visitors from suspecting that anything was out of the ordinary.

At the base of the walls were two wide, thick iron gates that were apparently the only way in and out of the prison, at least on this side of the building. Above the gates was carved an image of a woman with a ball and chain around her neck, wearing a shabby-looking prisoner's outfit that clearly identified her as Hona, the Goddess of Prisons and Prisoners. Hona was not a well-known goddess, but Darek knew who she was because he had once read that she established the first prison at the beginning of time to help humans keep their criminals from harming their communities.

I wonder if Hona knows that one of her prisons is now being used as a training ground for an army of prisoners, Darek thought. *Then again, she's probably too busy helping the other gods look for Uron to do anything about it.*

When Darek and his strange escort arrived at the gates,

they were met by four gatekeepers. Like the rest of the 'guards,' they were merely prisoners impersonating guards, and not very well, either, as their black armor appeared to be ill-fitting and strapped on incorrectly, though Darek didn't mention it.

"Halt," said one of the 'guards,' causing Darek and his escort to stop. He gestured at the prisoners surrounding Darek. "I know you guys, but who's the new guy? Never seen him before. New prisoner from one of the prison ships?"

The first prisoner, the one missing teeth, stepped forward and said, "Of course not. Don't you see who he is? Look at his face. Who does he remind you of?"

The lead gatekeeper frowned, but looked more closely at Darek's face. This made Darek uncomfortable, as he didn't trust the gatekeeper's sword (which, based on the dried blood on its blade, had probably been used fairly recently), but he kept up his appearance of confidence anyway. He didn't know if this was how Jakuuth usually looked, but considering that Jakuuth thought of himself as the Son of Grinf, he figured it was a good guess.

Then the lead gatekeeper shook his head. "Nope. That guy doesn't look like anyone I've ever seen before. Looks like he'd make great target practice, though."

The first prisoner waved his wand and the lead gatekeeper flew back into the gates suddenly. He hit the gates with a resounding *clang* of metal on metal and then fell to the ground. He did not get up, though he appeared to be simply stunned by the impact rather than dead.

"You idiot," the first prisoner said. He gestured at Darek. "You see this man? He's Darek Takren, the son of Jakuuth Grinfborn. Do you understand what that makes him? It makes him a quarter god, that's what it makes him."

"No way," said another gatekeeper. "I didn't know Jakuuth had a son."

"Well, now you do," said the first prisoner with a huff. "And he wants to see his father. So you'd better let us inside or I will let Jakuuth know just who tried to keep his one and only son from seeing him for the first time in years."

The remaining gatekeepers who hadn't been knocked unconscious immediately went to work opening the gates. They moved their unconscious friend out of the way and then began turning a huge wheel that slowly lifted the gates up. Darek was amazed at how efficient they were. He had thought that the prisoners of Rock Isle would be too undisciplined to be any good, but they opened that gate as if their lives depended on it.

Then again, the threat in that prisoner's words wasn't exactly subtle, Darek thought, glancing at the first prisoner, who seemed satisfied that he had scared some of his comrades straight.

Once the gate was open, Darek and his escorts passed underneath it. As they did so, Darek was aware that the remaining gatekeepers eyed Darek with fear and worry, as if they thought Darek would report their obstinacy to Jakuuth. Of course Darek wouldn't, seeing as he did not want to get them punished for a lie, but as long as it kept them from thinking about his own lie, he thought it good to let them think that for now.

They passed through the gate into a narrow, dark tunnel with a low ceiling. The tunnel sloped upwards, and with no steps for them to walk on, it was a much harder climb than it should have been. It didn't help that there was absolutely no light at all in the tunnel, as though whoever had designed it had decided that light was unnecessary. The only light was at the end of the passageway, through which the daylight streamed in.

The tunnel wasn't very long, for which Darek was thankful. Aside from the filthy scents that his escort gave off, Darek also picked up a strong blood smell in the tunnel itself. It smelled like someone had painted the walls, ceiling, and floor with blood, although it was too dark to know for sure if there was any truth to that thought.

As they drew closer to the exit, the sounds of what might have been battle entered Darek's ears. He heard people yelling, blasts of fire and water and steam, and the occasional very loud curse. Above the din was the voice of someone who might have been shouting orders, but the noises were so confused that it was impossible to tell for sure where one ended and another began. A loud *boom* actually caused the tunnel to shudder and shake, though no one on Darek's escort seemed to notice.

Because Darek was in no mood to walk into the middle of a prison yard brawl (which was what it sounded like out there), he asked the first prisoner, "What is all of that racket?"

"Training," said the first prisoner promptly, though

without looking at Darek. "Jakuuth demands ten hours of training per day. It is excruciating work. Very glad I got patrol duty today. It's boring, but not as hard."

Training, huh? Darek thought. *Makes sense. Jakuuth is raising an army here, after all. Then again, I wonder how you even train a bunch of the world's worst criminals to become an effective, unified army.*

Darek soon found out the answer to that question when he and his escort reached the tunnel's exit and stepped out into the light. Darek's eyes rapidly adjusted from the darkness of the tunnel to the light of the day. He fully expected to see the prisoners slaughtering each other while Jakuuth tried to organize them into some kind of coherent order.

But much to his surprise, what he saw down below in the prison yard was anything but an undisciplined mob of prisoners who couldn't stand each other. There were about three hundred in all from what Darek could see, each prisoner paired with a partner. The two partners faced each other like enemies in a battle, but rather than trying to kill each other, it looked like they were training together.

He saw one prisoner, a tall, lanky woman, try to shoot a fire bolt at her partner, a short, stout man. The man ducked to avoid the fire bolt, but rather than attack back, he gave her a thumbs up, as if she had finally gotten the hang of something that she had been working on for a while. The smile on that female prisoner's face was obvious even from Darek's position above the prison yard.

Another pair, two Nikons, if their red hair was any

indication, were not fighting at all, but rather sitting next to each other and drawing pictures in the dirt. No, not pictures, but maps and strategies, like they were planning to invade the Northern Isles. Considering how much they kept erasing each other's drawings and shaking their heads, they clearly disagreed with each other a lot, but their disagreement was more nonviolent than you'd think.

Not far from the arguing Nikons was yet another pair of people, Ruwans based on their pale skin and dark hair. They were practicing sword fighting, although when Darek saw their swords literally glowing with energy, he knew it was no normal sword fighting he saw. The Ruwans were practicing a type of swordplay called 'makhaimancy,' which involved a mage channeling pure magical energy through a sword specially designed to contain it.

And they're doing it remarkably well, Darek thought, watching as they parried each other's blows. *Makhaimancy is supposed to be one of the most difficult forms of combat magic a mage can learn, yet these two are practicing it as easily as if they have done it their whole lives.*

Yet they were nothing in comparison to the two prisoners about four or five dozen yards from where they stood. These two—one a man wearing grimy-looking glasses, the other a man without a shirt at all—stood facing each other, but they were not alone. At the bespectacled man's side was an absolutely massive column of water, far bigger than a mage of his size should have been able to conjure, while a blazing fire covered the shirtless man's body like a suit of armor.

No way, Darek thought, watching those two men below. *How did they do that? They don't even seem to be trying.*

The bespectacled man pushed his glasses up the bridge of his nose and gestured toward the shirtless man. The water column then shot toward the shirtless man like a cannon ball, but the shirtless man clapped his hands together and a massive wave of flame erupted from the palms of his hands.

The water column and fire wave met each other about halfway. The resulting collision resulted in a loud hissing sound and a thick cloud of steam obscuring the two training partners, although the steam cloud was quickly dissipated by a gust of wind that appeared to have come from the bespectacled man, who was now rubbing the steam off his glasses while the shirtless man's hands glowed with thick flame.

"Impressed?" said the first prisoner, giving Darek a grin that showed all of his missing teeth.

"I'm in shock," said Darek, shaking his head as he looked at the first prisoner. "This is the army?"

"The Limitless Army, as Jakuuth calls it," said the first prisoner, gesturing at the hundreds of prisoners down below. "He says that once we're done training, we will be the most fearsome army in all of the Northern Isles. Even the Carnagian Air Force and Aquarian Federated Army will not be able to stand against us."

The term 'Limitless' sounded familiar to Darek, but at the moment he was too distracted by all of the noise and smells to think too deeply about it.

"I thought I'd see just a bunch of undisciplined prisoners," said Darek, glancing at the training Army below. "But these ... they look like an actual army here."

"We weren't always like this," said the first prisoner. "When Jakuuth first arrived, we were always killing and raping and stealing from each other, some more than others, of course. And when he offered us freedom, we intended to keep our old ways and combine them with our new freedom to commit even worse crimes."

"That didn't happen, though, did it?" said Darek.

"Of course not," said the first prisoner. He sighed. "And for good reason. Your father quickly went to work stamping out all of those bad habits. It only took him a week to make clear that he was not going to tolerate any sort of raping, killing, or thievery in his Army for any reason whatsoever."

"I see," said Darek. "I just can't believe that my father managed to do all of this in two months."

"That's because he's the Son of Grinf," said one of the other members of his escort. "You haven't seen your old man for a while, but he's not the kind of guy you mess with. When he wants you to stop raping, killing, and stealing, he means it."

The prisoner said that while rubbing his side. Darek suspected that this prisoner had learned that lesson the hard way, though he didn't ask to see the scars.

The situation is worse than I thought, Darek thought. *If the prisoners are already a unified army, then I doubt it will be long before Jakuuth decides to start the invasion.*

Trying to seem as casual as he could, Darek asked, "So,

when is the Army supposed to begin its conquest of the Northern Isles?"

"No idea," said the first prisoner with a shrug. "Your father said we would head out when we were ready to head out. But if you ask me, I think it will be sometime soon, maybe next week, because Jakuuth has been pushing us harder than usual and has had more private talks with his lieutenants than he usually does."

Lieutenants? Darek thought. *Those must be the loyalists that the Ghostly God described, the ones who had escaped with Jakuuth. And if what this guy says is true, then the Army is almost ready to head out.*

Deciding he needed to see Jakuuth right away, Darek said to the first prisoner, "Good to hear. I thought I was going to be late for the conquest, but if all goes well, maybe I will be joining my father at the front of the Army as we kick down the doors of the Northern Isles."

"Yes, Mr. Takren, sir," said the first prisoner. "Right this way."

His escort began heading up a set of stone stairs to their left. Darek went up with them, but every now and then he'd glanced at the training Army below. He wasn't necessarily looking at the amazing magical feats that the prisoners—more like soldiers—were producing or even sensing their unusually high magical levels. He was looking for any sign of Aorja, just a hint of her blonde head anywhere in the crowd, but there were so many soldiers training so closely together that it was impossible to spot her, if she was even down there at all.

His eyes also wandered up to the huge back wall of the prison yard. It looked like it had been blown apart at one point and put back together in a way that looked normal at first glance but which, upon further inspection, appeared hastily done. He wondered what the story behind *that* was.

The escort took Darek up higher and higher, past rows of empty cells and up flights of stairs all the way to what looked like the main office at the top. Darek glanced at every cell they passed, expecting them to look grimy and dirty, but much to his surprise, each cell looked squeaky clean and neatly organized. Granted, he didn't have much time to stand and look at them too closely, but even just a cursory glance told him that Jakuuth had cleaned up these prisoners in more ways than moral.

In a few minutes, Darek and his escort reached the top of the flights of stairs that ran along the walls of the prison yard. From this spot Darek could now see the training Army even better than before, although his chances of spotting Aorja in particular were even worse than they had been before, so he gave up that task for now.

Up here, the strong wind caused Darek's robes to whip around, although as it was only a minor annoyance, he didn't pay much attention to it. Darek followed his escort down to the end of the walkway, toward a small, shabby-looking metal building that did not look like the kind of place where someone as powerful and well-known as Jakuuth would live. It had probably been the warden's office before Jakuuth arrived, though Darek thought that Jakuuth would have redecorated it to signal that he lived there.

"Here we are," said the first prisoner, gesturing at the metal building as they approached it. "Jakuuth ought to be in there right now talking with lieutenants about our future plans. But don't you worry, Mr. Takren sir. I'm sure Jakuuth always has time for his one and only son."

The first prisoner was smiling at him as he said that, like he thought it was so wonderful that he was getting to reunite a father and son who had not seen each other in years. Darek returned the smile, but he now wondered just how he was going to keep up this ruse once he actually met Jakuuth.

He'll know I'm not his son the minute he sees me, Darek thought as they drew closer and closer to the metal building. *Only question is, will he kill me right away or will he torture me first to find out who sent me here and then kill me?*

His grim thoughts were interrupted by the powerful energy levels he felt radiating from Jakuuth's headquarters. He almost stopped, the magical aura was so strong, but he didn't because he didn't want to attract unnecessary attention from his escort.

What is that power? Darek thought, now looking at the small metal building in bewilderment. *It feels like the Magical Superior's power level, but that makes no sense. Only one other mage in the world matches the Superior's power level and she is nowhere near here.*

Finally, Darek and his escort reached the small metal building. It had two windows on the front, but they were covered with tin shutters, making it impossible to see inside. Darek did hear voices talking, but they were too muffled and indistinct for him to identify who was speaking or what they were talking about.

The first prisoner rapped on the corrugated front door, making an unusually loud banging sound that made Darek want to cover his ears. "Hello! It's Stanzi here, with a very important guest who needs to see Jakuuth right away."

The voices on the other side stopped talking immediately. The next moment, the door opened, causing Darek to step back involuntarily when he saw who had answered it.

It was a young woman, close in age to him, with short, blonde hair and a wand in her right hand. She wore the same uniform that all of the prisoners did—a gray jumpsuit —but it seemed to fit her more loosely than it did the others, as if her uniform was a size too big.

Darek didn't focus too much on her clothing, however. He was staring into her eyes, which looked like the eyes of a bear that was about to kill its prey, eyes he had seen many times over the last decade, eyes he used to love and trust.

They were the eyes of Aorja Kitano, Darek's old friend.

"Stanzi, what do you—" said Aorja, before she met Darek's eyes and cut herself off abruptly.

"Hello, Miss Kitano," said Stanzi, smiling proudly. He gestured at Darek as the other prisoners moved out of the way to give her a better look. "Know who this is? He's Darek Takren, the son of Jakuuth. Isn't that amaz—"

Aorja drew her wand and pointed it at Stanzi. Without

warning, a blast of fire erupted from the wand and struck Stanzi in the chest. The blast was strong enough to send him flying off the walkway and into the prison yard below, a falling fireball whose screams of terror rapidly became indistinct the farther he fell.

Darek paid little attention to that. He reached for his own wand as quickly as he could, but Aorja grabbed him by the collar of his robes and dragged him inside. The last Darek saw of his escort before Aorja slammed the door shut behind them was the remaining eleven gathering at the edge of the walkway, pointing down at wherever Stanzi had fallen as cries of shock rose up from the prison yard from the training soldiers.

Chapter Nine

Durima's initial shock at seeing the banished God of Deception, Thieves, and Horses soon faded, replaced instead by a deep fear. She struggled to sit up, but then Hollech kicked her in the chin, a powerful blow that made her jaw burn with pain and forced her to sit back down.

"H-Hollech?" said Gujak, who hadn't even tried to move from his current position on the ground. "Wh-What are you doing here?"

Hollech let out an angry snort. "Don't tell me you forgot. I was banished here by that idiot upstart godling Skimif, for no reason other than I was trying to bring the world back to the way it once was."

As Durima massaged her aching jaw, she knew that that was somewhat true. Thirty years ago, shortly after Skimif had become the God of Martir, Hollech had formed a conspiracy with about a dozen other gods to overthrow Skimif. From what Durima had heard, the conspiracy had involved Hollech and his fellow deities causing chaos all over Martir to prove Skimif's inept leadership, which would then draw the Powers back to Martir and take away Skimif's divinity. His plan had been thwarted in part by a mortal known as Prince Malock, and as punishment for his crime,

Hollech had been banished beyond the Void by Skimif.

His banishment was supposed to last a thousand years, but when Durima saw how stringy Hollech's mane looked, how he seemed to be missing one eye, she began to wonder if he would even last another ten.

"But why did you call yourself the God of the Void?" said Gujak, holding his chained hands over his head like he thought that would protect him from Hollech's anger. "I thought you were the God of Deception, Thieves, and Horses."

"Correction: I *was* the God of Deception, Thieves, and Horses," said Hollech. He leaned forward, his sole equine eye widening unnaturally. "But then Skimif took away my powers, like a father taking away a toy from a child who is acting out. So now, I am the God of the Void, as none of the other gods have any influence here."

"So you can control the Void?" said Gujak in horror.

"Yes!" Hollech said, standing up straight. "Behold as I make the Void do my bidding."

He reached out with his non-glowing hand into the darkness. Durima and Gujak watched, waiting to see the Void react to Hollech's commands. Durima didn't see how it could be possible for a god to control the Void, but she did not want to accuse Hollech of lying, even though she knew that he probably wouldn't mind it.

Several minutes passed as they stared at Hollech's outstretched hand. Nothing happened; at least, nothing that Durima could see. She strained her ears, trying to hear anything, but the Void was as silent as always.

Then Hollech lowered his hand and looked down at them again. "Did you see that?"

"See what?" said Gujak before Durima could tell him to shut up.

"The Void bending to my will!" Hollech cried out, waving his arms up and down. "Didn't you see the darkness turn into a dragon and then become a perfect replica of yours truly? Are you two blind? Or just stupid?"

"Neither, my lord," said Durima hurriedly. "We saw the whole thing. Gujak here was just joking. He has a bad habit of doing that in these kinds of situations."

"What a terrible joke," said Hollech, shaking his head. "But I am glad you saw it. Truly, you now know that I am the God of the Void, not to be questioned or doubted."

Gujak glanced at Durima with an expression that clearly said, *What are you talking about?* But Durima just shook her head quickly, a nonverbal way of saying, *Just go with it. This guy is absolutely insane and you know it.*

"I, and I alone, rule the Void," said Hollech, raising his shining fist high above his head. "No one understands its intricacies and mysteries nearly as well as I do. The Void answers to one master, and that master is me."

Then Hollech pointed at Durima and snapped, "You. I remember you. What did you do for me back in the old days?"

Caught off-guard by Hollech's sudden topic change, Durima stuttered, "W-What?"

"What did I hire you to do for me back when I was in Martir?" Hollech said. "Answer quickly or I will toss you into the Void waters and see how well you can swim with those chains around your neck and limbs."

Durima thought fast. She did recall working for Hollech in her younger years, but it had been so long ago, perhaps a century or so, that she could barely recall what she had done for him. Combined with the stress of Hollech's threat, and for a moment she thought she wouldn't remember.

But then she did, and she said, "You hired me to kill this mortal man you didn't like. He blasphemed your name regularly and you couldn't stand that, so you gave me permission to kill him and his female partner."

"Did you do it?" Hollech asked, his voice lower and far more menacing than before.

"Yes, sir," said Durima, nodding. "I went to the man's house and burned it to the ground while he and his female partner were still inside. They had a baby, but I think it died as well."

"No, it didn't," Hollech snapped. He tapped the side of his head. "I remember. I raised that baby, who grew up to become my old servant Ramufa, but of course you don't remember him because I never hired you again. Ramufa was an infinitely better servant than you katabans, that's for sure."

Whether there was any truth to what Hollech just said, Durima didn't know. She decided it was better not to argue the point with him, as he could probably kill her if he wanted.

"Now tell me," said Hollech, his tone now more inquisitive than angry, "how many years has it been since

Skimif banished me beyond the Void? Are my thousand years nearly up yet?"

He asked that last question in a pleading voice, like a disciplined child asking if his punishment was almost over. It seemed like a very inappropriate tone for a god, of all beings, to use.

"No, Hollech, sir," said Gujak, shaking his head. "It's actually been thirty years since you were last banished."

"Thirty years?" said Hollech. He stomped the ground so hard that it cracked under his feet. He looked up and shook his fist at the sky. "Damn you, Skimif! Once I get out of here, I will do everything within my power to tear you limb from limb, you arrogant upstart of a godling! I will bring the entire wrath of the Void itself down on you! I—"

Hollech suddenly started coughing. He beat his fist against his chest, as if something was lodged in his lungs. He coughed and hacked so badly that Durima thought for a moment that he was about to die.

But then Hollech stopped coughing. He looked around for a moment, like he thought someone might have been watching him from the darkness. When he was sure they were alone, he looked back at Durima and Gujak, a more reserved expression on his face.

"Yes," said Hollech. "Well, thirty years is better than no years at all, I suppose. But that still leaves a solid nine-hundred and seventy years left. What am I supposed to do in the meantime?"

Gujak gulped. "Uh, whatever it is you've been doing now, sir?"

Hollech froze, like Gujak had just revealed the secrets of the universe to him. "You mean explore the deepest depths of the Void, cursing Skimif every minute of every day, and doing my best to avoid the Scavengers?"

"What's a Scavenger?" said Gujak.

"It doesn't matter," said Hollech. "Tell me, why were you two chained up together in a boat like that? Who sent you here? No, let me guess. It was a punishment for some crime you committed, but I cannot imagine how horrible that crime must have been if they decided to banish you two beyond the Void rather than mercifully execute you."

There was no way in hell that Durima would reveal to Hollech that she and Gujak had killed one of his sisters. One thing she did remember about Hollech was how protective he had been of his siblings, despite always playing tricks on them. If they told him the truth, he'd probably execute them himself.

Need a plausible excuse, Durima thought, looking around for any inspiration. *Not just any excuse, either. Hollech was the God of Deception. He can probably see straight through our lies. Doesn't mean we can't try, though.*

But Durima's thoughts were as dry as a well in a drought. She could not think of a good enough lie that would deceive the former God of Deception.

As it turned out, she didn't need to, because Gujak said, "We were kidnapped by a cult of katabans that worship the Void. They sent us here as their 'sacrifice' to the Void. It was very scary."

Durima was shocked at how quickly Gujak came up with that lie. He didn't even stutter once, although he did say it all quickly, as if he was afraid he would not get it all out if he hesitated even once.

And much to her surprise, Hollech nodded and said, "I see. Yes, I do recall, before my banishment, hearing about a bunch of dumb katabans who thought that the Void was worthy of their worship. I believe they called themselves the Empty, if I recall correctly, or something dumb like that. I see that Skimif apparently still allows them to exist. What a worthless God of Martir he is."

Durima did not let out a sigh of relief, as she did not want Hollech to suspect anything was amiss. She did, however, make a mental note to ask Gujak how he came up with that lie so quickly later.

"So I see that you two are as I innocent as I," said Hollech. "Allow me to free you from your chains, then. I'm not as obsessed with justice as my brother Grinf, mostly because his brand of 'justice' always ended up putting many of my followers behind bars, but if you are going to serve me here, then you would be better at that job if I freed you first."

Before Durima could ask when she and Gujak had agreed to serve Hollech, the banished god reached for the chains binding their bodies. He tore them off as easily as if they were paper, tossing them into the darkness somewhere out of sight as he did so.

A minute later, both Durima and Gujak sat on the ground rubbing their ankles and necks while Hollech stepped back and smiled at them. His smile looked odd on his equine face, even unsettling, although Durima did not say a word about it.

"Now, then," said Hollech. He began walking away. "Come with me. Tell me all that has happened on Martir during my absence."

Durima and Gujak exchanged looks before getting onto their feet and following Hollech. Durima still could not remember agreeing to serve Hollech, but as he probably knew the Void much better than either of them, she didn't think they had much choice but to follow him and hope for the best.

As they walked, Durima and Gujak shared as much as they knew about the changes Martir had experienced in thirty years to Hollech, who listened all the while. He showed little interest in most of it, except for when Durima mentioned that many of the gods were still unhappy with Skimif's rule, a comment which got a snort of approval from Hollech.

He showed some more interest when they got to Uron. Durima was very careful not to mention how she and Gujak had been the ones responsible for Uron receiving the God-killer. It required some careful word craft on her part, but Hollech didn't seem to notice she was lying, which was good.

"There is a being as strong as Skimif trying to destroy Martir?" said Hollech, his tone equally disgusted and excited. "Where is he now? What is he doing?"

"I don't know," said Durima, shaking her head. "No one

does. The gods have been searching for Uron for a year now."

"Has he killed any of my other siblings, aside from the Avian Goddess?" Hollech asked.

"Again, we don't know, sir," said Durima with a shrug. "We don't think so because we haven't felt the deaths of any other goddess or god, but we just don't know for sure."

"Hmm," said Hollech, scratching his chin. "I am torn. On one hand, I'd like to see this Uron fellow kill Skimif, but on the other hand, I don't want to see Martir destroyed. Where would I have to return to from my exile if that happened?"

Durima didn't know, so she kept quiet.

"Skimif should end my exile and bring me back to Martir to help," said Hollech. "Based on what you told me, this Uron fellow sounds like a tricky, deceptive being, and having once been the God of Deception myself, I bet I could see through any of his silly little tricks right away."

"I don't know, sir," said Gujak, looking over his shoulder every now and then, like he thought someone might be following them. "Uron still has the God-killer. Bringing you back would just give him another target, wouldn't it?"

Hollech slapped Gujak over the head. "Do not contradict me, katabans. Or I will leave you for the Scavengers to feast on. Trust me, the Scavengers are not clean eaters."

Gujak rubbed the back of his head where Hollech had slapped him, muttering as he did so, "Yes, Master Hollech, I'm sorry, I won't do it again, I promise."

Durima didn't like seeing Gujak get beaten like that, but

she also didn't want to cross a god who had obviously lost his marbles decades ago. Hollech's mention of the 'Scavengers,' however, did make her curious enough to want to know more about them.

So she asked, "Master Hollech, you mentioned something called the 'Scavengers.' What, exactly, *is* a Scavenger?"

Hollech stopped briefly and looked in every direction for a moment before resuming his pace. "Good question, servant. I don't know."

Durima almost stopped when she heard that. "What? But you said—"

"Let me clarify," Hollech continued. "I only call them Scavengers because that's what I saw them do on my first day in the Void. They tore apart the carcass of some corpse and left no sign that it had even been there. I've never seen them attack an already living being ... well, unless it attacks them first, that is."

"You mean there are creatures in the Void?" said Gujak, whipping his head back and forth as if he might catch a glimpse of some monster lurking the shadows. "I thought that the Void was empty of all life."

"Oh, the Void isn't quite as full as Martir," said Hollech, waving Gujak's concerns off. "But there are beings and creatures that live here, things that no Martirian eyes, whether mortal or divine, have ever seen."

"Such as the Scavengers, Master Hollech?" said Durima.

"Exactly," said Hollech, nodding. "I've never caught a full look at a Scavenger, as they hate the light and always stay in the shadows. From what I've seen of them, however, they are giant insects, almost like grasshoppers, and are very strong and capable of killing anything they want, though they tend to feast on things already dead."

"Where did the Scavengers come from?" Gujak asked in worry. "Are they also creations of the Powers?"

"Of course not," said Hollech. "I don't know what they are or where they came from. They were here when I was banished here and I imagine they'll still be here well after I return from exile. I believe they are native to the Void, if that is even possible."

Durima's paranoia kicked into high gear. She did not see or hear any of these Scavengers right now, but now that Hollech was telling her and Gujak about them, she realized she would have to keep her guard up at all times here. Especially since Hollech had implied that the Scavengers were not the only creatures that lived in the Void.

"Are they dangerous?" Gujak asked.

"As I said, they only eat dead creatures," said Hollech. "They never attack living creatures unless it is in self-defense. I learned that by watching a Scavenger tear apart another creature that had attacked it first."

"If that's the case, Master Hollech, then how did you lose your right eye?" Durima asked.

Hollech instinctively reached for his missing eye, then lowered his hand just as abruptly. "All I will tell you about that matter is that there are things in the Void that even we gods must be vigilant against. I will tell you more later, if it's relevant."

Durima could not help but shiver when she heard that, though she doubted Hollech or Gujak noticed. She didn't want to know what kind of creatures living in the Void were strong enough to wound a god. She doubted she would be able to sleep if that happened.

"What other kinds of creatures exist in the Void, sir?" said Gujak. "Besides the Scavengers?"

"I don't know," said Hollech with a laugh. "Oh, I've seen a few creatures, some that resemble dragons, others that resemble wolves, some that resemble nothing you could find on Martir, but trust me when I say that I doubt I've seen even one-tenth of the creatures that live here. They stalk in the shadows, making strange noises, fighting each other, sometimes fighting me. Every day is always a new adventure for me here."

Hollech said that like it was a fun thing. That confirmed Durima's suspicion that Hollech had indeed gone insane, although as usual she kept that thought to herself.

"The Void is a massive, massive place," said Hollech, gesturing at the darkness all around them. "I've been here thirty years, but I haven't even explored half of it. There is so much more to it that I could easily spend ten thousand years here and not even begin to scratch the surface."

"So you haven't seen the Powers or anything?" said Gujak. "Have you tried to locate them?"

"How would I ever do that?" said Hollech. "The Powers left Martir for good this time, I believe, and I have no idea where they could have gone. I originally tried to look for them, but I gave up when I realized that I would do better to wait near the Void's entrance than to wander aimlessly through the darkness for a thousand years."

"But how have you survived all these years, Master Hollech?" said Durima. "The Void is such a dangerous place. What have you been doing since your banishment?"

"Many things," said Hollech. He begin listing them off his fingers. "Asserting my dominance over the Void, avoiding the worst of the creatures that live here, cursing Skimif every chance I could get, planning my vengeance for when I will return to Martir, and gathering my new followers who obey my every command."

Durima frowned. "New followers? What do you mean by that?"

"You will see them soon enough," said Hollech, patting Durima on the head like a good dog. "But trust me, they are far better than any other servants who have served me. Except for perhaps Ramufa, although he is dead and has been dead for years."

"Where are we going, anyway?" said Gujak, looking ahead of them into the darkness. "You haven't yet said, Master Hollech."

"To my headquarters," said Hollech. "The place I've made my home and my personal fortress since the early days of my exile. We should be there any minute now ... although, considering how time doesn't work properly here, we might be hours away for all I know."

As it turned out, Hollech's initial estimate was correct. It was only minutes later that what looked like a massive stone gate appeared from the shadows. Hollech's light revealed gigantic stone columns that were cracked and withered, like they had been exposed to the weather, although from what Durima could tell, the Void had no real weather patterns to speak of.

"Here we are," said Hollech as he, Durima, and Gujak passed between the huge stone columns. "Castle Hollech."

He raised his light hand and brightened it, creating more than enough light for Durima and Gujak to see clearly what 'Castle Hollech' looked like.

Durima had expected the castle to be at least as big and imposing as the castles mortals used, but to her disappointment, there wasn't much to it. It was only two stories high, with a single turret rising from the center. It had no doors or windows, wasn't even painted any color. It resembled a stone box rather than a castle, as though whoever had designed it had tried to make it as simple as they possibly could. Strangely enough, there were at least a dozen holes in the ground, like some kind of digger worm had been through here recently.

"Did you build this yourself, Master Hollech?" Gujak asked, looking up at the banished god.

"Nope," said Hollech. "I found it on my third day in the Void, which, coincidentally, was also the day I stopped keeping track of how much time had passed here. No one was using it, so I took it as my own. It has kept me safe from most of the Void's threats."

"But who built it?" Durima said. She glanced over her shoulder. "And those stone columns back there and that gate. Who built all of this?"

"No idea," said Hollech. "I originally thought that these were leftover creations of the Powers, but upon closer inspection, I figured out that the architecture is unlike any Martirian style of building. That tells me it is something from some other world, maybe even from the world that existed before Martir. Who knows?"

Durima hated these kinds of mysteries. She wanted to know the facts, but it was clear that if even Hollech did not know who had built this place, then she was unlikely to get the facts that she desired.

"Why don't we go inside?" said Hollech as he resumed walking. "I want to introduce you to the rest of my servants. They will surely be glad to see that their Lord has found two new servants to help them carry out the orders I give them."

Once again, Durima and Gujak exchanged looks before resuming their following of Hollech. Durima wondered exactly what kind of servants that Hollech could possibly have found in the Void. After all, it seemed like every form of life in here was hostile towards him to some degree.

Maybe there's an entire intelligent species in here, Durima thought, her eyes trailing along the outline of Castle Hollech as they drew closer to it. *Like the humans or aquarians or us katabans. Maybe they even built this castle. That is probably what Hollech's servants are.*

Whoever had built Castle Hollech must have built the place for people much smaller than Durima or Gujak, because as they entered through the front door they were forced to duck to avoid hitting their heads against the door frame. Hollech, too, had to duck, although he did it much more naturally than them, probably because he walked through this doorway every day.

Upon entering the castle, Durima was struck by how tiny the lobby was. Their heads almost brushed against the ceiling and there was barely enough room for all three of them. If Hollech had a lot of servants, Durima guessed that this place had to get very full whenever they were all gathered here together.

The lobby was also very bare. Hollech's light revealed no furniture or carpeting, no banners or paintings on the walls, nothing except smooth, old stone that smelled like it had been freshly mined from a quarry. A few doorways split off from the lobby into other rooms, while a spiral stone staircase in the center of the room went straight into the ceiling, probably up to that tower that Durima had seen earlier.

"Here we are," said Hollech, spreading his arms wide as if they were standing inside a wide-open ballroom rather than a cramped lobby. "Castle Hollech, the only piece of civilization that the Void has not yet conquered."

It wasn't much to brag about, in Durima's opinion, but Hollech seemed genuinely proud of his castle. She glanced up the stairs, wondering if any of Hollech's servants were going to come running down when they heard his voice, but she didn't even hear any voices.

"My servants are upstairs, in the tower," said Hollech. "Since you will probably spend the next nine-hundred and seventy years serving me, I want you to know my servants as well as yourselves."

Hollech walked over to the stairs, Durima and Gujak trailing behind uncertainly. He began climbing the stairs, every footstep sounding like a horse hoof beating against the stone. The stairwell was rather narrow, but Durima fit just barely, while Gujak, with his slim body, had no trouble at all entering. They followed Hollech up the stairs, which seemed to go higher than they should have, although Durima thought that the Void was probably messing with her senses and making her feel out of whack for no reason.

The stairs were as dark as the rest of the Void; though thanks to Hollech's light, it was easy to see where they were going. As with the rest of the castle, there wasn't very much to see. The stone walls were eerily blank.

As they climbed the stairs, Durima listened hard for any sounds from above. Surely she and Gujak would be able to hear the servants moving above, wouldn't they? Even if Hollech's servants, whoever they were, were moving quietly, she thought she at least would have felt their magical energy signatures, if nothing else.

Then again, if these servants are from the Void, then they might not have normal magical signatures at all, Durima thought.

Finally, they reached the top of the stairs. A stone door, made of the same kind of stone as the rest of the tower, stood before them. It apparently wasn't locked because Hollech pushed the door open eagerly and stepped inside. Durima hesitated a moment, then followed, with Gujak right behind her, into the room itself.

"Durima, Gujak," said Hollech, gesturing at the room as

they entered. "Meet my servants. I have quite a few already, as you can no doubt tell, but I can always make room for more."

At first, Durima thought that Hollech must have been playing a trick on them. The tower room that they had stepped in had no other beings in it at all except for her, Gujak, and Hollech. The only things she saw was dirt; piles and pile of dirt, and based on the smell they gave off, not very fresh dirt, either.

Some of the piles were large enough for her to sit on; others were smaller than her foot. They were all placed in a circle in the room, doing absolutely nothing at all. Durima wondered if the dirt was some kind of living dirt found only in the Void, but the longer they stood there staring at it, the more Durima became convinced that the dirt was just dirt.

Gujak scratched the back of his head and looked at Hollech. "Um, Master Hollech? Where are the other servants?"

Hollech let out an offended whinny. "What do you mean, where are the other servants? Why, they're right here."

He gestured at the dirt piles. "See? All twelve of them, all sitting around right here instead of working, which they *should* be. Lazy bums."

Hollech kicked at one of the dirt piles, smashing it into pieces. The dirt scattered all over the floor, but it did not cry out in pain or make any noise.

"I never liked Quiet anyway," said Hollech, shaking his head. "That's what I called him, by the way, because he was always so quiet."

Durima nodded, although secretly, she was thinking, *Looks like Hollech really did lose his mind. What did the Void do to him in a mere thirty years?*

"Everyone, introduce yourselves to Durima and Gujak," Hollech ordered the dirt piles. "And don't be shy. They will be your new partners for the next millennia or so, so you'd better get used to working with them now."

Again, none of the dirt piles did anything. Durima almost thought that Hollech might just be playing with them, but when she remembered how he 'controlled' the Void earlier, she rejected that idea almost immediately.

"So, uh, Master Hollech," said Gujak. "What, exactly, do your servants do around here?"

"Nothing," said Hollech, glaring at the dirt piles as though they had insulted him. "Absolutely nothing. They sit around up here all day, in a circle like this, while I must do everything myself. I should fire them, but I think I would be in an even worse situation than I am now if I did. Do you understand?"

Frankly, Durima thought that Hollech's situation wouldn't change much if he 'fired' his servants. At best, Castle Hollech would be a little bit cleaner than it was now. At worst, Hollech wouldn't even have the pretense of company, which could potentially do all sorts of bad things to his already shattered insanity.

Before Durima could share this thought, however, Hollech started and looked out the window on the opposite side of the chamber. His equine features went from annoyed to horrified in an instant as his ears aimed forward, like he heard something horrible that only he could hear.

"What's the matter, Master Hollech?" said Gujak. "You look worried."

Hollech turned on his feet and immediately went stomping down the stairs. Alarmed by his unexplained behavior, Durima and Gujak followed, leaving behind the rest of Hollech's 'servants' to sit where they always sat.

"Master Hollech, please wait," said Gujak as Hollech, as if drawn by a magnetic force, ran down the stairs. "What did you see? Or was it something you heard?"

"No time to explain," said Hollech without looking back at them. "It's coming. We must prepare."

"What's coming?" said Durima, doing her best to keep up with him as they followed the banished god down the stairs. "Scavengers?"

Hollech shook his head. "It would be easy if it was the Scavengers. No, it's much, *much* worse than the Scavengers, I can tell you that."

Just as Durima was going to ask what was worse than the Scavengers, she heard what sounded like a blizzard of glass swirling through the air outside. It was shocking to Durima because it was the first sound she had heard in the Void that had not come from one of them, making her wonder briefly if she was imagining it.

Then Gujak asked, raising his voice over the sound as it grew louder and louder outside, "Why does it sound like glass is being shattered outside?"

"Because it *is* glass, you big idiot," Hollech replied as he jumped down the last few steps and landed on the floor.

"Now come on. Unless we get rid of it, we'll spend the next few months picking glass out of our bodies ... assuming we even survive this, of course."

Chapter Ten

Aorja slammed Darek onto the floor and pinned him there with her boot. Before Darek could even think, he felt Aorja's wand at the base of his neck, the heat of the energy radiating from its tip like Aorja was charging a powerful blast of fire like the kind she had shot at Stanzi seconds ago.

"How did you get here?" Aorja demanded, her voice angry in his ear. "Tell me or I'll blow your brains out right here right now."

"Aorja!" a feminine voice, scratchy and hoarse, Darek didn't recognize said. "What are you doing with that young man? Who is?"

"Interrogating an enemy spy, Rema," said Aorja, her tone full of venom. "I don't know how he got here or what he's planning, but I know this particular idiot well enough to know that it's not going to benefit us."

"Hold it, Aorja," said Darek, even though he knew nothing he could say would calm her down. "I'm not here to cause trouble, I—"

Aorja stomped on his back, causing Darek to gasp as she said, "Don't listen to a word he says. He's a student from North Academy and the whole reason I was thrown in this prison in the first place. He's nothing more than a goody-

155

two shoes who doesn't know when to stay out of other peoples' business."

"But you still haven't even told us his name," said that same voice from before, the one belonging to the being known as Rema. "Unless it's unimportant, of course."

"My name is Darek Takren," Darek gasped, ignoring Aorja's wand at his neck. "And I am here to see Jakuuth Grinfborn."

Darek did not know what to expect when he revealed his name to whoever was in the room. Though he had not heard Jakuuth speak, he hoped that the false Son of Grinf was here anyway. Because if Jakuuth was somewhere else, then there was a good chance that Darek would die today.

The room fell silent when he said his name. He didn't even hear Aorja say anything, even though she already knew who he was. He fully expected her to blow his head open or at least toss him down into the prison yard like poor Stanzi. He wondered if the Ghostly God might possibly intervene to save him, but when he thought about it some more, he realized that the Ghostly God would probably just find someone else to replace him if he died here.

Lord Xocion, please protect me, Darek prayed in his mind.

Then a voice—not Xocion's—spoke. "Did you say ... Takren, young man?"

The voice was somewhat older-sounding, though not too old. It reminded Darek of a book he had once read, which had described the voice of Grinf as that of a fiery furnace mixed with a clanging gavel. This voice, however, sounded more human than that, though the resemblance to Grinf's voice was definitely there.

Taking a chance, Darek looked up. The room he was in was fairly small. Two bookshelves, filled with what appeared to be record-keeping books, stood along the right wall, while a small, ripped sofa stood on the left wall opposite them. A large wooden desk, scattered with papers and books, stood near the back of the room. Behind the desk, on the left, was another door, though where it led to, Darek didn't know.

The room's furniture was not the only thing that caught Darek's attention, however. There were three other beings besides Aorja in here, people he had never seen before.

On the sofa sat a thickset woman with horns sticking out of her forehead. She wore a white dress that reminded Darek of the snow back in the Great Berg, although the dress was clearly a tight fit because he could see the shape of her large body a little too well through it. Her nose was long and pointed, almost like a bird's beak, which made Darek wonder just what the heck she was.

Leaning against the bookshelves opposite her was another female, but this one looked even less human than the fat one. She was taller and skinnier than her companion, almost skeleton thin. With her gangly arms, dark red skin, and crazy black hair, she reminded Darek of the pictures of the Dead Ones that he had once seen in a book.

And sitting behind the desk was none other than Grinf, the God of Justice, Metal, and Fire, himself.

Then Darek blinked and realized that the man sitting

behind the desk wasn't actually Grinf. He looked like Grinf, with his golden hair, his dark skin, his square jaw, and muscular arms. He even had a gavel that doubled as a ball peen hammer.

But the longer Darek looked at the man, the more he noticed hints of mortality in him. The man had aging lines in his face that no god would ever show, gray hairs poked out among his golden hair here and there, and he was hunched over slightly as if by age.

Even then, Darek knew that despite Jakuuth Grinfborn's aging body, he was not a force to be messed with. He sensed Jakuuth's magical energy levels, all right, and they were astoundingly high. He could think of only two other mages who had energy levels like Jakuuth and those were the Magical Superior and Yorak.

Impossible, Darek thought. *How did he get that strong? He's not blessed of the gods, like the Magical Superior and Yorak.*

Deciding to find out, Darek said, "Yes, Jakuuth, I said Takren. You heard right."

Jakuuth Grinfborn sat back in his creaky chair, a look of disbelief on his face. "Takren ... it has been decades since I last heard that name. I never thought I'd live to hear it spoken once more."

Then Jakuuth leaned forward, slamming his hands on his desk as he looked down on Darek with fiery eyes. "Why do you have that last name? Where did you get it from?"

"From my mother," said Darek, trying to keep his tone as cool as he could, even though he was terribly afraid.

"Jenur Takren."

The two strange-looking women looked at Jakuuth, as if they wanted to see what his response was.

Jakuuth's hands briefly pressed down on the desk before he pushed himself off. "Jenur Takren ... you are her son?"

"I am," said Darek. "And you ... you are my father."

Behind Darek, Aorja let out a gasp of disbelief. The two women also exchanged questioning looks, while Jakuuth ran a hand through his graying hair as if in shock.

"I ... I do not have a son," said Jakuuth, though there was a hint of doubt in his voice. "Jenur Takren and I ... no way. I would know if I had a son."

"It's the truth," said Darek in the most honest voice he could muster. "I would not be here if that was not so."

Jakuuth's arms fell to his sides and he stared at his desk as if his whole world had been turned upside down. "I do not remember impregnating Jenur. We were close, very, very close, but—"

"This idiot's lying," said Aorja, jabbing the tip of her wand deeper into the back of his neck. "Listen, Jakuuth, I knew Darek for nine years and he never once mentioned you as his father. And Jenur didn't mention you, either. I don't know what Darek's game is, but if he's lying like this, then it can't be any good."

Jakuuth looked up again, his eyes now alight with anger. "Aorja, I believe you are correct. Jenur and I were together, but we never had a child together. I would know even if Jenur had not told me."

That's when it hit Darek like a ton of bricks. The Ghostly

God had mentioned that Mom and Jakuuth had known each other, but until this exact moment, he hadn't realized just *how* they had known each other. The very thought of Mom and Jakuuth being together in *that* way ... well, it made his skin crawl, to put it lightly.

Then Jakuuth stood up. "Yes, I remember now. When I first attended North Academy prior to the Katabans War, Jenur already had a small child under her wing. I never cared about him as much as Jenur, but I do remember his name ... Darek Takren."

"What?" said Darek. He blinked rapidly. "But I don't remember you at all."

"You don't?" said Jakuuth, stroking his chin. "That makes no sense. I attended North Academy for almost six years, during which I spent a lot of time with Jenur and then with you. You had almost entered puberty by the time I was expelled; there's no way you could have forgotten about me."

Darek tried to think back to when he was a kid, but oddly, he found that part of his memory fuzzy and blank. Only a vague feeling of fear and anger smoldered in him when he thought back to those years, but the memories associated with those feelings were missing.

"He could be lying, Lord Jakuuth," the tall, skinny woman suggested, her voice as scratchy and hoarse as the one Darek had heard earlier. "He seems like the type who would."

"I doubt it," said Jakuuth. "While he may have been raised by the most deceptive woman in Martir, he likely is honest about not remembering me. Perhaps Jenur cast a memory spell on you that wiped away your memories of me ... without telling you, of course."

"My mom would never do that to me," said Darek. "Why would she? She loves me."

Jakuuth chuckled. "I thought the same thing when I first met her, but then she betrayed me. Just what I should have expected from a former member of the Dark Tigers, though I suppose I was too blind by my love for her at the time to notice."

The bitterness in his voice sounded as fresh as if it had happened yesterday, rather than twenty-four years ago. It made Darek wonder, just for a moment, if his mother was as good as he always thought she was. Even if she had been right in 'betraying' Jakuuth, if she had also wiped Darek's memory of Jakuuth without his consent, then what did that say about her character? What other unseemly things might she have done that Darek didn't know about?

"So can I kill him?" said Aorja, who sounded far too eager about murdering Darek for his liking. "After all, if he lied about this, he's probably hiding his true reasons for being here, which is to destroy us from within like the spy he is."

"I only said that so I could get to Jakuuth," Darek said. "I'm not here to cause trouble or anything. I just figured that the prisoners would treat me with respect if they thought I was a quarter god or whatever."

"Idiots," Aorja snapped. "I bet the Magical Superior himself could come here, claim to be the mail man, and those morons would take him straight to Jakuuth no questions asked."

"It would be wiser to kill him, Lord Jakuuth," said the tall, skinny woman. "He is a threat to our operations."

"Can I eat him?" said the thickset woman, eying him with hungry eyes. "I haven't had anything to eat in at least an hour. I'm already starving."

Jakuuth tapped his chin in thought. He appeared to be considering what his servants said, although whether he would actually order Aorja to kill Darek or not, it was impossible to know for sure.

"Killing Darek would do us no good," said Jakuuth, shaking his head. "At least right now. Instead, we shall interrogate him and make him tell us why he's really here."

"That's easy," said Darek as soon as Jakuuth finished speaking. "I heard on the grapevine that you were back and that you were building a new army with which you would use to conquer the Northern Isles. I wanted to join you because I wanted to become more powerful."

"That doesn't sound like the Darek Takren *I* know," said Aorja. Darek felt spittle from her mouth fall on his ear. "The Darek Takren *I* know would never in a million years join an army of rapists and killers just for power. He'd instead be here to stop us."

Darek bit his lower lip. This would have been so much easier if Aorja hadn't been in the room, breathing down his neck and seeing straight through his lies. Still, he couldn't confirm what she just said, otherwise the entire plan would fall apart completely.

So he said, "Well, the Darek Takren *you* know, Aorja, is gone. He died the night Uron rose from the grave of Braim Kotogs. This new Darek Takren wants the power to stop Uron, power the Magical Superior and the other teachers can't give to him. I think Jakuuth can, however, which is why I am here."

Darek was surprised to find how much of that lie he believed. He did want to get stronger, strong enough to help the gods defeat Uron, and he was frustrated by the fact that the teachers at North Academy forbid students from breaking through the ceiling and reaching new heights of magical power.

As for whether Jakuuth could give him that power ... he honestly did not know, but he said it with the same sincerity as the rest of his statement. After all, the best lies often had a little bit of truth sown in them, which made it impossible for anyone but the most astute of thinkers to see through.

The false Son of Grinf still stood behind his desk, a thoughtful expression on his face. Darek hoped Jakuuth believed him, but he would not know until Jakuuth spoke.

After several tense seconds of waiting, Jakuuth nodded. "I believe him. There is a sincerity in his voice that I cannot deny. Aorja, let him go."

"What?" said Aorja, her voice loud in Darek's ear, causing him to wince. "Why don't we read his mind first? If he's really telling the truth, then he should be okay with that."

"There's no need," said Jakuuth, waving off her suggestion with one of his scarred hands. "He is sincere and honest. Besides, he would be a complete imbecile to lie to me. I can sense his power level and it isn't very high. I could easily flash-fry him if I had to."

"But you won't," said Darek. "Because I'm on your side now. Don't know if I like the idea of conquering the Northern Isles, but if you can give me more power to help defend my world from Uron, I'll help you do it."

Jakuuth frowned. "Who said anything about conquering the Northern Isles?"

"What?" said Darek in surprise. "But I thought that's why you were training the Limitless Army."

"Of course not," said Jakuuth. "There are hundreds of powerful nations in the Northern Isles, each one with its own army. To try to conquer the entire Northern Isles, or even just one nation, with less than three hundred soldiers? That's not even counting the aquarians or the gods. To do so right away would be madness."

"Then ... then what *are* you planning to do?" said Darek. "Why are you raising this army if you're not going to conquer the Northern Isles?"

Jakuuth smiled. "Just because I am not going to conquer the Northern Isles immediately doesn't mean I'm not going to conquer anywhere at all. There are two places, in fact, that I will attack once the Army is finished training. Can you guess what those two locations are?"

Darek thought hard about it. "Um ... let's see ... I don't, actually, know which two locations you're thinking of conquering."

Jakuuth's smile turned into a scowl. "It's obvious, but let

me spell it out for you anyway: The Limitless Army, led by me, will conquer World's End and North Academy. We will split the Army in half in order to strike both places simultaneously."

Darek gasped. "World's End and North Academy? But why those two places?"

"That is also obvious," said Jakuuth, "if you would but think about my history with those two places. One is where I was rejected for stating the truth of my parentage; the other is where I was locked away for daring to act on that same truth. I will attack and destroy both places, wipe their memory from the world, just as they did to me."

"Especially World's End," said the thickset woman as she rubbed her belly. "They kept us locked under there for so many, many years, and without any really good food. It was horrible."

Darek wanted to get up and attack Jakuuth right now, but Aorja still pinned him to the floor. Besides, even if he did kill Jakuuth at this very moment, Aorja and those two strange-looking women would probably take him down before he could escape.

Thus, he said, "But how are you going to attack both places at once? No offense, but I don't think an army of trained prisoners is enough to take on a school that is home to the most powerful mage in the world and the island where the gods themselves are said to live."

Jakuuth sat back down in his chair and reclined in it. "It will be far easier than you think, Darek. The gods are too busy looking for Uron to pay attention to what we are doing, so that leaves World's End more or less undefended. As for North Academy, I do not fear the Magical Superior or his teachers, seeing as I am a Limitless and cannot be stopped."

"A what?" said Darek.

"Limitless," Jakuuth repeated. "It means I have exceeded my so-called 'natural' magical limits. It is how I became as powerful as I am today. And it is how I will destroy both World's End and North Academy."

Limitless ... Darek thought. *How come none of the teachers back in North Academy taught me about that? Can I become a Limitless?*

"Besides, you assume I am training these prisoners to be nothing more than highly effective soldiers," said Jakuuth with a chuckle. "That couldn't be farther from the truth. Once they are done training, they will be as Limitless as I. Limitless mages cannot be stopped, especially by mages who believe they are Limited, such as the Magical Superior or any of his teachers or students."

"Meaning that North Academy won't stand against us," said Aorja with glee. "A disciplined, well-trained Army combined with Limitless magical power will be able to overcome any obstacle. Even the katabans of World's End won't be able to stop us."

"Indeed," said Jakuuth, nodding. "Now, Darek, I can see that you are quite shocked indeed by learning about our true plans. Do you still want to join us? I will understand if you don't."

Darek did not answer right away. On one hand, he didn't want to destroy North Academy or kill anyone who lived in it. He had lived there his whole life, after all. It was his home and the many students and teachers who lived there were his family. He even had literal family there: his mother, Jenur Takren.

On the other hand, if Darek rejected Jakuuth's offer, then he did not doubt that Jakuuth would order Aorja to execute him. Or maybe that fat woman would eat him or maybe they would toss Darek to the Army and let them do with him as they saw fit. All Darek knew was that rejecting Jakuuth's offer would be useless; after all, the Limitless Army would try to conquer World's End and North Academy regardless of his decision.

Seeing that he had no other choice, Darek nodded into the floor. "All right, Jakuuth, I accept. I'll help you destroy World's End and North Academy, but in exchange, I would like to be trained as a Limitless, if that will give me the power to stop Uron."

Jakuuth put his hands together as if he was quite pleased. "Excellent, very good. After Aorja lets you go, we can start your training immediately. You have much catching up to do if you are going to reach the same level of power as the rest of the Army, but you seem like a smart man, so I doubt you will have much trouble learning the secrets of the Limitless."

Chapter Eleven

The sound of countless shards of glass cutting against the exterior stone walls of Castle Hollech was painful to Durima's ears. It sounded like a thousand children were tossing an equal number of glass balls at the castle, except these balls kept coming and showed no sign of letting up.

Thankfully, the Glass Blizzard, as Hollech called it, could not get into the castle. He had ordered Durima to block off the doorway and windows with her geomancy, which Durima was surprised to discover actually worked in the Void. She didn't question it, however, but simply used it to extend the castle's walls until they completely cut off all ways in or out of the building.

When she finished, Gujak was dancing around, as he always did when he was nervous, looking at the ceiling and listening to the muffled sound of glass cutting against stone outside.

"What *is* it, Master Hollech?" said Gujak as covered his mouth with his hands.

"A Glass Blizzard," said Hollech. "Weren't you listening? As far as I can tell, it's a natural weather phenomena of the Void. I never know when it will strike, but I do know that it is always deadly."

"Is that how you lost your right eye?" Durima asked.

Hollech shook his head. "Nope. But I did spend an ungodly amount of time picking glass from my body the first time I ran into it."

"How do we fight it off?" Gujak said with a gulp.

"That is exactly why I have you two here," said Hollech, gesturing at both of them. "I don't know how to scare it off. I only know how to hide from it and wait for it to pass."

"How long does it usually last?" Durima said.

"Hours, maybe days," said Hollech with a shrug. "I don't know. Time has no meaning in the Void."

"Maybe we can just wait it out," Gujak suggested. "I mean, Durima managed to seal the castle shut, so it can't get in, can it?"

"Perhaps not," said Hollech. "But I am the God of the Void and I do not want to be at the mercy of the Void's own weather patterns. Therefore, we are going to figure out how to beat it back."

I guess trying to stop the weather is about as crazy as calling a dozen piles of dirt your 'servants,' Durima thought, though as always, she was careful to keep that opinion to herself.

"But we've never done this sort of thing before," said Gujak. "I mean, not to question your greatness, Master Hollech, but just because our magic still seems to work here doesn't necessarily mean we can stop an entire Glass Blizzard."

Hollech slapped Gujak hard enough to knock him flat off his feet. "I don't care. As katabans, your whole point in life is to do what we gods demand that you do. I am starting to think that Skimif must have banished you beyond the Void as a way to punish me further by giving me such uncooperative, ineffective, complaining servants."

Gujak rubbed the side of his face where Hollech had slapped him while Durima said, "Master Hollech, I understand your frustration, but Gujak has a point. We've never faced a Glass Blizzard before, therefore we do not know how to handle it. Perhaps you could tell us more about what you know of it so we can effectively combat it."

Hollech sighed heavily. "Fine. I don't know much about the Glass Blizzard except that it is random and unpredictable. It lasts for as long as it wants and leaves when it is 'done,' whenever that is. It is highly painful and even more lethal."

"All right," said Durima. "But do you know what causes it? Such as the weather patterns that precede it?"

"No," said Hollech. "It always comes out of nowhere. Of course, if there are any weather patterns preceding its arrival, do you think I could see them in the Void?"

Durima shook her head, wincing slightly when she heard a particularly loud shattering sound outside. "No, sir. I was just wondering if there might be a way to predict its arrival."

"Well, there isn't," said Hollech. He gestured at the walls. "It comes and goes when it feels like it. There is no pattern to its arrival or departure at all."

Durima scratched her chin as the Glass Blizzard's shattering sound grew to a roar outside. "Then maybe it's not a natural weather phenomena at all. Maybe it's actually a thinking, intelligent being in the form of glass."

"Impossible," said Hollech. "If that was true, I think I would know. I've had to endure it for thirty years and it hasn't shown even the slightest hint of intelligence to me."

"You mean there isn't even a god or goddess controlling it?" said Gujak.

"Of course there isn't," said Hollech, jerking his thumb at his chest. "*I* am the only god in the Void. There are no other gods here, nothing except those freaky godly wannabees anyway."

"Freaky godly wannabees?" said Durima. "What do you mean by that?"

"I'll tell you later, after we deal with this Glass Blizzard," said Hollech. "Now, come up with a plan to get rid of it or I will toss both of you out there and let it have you. I might just do that anyway since I'm in such a bad mood right now."

Durima looked at the blocked off doorway. Outside, she heard the Glass Blizzard swirling and howling, the sound so loud and awful that it made her want to cover her ears and hide until it went away. Yet she knew that Hollech was not joking when he said he'd throw them out there if they didn't come up with a plan quickly.

How do you stop a Glass Blizzard? Durima thought. *Maybe melt the glass? But can I even generate enough heat to do that? I don't even know how big the damn blizzard is.*

That reminded Durima of a problem she had felt earlier. Although she had succeeded in closing off the door and windows with her geomancy, the effort had taken a lot of energy out of her, far more than it normally did. She sensed that, while it was indeed possible for her and Gujak to use their magic here, it was exceptionally harder than it was in Martir. It felt like trying to pull up a boulder from the bottom of the sea, although the fact that she could use it all was something of a miracle to her, as there were no gods in the Void to generate magical energy for her to use.

Except for Hollech, Durima thought, glancing at the banished god, who was now impatiently tapping his foot against the stone floor. *But I don't sense as much magical energy from him as I normally do from the other gods. Skimif must have taken away more than just his authority over his dominions.*

But all of that was irrelevant to her current situation. Right now, she and Gujak needed to figure out how to destroy a Glass Blizzard or at least scare it away.

She looked at Gujak, who appeared to be thinking hard about what they needed to do.

"Any ideas?" Durima asked.

Gujak shrugged. "Nope. How about you?"

"Think harder, both of you," Hollech snapped, causing Durima and Gujak to look at him. "What do you think I'm paying you two for?"

You're not paying us at all, actually, was what Durima wanted to say, but knowing how volatile Hollech could be, she said, "Yes, sir. We'll get back to it right away."

"Good," said Hollech. "Because once you two figure out how to do that, then the entire Void shall tremble beneath my feet."

Durima walked up to the sealed door and pressed her right ear against it before immediately taking it off. The sound of the glass shattering against the castle wall's outside had been ridiculously loud and had done nothing to help her understand how to get rid of it better. She had thought it worth a try, at least.

"Sir, there's really not much we can do against it," said Gujak, rubbing his right arm. "I think all we can do is wait it out."

"Wait it out?" said Hollech. He whinnied angrily. "I will *not* wait it out. If you two are simply going to waste my time by telling me you can't even get rid of a Glass Blizzard, why, I—"

Without warning, the sounds of glass shattering and cutting the walls of Castle Hollech outside ceased as abruptly as it had came. Everyone went quiet, listening hard for the Blizzard to start up again, but as time went on, it seemed as if the Glass Blizzard had left for good.

"Why did it stop?" Gujak asked in a low, frightened-sounding voice. "Where did it go?"

Hollech walked up to the walls and put his ear again where one of the windows had been, just like what Durima had done a moment ago. He seemed to listen hard; then his equine eyes widened and he stepped back from the wall.

"Get back," Hollech hissed at Durima and Gujak. "*They* are here."

Durima and Gujak backed away from the walls, though Durima could not help but ask, "Who are *they*?"

"Shh," Hollech said, holding a hoofed finger up to his lips. "If we speak too loudly, they will hear us."

Hollech looked dead serious, but Durima could not help remembering how crazy he had acted today. Sure, there might be some new dangerous Void creatures out there, but this warning was coming from the same god who claimed that a dozen piles of dirt were his lazy, no-good servants. Durima did not think it unreasonable to be more than a bit skeptical about his claims.

At least, she thought it was reasonable until she heard loud *boom* against the wall opposite them. Another *boom* and cracks appeared in it.

"Get ready," said Hollech as he held up his fists. "Once they break through, they will not hesitate to kill us all."

"K-Kill us all?" said Gujak, looking at Hollech in alarm. "What do you—"

A third *boom* and the wall before them crumpled into pieces as the loud roars of monsters assaulted Durima's ears like cannon fire. Something long and dark shot out of the darkness and wrapped around Gujak's waist, but Durima snapped it with her teeth before it could pull him in and the tendril returned into the darkness.

But that wasn't the only thing that tried to get inside. A creature that appeared to be made entirely of metal jumped inside, but Hollech was faster than it. He jumped at it and kicked it in the gut, denting its stomach, before grabbing its head and snapping its neck in an instant.

Yet even as the creature fell dead at his feet, more strange tendrils—these ones like vines—launched out of the shadows at Hollech. They wrapped around his wrists as some huge, ugly-looking green monster with a mouth as big as Durima entered Hollech's light before the banished god kicked it in the tongue. The creature yelped in pain and retreated.

Just as it left, another beast appeared, this one resembling a human combined with a horse. Instead of attacking Hollech, however, it went for Durima and Gujak. Gujak screamed in fear when he saw it, but Durima leaped at it and punched it with all her might. The weird monster staggered backward before Durima hit it again so hard that it retreated with a loud whimper.

Panting, shaking her aching fist, Durima stepped back as a horrible, foul-smelling toxic stink filled her nostrils. A second later, some kind of muck creature peaked its head through the gap in the wall, its mouth revealing row upon row of ugly jagged, metal teeth before Hollech punched it, causing it to go back into the shadows like it hadn't been there at all.

"Quick!" Hollech snapped, looking over his shoulder at Durima and Gujak. "Repair the wall now while there's a break in the attack!"

Durima didn't hesitate. She slammed her fists into the stone floor and sent a burst of geomancy into it. The earth energy traveled to the remains of the wall, which immediately began repairing it. A clawed hand reached for Hollech, but he swatted it away, and just in the nick of time, too, because soon the stone wall was back to normal now.

"But how is it going to hold?" Gujak asked even as

another familiar *boom* sound echoed through the castle. "What's to stop them from breaking through it again?"

Hollech placed his hands against the rebuilt wall. A bright glow swept over it before vanishing. Then the god stepped back from it, putting his hands on his knees as though he was tired, even though gods couldn't get tired.

"There," said Hollech, brushing some loose hairs from his mane out of his eyes. "That is a reinforcement spell. It isn't my specialty, but it's something I've learned how to do ever since I discovered that it's about the only thing that keeps those bastards out. Should last for a week or so at least."

"But what *were* they?" said Gujak. "And why did the Glass Blizzard leave all of a sudden?"

"I don't know why the Glass Blizzard left," said Hollech. "But I do know what those *things* are. They are what I like to call 'half-gods.' Those freaky godly wannabees I told you about earlier."

"Half-god?" Durima repeated. She glanced at the dead metal creature lying on the floor near the wall. "You mean like a godling?"

Hollech let out a disgusted sound. "Of course not. A godling is a mortal turned into a god. A half-god is … well, I like to think of it as an incomplete god, if you will."

"Incomplete?" said Gujak. "What does that mean, sir?"

"It means exactly what 'incomplete' means," said Hollech, now looking at Gujak as if he was an idiot. "Unfinished. Abandoned. Forgotten. Missing parts. A potential for greatness that was never realized."

"But gods can't be incomplete, sir," said Gujak. "All of the gods on Martir, including yourself, are complete, aren't you?"

"My siblings and I may be that way, but these creatures are not my siblings," said Hollech. Then he paused. "Although in a way, they are. After all, those creatures we just fought off? The ones that tried to kill us? They are also creations of the Powers, just like you and me."

"But I thought that there weren't any creations of the Powers in the Void," said Gujak, who had by now backed well away from the rebuilt and reinforced wall. "I mean, aside from you, obviously, Master Hollech."

Hollech walked over to the dead metallic being lying on the floor and kicked it over onto its back. In the light from Hollech's hand, the metallic being's wide, crazy-looking mouth and deep black eyes made Durima turn away in disgust.

"I thought so, too, until I ran into these guys after my first week here," said Hollech, gesturing at the dead half-god at his feet. "I don't know the full story behind these beings, but I do know they were created by the Powers like you and me. I've sensed magical energy in them similar to the kind my siblings and I generate, though they are only half as strong as us."

"Why aren't they in Martir?" Gujak asked, his eyes now fixed on the dead half-god. "Why are they here in the Void?"

"As I said, I don't know their full story," said Hollech. "From what a half-god I once captured told me, the half-gods are unfinished gods that the Powers grew tired of.

Some are prototypes of us final gods—this one here looks like a prototype of my sister—but not all of them are. The Powers didn't want to destroy them or put them in Martir with the rest of their completed creations, so they simply abandoned these half-gods in the Void indefinitely."

"How many of them are there?" said Gujak.

"Numerous," said Hollech. "I suspect that the half-gods have lost their minds after being in the Void for so long and so have split up into various packs that are at constant war with each other. They're little more than beasts now, easy to manipulate, but not easy to defeat."

"That's creepy," said Gujak. "How have you been fighting them off for so long?"

"By being smarter and stronger than them, obviously," said Hollech with a snort. "Even without all of my original powers, I am still head and feet above them. They are an annoyance, however, and one I have been meaning to dispose of for a long time now."

"Well, I'm glad they can't get into here now," said Gujak. "They're too much, on top of everything else."

Durima looked at the newly-repaired wall and frowned. "Master Hollech, how long are we going to stay in here? How will we know when it's safe to venture outside of the castle and into the rest of the Void?"

Hollech whinnied. "Safe? It is *never* safe to travel into the rest of the Void, Durima. Never. But you are correct that at some point we will need to leave. Otherwise, we'll all go crazy."

Gujak and I will go crazy, probably, Durima thought,

178

but I'm afraid that you have already gone over the deep end, Master Hollech.

"We will wait a few hours," said Hollech, gesturing at the wall. "The half-gods usually give up fairly quickly, as they lack the patience necessary to be truly effective hunters. After those few hours are up, we will go hunting."

"Hunting, Master Hollech?" said Gujak. "Hunting for what?"

Hollech's equine face broke into a hideous smile. "Hunting for half-gods, of course. With you two at my side, killing every last one of those bastards should be quite easy. But before we do that, come with me and I will give you the weapons and equipment necessary to kill those unfinished deities as easily as if they were insects."

Chapter Twelve

Darek Takren followed Jakuuth down the walkway that clung to the inner walls of the prison like a grapevine. Behind him, Aorja followed, every now and then muttering something under her breath, though he could not tell what she was muttering about exactly because of the noise from the training prisoners below.

I can guess, though, Darek thought, remembering how Aorja had pinned him to the floor of Jakuuth's office earlier.

As for their destination, Jakuuth had said that Darek would need to be personally trained by him in order to catch up with the rest of the soldiers in time for the invasion. So Jakuuth was leading Darek to a room underneath the prison, away from everyone else, where he could give Darek the personal training and attention that he needed.

And despite knowing full well just how awful and evil Jakuuth's plans were, Darek could not help but feel excited about the prospect of learning how to become a Limitless. He was sure that he had heard that term somewhere before, but he could not recall where. At the very least, he knew that the teachers at North Academy had never taught him about the concept, not even his own mother.

Rather than heading down to the prison yard itself,

Jakuuth led Darek and Aorja into another entrance that Darek had not noticed before. It was a blank, metal door located about halfway between the top of the prison's walls and the prison yard below, with nothing to indicate that it led anywhere special.

The door opened with a loud creaking noise, like the hinges had not been oiled in years, as Jakuuth, Darek, and Aorja entered. They had entered a metal hallway well lit by orbs of light trailing along the ceiling, which revealed that the hallway was cramped, dirty, and smelly. There was even a fist-shaped dent in the right wall, although neither Jakuuth nor Aorja offered to explain it, perhaps because they didn't know how it had gotten there themselves.

Darek wished that Aorja was in front of him, rather than behind him. He didn't want to look at her so much as he didn't like having someone who hated him where he couldn't see her. She technically didn't need to come at all as far as Darek could tell, but she had insisted upon following them because she wanted to make sure Jakuuth would be safe.

Not that he needs the extra protection, Darek thought as they walked. *He could probably kill me with both hands tied behind his back and his eyes gouged out by a chimera.*

"Where are we going?" Darek asked. "I mean, where exactly?"

Jakuuth didn't look over his shoulder as he said, "We're going beneath the prison. There's too much noise and chaos outside for me to train you properly. I am going to teach you how to exceed your limits in a place where we can have enough silence to allow us to concentrate."

"Right," said Darek. "How long will this training take?"

"It depends on your individual strengths and weaknesses, of course," said Jakuuth as they walked down a short metal staircase to a lower part of the hallway. "Some of the prisoners caught on quickly, others took much longer. With me as your teacher, it should not take very long to complete your training in time for the invasions of North Academy and World's End."

Darek glanced over his shoulder at Aorja. She wore an ugly, mean-looking scowl, but she didn't have her wand out pointing at him at least. That was good, although that didn't mean Darek felt safe enough to try anything down here.

"So is Aorja a Limitless as well?" Darek asked, addressing this question to Jakuuth.

"I'm right here," Aorja snapped, before Jakuuth could say anything. "And yes, Jakuuth taught me how to be a Limitless. He even made me one of his trusted lieutenants because he was so impressed by my loyalty to him."

"That is true," said Jakuuth. "Aorja was one of the first to become a Limitless, hence why I consider her an important—although certainly not expendable—member of the Army."

Either Aorja didn't catch the 'certainly not expendable' part or she didn't care because she said nothing about it. If Darek had been in her position, he would have been worried if he had heard Jakuuth say that about him.

Then again, Aorja is downright insane, Darek thought. *She probably interpreted it as meaning something else entirely.*

"I will answer any other questions you have once we are actually beneath the prison," said Jakuuth. "For now, we walk in silence."

Ten minutes of walking in silence later, descending deeper and deeper into the bowels of Rock Isle, they emerged into a wide-open, though incredibly dark, room. Like the rest of the prisoner's interior, this room was plated with metal on the walls, ceiling, and floor. It was apparently completely empty, although the smell of rotting meat and ikadori peach juice told Darek that this room must have at one point been a storage room, though it seemed like the prisoners must have eaten all of the food if its absence was any indication.

The trio walked down the metal staircase leading from the room's entrance down to the room's floor. Jakuuth walked with a much heavier step than either Darek or Aorja, because every time he stepped on one of the metal steps, it sounded like a hammer clanging against a metal sword fresh from the forge.

Once they reached the bottom floor, Jakuuth gestured toward the middle of the room. "Go over there, Darek, and we can begin your training."

Darek did not move right away, however. "I still have some questions about what being a Limitless actually means."

Jakuuth frowned, as if he did not want to waste time talking, but then he nodded. "Fine. Understanding what it means to be a Limitless is the first step in breaking through the ceiling; therefore, ask whatever questions you might have about it and I will do my best to answer."

"All right," said Darek. He crossed his arms over his chest. "I was always taught that every mage has Limits to the magical energy he or she can use. Those Limits vary from individual to individual, obviously, just like anything else, but those Limits are there and they are very real."

"Ah, yes," said Jakuuth, rolling his eyes. "The Pillar of Energy, also known as the Sixth Pillar of Magic. I assume you know that it was added much later after the rest of the Pillars were decided by the First Council of Martirian Mages five hundred years ago, yes?"

Darek shook his head. "I didn't know that."

"Yeah," said Aorja in disgust, brushing a few stray strands of hair out of her eyes. "They didn't teach us that at North Academy because they didn't want us to get too uppity or powerful, not because they were concerned about our health."

Darek looked at Aorja in surprise. "How do you know that?"

"She knows that because she knows me," said Jakuuth, placing a hand on his chest. "The reason I was exiled from the school was because I claimed to be both the Son of Grinf and a Limitless, which are as factual as stating that the sky is blue and the sun is bright. They didn't want me teaching the other students things they didn't approve of."

"Really?" said Darek, scratching the back of his head. "But why would they do that?"

"It's obvious," said Jakuuth in a bitter voice. "The

Magical Superior is an ego-centric control maniac who thinks that because he is powerful and connected to the gods, that means that whatever he believes or says is true. Because he is too weak to breach his own Limits, he thinks no one can do it and so discourages his students and teachers from ever trying it."

"Spot on," said Aorja. "I always knew that the Magical Superior was nothing more than an ancient blowhard. Always."

Darek did not agree with that characterization of the Magical Superior at all, but knowing how dangerous it would be to disagree too strongly, he said nothing. Besides, the seeds of doubt had already been sown in his mind and he was beginning to wonder if there was any truth to Jakuuth's claims.

"North Academy has a reputation for teaching students how to be the best, but that is only from within the Limited worldview," said Jakuuth. "The Limitless have always been a minority, at least since the time that the Sixth Pillar was added after the First Council by Limited too weak to break through their own Limits. Every other magical school teaches the Sixth Pillar to its students, which is why so many mages are weak and ineffectual despite drawing upon the powers of the gods themselves."

"They burn Limitless literature," said Aorja. "You can't get a job teaching the secrets to Limitlessness in any school because no one believes it can be done."

"Then how did you learn how to do it, Jakuuth?" said Darek, looking at the false Son of Grinf with confusion. "If you didn't have any teachers to teach you or books to read, I don't see how you did it."

Jakuuth looked up at the ceiling as if it were a bright, open sky. "I am the Son of Grinf, of course. My divine side has a clarity that most mortals lacked. I knew that I was not Limited to whatever arbitrary power level that my teachers or anyone else designated me because my father is not Limited. I searched out a teacher, an old woman living by herself on the obscure island in the south known as Destan, where I learned everything I needed to know about how to become a Limitless."

Then Jakuuth sighed. "Sometimes, I miss that old woman. When I escaped from World's End two months ago, I went to Destan, where I learned she had died ten years previously. She was one of the few mortal mages who continued to practice Limitlessness, though she chose to live in seclusion to avoid the wrath of her fellow Limited mages."

Darek had no idea who this old woman was, but he thought it was kind of sad that she had been forced to live that way just because the other mages didn't agree with her. Darek wanted to ask what her name was, but then he realized it was a useless question and so disregarded it.

"But I don't think I have actually defined what being a 'Limitless' means just yet," said Jakuuth. "A Limitless mage is a mage who believes that, contrary to the Sixth Pillar, we mages do not have any actual Limits except the ones we place on ourselves. We believe that any mage, with hard work, can learn to break through the 'ceiling' and grow to previously unimaginable heights of pure magical power."

"So that's what being a Limitless means?" said Darek. "Breaking through the ceiling? But isn't that dangerous?"

"Only if you're an idiot who has no idea what they're doing," said Jakuuth. He placed one hand on Darek's shoulder and looked him straight in the eyes. "All those stories of mages falling into comas after breaking through the ceiling? Simply examples of mages who, due to a lack of training, did not understand how to achieve Limitlessness."

Darek almost shuddered under Jakuuth's touch, but he stayed still so as to not arouse the suspicion of Jakuuth or Aorja. "I tried to break through the ceiling earlier today, during my graduation. I ended up falling into a coma."

"I know that," said Jakuuth. "Not because I was there, but because your obvious interest in becoming a Limitless led me to conclude that about you. The only types of mages, in my experience, who are interested in becoming Limitless tend to have a history of doing it by themselves, often with disastrous results, until they find a teacher or book that shows them the proper way to do it."

"I knew it," said Darek. "My mom, Jenur, got onto me about it when I woke from the coma, but I knew I had been doing it wrong."

Jakuuth's frown turned into a scowl. "Yes. Jenur believed in the limits of magical power back in our younger days as well. I suppose it was too much for me to expect her to have changed her mind over the years. Combine her stubborn nature with living and teaching in North Academy all day every day and I doubt she can be convinced that it is possible even if you showed her how to do it."

"Some people are just so dumb," said Aorja. "Especially Jenur. So shortsighted and narrow-minded."

"Hey," said Darek. "Mom's not that shortsighted or narrow-minded. She just doesn't know any better, that's all."

"Stop arguing, you two," said Jakuuth as Aorja opened her mouth to respond. "You will be working together very closely from now on, which you can't do if you're constantly nipping at each other's heels."

"Yes, Jakuuth, sir," said Aorja in a reluctant voice. "I won't argue with Darek anymore."

"Good," said Jakuuth. "Now, Darek, do you have any other questions or should we begin the training now?"

A memory flashed in Darek's mind, a memory of when he broke through the ceiling earlier. He remembered how amazing he had felt, at least for a short period of time, and then he remembered that mysterious skeleton that had appeared and spoken to him briefly before he fell unconscious.

"When I broke through the ceiling today, I saw ... something," said Darek.

Jakuuth raised an eyebrow. "Something? What might that something be?"

"A skeleton," said Darek. "At least, I think it was a skeleton. It looked like a skeleton, but it talked and acted like a person. Do you know what that might have been?"

Jakuuth stroked his chin, looking somewhat distressed by Darek's question. He clearly knew what it was or at least had a sneaking suspicion, though he appeared reluctant to say anything about it if the way he turned his body away from Darek was any indicator of how he felt.

"Seeing that skeleton when you break through the ceiling is rare," said Jakuuth. "Even among Limitless, it's not something you see every day. As for what it is ... it is one of the few mysteries of Limitlessness that even I do not know the answer to."

Darek did not believe that for a second. No wonder Jakuuth considered himself the Son of Grinf rather than the Son of Hollech; he was a terrible liar. His body language clearly said that he knew exactly what Darek had seen and refused to talk about it, though why, Darek couldn't imagine.

He was tempted to push the issue, but he decided that it was not very important at the moment. Maybe later, after he had grown closer to Jakuuth, he would ask again.

Assuming I don't just kill him, of course, Darek thought. *Remember, Darek, that's the whole reason you're here. You're supposed to kill him because without his leadership, the Limitless Army would fall apart completely. Just keep your eyes open for a good opportunity to attack.*

"Now, then," said Jakuuth. Once again, he gestured toward the middle of the room. "Go stand over there. I will give you further instructions once you are positioned correctly."

Darek did as Jakuuth asked, walking over to the center of the room, which was difficult to find at first due to the low light conditions of the room. Once he was positioned where he needed to be, he looked back toward Jakuuth and Aorja and asked, "What next?"

"Next, we begin training you to become a Limitless," said Jakuuth. "Draw your wand. You will need it to perform the next step."

Darek did so. "Done."

"Good," said Jakuuth. "Now, we need to work on defining your Limits."

Darek frowned. "Defining them? Why should I define my Limits if I am going to break them?"

"Because you need to define them in order to break them," said Jakuuth. "How else will you be able to break through the ceiling if you don't already know your own Limits?"

"Well, I know what they are already," said Darek. "Because I broke them already. Doesn't that already make me a Limitless?"

Jakuuth shook his head swiftly. "Not necessarily. Becoming a Limitless is more than just breaking through the ceiling once. It requires abolishing the belief that you have Limits to your power, and to abolish that belief, you must break through the ceiling again and again until you no longer believe it."

"But I already believe I don't have any Limits," said Darek.

"No," said Jakuuth. "You do; otherwise, you would be far more powerful than you are now. Your subconscious continues to believe in Limits because that is what it was taught for decades ... and it is time to destroy that belief in the only way you can: With cold hard experience."

Darek gulped. "That sounds dangerous."

"Greatness is always dangerous, Darek," said Jakuuth. Then he looked at Aorja. "Aorja, would you please stand opposite Darek? I want you to help him transcend his Limits."

Aorja obeyed without saying a word, although she didn't look very happy about it. She went over to the center of the room and stopped about a dozen feet from Darek, where she drew her wand and held it before her just like Darek.

"Now, Darek, you and Aorja are going to be training partners," Jakuuth continued, "which is the real secret to achieving Limitlessness. It is impossible to do on one's own without falling unconscious. If you have a partner, however, it becomes exceptionally easier to do so."

"How does having a partner make exceeding your Limits easier?" said Darek, glancing at Aorja. "Is she going to share her magical power with me or something?"

"No," said Jakuuth. "What Aorja will do is keep you going. That is to say, she will give you motivation not to let up. The reason so many mages fail to achieve Limitlessness is because they try once, fail, and never try again. Having a partner to support you is essential to achieving Limitlessness without killing or hurting oneself."

"I have to be his partner?" Aorja said in disgust. "I respect you, Jakuuth, but Darek's ... well, you know our history. How am I suppose to get along with him?"

"Are you questioning my orders, Aorja?" said Jakuuth in a sharp tone. "I thought you had vowed to obey me no matter what."

Aorja closed her mouth, but she still didn't look happy about it. Darek wasn't thrilled about working with her either, although unlike her, he knew better than to question Jakuuth. The Son of Grinf appeared reasonable on the surface, but if what the Ghostly God had told Darek was true, than Jakuuth was infinitely more dangerous than he looked.

"Your first step in achieving Limitlessness, then, is to use up as much of your magical energy as possible in as little time as you can," said Jakuuth. "You must reach the ceiling of your Limits, which you should be able to do with little problem, seeing as you've already done it once before."

Darek hesitated. He remembered all too well how weak he had felt after breaking through the ceiling earlier. His knees grew weak at the very thought, like he was already about to break through the ceiling, even though he was near full magical power at the moment.

"Don't worry about hurting Aorja," said Jakuuth as he folded his arms behind his back. "She is strong enough to handle whatever you, a Limited mage, can throw at her."

Darek looked at Aorja again. She held her wand up in front of her like a sword. She didn't seem at all afraid of him, which meant that Jakuuth was telling the truth.

Still, Darek remembered how, back in North Academy, he had always been a little bit stronger than Aorja in terms of pure magic. He recalled how he had hurt her once while they were practicing botamancy. He had conjured a thick spiky plant that had cut her left arm; not a serious injury, but it had been the first time Darek remembered hurting a friend unintentionally.

Of course, that had been years ago, when he and Aorja had been young students with far less experience than they had now. No doubt Aorja was perfectly capable of protecting herself, especially now that she was a Limitless.

Besides, Darek, don't you remember how she tried to kill you, Jiku, and Mom? Darek thought. *If she gets hurt, it will be nothing compared to the pain that her betrayal has caused you and everyone else back in North Academy.*

With that thought in mind, Darek began to consider which spells he wanted to use against Aorja. He would have to try something powerful in order to expend as much energy as he possibly could. He thought about encasing her in a block of thick ice, but that would definitely kill her, so he would have to do something else.

"Come on, Darek," said Aorja, waving her wand at him impatiently. "Are you going to get started or are you going to stand there and look like an idiot?"

"Fine," said Darek. "Then let's begin, shall we?"

Drawing on as much of his magical energy as he could, Darek fired a beam of pure ice at Aorja. The ice zigzagged through the air, but Aorja jumped out of the way in the nick of time. The ice beam struck the spot where she had been standing, leaving a thick icicle as tall as her in her place.

"Good show, Darek," said Jakuuth, clapping. "How do you feel?"

"Pretty good," said Darek, looking at Jakuuth. "Why?"

"You need to get tired," said Jakuuth. He held up a hand

and closed his fist tightly. "Push yourself. Push yourself to the very limits of your power. Do what you did back in North Academy to achieve that power."

A powerful fear rose up in his body at the thought of breaking through the ceiling again. He didn't want to fall into a coma again, or worse, see that mysterious skeleton once more.

But his desire to become a Limitless overwhelmed his fears and he nodded. "All right. I'll try again."

"Good," said Jakuuth. "And Aorja, if Darek appears to be on the verge of fainting, help him, won't you?"

Aorja did not look like she wanted to help Darek; she said nonetheless, "Yes, Jakuuth, sir."

This time, Darek did not hesitate or stop. He drew upon as much of his power as he could, sending more and more ice flying from the tip of his wand. Instead of aiming for Aorja, he aimed for that spot opposite him where the ice chunk stood, adding more and more ice to it as time went on.

With both Jakuuth and Aorja watching him intently, Darek kept pouring as much of his power out of his body as he could. He was vividly reminded of earlier, when he had broken through the ceiling and fell into a coma, except this time he wasn't even bothering to hide his magic use. After all, there were no teachers here to stop him, so he could use as much magic as he pleased.

As the chunk of ice grew larger and larger, the room became colder and colder. Aorja shivered and hugged herself, while Jakuuth merely continued to watch as if the temperature wasn't falling rapidly at all. Darek felt himself reach the halfway point again, which alarmed him as it had taken him much longer to reach that point before.

Don't stop, Darek told himself. *Just keep going. You'll be safe. Jakuuth and Aorja will help. That's what they're here to do.*

Still, he found it exceptionally difficult to keep going. It was like his body was rebelling at the very thought of him breaking through the ceiling again. His arms and legs became as weak as twigs when he thought about it, but he continued to pour energy from himself at an accelerated rate.

"Good, Darek," said Jakuuth. "Very good. I can sense you've almost depleted your energy reserves. Not much longer now."

The ice chunk was now much bigger than Darek, Aorja, or Jakuuth. It hadn't yet reached the ceiling of the large underground room they stood in, but it was getting close. Darek briefly wondered how they would get rid of it after he was done here, but he banished the thought from his mind in order to focus on getting rid of all of his magical energy.

He pushed more and more, until soon he figured he had only a quarter of his normal reserves left. He wondered for a moment why he was able to drain himself so quickly. Was it an aftereffect of his earlier attempt to break through the ceiling or was it because he was now focusing as intently as he could without distraction?

Either way, he was now rapidly close to depletion again. As before, he felt weak, like he hadn't eaten a good meal in weeks. He wanted to drop his wand and fall to the floor, and he probably would have, had he not felt a warmth in his body that he did not recognize, a warmth that gave him enough energy to keep standing.

Surprised, he looked in Aorja's direction and saw she was pointing her wand at him. He remembered that Jakuuth had given her orders to help him stay on his feet. He had not expected her to actually listen to Jakuuth's orders, but he appreciated it nonetheless. It reminded him of their younger years, when they had both been students and friends in North Academy and had worked together.

"Very low now," said Jakuuth, rubbing his hands together in anticipation. "Just a little bit more."

"I can't ..." Darek coughed. "Jakuuth, I can't do it, even with Aorja's help. It hurts."

He was telling the truth. His chest felt tight and his wand seemed to burn his hand. He felt like he was falling apart. He hadn't felt this way earlier, which made him wonder if something in his body had changed as a result of his earlier attempt to break through the ceiling.

"You can, Darek," said Jakuuth in a soothing, encouraging voice. "You can. With Aorja and me here, you should be able to break through the ceiling without experiencing any of its negative side effects. Unlike your teachers, I know what I am doing here."

Darek nodded to show he had heard, as he was too tired to even speak. He returned his focus to draining himself, until soon his whole front vision was taken up by the massive ice chunk before him, which now resembled a rough mountain in shape.

Aorja's warmth still glowed within him, which he was now sure was the only thing keeping him going at this point. He just wanted to fall down and fall asleep, or maybe fall into another coma. He was practically empty now, but rather than slow down, he sped up.

There it was. He used up the last of his magical energy. He could barely think straight now. His whole body shuddered. He had nothing left, yet he still forced himself to pour more and more. He wished he had never tried this again, but it was too late to turn back now.

"You are empty," said Jakuuth in a pleased voice. "Excellent. That is the first step to achieving Limitlessness, and you did it in good time, my friend."

Darek couldn't think now, but he did manage to say, "What's ... next?"

"Next? Keep doing what you are doing," said Jakuuth. "Pour more and more of your energy out."

"But ..." Darek shuddered again. "How ... I'm empty ..."

"Aorja will aid you there," said Jakuuth. "Aorja? Give Darek a hand."

Aorja sighed reluctantly, but deep inside, Darek felt her warmth rising within him. It gave him the strength to stand up and stay conscious, even though all he wanted to do was lie down and fall unconscious. His head burned so much that it felt like his brain was melting.

"Now, Darek, how do you feel?" asked Jakuuth.

"Better," Darek said, his voice stronger now. "But ... still ... not ... perfect ..."

"Normal," said Jakuuth. "That's how you feel right now. Every mage who attempts to achieve Limitlessness goes through what you are feeling right now. Right now, we're going to work on upping your Limits, as you won't be able to achieve true Limitlessness right away."

Darek blinked. Hot sweat was starting to roll down his face, but he couldn't lift his arm to wipe it away even with Aorja's support. "How ... will ... I—"

"How will you know when you've upped your Limits?" said Jakuuth. "You will feel it, don't worry. It will be a bit scary at first, but once you've upped your Limits, it won't be long before you become a fine Limitless yourself."

But despite what Jakuuth said, Darek couldn't sustain this effort. It was too much for his body. Although Aorja's magic was helping, it was only a crutch and he could sense that it was not working as well as it should have. He sensed that he was getting close to breaking through the ceiling now, but he knew beyond a shadow of a doubt that he couldn't make it this time, not when every fiber in his body was raging against this abuse.

So Darek gave up. He dropped his wand and fell to his hands and knees. The warmth in his body from Aorja's magic vanished, almost making him black out. He gasped for breath and wiped the sweat from his brow, but that did little to make him feel better.

He heard someone walking toward him and he gathered enough strength to look up. Jakuuth was walking toward him, looking as angry and disappointed as Mom used to look whenever Darek, as a child, had done the wrong thing.

He wanted to explain to Jakuuth why he gave up, but his mouth was too weak to form coherent words.

"Why did you give up, Darek?" said Jakuuth as he approached him. "Weren't you listening to a word I said?"

Darek couldn't even nod. It was taking almost all of his strength just to stay conscious. Didn't Jakuuth realize that?

"I see you are too weak to respond," said Jakuuth. He put his hands on his hips. "In that case, perhaps you are too weak to become a Limitless. At the very least, I can't have a weakling like you in the Army. Every soldier needs to haul their own weight, and if you can't do that, then I am afraid we will have to deal with you the hard way."

Darek's eyes widened. He managed to say, "Hard ... way?"

"You know what I mean," said Jakuuth."You lied about your parentage to get here. As the Son of Grinf, I should not tolerate such awful lies. I only tolerated that one because I saw potential in having you around, but now I am starting to think that that potential was a lie as well."

Darek gulped, although his mouth was too dry for that to do any good.

Jakuuth raised his gavel. "Do you know what this is, Darek? This is the Gavel of Grinf, or rather, an imitation of it that I made decades ago when I first learned of my true parentage. It acts as my wand, but it can also smash open skulls very well."

Darek realized where Jakuuth was going with this. "Please ... don't kill me ..."

"Why shouldn't I?" said Jakuuth. He patted the gavel's

head. "It would only be just. My father would not hesitate to punish a liar like yourself, no matter how valuable you might be normally."

"I can do it," Darek gasped. Those four words alone were enough to hurt his throat, but he kept talking. "Please ... give me another chance ..."

"Why should I?" said Jakuuth, tilting his head. "I did not initially invite you to join the Army. Your jumping in has forced me to put off the invasions for another month at least. If you aren't willing to put in the effort to achieve Limitlessness, then you are less than useless to me."

Darek glanced at Aorja. She had lowered her wand now, holding it in both hands as she watched their conversation with interest and excitement. She was probably looking forward to seeing Jakuuth kill Darek, so Darek could not rely on her for help.

"Knowledge," said Darek, looking back up at Jakuuth. "Knowledge of North Academy."

"So does Aorja," said Jakuuth. "She has already told me everything she knows about North Academy's defenses. I doubt there is anything new that you could tell me."

Darek bit his lower lip. He could not think of any major changes that had been made to North Academy's defenses since Aorja's banishment, so Jakuuth had a point.

Jakuuth raised his gavel higher. "I will make this quick so that Aorja and I can return to the surface and begin the preparations to transport the Army to North Academy and World's End."

Panic rose in the pit of Darek's stomach. He reached out

and wrapped one weak hand around Jakuuth's ankle, saying as he did so, "No ... please ..."

Jakuuth actually hesitated. He looked down on Darek's hand as if he had never seen it before. Not that Darek could take advantage of that. He was much too weak to do anything. Even just grabbing Jakuuth's ankle had taken a lot out of him, more than he thought it would.

Yet Jakuuth still held his gavel above his head. The muscles in his arms were tense, like he was going to bring the gavel down any minute now. His eyes were still locked on Darek's hand, but Darek had no doubt that Jakuuth could kill him in one blow even without looking at him.

Then Jakuuth lowered his gavel to his side. "You have a drive to survive. Even when the odds are clearly against you, you still think you can do it."

Without warning, Jakuuth lashed out with his left boot. The boot crashed into Darek's jaw, causing him to let go of Jakuuth's right ankle and fall flat on his back. His jaw ached, like it had been smashed by a metal pipe, and Darek's head spun. He couldn't even focus on anything because he was in such pain.

Jakuuth's face appeared above him, looking as solemn as the gods. He reached down with one hand and brushed something wet and hot from Darek's lips, which Darek's sluggish mind realized was blood.

"I will not kill you today, Darek Takren," said Jakuuth. He held the drop of blood on his finger in Darek's face. "I sense that you will be worth the time and effort I will need to put into training you. But I am only going to give you this one last chance, and if you toss it away like so much garbage, you will see far more than a single drop of blood flowing from your body."

Then Jakuuth looked up. "Aorja, get Darek to the medical room, where he will rest until he feels strong enough to try again. If there are any problems, you know where to find me."

Then Jakuuth walked out of Darek's line of sight, replaced almost immediately by Aorja. Her violet eyes were angry, like she was annoyed by the fact that she had to take care of Darek, but as before, she did not complain or object. She didn't ask if Darek was all right or even how he felt, though that didn't surprise him at all.

As Aorja used telekinesis to cause Darek to hover off the floor, Darek wondered if the Ghostly God had sent him on this mission because the southern god believed he could actually complete it or if he had sent Darek here in order to die.

Either way, it looks like killing a Limitless mage who may or may not be the real Son of Grinf is going to be much more difficult than I thought, Darek thought as Aorja began hovering him away from the ice chunk and toward the exit. *Much,* much *more difficult. Maybe even impossible.*

Chapter Thirteen

Durima did not like the Void metal armor that Hollech had given her. Not that it wasn't practical; oh, it was. It was thick, but not so thick as to be suffocating. It was flexible and covered most of her body. The few spots it didn't cover, such as her armpits, were so difficult to hit that she didn't feel frightened or worried that she could get hurt by leaving them exposed.

What she didn't like about it was how it had clearly been designed for someone smaller than her. As flexible as the armor may have been, it was still tight against her body and limbs—nor was it padded, either, which only added to her discomfort.

She glanced at Gujak, who walked beside her. His armor seemed to fit him much better than hers did. He looked less like a walking tree now and more like a warrior heading off to battle against the enemy army. Of course, it was hard to see him well due to the darkness of the Void, but she had seen him back in Castle Hollech and so remembered exactly how he had looked with the armor on.

Ahead, Hollech led them like a general of an advancing army, although quietly so. He walked so silently that Durima sometimes feared she would forget him if she stopped or looked away. Like Gujak and she, he wore Void metal armor, although he didn't wear as much as they because he seemed to believe that he didn't need it due to his divine nature.

The three of them had been walking through the Void for quite some time now, although again Durima had no idea how much time had passed exactly. Hollech had said that he was leading her and Gujak to the 'nest' of the half-gods, a canyon located not far from Castle Hollech that he had once visited years ago after a half-god attack convinced him that he needed to learn more about them in order to survive.

That was why Hollech had given her and Gujak the armor they wore. After the half-gods' earlier attack, Hollech had shown Durima and Gujak a cache of armor and weapons that he had found stashed away in one of Castle Hollech's hidden rooms. He had claimed that he did not know who or what had put that equipment there, but that he had been keeping it safe in the event that he would need it. He had muttered something about his useless servants not being able to wear any of it, which Durima had chosen not to comment on.

Durima saw the logic behind Hollech arming them. Their equipment was made out of Void metal, a substance that was exceedingly rare in Martir, known for the simple fact that none of the gods, not even Grinf, could break it. Durima had only seen Void metal in person a handful of times over her three centuries of life, so she had been quite shocked when she saw the piles and piles of swords, axes, helmets, shin guards, and other equipment in that room in Castle Hollech. By wearing armor made of the substance,

Durima and Gujak were guaranteed a certain invulnerability that they would otherwise not have.

Still, even with their Void metal armor and weapons, Durima wondered how she and Gujak could possibly help Hollech kill these half-gods. Hollech had assured them that half-gods could be killed by non-divine beings such as katabans, but she didn't see how Hollech could know that, seeing as it was unlikely that he had seen a mortal kill a half-god in the Void.

And of course, Hollech is also completely nuts, Durima thought, eying the back of the banished god as she followed him. *I wouldn't be surprised if he starts to tell us that the secret to defeating the half-gods is to feed them week-old cake.*

For that matter, Hollech had not told them how many half-gods there were. He had said that the half-gods were numerous, but whether 'numerous' meant twenty, thirty, fifty, or even one hundred, Durima didn't know. She suspected that Hollech didn't know, either, though he obviously was not going to admit that.

Every now and then, Hollech would hold up a hand signaling Durima and Gujak to stop. They would do so, and then the three of them would listen for whatever Hollech had seen or heard. Most of the time, it was nothing, although once Durima heard what sounded like a giant grasshopper walking nearby, no doubt one of the Scavengers that Hollech had mentioned earlier.

Aside from the sound of the occasional Scavenger and their own footsteps and breathing, Durima heard no other noises or sounds in the Void. There wasn't even a light breeze blowing through, although that didn't mean that it was warm. On the contrary, the Void was icy, almost as cold as the Great Berg, or perhaps as cold as a long-dead corpse.

Regardless of the climate, Durima was almost certain that she, Gujak, and Hollech were going to be attacked at any moment. While Hollech moved with the silence of a thief, Durima and Gujak, in their Void metal armor, were more like crashing piles of pots and pans, even though both of them were trying their best to be as stealthy as possible. No half-god or Scavenger emerged from the shadows to claim their lives, but that hardly made Durima feel better.

It reminded her of the War, when she and some of her fellow soldiers had been traveling through enemy territory at night. Of course, the King's Desert had been much louder than the Void, with scorpions scuttling across the sand, dune wolves howling at the moon, and the ever-present sound of the sand shifting beneath their feet—not to mention hotter as well.

Just as Durima was about to ask Hollech how much farther the canyon was, Hollech stopped and said, in a short, harsh hiss of a voice, "Stop."

Durima and Gujak did so. Durima reached for the short sword at her side. She technically didn't need it, seeing as her claws were more than enough for dealing with most enemies. But it was made of Void metal, so she thought it would give her an advantage over any half-gods they ran into.

"What is it, sir?" Gujak asked, his voice almost too low to

hear.

Hollech pointed. "Light."

Durima blinked and looked around Hollech. He was right. Coming from down below them was a small light, like the glow of a campfire in the middle of the night, though unlike a campfire it changed colors rapidly. Every now and then creatures would dance past the light, briefly obscuring it, but never for very long.

By her side, Gujak trembled, his Void metal armor clanking like tin. "What is—"

"Shush," Hollech snapped. "Or do you want the half-gods to find us?"

Gujak gulped, but for once he kept quiet.

"That's the group of half-gods that's been giving me hell ever since Skimif banished me here," said Hollech, gesturing toward the light. "Has to be. This is their canyon. But I don't understand the light."

"What do you mean?" Durima asked, keeping her voice as low as a whisper.

"The half-gods never create light," said Hollech, shaking his head. "They are creatures of the Void, which means they despise light. It's how I've been keeping them at bay for so long. I didn't think they even knew how to start a fire."

Gujak looked over his shoulder. "Are there any trees in the Void you could use to make a fire out of?"

"No," said Hollech. "I don't like this, not one bit. Someone taught them how to do it. I don't know who or why, but I am going to get to the bottom of this regardless."

Hollech took off toward the light, still silent, although

much more quickly than he normally did. Durima and Gujak increased their speed to catch up with him, although they ended up making more noise than Durima liked.

Despite the absolute blackness of the Void, Hollech managed to lead Durima and Gujak down into the canyon without any trouble. Soon they reached the bottom of the canyon, at which point Hollech began leading them from boulder to massive boulder so they would not be seen.

The closer they drew to the light, the better Durima saw of the canyon. Half-gods were still dancing around the light, but there was no music playing, except for the occasional growls and screeches of the half-gods themselves. From their position behind a boulder, Durima counted about a dozen half-gods visible in the light, but she heard more dancing in the shadows like puppets.

The sounds of their dancing was a terrible farrago of noise. Durima picked out the sound of sludge slopping against the earth, metal boots clinking against each other, and wooden shoes tapping against a rock. There was no unified method to the dancing, at least none Durima could see. It was a free-for-all, each half-god dancing as he or she saw fit.

"Oh my gods," said Gujak, peering from around the boulder with Durima. "Why are they all dancing? Master Hollech, is this normal behavior for the half-gods?"

Hollech was also peering around the boulder, but on the other side, so Durima could not see his expression. "No, of course not. The half-gods never dance. I didn't even know they knew how to dance ... well, they clearly don't, considering their dance moves, but you know what I mean."

Durima squinted at the light. It looked like a normal fire, but every now and then its color would change. Not only that, but Durima thought she saw faces in the fire or images of beautiful crystalline buildings that she had never seen anywhere in Martir. Every time the color or image changed, the half-gods would let loose another chorus of their chilling song and dance even more frantically, as if this was the last day of their lives.

She caught the expression of one half-god, who looked like some weird cross between a wolf and a golem. There was no mistaking the sheer look of terror on its face, as if it was being forced to dance against its will.

"Someone is behind this," said Hollech's voice, which was right behind Durima.

She pulled her face from around the boulder and saw Hollech standing behind her. The light of the fire did not extend to behind this boulder; nonetheless, Hollech's luminimancy provided enough light for her to see his angry equine face.

"We know that, sir," said Durima. "But who?"

"I have no idea," said Hollech. "But once I find out who it is, I will force him to tell me how he tamed the half-gods and then kill him and become their king."

"Uh, Master Hollech?" said Gujak, who was still peering around the side of the boulder. "I think you'll get a chance to meet their leader, or at least see him, very soon."

"How do you know that?" Hollech said, putting his hands on his hips.

"Because I see him right now," said Gujak. His wooden teeth were chattering now. "And I think ... I think I know who he is."

Durima and Hollech looked around the boulder with Gujak as best as they could. Durima had to get low to the ground to allow Hollech room to look over her, so she got the first glimpse of whoever the leader of the half-gods was.

And when she did, all her hope practically drained away from her like water in the sink.

The half-gods had stopped dancing now, all standing around the fire as if waiting for something. There was a new being in their midst, a humanoid being who walked around the fire as if it was nothing more than a small candle. He was silhouetted against the flame, but Durima had no trouble recognizing those muscular arms, nor could she forget the smell of death that seemed to follow him wherever he went.

"Who is he?" Hollech asked, looking at Gujak and Durima impatiently. "Do you two know who he is?"

As usual, Gujak was too afraid to speak. In fact, he was so afraid that he wasn't even shaking. No doubt he remembered what the leader of the half-gods had done to him last year, a memory even Durima could not forget if she tried.

She did not want to say his name, but there was no hiding it from Hollech.

So Durima said, in a voice little more than a whisper, "That, Master Hollech, is Uron. You know, the guy we told you about earlier? The one who killed two of your sisters?"

Hollech gripped the side of the boulder more tightly, though whether it was out of anticipation or fear, Durima didn't know. "So that's Uron, eh? He doesn't look that powerful."

"Not to disagree, Master Hollech, but he could go toe-to-toe with Skimif himself," Durima pointed out. "Which is to say that looks can be deceiving."

"Why is he here, then?" said Hollech. "Why isn't he back in Martir killing my siblings? Did he come here to kill me? I bet he did. He probably sees me as a threat."

Durima sighed internally. She did not see how Hollech, who despite his strength was essentially a depowered god, could be a threat to Uron in any way, shape, or form. But as always, she kept that thought to herself.

"What should we do, Master Hollech?" Gujak asked. Although he was clearly trying to be quiet, his voice became higher nonetheless. "Run?"

"Of course not, you cowardly katabans," said Hollech, glaring at Gujak. "We stand here and wait to see if Uron is going to say anything to the half-gods."

Just as Hollech finished speaking, Uron spoke. Although Uron's voice sounded different from how Durima remembered it—it wasn't as ancient-sounding as it used to be and had lost much of its hissing overtone—she still had no trouble recognizing his voice at all.

"My humble servants," Uron said, still walking around the fire. "I see you have all made it today or tonight or whatever the time is here in this timeless place. But of course you did. None of you would dare defy me by refusing to come, now would you?"

The half-gods shifted uneasily, as if they wanted to run but were afraid of angering Uron. The fire continued to crackle, though it no longer changed colors or images quite as fast as before.

"Of course you wouldn't," said Uron. "Not after you've seen my full power. Even you half-gods, with only half the brains of a full god, know that I could easily end all your lives here, at this very moment, just as you deserve."

Durima stepped back involuntarily, but then she felt powerful, hoofed fingers grab her fur and looked up. Hollech's eyes were fixed firmly on Uron, although he must have noticed that she was about to run, because why else would he grab her like that?

"But enough with the reminders of your servitude to me," said Uron. "Tell me, has anyone here ever seen the sun?"

None of the half-gods answered, though a few exchanged looks as if they did not know what Uron was talking about.

"Of course you haven't," said Uron. He stopped and spread his arms. "You, all of you, have spent your entire lives in this dark, wretched place. You were placed here only because the Powers, in their infinite wisdom, did not want anyone to see their ugly, unfinished, and abandoned projects. But you all know that."

Uron must have struck a chord because some of the half-gods nodded in agreement, though as a whole the half-gods were as still as statues.

"The sun is a beautiful thing," said Uron, raising his

arms as if to indicate its size. "It is like this fire, except a thousand times larger. It is one of the best privileges of living on Martir, one that has been denied to every one of you half-gods over the centuries."

Is he trying to incite the half-gods to rebel? Durima thought. *He's talking to them as if the gods had been intentionally oppressing these guys.*

"But if you follow me, then that privilege, and so much more, will be yours," said Uron. He lowered his arms. "But I can see the looks of boredom and confusion on your faces. You know all of this, have known it for a year, and are probably wondering why I bring it up again."

Because you're an insane god murderer who likes to listen to the sound of his own voice? Durima thought.

"Because the time is nigh," said Uron. "In another month, I will lead you into Martir, where you will be able to live as freely as any of the gods. Isn't that what you all want, deep down inside?"

The half-gods began muttering among themselves. It sounded like they agreed with Uron, although it was hard to tell because based on what Durima could hear, they were not speaking in any Martirian language.

"The gods will not even see you coming," said Uron. "You will emerge from the Void like the sun rising from the east. You will tear down the jewel of the Powers, that city on the edge of the world, known as World's End. The creation that symbolizes the Powers' utter hatred of you, as it was designed to be a home for the gods, a place where unfinished creations such as yourselves were never allowed to set foot."

Gujak whimpered, causing Durima to slap her hand over his mouth to silence him before he gave away their position. Thankfully, neither Uron nor any of the half-gods appeared to notice.

"But not yet," said Uron, shaking his head. "The time is not yet ripe. We have allies in Martir, allies who are not ready to strike. Once they are, I will know ... and then the gods will know that even unfinished creations are not to be reckoned with."

Uron said that while raising his right hand up. The light of the fire reflected off the silver gauntlet covering his hand, the gauntlet known as the God-killer. It had been a long time since Durima had seen that awful object in person. It sent chills up her spine, like the kind she had felt during the War whenever she saw the corpses of her fellow soldiers lying in the dirt.

The half-gods began moaning and growling and shouting in excitement, like Uron had just finished giving the most inspirational speech ever. They immediately resumed dancing, but whereas most of them had looked scared and confused before, now every half-god seemed to dance with mad delight, as if they were eager to begin their conquest of Martir right away.

And still the fire burned, a greenish hue now, bathing all of the half-gods and Uron in its sickening light. An image of a man who looked like Grinf appeared in it briefly before dissolving into nothingness.

Hollech pulled Gujak and Durima back behind the

boulder. He looked them both in the eyes, his own orbs burning with an untold madness that seemed to radiate like the heat from the fire.

"Did you two hear all of that?" Hollech hissed, forcing Durima to listen hard in order to hear his words above the din of the dancing half-gods. "Uron is going to lead the half-gods to destroy World's End. The bastard."

"Won't your fellow gods be able to stop them?" Gujak asked. His voice wasn't quite as high as it used to be, but it did tremble slightly. "I mean, the half-gods aren't as strong as you and your siblings, right?"

"Under ordinary circumstances, I agree, this would hardly be a threat worth getting upset over," said Hollech. "But you told me that this Uron fellow has the God-killer. Do you think any of my siblings or Skimif will even try to fight the half-gods, knowing that Uron is leading them?"

"No," said Gujak. "But—"

"So you see the problem," said Hollech. "I have no idea how he intends to pass through the Void, seeing as it is sealed from this side, but given his confidence, I have no doubt he's already got a plan all figured out for that."

"Then what do we do?" said Gujak. "I am sorry, Master Hollech, but it's not like we can stop him. He could kill you."

"I am thinking," said Hollech with a snort. "Unlike you, I have an actual brain up here. I will come up with a plan, no worries there."

Durima frowned. "Master Hollech, forgive me for my skepticism, but are you sure you are in any position to come up with a plan?"

"Why would you say that?" said Hollech, glaring at Durima. "Are you implying I'm dumb?"

Durima held up her hands in a pacifying way. "No. I was just saying that the Void might have possibly affected your sanity enough to make any plan you come up with highly ... er, questionable."

Hollech's eyes bugged out of his head as he looked down on Durima. "Me? Come up with *questionable* plans? Katabans, I will have you know that I, the God of the Void, came up with a plan that, had it not been for a certain mortal prince who shall remain nameless, would have resulted in Skimif losing his unearned powers and the hierarchy of the gods being restored to its original form. Are *your* planning credentials on that level? I think not."

Durima flinched under Hollech's angry eyes, but she didn't back down. "I did not mean to imply anything like that, Master Hollech. I was just saying that I think we should take the time to plan our next moves. Uron is a dangerously clever being, and if we don't plan correctly, we could all get killed."

Hollech slammed one of his fists into the boulder, creating a small crater in it. Durima hoped that none of the half-gods had heard it, but all she heard was the mad and seemingly endless dancing and singing of the half-gods.

"I know what I am doing," said Hollech. He pointed a shaking finger at Durima. "Don't question me. A katabans's place is to support the gods at every opportunity, not to question us. Do you understand?"

"I do, Master Hollech," said Durima. "But—"

Hollech slapped Durima across the face. The blow made a clanging sound against her helmet as she staggered to the side, while Hollech breathed in and out hard as if he could barely control his anger.

"Again, do you understand that?" said Hollech.

This time, Durima nodded slowly, even though her head hurt like hell. "Yes."

"Good," said Hollech. "Now, gather round, because I have just come up with the most brilliant plan in the—"

He paused. He paused so abruptly that for a moment Durima was certain that she had somehow missed the rest of his sentence, but when she glanced at Gujak, she saw that he was waiting patiently for Hollech to continue just like she was.

Then she realized that the dancing and singing of the half-gods had ceased. The silence of the Void had returned, eerier and more unsettling than ever.

It didn't take Durima long to figure out what had happened. Although she did not want to, she turned to look around at their surroundings.

On every side, half-gods surrounded them. Due to the poor lighting, she could not see all of them, and of those she could see, she could not see much. Still, she saw enough of them to conclude that she, Gujak, and Hollech could not escape unless they fought through every last one of the half-gods in the area.

Standing before the half-gods was Uron himself. The low glow of Hollech's hand revealed a serpentine face twisted in a triumphant and eager smile.

"Durima, Gujak," said Uron, as if addressing old friends. "Long time, no see."

Chapter Fourteen

It was a day later that Darek, having fully recovered from his failed attempt to break the ceiling yesterday, found himself walking alone in a fairly obscure part of Rock Isle. Rock Isle was almost entirely dominated by the massive stone prison which housed all of the prisoners, but there was a small part of it that was still wild and free, that same rocky beach where Darek had turned up when the Ghostly God had teleported him here the day before.

As for why Darek was alone, that was easy. When he had gotten up this morning, Aorja had told him that he was supposed to go meet Jakuuth in the underground storage room where they had trained the day before. Darek fully intended to do that, but first, he told Aorja that he needed to use the bathroom and that he had to do it away from everyone else for the sake of his privacy.

Thankfully, Aorja had let him go and none of the other prisoners had followed him or asked him where he was going. Not that he expected them to; after all, when he emerged from the medical room, he had seen all of the prisoners training in the prison yard below, almost as if they had been training all night long.

Of course, Darek wasn't actually going to relieve himself. He had not eaten anything since early yesterday morning, shortly before his first attempt at breaking through the ceiling. His stomach was as empty as the catacombs under North Academy. His appetite was not helped in the least by the fact that he had tried to break through the ceiling twice in one day.

The real reason he was going out alone was so he could contact the Ghostly God. Last night, while he slept, Darek had had a dream in which the Ghostly God had demanded that he report his findings on Jakuuth to him right away.

How Darek would contact the Ghostly God, he did not know. All he knew was that the Ghostly God had shown him this beach in his dream, telling him it would be a good spot to meet without fear of being seen by the others. Of course, Darek would have to be quick, otherwise he ran the risk of raising the guards' suspicions.

So Darek walked across the rocky beach, toward the outcropping rocks at the other end. The waves of the Crystal Sea washed in and out, getting water into his shoes and making wet sand cling to his ankles, but he ignored it as he walked to the place he had seen in his dreams.

The cove was small and rocky, but it did block him from the view of the prison, which was good. He saw some clams sticking out of the sand as he went under the cove's overhang to make sure he was out of the guards' sight. There was no sign of the Ghostly God anywhere.

Where is he? Darek thought, glancing to the left and right, even though the cove was so small that he didn't even need to do that to see that he was alone. *Just like a southern god. Tells you to meet him and fails to show up.*

"We southern gods are not *that* unreliable, Darek Takren," said a voice in his ear.

Darek jumped, but it was an awkward jump and he ended up falling on his behind on the wet sand. He immediately got up, brushing the wet crusty sand off his behind as he looked around for the Ghostly God, though he only saw mist everywhere he looked.

"Where are you?" said Darek, keeping his voice low so it wouldn't carry up to the prison.

"I'm the mist, idiot," the Ghostly God hissed. "Remember, I'm the God of Mist as well. This was the only way I could get here without Jakuuth or any of his minions noticing."

Darek didn't like speaking to mist, as it made him feel silly, but he nodded and said, "Oh, right. I forgot about that."

"Yes, I see that you did," said the Ghostly God. "That makes you almost as bad as Durima and Gujak. But I digress. Tell me what you've learned so I may report it to Skimif and the other gods."

As quickly as he could, Darek related all that Jakuuth had told him since arriving there. It was hard to tell if the Ghostly God was listening or not, mostly because his mist form had no face or body, but Darek assumed he was.

When Darek finished, the Ghostly God said, "So he is planning to attack North Academy *and* World's End, with a mere three hundred mages?"

"Limitless mages," Darek corrected, "who are also among the worst criminals in the Northern Isles."

"I can't see that succeeding, no matter how 'Limitless' his mages may be," said the Ghostly God. "Jakuuth is most likely blinded by his desire for vengeance. While I can't speak for your school, I do know that World's End will never fall, as it is the only city in Martir that has never been besieged."

"He sounded confident about that, though," said Darek, glancing over his shoulder just to make sure no one was nearby eavesdropping on their conversation. "He seemed to think that the Limitless Army would have no trouble destroying both places."

"Either he's arrogant—not at all unlikely, considering he thinks he's the Son of Grinf—or he has a trump card no one knows about yet," said the Ghostly God. "And I am afraid to say that it is very likely at this point that he has a trump card, if what we gods have found is any indication."

"What have you and the others found?" said Darek, leaning forward eagerly.

"That's the thing," said the Ghostly God in a troubled voice. "Although every single god in both Pantheons has been searching for Uron high and low, we haven't found even the slightest hint of him anywhere. Skimif has concluded that Uron has left Martir, though he will undoubtedly return at some point."

"But why would he leave Martir?" said Darek. "Doesn't he want to destroy everything? Where could he have gone?"

"That is just as much a mystery to us as it is to you," said the Ghostly God. "He probably went through the Void, as it is the only way in and out of Martir."

Darek scratched the back of his neck nervously. "That means there must be something in the Void that he wants, right?"

"Undoubtedly," said the Ghostly God. "But Skimif, as usual, has been debating with himself whether or not to send some of us gods into the Void to search for him. He has even considered contacting Hollech to see if he would be willing to help, though considering how much Hollech hates Skimif, I doubt my devious brother would accept any such offer, even if it was in exchange for a reduced sentence."

"What does this have to do with Jakuuth?" Darek asked.

"We suspect that Jakuuth and Uron may be working together," said the Ghostly God. "Uron may have freed Jakuuth from his prison beneath World's End. In exchange for that freedom, Jakuuth might have agreed to work with Uron to destroy World's End."

"But why would Jakuuth work with Uron at all?" said Darek. "I understand Jakuuth is angry at everyone, but doesn't he know Uron will kill him as soon as he is no longer useful to his plans?"

"You know how arrogant Jakuuth is," said the Ghostly God. "It's a common feature among the Limitless. They think they're so much smarter and stronger than everyone else that it often blinds them to their true failings. The fools."

"So you think Jakuuth thinks he's stronger than Uron," said Darek.

"Most likely," said the Ghostly God. A sigh caused the

mist to shimmer slightly. "It will be satisfying to see Uron kill Jakuuth, I suppose, once this is all over with—assuming, of course, you do not get to him first."

Darek rubbed his arm. "I ... I don't think I can do it, Master."

"Do what?" said the Ghostly God.

"Kill Jakuuth," said Darek. "He's just so powerful and I've just never killed anyone before."

"We discussed this before," said the Ghostly God in an uncompromising tone. "I don't care whether or not you've killed anyone before. Jakuuth needs to die. You already agreed to be the one to do it, no matter how hard it might be."

"All right," said Darek in a reluctant voice. "I just don't know if I will be able to find an opening."

"You will," said the Ghostly God. "Jakuuth is arrogant. As you grow closer to him, he will let his guard down long enough for you to stick the knife in his gut and twist."

"If you say so," said Darek.

"Besides, wasn't your mother an assassin?" said the Ghostly God. "What was it, a Black Cat or something like that?"

"Dark Tiger," Darek corrected. "But she's my adopted mother. It's not like I inherited her killing skills or anything like that."

"True enough, but killing another being honestly isn't that difficult," said the Ghostly God. "I should know, as I killed my sister, the Goddess of Mist, back in the Godly War. How else do you think I became the God of Ghosts *and* Mist?"

The Ghostly God seemed to consider that encouraging, although all that told Darek was that the Ghostly God must have killed his own conscience at some point if he thought bragging about murdering his sister was inspirational.

"Right," said Darek. "Well, what is going on in North Academy? Does everyone know I'm missing yet?"

"Most likely," said the Ghostly God. "Though I will be honest: I don't know, seeing as I couldn't care less about what they are doing. I doubt they're in any sort of trouble, if that's what you're worrying about."

Darek frowned. "I just want to know if anyone was worried about my disappearance. I vanished on the day of my graduation, after all. Surely people would start talking about that."

"Maybe they are," said the Ghostly God. "Maybe they aren't. I don't live there or pay attention to what happens there much, so how should I know? Nor does it matter. You can complete your mission without knowing about the sorts of strange rumors your peers might have made up about your disappearance, can't you?"

Darek was about to say yes, but before he did so, he heard light footsteps against the sand. Someone was coming, but who, he didn't know.

"I must leave," the Ghostly God whispered. "I will let Skimif know about Jakuuth's plans. Just keep doing what you are doing and always keep an eye out for a good opportunity to kill Jakuuth."

Darek couldn't tell whether the Ghostly God had left or

not, as the mist was still there, but it didn't matter. A moment later, Aorja appeared from around the rock, eying Darek skeptically as he stood there ankle-deep in the sand.

"I heard you talking," said Aorja. "Who were you talking to?"

Darek, avoiding Aorja's eyes, began pulling his feet out of the surf, saying as he did so, "Oh, it was nothing. I was just talking to myself. You know how I do that sometimes."

"Right," said Aorja, though she didn't sound like she believed him. "If you're done here, it's time to go back to the prison. Jakuuth is getting impatient and you don't want to know what he does to people who make him impatient."

"Sure," said Darek. "Just lead the way, Aorja, and I will follow right behind you. No more wasting time."

Aorja rolled her eyes, but then turned and began walking away. Darek hastened to catch up with her, his wet shoes squelching against the sand, but even so, he did cast one last look over his shoulder at the mist as they walked up the beach toward the prison. He wondered if killing other people, even someone like Jakuuth, would ever become as easy for him as it was for the Ghostly God, or if that was even a good thing.

He decided that he would worry about that later, after Jakuuth was no longer a threat to North Academy and World's End.

Chapter Fifteen

"So you are Uron," said Hollech, stepping forward, apparently without fear. "The one who killed my sisters and who has scared the rest of my siblings worse than anything since the Sleeping Beast."

"I do not usually identify as such," said Uron. "But yes, that is accurate. And you are Hollech, the God of Deception, Thieves, and Horses, correct?"

"*Former* God of Deception, Thieves, and Horses," said Hollech. He gestured at the darkness all around them. "Now, I am the God of the Void, which makes me stronger than all of the other gods combined. Fear me."

Durima bit her own tongue to keep from calling Hollech an idiot. A suicidal idiot, at that, considering who he was talking to.

Does Hollech want to die or does he actually believe what he's saying? Durima wondered.

Uron stroked his chin, his yellow eyes glittering with amusement. "The God of the Void, hm? I did not know such a thing existed."

"Now you do," said Hollech. "So, will you stand down and flee or face the ungodly powers that I command? I will use the Void to crush you if you continue to stand in our way."

"Very interesting," said Uron, his tone sarcastic. "Tell me, how did you gain control of the Void? After all, it is not a creation of the Powers. It existed before Martir, probably even before them."

"Because I conquered it," Hollech said, gesturing at the darkness all around them. "I have lived here for thirty years, surviving when I did not even know where I would lay my head the next day. By right of conquest, the Void is my new domain."

Uron folded his arms across his chest. "None of the half-gods told me that you were the God of the Void. They told me all about a lunatic deity living in a stone castle by himself, however."

"Lunatic?" said Hollech. "That's it. I will crush you here and now and show everyone why I am still a god to be feared."

Hollech thrust his arms forward, saying as he did so, "Feel the weight of the Void crush your body! Feel it!"

The half-gods appeared to believe Hollech's warning, because they began looking around in fear, like they thought that the Void would attack them at any second. Uron simply stood there, a bored look on his face, as Hollech continued to hold his arms out before him.

A minute passed before Uron sighed. "Is that all you've got? For being the God of the Void, you certainly are, how should I put it, pathetic."

Hollech looked down at his hands in surprise. "Why didn't the Void kill you? It is under my command. This makes no sense."

Durima would have said, *Well, actually, it does,* but she had a feeling that Hollech would not appreciate that.

Uron flexed the God-killer around his right hand. "Why don't I show you true power, rather than that fake power you tricked yourself into believing you have?"

Uron leaped at Hollech, holding the God-killer out before him like a sword. Hollech looked too stunned to move, as if he was starting to question his whole existence.

Durima, however, did not hesitate. She ran at Hollech and slammed into his side, sending them both stumbling into the dirt as Uron landed on the spot where Hollech had stood just moments before.

That blow must have been enough to snap Hollech out of his shock, because he shook his head and looked at Durima. "Did you save my life?"

Durima nodded and jumped to her feet, dusting the dirt off her fur as she said, "Yes, I did. Now get up because the fight's not over yet."

As Hollech pushed himself up, Uron turned to face them, a look of minor annoyance on his face. "You are only delaying the inevitable. It won't be long before I kill all of the gods in Martir, including you."

"You won't get away with it," said Hollech, shaking one fist at Uron. "The Void may refuse to respond to my commands, but that does not mean I cannot defeat you."

"Defeat me?" said Uron. "How? Didn't Durima and Gujak tell you that I am as strong as Skimif?"

"I will find a way," said Hollech. "I *always* find a way."

Uron shook his head and slammed the God-killer into his other fist. "Forget this. I will finish both of you off and then let the half-gods feast on your corpses. You are all very hungry, aren't you, boys?"

The half-gods growled and roared in hunger, a terrible sound that was too loud for Durima's tastes.

Then, without warning, tree roots burst from the ground under Uron's feet. They burst through the earth so fast that even Uron had no time to react. In another moment, they had wrapped themselves tightly around Uron's body, forming a kind of wooden cocoon around him that kept him rooted where he stood.

"What is this?" Uron said, looking down at the roots in surprise. "Where did these roots come from?"

Durima looked around Uron and saw Gujak standing behind him, an intense look of fear on her friend's face. He was holding his hands out, which proved that he was indeed the person who had summoned those roots. But when his hands shook, it became clear that he could not hold Uron for long.

"G-Get him, guys," Gujak said, his teeth chattering. "I can't hold him forever."

Hollech didn't even hesitate. He drew his Void metal sword, long, thick, and sharp, and ran at Uron with all his might. Durima realized too late that Hollech was gone, so by the time she reached out to stop him, he was out of her reach.

Uron struggled against the roots, even breaking apart a few of the weaker ones, but his progress was slow. Soon

Hollech was before him and, in one smooth motion, shoved his sword directly into Uron's heart, pushing it in all the way up to the hilt. The snapping of wood signaled that the sword had even pierced through Uron's back, though Hollech did not cease pushing down on it.

"Die, you wicked otherworlder," Hollech said, his voice clear and hateful. "I may not be as strong as Skimif, but this Void metal sword should certainly be more than enough to end your pathetic little life once and for all."

For a moment, Uron's facial expression was genuinely shocked. He coughed, and some kind of liquid, maybe blood (although Durima didn't know if he had blood), came out of his mouth. The half-gods, meanwhile, watched the whole event in silence, though how long that would last, Durima didn't know.

Did Hollech actually succeed? Durima thought, unable to believe what she was seeing. *Did he* actually *kill Uron?*

Then Uron's lips twisted into a smile. "Nice ... try, Hollech. You genuinely ... hurt me. But I am no mere mortal. A sword through the heart means nothing, for I have no heart."

That ominous pronouncement was followed by the bursting of wood, which Durima realized too late was the God-killer breaking through the root cocoon wrapped around Uron. The fingers of the God-killer wrapped around Hollech's neck, causing Hollech to whinny in fear as Uron lifted him up off his feet.

"Don't be afraid, Hollech," said Uron, his breathing somewhat ragged. "You will soon join your two sisters in the afterlife. Isn't that wonderful?"

Hollech kicked and brayed, but Uron didn't let go. He merely tightened his fingers around Hollech's throat; the next moment, Hollech slowly began to disintegrate just like the Spider Goddess had. The disintegrating effect started at his shoes and slowly began making its way up Hollech's legs, until soon it reached his waist, and then his chest.

The banished god did not get a chance to say his last words. The disintegrating effect soon consumed his chest and head, leaving nothing except a pile of dust before Uron's root cocoon.

"Master Hollech!" Gujak screamed. "No!"

Durima didn't scream, mostly because she knew that that would be useless. Instead, she drew upon what little magical energy she could and summoned a burst of bright, white light that blinded her and, from the sound of it, everyone else as well.

She heard Uron breaking through the root cocoon and knew he would be free in minutes if not seconds. So she dashed by him, her eyes closed to avoid getting them harmed by her own light, and grabbed Gujak, who was still screaming Hollech's name. She hauled him over her shoulder and then took off in a random direction, barreling past the slimy body of a half-god that shrieked in surprise when she knocked him over.

Durima didn't have a particular destination in mind, largely because the flash burst she had set off was still in effect. She just ran and ran, hoping to get out of the reach of Uron and his half-gods, willing to go anywhere that they weren't.

Even so, she could not help but feel that with Hollech out of the way, there was literally nothing to stop Uron and his half-gods from destroying World's End now.

And even worse, there was nothing she or Gujak could do to warn the Martirians of their impending doom. Nothing at all.

Chapter Sixteen

One month later ...

Ever since achieving Limitlessness, Darek didn't know how he had ever lived without it. Whenever he woke up in the morning, he didn't drag as he usually did. He got up, went down to the prison yard where breakfast was served (nothing more than slop and some kind of mystery meat, although it was good enough for him), chatted with a few of the other soldiers, and then found a partner and began another long day of training in the Limitless Army.

Much to his surprise, it had only taken him one week after arriving on Rock Isle to achieve Limitlessness. He had been training with Aorja, under the careful supervision of Jakuuth, when he broke through the ceiling again, but rather than fall unconscious, his high had stuck with him.

That was exactly what being Limitless felt like: An endless high. As a Limitless, colors such as Jakuuth's red robes were vibrant and richer, sounds were amplified so well that he could hear even the heartbeats of his fellow soldiers during training, and even the subtlest changes in temperature did not escape his notice. Not only that, but he could go much longer without food; once last week, he trained the whole day without eating so much as one morsel of mystery meat.

He now understood why the Limitless Army was so organized and disciplined. When you looked at the world from the perspective of Limitlessness, all of those petty disagreements and arguments that divided people no longer seemed quite as important. He almost began to feel a kinship with his fellow soldiers, as if they weren't guilty murderers, thieves, and rapists, but brothers-in-arms who would do anything for each other.

Except for Aorja. Though his Limitlessness had made him feel closer than ever to the Army, Aorja still treated him like the spy he was. She always avoided him whenever she could, even at mealtimes, and glared at him every time she saw him.

Granted, Darek would sometimes return the glares, as he wasn't exactly fond of her, either. Still, sometimes, when he was lying in his cell at night, trying to go to sleep over the snoring of his cell mate (a former murderer who called himself Slash), he found that he wished he and Aorja got along better. Yet she clearly didn't want to rebuild their friendship, so most of the time he forgot about it in favor of focusing on his daily training.

So Darek was quite surprised when he felt someone shaking him awake and, upon opening his eyes, saw Aorja standing above him. Her blonde hair was tied back in a knot behind her head, putting her impatient features into sharp relief as she stopped shaking him.

"Aorja?" said Darek, rubbing the sleep out of his eyes

with a yawn. "What are you doing here?"

"Jakuuth told me to wake you," said Aorja. She jerked her thumb over her shoulder. "Today is the first day of the invasion. He told me to make sure that every soldier was awake and ready to leave for North Academy immediately."

Darek craned his neck. "Aren't we going to invade World's End, too?"

"Yeah," said Aorja. "But not you or me. He wants us specifically to join him on the assault on North Academy. He probably wants to have our knowledge of the school on hand so we don't get taken by surprise by any unexpected traps set by the students and teachers."

"How could they possibly set traps for us?" said Darek. "It's not like they know we're coming, right?"

Though Darek said that, he knew it was probably false. The Ghostly God had most likely told Skimif and the other gods about Jakuuth's plans. Darek did not know for sure, but he could see Skimif or one of the northern gods going to the Magical Superior and warning him about the Limitless Army. If so, then Darek began to doubt whether the Army would win today.

We may be the Limitless Army, but that doesn't mean we're invincible, Darek thought as he sat up and tossed the rough cotton blanket off his body.

"Go to the prison yard," said Aorja, already heading for the open door of his cell. "Jakuuth said that that is where everyone is supposed to gather. He's going to give one last speech before we leave, so don't miss it."

Darek watched her go, rubbing his sleeveless arms.

Aorja sure seemed to be in a hurry, though he understood that completely. She most likely didn't want to be in the same room as him for even five minutes.

So Darek jumped off his cot, pulled on his mage robes, washed his face and hair in the smelly basin in the corner of the cell, and then stepped out of his cell onto the walkway just outside it.

Under the first rays of the morning sun, Darek saw that most of the soldiers were already present. Most of them stood around talking, simply passing the time until Jakuuth decided to speak. As he walked down toward the prison yard, Darek also noticed Jakuuth standing on a makeshift wooden stage, deep in discussion with his two lieutenants, the twin katabans sisters known as Rema and Gonar, respectively.

Darek slowed when he saw those three, dread rising in him despite his best efforts to hide it. As always, Jakuuth looked firm and in charge, his mouth moving quickly as the lieutenants listened to whatever he was telling them. Jakuuth seemed to notice Darek, however, because he briefly waved at him, forcing Darek to wave back to avoid raising suspicions. Then Jakuuth returned his attention to Rema and Gonar.

Over the past month, Darek had indeed grown close to Jakuuth, just as he had planned. Jakuuth had been quite pleased with Darek's progress, claiming that Darek had achieved Limitlessness faster than any of the other prisoners on Rock Isle. Darek did not know if that was true; he suspected that Jakuuth only praised him because he was

Jenur's son, despite Jakuuth's obvious bitterness towards his mother.

As a matter of fact, Darek was starting to think that Jakuuth saw him as a son figure. And, as much as Darek hated to admit it, he found himself more and more looking to Jakuuth as a kind of father. It made no sense, but over the past month Darek found himself thinking about what Jakuuth would do in certain situations, as if Jakuuth was the pinnacle of purity and moral behavior.

It made some sense. Although Mom had raised Darek well and good, he had never had an actual father of any sort. He had always treated the Magical Superior as more of a grandfatherly figure than anything due to the Superior's ancient age. Even as a child, Darek had always wanted a father, but he thought he had abandoned that desire after becoming an adult himself.

I guess even adults still want parents, Darek thought. *I wonder if Mom ever misses her father.*

This was a problem, though. If Darek couldn't kill Jakuuth ... well, then the entire mission was jeopardized and he would have to abort. He didn't know how to do so, however, because that would mean leaving Rock Isle and he knew for a fact that the nearest island was too far away for him to teleport to.

He didn't risk sending a gray ghost to contact the Magical Superior or the Ghostly God for assistance, either. Despite his reservations, Darek was confident that he could kill Jakuuth. He seemed to trust Darek more than anyone else in the Limitless Army, aside from Rema and Gonar.

True, Jakuuth did not share all of his secrets and thoughts with Darek, but Darek knew that Jakuuth did not suspect him to be a spy, at least.

Maybe I'll even kill him today, before we leave for North Academy, Darek thought, touching his wand, which hung off his belt. *That would be perfect ... well, until the Army tears me to shreds after finding out about it, anyway.*

That was another problem he faced. The Limitless Army worshiped Jakuuth like a god. Every soldier seemed to believe that Jakuuth was indeed the Son of Grinf. Not that Darek questioned it openly; he had seen one soldier question Jakuuth's true parentage, only for that soldier to be lashed to the rocks on the beach, where he was pecked to death by the sword seagulls that made their homes on Rock Isle's coves.

If Darek killed Jakuuth today, here on Rock Isle, then he would have to do it in private and find a way off the island quickly after performing the deed. If he was too slow, the Army would find out what he did and would destroy him.

Maybe the Ghostly God will provide a way for me to get off the island after that, Darek thought, slowing his pace due to a couple of other late-comers walking ahead of him. *But I don't recall him ever saying what we'd do* after *I kill Jakuuth.*

He had the sinking feeling that he would be on his own when it came to escaping Rock Isle after killing Jakuuth; assuming, of course, he succeeded in killing him today at all. He just couldn't keep thinking about what would happen if he tried and failed. No way in hell would Jakuuth merely shrug it off. Jakuuth was as justice-obsessed as your average Grinfian, perhaps more so due to his belief that he was the son of the God of Justice himself. He would not take an attempted assassination from one of his favorite soldiers well.

When Darek reached the prison yard, he was about to take up a spot near the back (as he was not interested in going to the front), when a clawed hand fell on his shoulder, causing him to whirl around in surprise.

It was Rema, the tall, skinny, red-skinned katabans lieutenant who always seemed to be at Jakuuth's side. Darek hadn't heard her walk up to him, but over the past month he had learned that katabans could move as quickly and silently as they wanted. He suspected it was some kind of magic at work, though that didn't stop him from being surprised every time Rema or Gonar appeared behind him like that.

"What do you want?" Darek asked. He knew how hostile those words sounded, but he didn't care, as Rema had always creeped him out.

"Jakuuth asked me to tell you to join him on stage," said Rema, gesturing toward the makeshift stage at the front of the crowd. "He wants you to stand by him while he gives the Army one last speech before we begin the invasion."

Darek groaned internally, but he knew better than to reject Jakuuth's offer. Jakuuth did not take rejection well, to put it lightly. Darek had once heard a story about how, during Jakuuth's first week in Rock Isle, one prisoner had refused to obey an order Jakuuth had given him. The prisoner had then been turned into ash and his ashes scattered over the sea.

So Darek nodded and said, "All right, I'll—"

He cut himself off when he blinked and realized that Rema was no longer there. A quick glance in the direction of the stage showed him that Rema now stood next to her sister Gonar. He hated it when she did that, but rather than complain about it, he walked around the perimeter of the Army toward the stage at the front.

As soon as Darek climbed onto the stage, Jakuuth walked over to him and held out a hand, a smile on his aged yet handsome features. "Darek, good to see you. How did you sleep last night?"

Darek shook Jakuuth's hand. "I slept well. How about you?"

"Oh, you know I'm not as young as I used to be," Jakuuth sighed, rubbing his back as he said so. "Even we Limitless suffer from the effects of age, after all. But I am still in good enough shape to lead the attack on North Academy, so don't worry about me."

Jakuuth slapped Darek on the shoulder good-naturedly as he said that, while Darek just smiled and nodded. Jakuuth could certainly be friendly when he wanted to, but Darek just couldn't forget how Jakuuth had threatened to bash his head in with his gavel if he failed to achieve Limitlessness. Nor could he forget that sooner or later, he would have to kill Jakuuth.

"Now go stand by Rema and Gonar over there," said

Jakuuth, gesturing at the sisters. "Aorja will be here to join us shortly, and once she gets here, I will begin the speech."

Darek nodded again and walked over to stand by Rema and Gonar. The two sisters were talking with each other, but it was in that strange language that all katabans spoke in. It sounded like shrieks and clicks to him and reminded him of Durima and Gujak, those two katabans who he had not seen or heard of in over a year.

Wonder how they're doing now, Darek thought as he stood beside Gonar, who did not seem to have noticed his arrival. *I bet they're doing far worse than me, unless they're still on the run for killing the Spider Goddess.*

A moment later, Aorja climbed onto the stage, spoke briefly with Jakuuth about something Darek couldn't hear, and then went to join Darek, Rema, and Gonar. Rather than stand next to Darek, she took up a spot next to Rema. This in spite of the fact that Darek knew that Aorja despised Rema, though why, he didn't know. He suspected it was just another female rivalry that he couldn't understand.

She must really hate me if she wants to stand next to Rema instead of me, Darek thought. He found that that thought hurt, even though Aorja's hatred of him wasn't a secret.

Now that everyone was present, Jakuuth raised his gavel. That motion alone silenced the entire Army, which up until this point had been a loud mass of talking, joking, and training, in the case of a few of the more disciplined soldiers who had seen this waiting period as the perfect opportunity to work on a few spells they hadn't yet perfected.

"My Limitless Army," said Jakuuth, his voice booming over the crowd, his back to Darek and the others. "For three months, we have been training every day to become a powerful Army of disciplined soldiers, the best in all of Martir. When I first arrived here, you all were nothing more than a collection of the world's worst rapists, murderers, thieves, ship saboteurs, and assassins, easily the least likely candidates to make a disciplined Army out of."

Aorja was nodding, like she agreed. Darek agreed as well, though he was too busy wondering if he could kill Jakuuth now and get away with it, to nod.

"But I have always had faith in my ability to train anyone in the path of Limitlessness," said Jakuuth. "It was hard work, as you all know, but it was also well worth the effort. Even now, I can see us storming North Academy and World's End, not as an undisciplined mob seeking vengeance on those who harmed us, but as an effective and united Army the likes of which the Northern Isles has never seen before."

Darek did not doubt that, although he would not have put it in so cheery terms himself. After all, a large part of the reason that the Limitless soldiers listened to Jakuuth was because he was such a harsh and unyielding leader. Sometimes Darek wondered if the Limitless Army could work together to overthrow Jakuuth, but then he dismissed the thought every time. Jakuuth was strong and powerful, far more so than any one of the Limitless. No doubt he had some way of dealing with rebellion, should he ever need to.

"Even better, I can confirm that we will not be alone,"

Jakuuth continued. "The squad that will invade World's End shall be aided by allies I made a while ago. I will not say just yet who these allies are, but rest assured that they will support us when we attack the Throne of the Gods. Powerful allies, too, who are not afraid of the pathetic katabans 'navy' that is currently protecting World's End as we speak."

Uron, Darek thought. *Has to be. But why does he say 'allies,' plural? Does that mean that Uron has his own army? Where would Uron even get an army? Perhaps more importantly, how could he keep it hidden from the gods for so long?*

"The North Academy force will not have similar backup, but we won't need it," said Jakuuth, in a loud, mocking voice. "The students and teachers of North Academy all believe in the false Sixth Pillar. They believe they are Limited and incapable of growing stronger. Because of this, we will crush them as a boulder crushes an ant. Even the so-called Magical Superior will fall before us."

Darek cast a quick glance in Aorja's direction. She was smirking, as if imagining what the Magical Superior would look like dead. Darek balled his hands into fists, but said nothing.

"Nervous?" Gonar muttered, causing him to look down at her. She was chewing on some kind of bone, though it was stuck too deep within her mouth for him to tell what it might have belonged to.

Darek shook his head and muttered in return, "No."

"You don't need to be, you know," said Gonar as the

Army cheered on Jakuuth's proclamation of the Magical Superior's death. "Jakuuth has it all figured out. But if you're still nervous, I have some extra fingers in my pocket here I could share with you. They always help me calm my nerves, even when I'm not hungry."

The short, fat katabans patted her pocket. Darek grimaced, remembering Gonar's disturbing habit of collecting human fingers to carry around as snacks. He had heard that she had taken the fingers from prison staff after Jakuuth overthrew them ... before killing them, of course.

Before Darek could decline her offer as politely as he could, Jakuuth's voice boomed again, causing him to start and return his focus to the Limitless leader's speech.

"Once we conquer North Academy and World's End, we will then move onto the rest of Martir," Jakuuth continued. "Nation after nation will fall before us like wooden blocks stacked unevenly on top of one another. The gods themselves, weakened by the destruction of World's End, will be incapable of stopping us. I promise to give each individual soldier their own island to rule as you see fit, to answer to no one but yourselves and me."

The Limitless Army whooped and roared their approval, a few banging their swords and shields together just to add to the noise. Darek normally would have been skeptical about the idea of three hundred odd men and women conquering the whole world, but when he felt his own Limitlessness, his doubt faded, especially if they managed to add other mages to their ranks at some point.

"I mean to keep this speech short and to the point," said

Jakuuth. "We have spent more than enough time thinking and training and planning and talking. In another hour, after everyone has filled their bellies with the prison food and gathered all of their equipment, we will begin the invasion of North Academy and World's End. Therefore, I dismiss you all to eat and prepare, but only for an hour. Once that hour is up, I expect to see every head back here ready to go to your designated location."

As soon as Jakuuth finished speaking, the Limitless Army broke up. Half of them climbed back up the walkways to their cells, likely to gather last minute provisions that they may have forgotten in their haste to gather for Jakuuth's speech. The other half went over to the large boiling pot of slop and meat located on the other side of the prison yard, getting into a neat line so that each soldier could get his fair share.

Darek saw his chance. He broke from his place next to Gonar (who was now eating one of the fingers she had offered him earlier) and walked up to Jakuuth, who had just turned around at that exact moment.

"Great speech, Jakuuth, sir," said Darek with the most winning smile he could muster. "You did great. I am sure the rest of the Army will keep your speech in mind as they attack our enemies and begin our conquest of the world."

"Thank you, Darek," said Jakuuth. "But please, don't call me 'sir.' We're so close now, why, I think we can just call each other by our first names, don't you think?"

He's in a good mood, Darek thought. *Should be easy to get him to do whatever I ask.*

So Darek nodded and said, "Of course, Jakuuth. I was just wondering if we could speak in private somewhere, perhaps back in your office. There's something I'd like to talk with you about, but I don't want to do it where everyone can hear it, as it's private."

"Private?" said Jakuuth. He glanced over his shoulder at the long line of soldiers waiting for their food, as if he was hungry as well. "Very well. I know you wouldn't be asking me this if it wasn't serious, Darek, so I will grant you that request."

"Where are you two going?" Aorja asked.

Darek almost jumped. Aorja was standing behind him, suspicion painted all over her face. She had her hands on her hips, just like how Mom had looked in Darek's younger days whenever she thought he was up to no good.

"To speak in private in my office," said Jakuuth. "It's fine, Aorja. Go and join the other soldiers for breakfast. I doubt we'll talk for more than five minutes, if that."

Aorja frowned. "Are you sure you don't want me to come with you, sir?"

"Absolutely," said Jakuuth. Then he put one hand on Darek's shoulder. "Now, let's go and get this over with quickly. I was serious when I said that I wanted everyone here in an hour, so why don't we head up to my office and get this over with right away?"

When Darek blinked again, he and Jakuuth no longer stood outside on the makeshift wooden stage. Instead, they stood inside the small office where Darek had first met Jakuuth a month ago. The curtains were drawn and the door was closed, making it quite black inside until Jakuuth snapped his fingers and several candles on his desk lit up, allowing Darek to see Jakuuth's aged, curious face.

"All right, Darek," said Jakuuth with a yawn. "What is it you would like to talk about?"

Darek's nose twitched at the smell from the candles. It was like chocolate and dirt, a smell which irritated him greatly. His fingers curled, but he did not grab his wand. Even though this was the perfect opportunity to do so, he could not bring himself to kill Jakuuth right now.

So Darek said, "When we attack North Academy, will you spare Mom?"

Jakuuth's expression quickly turned into a raging scowl. He grabbed Darek's shoulders roughly and snarled, "You mean the woman who betrayed me? The woman who is the very reason I spent the last three decades locked away beneath World's End, like some kind of disgusting cripple that no one wants to look at?"

Although Jakuuth was clearly older than Darek, that didn't mean he was weaker. His hands, large and strong, gripped his shoulders so hard that Darek almost thought that the Limitless leader was going to crush him to death.

But then Jakuuth let go and stepped back. His chest heaving up and down, Jakuuth said, "I apologize for manhandling you, Darek. Your mother and I ... we used to be close. We were young and carefree and I thought ... never mind."

"Uh, sure," said Darek. He realized he had grabbed his wand, which he quickly let go of so Jakuuth wouldn't get suspicious. "I was just wondering if we could spare Mom. I don't want her to die because ... well, you know."

Jakuuth ground his teeth, but then he said, in a forced calm voice, "I understand how you feel. When I was younger, I cared about my own mother, too."

"You had a mother?" said Darek, though he wasn't sure why this came as a surprise to him.

"Of course I did," said Jakuuth. "Remember, I am half-human, half-god. My godly half came from Grinf, while my human half came from my mother. As much as I loved her, she never understood my greater destiny as the Son of Grinf."

Or she understood you were crazy, Darek thought, but aloud, he said, "Is she still alive?"

"No," said Jakuuth, shaking his head. "When I broke out of prison two months ago, my first stop, before Rock Isle, was Carnag, my home island, sometimes known as Grinf's Court. I sought out my mother, only to discover that she had died ten years back due to her old age. I visited her grave, where I left her flowers and prayed to my father to give her soul peace."

He looked at his feet as he said that, as if he was still back in that Carnagian graveyard looking down at the grave of his deceased mother. It almost made Darek feel sorry for him, which made it even more difficult for Darek to look for an opening in which to strike.

"But understand this, Darek," said Jakuuth, looking up at him. "Do not let your love for your mother blind you to the kind of woman she is. She is deceitful and treacherous.

She will grow close to you, even love you, and then toss you aside when she learns who—no, what—you really are. She is a propagator of the limiting beliefs that keep us mages from achieving our true power. She is a witch."

"She's not that bad," said Darek, although he made sure to keep a conciliatory tone to avoid angering Jakuuth. "I know she can be a bit bossy and stubborn, but I think killing her would be a huge mistake."

Jakuuth shook his head. "You still don't understand. Do you think I'm just some mad, would-be dictator who wants to impose his beliefs on the world? Do you think I am doing all of this because I desire power above all else? Do you think I want to destroy North Academy because they rejected me so many years ago?"

Yes, yes, and yes, Darek thought. *You're nothing more than a crazy sick bastard who is leading an army of other crazy sick bastards to destroy a school full of innocent teachers and students.*

But Darek made sure not to utter a word of that thought. He said instead, "Well, no. I just thought—"

Jakuuth held up a hand. Darek tried to speak, but he realized that Jakuuth had taken away his ability to speak, at least for the moment.

"I do this because I am the Son of Grinf," said Jakuuth. "The Son of Grinf, and a mage of Martir. When I first discovered the truth about Limitlessness, when I saw with my own eyes how the Magical Superior and his teachers—among many, many others—spread the falseness of the Sixth Pillar, I knew beyond a shadow of a doubt that it would be unjust to let this lie continue unabated. Justice cannot tolerate lies; therefore, I could not tolerate the Sixth Pillar of Magic."

He looked up at the ceiling again, like he could see into the sky and beyond. "I participated in the Katabans War so many years ago because I believed that by working with the katabans, I might first be able to spread the message of Limitlessness through them. The katabans, if you don't know, also believe in limits to their magical power, but Limitlessness is less controversial among them than it is among us."

Jakuuth turned and walked over to one of the curtained windows. He peeked out it, like he thought someone might be listening in. Darek felt his speech return to him, but he decided to keep quiet and listen to Jakuuth's story.

But his back is to me, Darek thought. *Just snap up my wand, aim it, and hit him with a good fire blast. He could be dead in five minutes.*

Then Jakuuth turned around again, thereby making Darek's plan moot. "I provided one side of the War with the knowledge of Limitlessness so they could destroy their enemies quickly. I kept my involvement a secret from Jenur and everyone else ... until that meddling King Malock discovered my plans and revealed it to all."

Jakuuth's eye twitched. "I thought about destroying Carnag Hall, King Malock's dwelling place, when I went to visit Carnag after I escaped from World's End, but I knew it would only bring unnecessary attention to me. But rest assured, after North Academy is buried in ice and World's

End is a ruin, Carnag will be the first Northern Isles nation to fall."

Darek had never met King Malock, although he knew that the King of Carnag was a good friend of Mom's. He was glad, therefore, that Malock was still alive, though he didn't doubt the authenticity of Jakuuth's promise to destroy Carnag.

"It was because of King Malock that Jenur rejected me," said Jakuuth. "She didn't like what I was doing, even when I told her it was for the greater good. But now, I will be able to resume my great plan to bring the good news of Limitlessness to all mages, human or aquarian, and it will be under my just rule that we mages of Martir will reach new magical heights, perhaps even become equal with the gods themselves."

Darek didn't know how much time had passed. He guessed it had been fifteen or twenty minutes; even so, he knew that Aorja or Rema or Gonar or someone else would soon show up to find out what was taking Jakuuth and Darek so long. Therefore, Darek had to act now if he wanted to get out of here without anyone interrupting or stopping him.

So Darek said, "Then I guess that means I can't convince you to spare Mom or anyone else at North Academy."

"Of course not," said Jakuuth. "Unless they agree to become Limitless themselves, but I know how thoroughly the Magical Superior indoctrinates his students into the Limited belief system. When they see us, they will not stop and question whether they are wrong and we are right. They will fight, and to the death, most likely, because that is what they were trained to do."

"So you won't even offer them a chance to survive." Darek stroked his wand in his belt.

"Yes," said Jakuuth. "You are absolutely corre—"

Darek didn't hesitate. He drew his wand out of his belt, aimed it at Jakuuth, and unleashed a freezing blast of ice in one smooth motion. The ice flew through the air at Jakuuth, moving too fast for him to dodge.

And when the ice struck Jakuuth, it exploded, covering his entire body from head to foot. He didn't even get a chance to scream as the ice grew so thick that Darek couldn't even see him through it. In a couple more seconds, the ice ceased expanding, though its presence did cause the temperature in the room to drop considerably.

With a chill seeping into his bones, Darek lowered his wand and put it back in his belt. Instead of running, however, he took a moment to stand there and stare at the ice block, scowling at it.

The Ghostly God was right, Darek thought. *Killing another being really isn't that difficult, although I guess it would have been harder if he had not insulted my mother so much.*

Then two familiar strong hands—Jakuuth's hands—grabbed his shoulders and shoved him forward. He smashed into the ice block, but before he could recover, one of the hands grabbed the back of his head and smashed his face into the ice again and again. The blows were swift and furious; on the fourth blow, Darek's nose broke, causing blood to leak into his mouth, but there was nothing he could do to stop Jakuuth from continuing to smash his face into the ice.

Then Jakuuth stopped slamming Darek into the ice block and shoved him onto the floor. Darek crashed onto his side, too weak from the repeated blows to get back up. His consciousness rapidly slipping, Darek's eyes darted up in time to see Jakuuth standing above him, his gavel in his hands.

"Teleportation," said Jakuuth with that same evil smile of his, "in case you're wondering how I got out of that pathetic ice block you made."

Darek groaned.

"It doesn't matter," said Jakuuth. "I suspected you might try to betray me at some point, as your appearance on the shore of Rock Isle seemed a little too convenient, even though I hoped you would not. That you would wait until the last minute to try to kill me is exactly the sort of deceitfulness I should have expected from the son of Jenur."

That was the last thing that Darek heard Jakuuth say, because the last of his consciousness slipped through his fingers like sand and everything around him went black.

Chapter Seventeen

Durima lay underneath the heavy, dark sand along the shore of the Void that her and Gujak's tiny boat had washed up on ... well, she didn't know how long ago that had been. It could have been a day ago, a week ago, hell, maybe even a year ago. Time in the Void was as ill-defined as the ramblings of a lunatic.

Beside her, Gujak also lay under the sand, having just finished complaining that the sand had gotten into the crooks of his body and would be hard to wash out later. Durima had no sympathy for him, however, because he clearly didn't understand how difficult it was to wash sand out of a fur coat like the one that she had. It made her wish that they hadn't ditched the Void metal armor Hollech had given them, which they had disposed of largely because they were not planning to fight the half-gods directly. Though at least the armor could have kept most of the sand out of her fur.

Regardless of their levels of discomfort, Durima knew they would have to bear it silently. Making even one unnecessary sound could ruin their entire plan. It would even get them killed, and getting killed was the last thing on Durima's list of things to do today.

They had been lying in wait here for hours (that was

what Durima estimated, though again, she was not sure because of the Void's fluid time). There was still no sign of the half-gods or Uron anywhere. They didn't even know if this was the spot where Uron and his minions would depart from in order to get to World's End. Void Beach, as Durima called it, seemed to stretch on forever in both directions.

Though I suppose even if we knew exactly where they planned to set sail from, it might not matter, Durima thought. *We're two katabans trying to stop a being as powerful as Skimif and an army of unfinished gods. Our chances of survival are slim, at best.*

Their plan was simple. When Uron and his half-gods showed up here, Durima and Gujak would use their magic to set off a series of traps that would hopefully distract and maybe even frighten the half-gods. Then Durima and Gujak would hop into their little boat (the motor of which Gujak had managed to repair) and head for the Void's exit, where they would they emerge back into Martir and warn the gods of Uron's coming.

They would have put this plan into action much sooner, but several factors had prevented them from doing so. First, with Hollech's death, Castle Hollech was no longer a safe place for Durima and Gujak to stay. There was simply no way to defend it from the half-gods, which had forced Gujak and her to find another hiding place in order to avoid Uron and his minions.

That had taken them a while, but eventually they had found a cave well away from the place where Uron and the half-gods had been gathered. There, Durima and Gujak had hid for a long time, hoping that none of the half-gods would stumble upon them. Or any of the other creatures that lived in the Void, for that matter, creatures they heard moving around outside of their cave just when Durima and Gujak thought they were safe.

But of course, Durima didn't want to stay there forever. She may have been exiled from Martir, but it was still her home and she still wanted to save it. So she coaxed Gujak into helping her come up with some sort of plan for them to warn Martir about Uron and the half-gods, although that had taken her quite a while due to Gujak's fear of Uron making it almost impossible for him to think rationally.

After coming up with the plan, Durima and Gujak had had to find their boat again. Due to the darkness of the Void, that had taken even more time, but they did eventually find it and even fixed it. Gujak had wanted to leave as soon as they could, but Durima had resisted that suggestion.

Granted, it probably would have been more reasonable for them to take the boat and get out of the Void before Uron or his half-gods showed up. That way, they would have had plenty of time to warn the gods about Uron's army of half-gods, maybe even redeem themselves as heroes.

"But how can we prove that the half-gods will attack?" Durima had said at the time. "If the gods see us, they'll just kill us or throw us back into the Void. We can't leave now."

"What do you suggest we do, then?" Gujak had asked. "Try to stop the half-gods ourselves? Let them leave the Void and then tell the gods about the army of half-gods they are probably already fighting?"

For once, Gujak had made an excellent point. Stopping the half-gods themselves was completely out of the question. If Hollech had been fighting them off by himself for thirty years with little success, there was no way that two katabans could possibly stop them, especially if they were led by Uron.

Nonetheless, Durima had said, "We'll confuse and scare the half-gods. Make them think that there are more of us than there really are. They don't seem all that smart or clever, so it shouldn't be hard to do."

"But what about Uron?" Gujak had asked. "He's way too smart. He'll see right through our plan."

"Not unless he's too busy trying to reorganize the half-gods to stop us," Durima had argued. "Remember, he's not going to try attacking World's End on his own. So if we can scare the half-gods into a disorganized frenzy, it might give us enough time to get out of here before Uron rallies them again."

After that, Gujak had agreed, although reluctantly, as he seemed to think that they were going to die no matter what. That may have been true, but Durima figured they would probably die if they left the Void too early as well, as she doubted the gods or Katabans Council would happy to see them.

Of course, another reason they had not left immediately was because Durima was not quite sure that they could. After all, if the Void's exit was open, then Hollech would have probably left ages ago. She vaguely recalled Erich telling her and Gujak that the Void was locked on the inside to keep people from getting out.

Even if our plan works, we might fail anyway, Durima thought. *Not like we have much of a choice, though. We'll just have to hope for the best.*

Gujak poked her in the side, causing her to shift her eyes in his direction. "What?"

"Do you hear that?" said Gujak, his voice muffled under the sand. "The half-gods."

Durima listened as hard as she could. All she heard was the waves of the sea washing up on the shore. Then she felt vibrations in the sand, like an army marching into battle, and a moment later she heard the sounds of dozens of beings walking across the sand. She had a hard time gauging how far the half-gods were from their current position, but if she could feel and hear their movements now, then they were probably closer than she thought.

"Got the decoys ready?" Durima whispered to Gujak.

Gujak nodded. "Yes."

"Really?" said Durima. "I just want to make sure so that you don't end up freaking out at the last minute and messing everything up."

"I w-won't," said Gujak, though his voice trembled. "I've got my fears under control. I won't panic. I promise."

"All right," said Durima, although deep down she wasn't so sure she believed him. "Get ready to activate the decoys any minute now, just like what we talked about earlier."

Gujak nodded and turned his attention back to the sounds of the advancing half-god army. Durima was amazed at how silent the half-gods were. There was no cheering or chanting, nothing to indicate that an army of freaks was moving to destroy the Throne of the Gods. The only clue was the sounds of their feet beating against the sand and the vibrations in the ground.

The worst part about the Void was that it had no natural light, not even tiny stars in the sky to offer illumination. Timing their diversion right was going to be difficult, very difficult. If Durima and Gujak put their plan into action too soon, they risked giving the half-gods time to react; too late, and they would be dead.

So Durima, using her geomancy, sent a wave of energy through the ground to see if she could figure out how close the half-god army was. The wave soon returned to her, much sooner than she expected, which told her that they would have to act soon.

"Okay, Gujak," Durima muttered, keeping her eyes firmly on the direction the army was coming in. "As soon as I give the signal, I want you to activate the decoys, all right?"

Gujak nodded again, a confident expression on his face that Durima was unsure she should believe. She would just have to trust that Gujak would do as he said, a rather depressing thought, as she rarely trusted Gujak to do anything effectively in stressful or tense situations like this one.

So Durima summoned a tiny orb of light in her right hand. She wasn't much of a luminimancer, but she had worked for Nimiko, the God of Light, once, and he had taught her more than a few tricks about how to use light magic effectively. She just hoped that she remembered everything he had taught her.

Without waiting another moment, Durima hurled the light orb toward the army. She heard the army stop, heard some of the half-gods growl in surprise, but before they had a chance to react, the light orb exploded.

It wasn't a fiery explosion, however; in fact, as Durima covered her eyes to avoid getting blinded, she doubted it even hurt. However, the explosion did light up the area as bright as day, and if it worked as it was supposed to, the half-gods would be too blinded by the orb to react.

As soon as she heard the half-gods shriek and scream in shock and pain from the light explosion, Durima said, "Gujak, decoys, now!"

Thankfully, Gujak hadn't just been talking earlier. He pressed his hands against the sand and, as the light faded, Durima saw two dozen or so wooden replicas of herself and Gujak sprout out of the sand before the half-god army. Some of the half-gods that weren't stumbling around blinded by the light ran away as soon as they saw the decoys, while others ran into their blinded brethren and fell over.

It wasn't over yet, however. Durima punched the sand and another dozen or so decoys—these ones made out of stone—burst out of the sand like snake worms. One of the half-gods did shoot a lightning bolt at one of the stone decoys, shattering it into pieces, but for the most part, the half-gods were too shocked and confused to realize that the decoys were nothing more than rock and wood.

"Let's go now before they recover," said Durima. "Come on!"

She stood up, sand tumbling off her back, and hauled Gujak out of the wet sand as well. The two of them turned around and headed directly for their little boat, which was beached on the sand behind them, ready to go as soon as they were.

The two katabans worked together to push the boat into the waters of the Void, which were warm for some reason. As soon as the boat was in, Durima and Gujak hopped into it, causing the boat to shake before they managed to right it.

As soon as the boat was steady, Gujak activated the engine, which roared to life and sent the boat gliding away from the shoreline and into the dark waters of the Void. All the while, the cries of anger and shock from the half-gods echoed from the darkness of the Void, occasionally punctuated by bursts of flame or flashes of light from the confused unfinished deities as they attempted to fight an enemy that wasn't real.

Grinning, Durima turned to look at Gujak. "Doesn't look like those idiots are going anywhere anytime soon, now does it?"

Gujak nodded, but his eyes were wide, like he had just narrowly escaped a wild animal. "Y-Yeah. I can't believe that actually worked. I thought for sure something would go wrong and we'd die."

Durima sat back in the boat, though she was careful to keep her weight distributed evenly to avoid upending it. "I know what you mean. During the War, very few of our plans ever went exactly the way we planned them. But sometimes, Dranyx's luck really is with us, even in the Void."

"I guess you're right," said Gujak. Then he frowned and looked over his shoulder back toward the beach, where the half-gods were still fighting in a confused mess. "But where is Uron? Did you see him when your light bomb went off?"

"No," said Durima as she dusted off some sand from her shoulders, though she had so much of it in her fur she doubted she would ever be totally free of it. "I just assumed he was caught in the middle of it. Most likely the half-gods are attacking him in their confusion."

Gujak gulped. "But what if Uron isn't with them at all? I know he said he was going to lead the half-gods to victory, but maybe he changed his mind between then and now. Maybe he decided to go to Martir and wait for the army to arrive."

"That's silly," said Durima. "Uron has no reason to go ahead of his army. That would mean ruining the element of surprise, which is the only thing that he's got going for him at the moment. Why would he give the gods even a moment's notice?"

"You are absolutely correct, Durima," said an ancient, vaguely serpentine voice behind her. "That would hardly be a smart move on my part, which of course is why I am not doing it."

Durima did not want to turn around, but she did anyway. She also activated her luminimancy as she did so, making one of her fists glow so that she and Gujak could see who had spoken.

Standing in front of the boat was Uron; actually, he wasn't really standing. He was walking backwards on the water, his arms folded behind his back, managing to keep a step ahead of the motorboat. His yellow eyes, as snakelike as ever, glowed in her light, though his purplish-black skin seemed to absorb all illumination that came upon it, making it look like Uron was nothing more than a floating pair of eyes in the darkness of the Void.

"Uh oh," said Gujak with another gulp. "We're dead."

Uron smiled. "Yes, you are."

He kicked the boat's prow. That blow upended the boat, tossing Durima and Gujak out of its body and into the water beneath it.

Durima and Gujak fell into the water with a splash. Durima tried to swim, but her fur was getting wet and weighing her down. In addition, the water felt strangely thick, as if she was swimming in a sea of mud. She found it difficult to stay afloat no matter how hard she kicked her legs.

"Help!" Gujak cried out, splashing around nearby. "The water ... it's pulling me in!"

Durima reached out and grabbed Gujak's arm instinctively, but that turned out to be a mistake. With Gujak's weight now added to her own, Durima began rapidly sinking beneath the dark waters of the Void, which pulled at her legs like the tentacles of a kraken dragging a ship to the bottom of the sea.

The last thing she saw, before her head went under

completely, was Uron standing above them on the water, his smile never wavering until the blackness of the Void claimed Durima's vision completely.

Chapter Eighteen

If Darek was not dead yet, he figured that he would be soon. After all, why would Jakuuth spare his life, after Darek's botched attempt at assassination? It wouldn't take Jakuuth, a Limitless, very long to end Darek's life. Indeed, for all Darek knew, he was already dead and the empty blackness he saw was the only thing that lay beyond, making he wonder if that meant that the Heavenly Paradise was indeed a myth.

The last thing Darek recalled was getting his face smashed into the ice block that he had tried to kill Jakuuth with. A hot pain in his face told him that he had still not yet recovered from it; however, that was irrelevant because it just occurred to him that he had to still be alive if he was capable of feeling pain like that.

Does that mean Jakuuth hasn't killed me yet? Darek thought. *Or does it mean that he wants me to be awake so he can see how I look before I die?*

Neither option was very appealing to him, but Darek was too curious to keep his eyes closed. If there was even the slightest chance that he was still alive and in some position to stop Jakuuth before he went to North Academy, then he would have to risk opening his eyes.

His eyes flickered open. The first thing he saw above him

was the ceiling of Jakuuth's office. That told him that Jakuuth had not moved him out of the office, though why, he couldn't say. He doubted it was due to any benevolent intentions on Jakuuth's part, however.

He tried sitting up, only to discover that thick heavy metal chains were tied around his arms and legs. He couldn't budge at all. It was like he had been chained down to a mountain. He wondered if he could use his magic to destroy or weaken the chains, although without his wand (which appeared to have vanished), he was not certain he could do it without harming his body.

He heard someone start nearby and looked to his right. Aorja was sitting on the sofa, with both her feet on it as if she was afraid of mice on the floor. An opened book lay on the seat next to her, although he didn't know what that book was.

"Damn it," said Aorja as she lowered her feet back onto the floor. "I was hoping you wouldn't wake up until Jakuuth returned."

Darek blinked. "Aorja? What are you doing here? Where is Jakuuth?"

"He left," said Aorja, rolling her eyes. "Duh. He took half of the Army to attack North Academy. That was maybe half an hour ago, I think. He left me here to keep an eye on you while he was away, even though I wanted to come along and help."

Darek struggled against his bonds, but they were still too heavy for him to move. "Aorja, we have to stop him. Jakuuth is insane. He's going to kill everyone."

Aorja raised an eyebrow. "You think I care about the Academy or the Magical Superior or anyone else there? If it were up to me, I'd be fighting alongside Jakuuth, helping him burn that damn school to the ground."

"If you let me go, we might be able to get there in time to stop him," Darek suggested. "If we do, then the Magical Superior might be willing to forgive you for your crimes against the school."

Aorja sighed heavily. "Why do you think I want the Magical Superior's forgiveness? What I want is to see that old coot's head on a silver platter. That's the only thing that would make me happy at this point."

Darek gritted his teeth. "I don't think you understand. This is more than just North Academy being destroyed. There's a good chance that Jakuuth is working with someone who wants to destroy all of Martir and he doesn't even realize it."

"Who would want to destroy all of Martir?" said Aorja. "You're making stuff up now just to scare me enough to let you go. How pathetic."

Aorja picked up her book and resumed reading it, a clear sign that she was not interested in continuing the conversation. While Darek didn't like talking to her, he knew that convincing her to let him go was his best chance at getting free.

"Come on, Aorja," said Darek. "You know how crazy Jakuuth is. Do you really want to support him? Don't you care about *anyone* at North Academy?"

"Jakuuth promised each of us Limitless our own islands

to rule after we conquered Martir," said Aorja, turning the page of her book without looking up at Darek. "He specifically promised me the Great Berg, as I think it would be a good place to build my own castle after North Academy is little more than a memory. Lots of room to build, after all."

Darek scowled, but said nothing to that. He didn't know how he could possibly convince Aorja to free him now. He couldn't appeal to her conscience (which he was pretty sure she had murdered at some point) and he didn't have anything to offer her that she'd want. Yet Darek couldn't escape on his own, and even if he could, he would have to fight her in order to leave for North Academy.

No guarantee I'd win a fight against her, Darek thought. *She has way more experience as a Limitless than I do. Plus, she has a wand and I don't. So I* have *to reason with her somehow, but there's no time to reason with her if Jakuuth is already at the school.*

He considered possibly calling out to the Ghostly God or Xocion for help; however, when he thought about it, he doubted it would work. If World's End was under attack by Jakuuth's forces, then the gods were no doubt preoccupied with keeping their city safe. Especially if Uron was part of the attack, which meant that Darek was on his own, as usual.

So Darek tried to think about Aorja as a person. He had known her for nine years, after all, and had grown quite close to her in that time. There had to be something he could say or do that would convince Aorja to let him go.

Some part of her that he could exploit—he would readily admit that that was what he was trying to do—in order to regain his freedom.

Aorja is a mousimancer, Darek thought. *That makes her a servant of Yaona, the Goddess of Music. She was always good with a guitar and had an excellent singing voice. I remember one time she told me that she wanted to become a famous singer in the Northern Isles after she graduated or at least serve as a priestess of Yaona on some island somewhere.*

Unfortunately, right now Aorja didn't seem to be in the mood to sing or play a guitar. He wasn't even sure that she did that anymore, now that she was no longer in North Academy. For all he knew, she might have forsaken Yaona after coming to Rock Isle and was now serving some other god or goddess, or perhaps just serving herself.

Seems like there's nothing I can do, Darek thought, tugging at his chains ineffectually. *Except wait for Jakuuth to return, probably carrying the heads of Mom and the Magical Superior as trophies of war.*

That sapped his motivation as well as anything. This feeling of hopelessness sparked a memory of when he had been five-years-old, although it was too vague for him to remember why he had felt that way at that age. No doubt something terrible had happened then, just as terrible as what was happening to him now.

No, Darek thought, shaking his head. *This* isn't *hopeless. I am a Limitless. That means I can do anything. I may not have a wand, and I may not be as powerful as Aorja, but that doesn't mean all hope is lost. It's time to draw upon some of that Limitless energy and see what I can do.*

That was easier said than done. Although he had been a Limitless for a while now, his body still reacted negatively to the idea of going over his original Limits. There was also the fact that Aorja would no doubt notice him using his magic to escape, which meant that he would have to distract her.

While Darek began to focus on loosening the chains around his ankles and wrists, he said to Aorja, "So, what is that book you're reading?"

Aorja still didn't look up at him. "None of your business."

"That's an odd name for a book," said Darek. "Who's the author? Is it Rude Impoliteness?"

Aorja looked up at him with a glare as sharp as any knife. "Don't joke around with me. Jakuuth gave me full authority to treat you as I see fit. If you make a bunch of stupid jokes like that one, I will shut you up myself."

"I was just trying to make conversation," said Darek. He felt the chains around his wrists and ankles loosening ever-so-slightly, giving him more motivation to keep Aorja distracted. "Did Jakuuth say when he was going to return?"

"In his words, 'after North Academy is a graveyard and World's End is a ruin,'" Aorja said. She pouted. "I have no idea how long that will take, but it would probably be a lot faster if he had allowed me to come along and help."

"It is unfair that Jakuuth left you here, I agree," said Darek, nodding. "I know how much you were looking forward to destroying North Academy. You must be very disappointed."

Aorja eyed him as if he was a trickster trying to swindle her out of her money. "I'm not an idiot, Darek. I know when you're trying to distract me. We lived in the same dormitory for years."

"I'm not trying to distract you, though," said Darek. "All I am doing is agreeing with you that you would be better suited leading the Limitless Army into battle rather than playing prison guard here with me."

"Got that right," said Aorja as she lowered her book. "Sometimes I wonder if Jakuuth actually knows what he's doing. I don't see why he couldn't have left Rema or Gonar here to watch you instead. He gave them command of the Army that's going to World's End."

The chains' pressure on Darek's wrists and ankles had lessened considerably by now; in fact, he thought he might be able to slip his hands and feet out if he wanted to. Yet he didn't want to try anything too sudden, at least until he was sure that Aorja was completely distracted. That meant he needed to talk with her a little bit more, just to be safe.

"Probably he thought you knew me well enough to see through any tricks I might try to use to escape," said Darek. "By the way, why did Jakuuth leave me alive? Why didn't he just kill me?"

"How am I supposed to know that?" said Aorja with a shrug. "Though if I had to say, I think he actually still likes you. He probably remembers how much he loved your mom, so maybe he decided to let you live a little longer to honor her or something."

"Maybe," said Darek. "I thought for sure that leaving me alive would constitute a security hazard, but I guess he's confident that there's nothing I can do to stop him now, even if I were to escape."

"I wouldn't say so," said Aorja. "If he thought you couldn't stop him, he wouldn't have left me here to babysit you. He just doesn't want you underfoot."

The chains around Darek's ankles and wrists jangled slightly as he moved his body to a more comfortable position, but it was a very slight sound, so low that Aorja didn't seem to hear it. Still, Darek did not feel comfortable attempting to escape just yet. He needed to be absolutely sure that Aorja was distracted before he tried anything.

"Presumably, then, if I escaped, it would be a big problem," said Darek.

"Presumably," said Aorja. "But that's irrelevant. You're chained up and I am not going to let you escape. Jakuuth would skin me alive if he found out I let you go."

"First the Ghostly God, now Jakuuth," Darek observed. "It really seems like you have a thing for following cruel, unreasonable masters who don't actually care about you."

Aorja folded her arms across her chest. "Jakuuth is handsome, despite being so old. Why do you think I'm so loyal to him? Well, that, and he has given me far more power than I could ever have gotten on my own. If he didn't actually care about me, he wouldn't have given me such an important place in the Limitless Army."

"Or he's just manipulating you," Darek suggested. "You're very insecure, you know, which makes you exactly the sort of person who would be easy to manipulate."

Aorja threw her book on the floor with a loud *clunk* and stood up. Glaring at Darek, she said, "I am *not* insecure."

Darek shrugged as best as he could on his position on the floor. "If you say so."

Then, moving as fast as he could, Darek pulled his right hand out of its chain and pointed at the book. He activated his telekinesis and sent the book flying into Aorja's face.

Aorja didn't even try to dodge it. She looked down just in time to get hit directly in the face by the thick tome, causing her to fall back onto the sofa she had been sitting on. Slumping in the sofa, she was clearly out for the count, especially with her nose, which looked quite broken.

Darek slipped his left hand and feet out of their chains and stood up. Rubbing his wrists, he looked around for his wand before spotting it on Jakuuth's desk. A flick of his wrist and the wand flew back into his hand immediately.

After examining his wand to make sure it was still in one piece, Darek looked at Aorja again. She was quite still and didn't seem likely to get up anytime soon; nonetheless, Darek didn't trust her. Using what little metomancy he knew, Darek manipulated the chains to wrap themselves around her body. He doubted that would hold her for long—if he could escape from that, then she probably could, too—but for now it would have to work.

Then Darek ran to the door, opened it, and stepped outside. The prison yard below was completely empty, looking as abandoned as the ruins of the tiny town of Yurima in the Great Berg. Aorja had been telling the truth about the Limitless Army leaving, a truth he had hoped was false until he saw the proof of it for himself right now.

Darek gripped his wand tightly. How was he supposed to get from Rock Isle to the Great Berg? True, as a Limitless, his ability to teleport was no doubt much stronger than normal; even so, it would probably take him many days to teleport from island to island until he got to the Great Berg, and likely another day until he got to North Academy, which was located at the northernmost end of the Great Berg.

And I don't have even one day, Darek thought. *Jakuuth's Army is already there. They're probably destroying the campus and killing people even as I think this.*

Darek looked up at the sky and called out, "Hey, Ghostly God! A little help?"

No answer.

"Xocion? Skimif?" Darek said. "Anyone?"

Again, no answer.

Then Darek remembered that half of the Limitless Army was in World's End, likely working alongside Uron's army. No doubt all of the gods, northern and southern, were busy defending World's End from Jakuuth and Uron's forces. Maybe they even had orders from Skimif not to bother with anything else.

Looks like I'm on my own again, Darek thought. *If it's too late for me to go back to North Academy, maybe I could go to Carnag or Itrija or one of the other Northern nations. Or maybe I could send a gray ghost to Archmage Yorak and ask for her assistance, although I doubt the*

Institute mages will be able to get to the school in time to help.

That was when Darek heard the sound of bone clacking against the metal walkway. Puzzled, he looked around, but did not see anyone else in the area. Yet he heard the sound as clear as day, making him wonder if he was losing his mind or if the sound was being blown in from the sea on the other side of the massive prison wall opposite him.

"Darek Takren."

Darek went still. He recognized that clacking voice, even though it had been a while since he last heard it. It was not a voice he had expected to hear again, and for a moment, he thought he must have imagined it until a skeleton materialized next to him, its eyes glowing green, its mouth smiling as widely as always.

Darek aimed his wand at the skeleton, even though he wasn't sure if it was a threat or not. It just stared at the end of his wand for a moment before looking up at him, as if confused. It was hard to tell, however, because its expression never changed.

"What are you doing here?" said Darek, taking a step back. "You're the skeleton I saw when I first broke through the ceiling a month ago, aren't you?"

The skeleton made a bony, clacking sound like a laugh. "You remember. I thought you might have forgotten about me in all of the excitement. I'm ready to take you back up on that earlier offer to fight me, by the way."

"I don't remember making any such offer," said Darek. "Even if I did, I'm in no mood to fight you. If you haven't noticed, I need to get to North Academy right away to stop Jakuuth and his Army of Limitless thugs."

The skeleton stroked his chin. "Yes, I know. And then there is Uron and his half-gods in World's End causing trouble for the gods down there. These are desperate times, it seems, for everyone who calls Martir home."

Darek had no idea what a 'half-god' was, but he nodded anyway. "Since you seem to be so well-informed, I hope you understand why I don't have any time to play with you at the moment. Maybe we can pick this up later."

"I didn't come here just to fight you," said the skeleton. He put one finger on Darek's wand, sending a jolt through Darek's arm. "I only said that to see your reaction, which was exactly what I hoped it would be."

Darek didn't understand what that jolt meant, but he said, "Okay, it looks like you're not leaving. Cool off."

Darek jabbed his wand in the skeleton's face, but nothing came out of the tip. He did, however, bump the end of his wand in the skeleton's forehead, making a hollow echoing sound like a coconut.

The skeleton rubbed his forehead as Darek looked down at his wand in disbelief. "That didn't hurt, but it was annoying and silly."

"I don't understand," said Darek, looking back up at the skeleton. "Why can't I use my magic against you?"

"I disabled it," said the skeleton. "Not forever, mind you. Just long enough to ensure you won't try to hurt me, though to be honest, even if I didn't do that, you wouldn't even be able to scratch me with that level of magic."

"Disabled it?" said Darek. He tried conjuring just a tiny ice cube, but nothing appeared. "No way. Impossible. You can't disable magic. That's not how magic works."

"Magic works more or less the way I say it does," said the skeleton. "One of the perks of being the God of Mystery and Magic."

Darek's eyes narrowed. "Wait, you mean you are the Mysterious One spoken of in legend? I thought you were just a myth."

"Everyone says that," said the skeleton with a shrug. "Even the other gods say it. Truthfully, I'm as real as anyone, although there are times where it feels like I am not."

"I don't understand that," said Darek as he lowered his wand. "But I guess I don't have to. What are you doing here, so-called 'Mysterious One'? Are you going to stop me? Why aren't you helping your brothers and sisters on World's End?"

The Mysterious One shook his head. "I'm here to *help* you, Darek Takren, not stop you. That's the same reason why I appeared to you back in North Academy. I didn't want to see you go down the same route as Jakuuth, which is partly my fault."

"What does that mean?" said Darek.

"It doesn't matter," said the Mysterious One. "What does matter is getting you to North Academy, and fast. You should be able to help turn the tide, seeing as you know the Limitless Army better than your friends do."

The Mysterious One held out a hand as if to grab Darek,

but Darek stepped back out of his reach.

"You didn't answer my other question," said Darek. "Are you or are you not going to help the other gods? You know, your siblings?"

The Mysterious One sighed. "But I *am* helping them. Just not in an obvious way. And please don't call them my 'siblings.' I never said they were such."

"But I thought all of the gods were related," said Darek. "Except for Skimif, obviously, but besides that I thought every god and goddess were family."

"I've said far too much," said the Mysterious One. He looked up at the sky apprehensively, as if he didn't want to be caught in the middle of wrongdoing. "I'm technically not even supposed to be here. So I better send you to North Academy quickly. Then I must go."

Darek opened his mouth to ask more questions, but then the Mysterious One snapped his fingers.

All of Darek's surroundings—Jakuuth's office, the walkway underneath his feet, the prison yard below, the Mysterious One—vanished, immediately replaced by the tall Walls and heatstone buildings of North Academy ... and an all-out war.

Chapter Nineteen

Cold. That was what Durima felt as she and Gujak sank beneath the waters of the Void.

Not 'cold' as in the temperature, but cold as in a cold intelligence. All around her, Durima felt something watching them, an intelligence that was far older and much colder than any god. It was too dark for her to see what it was, but something told her that even if it was as bright as day under here, she wouldn't be able to see it because the intelligence was a part of the water itself.

An intelligent sea, Durima thought. *No, not a sea. The Void itself.*

Yes, that was it. The spirit of the Void, if it could be called that, was the sea in the Void. She could feel its darkness filling her lungs, attempting to smother her and Gujak, too, although with Gujak it was hard to tell because of the shadows. That he was so still, however, told Durima that she was on her own for now.

She swiped her free claw through the water, but it was a useless gesture. She couldn't hurt it, but it could hurt her. Her fur grew heavy with wetness and her legs were too weak to kick against the water. Her mind slipped in and out of consciousness, the way it did whenever she went to bed at night.

Sleep, an unfamiliar, feminine voice whispered in her mind. **Rest. There is nothing you can do now. Stop resisting. Allow the Void to claim you as its own.**

The voice—more like a feeling put into words—was seductive, tempting as gold. Durima almost closed her eyes in obedience to its coaxing, but then she forced them open. She couldn't breathe, and it didn't seem likely that she and Gujak would escape, but damn it if she was just going to let anyone kill her before she was ready to die.

But despite her best efforts, her muscles relaxed. The Void filled her with its darkness, filled her like a cup of water. She gradually began to forget what she was doing or where she was. All Durima wanted to do now was sleep, as the sweet, gentle voice had suggested.

Before she closed her eyes completely, she felt a boney, thin hand grab hers. Then the hand pulled, and a moment later, the darkness and water of the Void vanished. Durima felt like she was being pulled through mud, like the Void itself was trying to keep her and Gujak with it, but then Durima felt light and heat on her back and she landed face first on a hard wooden surface underneath her.

Gasping for air, Durima looked to her right. Gujak lay next to her, also gasping for air, coughing out an inky black water that resembled crude oil. She herself coughed out much of that water as well, although for some reason she didn't seem to have inhaled as much of it as Gujak.

"By the gods," Gujak gasped, his voice hoarse. "What ... what happened?"

Durima shuddered. "I ... I don't know. Somehow, we're

alive."

"All thanks to me," said a voice above her that she didn't recognize. "Though I don't expect you to thank me if you don't want to."

Durima looked up at the source of the voice, but as she did so, she found herself staring up at the sun in the sky.

Wait ... Durima blinked. *The sun?*

She sat up, her fur dripping wet, as she looked more closely at the sky. Yes, that was indeed the blue afternoon sky of Martir, which ended at the black wall that was the entrance to the Void about a thousand or so feet from them. The sun was in the sky, shining as brilliantly as ever; in fact, after so long in the Void, to her the sun looked brighter and more beautiful than ever. She had forgotten how much she enjoyed feeling its rays shining down on her body, drying her fur and warming her skin underneath.

Then she looked down at what she and Gujak were on. It was some kind of wooden boat, similar to the one that had taken them into the Void, although it was much bigger and seemed less prone to teetering than theirs had. It floated gently on the waves of the sea, waves as clear as crystals.

Finally, Durima looked up at whoever their savior was, saying as she did so, "Whoever you are, I have to thank—"

She stopped mid-sentence when she saw who stood before them. Her feelings of happiness at returning home went down the drain as she looked up at the glowing green skeleton that stood above her, a skeleton which she had never seen before in her life.

"Hi there," said the skeleton, waving at her as if he did

this sort of thing every day. "You look surprised."

"Durima," said Gujak, his voice as high as it always was whenever he was afraid. "Why is there a walking, talking skeleton on the raft with us?"

"Because I saved you two, naturally enough," said the skeleton. "I understand that my appearance is somewhat disquieting, but rest assured I am on your side. After all, I am the God of Mystery and Magic and you two are loyal katabans servants of the gods."

"The Mysterious One?" said Durima. She coughed again, causing more of that ugly black water to spew from her lungs. "Im—"

"Impossible?" the Mysterious One finished for her dryly. "A myth? I'm afraid I've been called both of those things today by someone already, so you can save your breath for more important questions."

"I knew it," said Gujak, causing Durima to look at him and see a big smile on his face. "I knew it! The Mysterious One *is real*. He's not a myth after all. I was right."

"Yes, yes, good for you," said the Mysterious One. Then he leaned down toward them slightly. "Now tell me, do you two feel up to saving the world today?"

"What kind of a question is that?" said Durima.

"A very relevant one, considering our current situation," said the Mysterious. He gestured to their right. "You might want to take a look at World's End."

Though Durima didn't trust this 'Mysterious One' (who she didn't actually think was the real Mysterious One), she nonetheless looked in the direction he had indicated.

Almost as soon as she did, she regretted doing so.

She was looking at World's End, but it no longer looked like the majestic Throne of the Gods that Durima had always known it as. Smoke and flames rose from the tops of the various skyscrapers, with one of the taller buildings having a giant hole in it, as if a titan had punched out its center. Bursts of lightning, flame, water, and every other kind of magic lanced from building top to building top, as if two separate armies were duking it out in the city itself.

Even the waters around World's End were hardly peaceful and tranquil. Several of the katabans battleships Durima had seen prior to her and Gujak's banishment lay in ruins in the water, their hulls burning, with no sign of their crews anywhere. A massive kraken stood amidst most of the wreckage, but then Durima looked at it again and realized that that wasn't a kraken at all, but rather a giant half-god that resembled a kraken mixed with a tiger.

The half-god smashed its tentacles against the sunken ships, roaring like a tiger before it was cut off by a splash of water in the face. An actual kraken had risen out of the sea now opposite the half-god, but it was twice as large as a normal krakens and three times as huge as the biggest battleships in the katabans navy.

That was no mere kraken. The magical power radiating from it pegged the beast as none other than the Kraken Goddess, Goddess of Kraken, Fish, and the Storm. Durima recognized her because she had served the Kraken Goddess once. She watched as the Kraken Goddess lunged at the tiger/kraken half-god, wrapping her tentacles around it and dragging the monstrosity beneath the waves in a violent struggle that sunk what little debris of the battleships remained.

Then a massive, earsplitting explosion caused Durima to look back at World's End itself again. A chunk of the roof of one of the skyscrapers had been blasted off completely, falling down into the streets below. Durima did not hear it fall, but she did not doubt that it would crush many innocent katabans, assuming that the city's inhabitants had not evacuated as soon as the battle started.

"Oh my gods," said Gujak, putting his hands against his mouth. "What's going on there?"

"The first war to ever bring its battle to World's End's shores," said the Mysterious One in a flat voice. "Half of the invading force is something called the 'Limitless Army,' essentially a group of the Northern Isles's worst criminals trained by Jakuuth Grinfborn, though this part of the Army is led by two katabans sisters known as Rema and Gonar."

"Grinfborn?" said Durima. She scowled. "I thought he was in jail."

"He escaped a while ago," said the Mysterious One. "And of course, the other half of the army is the half-gods, led by Uron. The Limitless Army attacked from the north and the half-gods struck from the south. No one saw them coming, not even Skimif, which is why World's End is in such terrible condition."

"Where are the gods?" said Durima. "Who is fighting the enemy?"

"The gods are there," said the Mysterious One. "Not

quite as many as they need, perhaps, seeing as most of the gods are still afraid of Uron, but they're there nonetheless. The Soldiers of the Gods are also present, though their numbers are rapidly dwindling because they're not as strong as the Limitless mages or the half-gods. Skimif is there, too, and is probably the only reason why Uron hasn't succeeded in demolishing the entire island yet."

"What about the people?" said Gujak. "You know, the katabans who live there?"

"From what I've gathered, quite a few were killed in the initial attack due to being unprepared for the assault," said the Mysterious One. "But when the gods came in and began fighting off the Limitless and the half-gods, most of the katabans evacuated via the ethereal. They're currently migrating due north, though where they're going, I can't say."

"Probably trying to get as far away from this war as they can," said Durima, shaking her head. "How long has this battle been going on?"

"Not long," said the Mysterious One. "Half an hour at most. Nonetheless, as you can see, World's End is already dangerously close to falling. That's why I saved you two, so you could save it."

Durima laughed. "Us? Mysterious One—if that's your real name—you do know *why* Gujak and I were banished beyond the Void, yes?"

"I am aware of your accidental killing of the Spider Goddess," said the Mysterious One, nodding. "So?"

"So the gods will kill us if we tried to help," Durima said.

She was starting to get the feeling that the Mysterious One wasn't the brightest god in the Southern Pantheon. "And even if they did allow us to help, what are two weak katabans supposed to do against Limitless mages, an army of half-gods, and Uron himself?"

"You two are wild cards," said the Mysterious One. "Uron thinks you're dead, so you can use that to your advantage."

Durima frowned. "How the hell are we supposed to do that? Are you suggesting we attack him and hope he is too surprised to kill us?"

"I am suggesting nothing," said the Mysterious One, holding up his hands as if to pacify Durima. "I trust that you two will be able to come up with a way to stop Uron. If you can take him out, the half-gods will become afraid and disorganized, which will make it easier for the gods to defeat them. The Limitless mages will fall even more easily, because despite their power, they are still mortal and therefore not even half as strong as the gods."

"So the only reason that Uron's army is causing so much trouble is because the gods are too afraid of Uron to go all out?" said Gujak.

"Exactly," said the Mysterious One, nodding. "Skimif is currently fighting Uron, but it's only a matter of time before Uron touches Skimif with the God-killer. I trust that you two realize exactly what would happen if Skimif died today."

Durima remembered how frightened the other gods had been when they had learned of the Spider Goddess's death. And the Spider Goddess was one of the more obscure goddesses, hardly as respected or famous as Skimif.

"Will you fight alongside us, Mysterious One?" Gujak asked. "If we're going to fight Uron, we'll need all the help we can get."

The Mysterious One shook his head. "I've never been much of a fighter. I stayed out of the Godly War, avoided getting caught up in that apocalypse mess thirty years back, and am in no mood to possibly die at Uron's hands today. I've done as much as I should, and probably more."

"But this is your world, too, isn't it?" said Gujak. He pointed at World's End. "Won't you help your brothers and sisters on World's End save Martir? They could use your help."

The Mysterious One made a clacking, rattling sound, which might have been his way of chuckling. "My world ... oh, that's rich. No, Martir isn't my world, but I do care about it nonetheless."

"Aren't you a god, though?" said Gujak. "Aren't all gods from Martir? So doesn't that mean that this *is* your world?"

"Let's change the subject," said the Mysterious One. "I'm rarely this talkative, so why don't I just get you two to World's End, where you can help Skimif get rid of Uron?"

"Assuming there's anything we can actually do about Uron, of course," said Durima, glancing at the war-torn city.

"Just think," said the Mysterious One, tapping the side of his head. "What can you do to help get rid of Uron? There has to be something."

Durima scowled. She wanted to say that there was literally nothing that she and Gujak could do, that Uron was far above their power level, and that any attempts on their part to stop Uron would only end in their deaths.

Then a thought occurred to Durima, a plan that she had never considered before but which suddenly caught her attention. She looked at Gujak and said, "I've got an idea."

"What is it?" said Gujak. "Does it involve us fighting Uron?"

"Not really," said Durima, shaking her head. "If it works —and it might not—it should end with no one fighting Uron. We'll need to work together to do it, though. Are you in?"

Gujak scratched the back of his neck and looked toward World's End as the rooftop of another skyscraper went flying sky high. "I have a feeling I'm going to regret this ... but okay."

Durima then looked up at the Mysterious One again. "We will need your help for this one."

The Mysterious One shook his head. "Can't guarantee that. As I said, I normally keep under the radar; in fact, most of my fellow gods don't even believe I exist. But I suppose I can assist you in some minor way here, if necessary and if it will help us save Martir."

"Good," said Durima. "Because I am going to need you in case Gujak fails. So you two, gather round and I will tell you about my plan. We'll have to be quick; I have no idea how long Skimif and the gods can keep Uron and his forces at bay. If we don't get this plan rolling right away, everything we know will be destroyed."

Chapter Twenty

Everywhere Darek looked, mages were fighting mages. Near the First Dorm, Jiku was fighting Raka, while on the steps of the Arcanium, Irliza, the pyromancy teacher, was fighting Rujan. Bursts of magical energy flew through the air, only to explode and rain flame and heat on anyone who was unfortunate enough to be underneath them when that happened.

Quite a few bodies already lay unmoving in the courtyard, most of them Darek's fellow students, though he saw a few Limitless soldiers as well. The library's front doors had been blown off their hinges completely, allowing Darek to hear the sounds of people battling inside. The statue of the God of Reading lay across the steps of the library, broken in half straight down the middle, smoking like it had been on fire not too long ago.

He ducked to avoid a thick vine that went shooting off from a duel between a Limitless soldier and Noharf Ximin nearby, then jumped onto the path as the grass under his feet caught fire. No one seemed to have noticed him yet, not even the Limitless, but that was good because Darek needed to find Jakuuth, and fast.

Then he saw the goalposts from the sports field come flying over the dorms. One of the goal posts struck the Third

Dorm, smashing through the roof (no doubt into Darek's and Jiku's room, unfortunately), while another impaled itself in the ground nearby, missing Darek by a few feet. The impact of the second goalpost sent dirt and grass into the air, forcing Darek to hold his arms up over his eyes to avoid getting the dirt in his eyes as the soil and grass rained down on his head.

He looked desperately around the area, searching for Mom or the Magical Superior or Jakuuth, but all three seemed to be absent. He did, however, see one of the Limitless soldiers unleash a burst of flame at one of the younger students, instantly incinerating that student without another word.

Without thinking, Darek swung his wand at the Limitless soldier. The soldier suddenly became a solid block of ice. Then Darek swung his wand again and the ice block shattered, turning the soldier into little more than chunks of frozen meat that lay scattered all over the courtyard.

Don't get distracted, Darek thought. He looked up at the Arcanium, which was the only building that seemed to have avoided taking any serious damage yet. *Find Jakuuth. Kill him before he kills Mom or the Magical Superior or anyone else.*

To find out where Jakuuth was, Darek ran toward the steps of the Arcanium, where Jiku was still in combat with Raka. Although both mages were hardly spring chickens, they still jumped around the steps a lot, dodging each other's magical blasts and countering with devastating spells of their own. The steps had large holes in them and smelled like burnt stone, though Darek ignored that smell as he aimed his wand at Raka and jerked it upward.

His telekinesis caught Raka by surprise and sent her flying. He then jerked it downwards, slamming Raka into the steps of the Arcanium as hard as he could. A sickening cracking sound shot from Raka's body when she crashed into the steps, no doubt every bone in her body breaking from the fall. If she wasn't dead, then she at least wasn't going to be getting up again anytime soon.

Jiku, who had stood there momentarily too surprised to move, shook his head and ran down the steps toward Darek, a big smile on his middle-aged face.

It was the only good-looking thing about him. Jiku's robes were torn and burned away in some places. His hair was as messy as mud and parts of his skin were burned or cut. Blood leaked from his nose and he seemed to walk with a minor, almost unnoticeable limp, not to mention he smelled like blood and smoke.

"Darek!" said Jiku, his tone joyous as he and Darek met at the foot of the steps. "Where have you been for a month? We're under attack!"

"I know," said Darek, nodding. "No time to catch up. What's the situation like?"

Jiku frowned as the screams of someone—whether a Limitless or a fellow Academy student, Darek didn't know—pierced the air, only to be drowned out by an explosion. "I've lost track, but last I checked, the Sixth and Fifth Dorms are little more than rubble, Guardian was destroyed *again*, Junaz is missing, and Eyurna ... Eyurna was one of the first killed in the initial attack."

Darek grimaced. Eyurna was the school panamancer and head of the medical wing, but unfortunately, he had no time to mourn her death right now. "Where is Jakuuth?"

Jiku frowned. "Who?"

"The guy who led the assault," said Darek in frustration. "Middle-aged, looks kind of like traditional Carnagian portrayals of Grinf, extremely crazy and powerful?"

"Oh," said Jiku, nodding. "That's right. I do recall seeing someone who looked like Grinf run into the Arcanium around the start of the battle. I thought my old eyes were playing tricks on me."

He's gone after the Magical Superior, Darek thought. *That has to be the reason why the Superior isn't out here.*

"And Mom and the Superior?" Darek asked.

"Not sure," Jiku admitted. He gestured at Raka's lifeless form. "Too busy fighting this old hag to keep track of everyone. They might be in the Arcanium."

"I need to go help them," said Darek. He put a hand on Jiku's shoulder. "You stay here and help the others. If I can take our Jakuuth, we should be able to win this."

Jiku saluted. "Sure thing, Darek. Teach that bastard what happens when you mess with North Academy mages."

Darek nodded and then ran up the steps toward the Arcanium, hoping against hope that he would get to the Magical Superior's study in time to save him.

Upon entering the Arcanium, Darek expected to see the lobby as wrecked and destroyed as the rest of the campus.

Yet he didn't see any sign that Jakuuth had even been here. The fountain in the center of the lobby was in one piece, the Wall of Mastery at the very back appeared to be in order, and the walls and floor showed no scars or signs of battle.

It was eerily quiet in the lobby, even with the doors open and the sounds of battle raging outside. It was like the Arcanium was somehow separate from the rest of the campus, like Darek had stepped into another world entirely.

Then he smelled burnt flesh wafting down from above and looked up. Attached to the ceiling by some kind of strange green goo was one of Darek's fellow students or teachers, though it was hard to say which or who because the mage in question was blackened to the point of obscurity. The sight made Darek want to run, as that was clearly the handiwork of Jakuuth; nonetheless, he ran toward the hallway to the left of the Wall of Mastery, determined to get to the Superior's study as fast as he could.

The halls of the Arcanium were even quieter than the lobby; he could no longer hear the screams of dying mages or the magical explosions outside now. Of course, Darek remembered that the Arcanium's halls were enchanted to be soundproof in order to help students focus on their learning. Still, if Darek hadn't known about the battle outside or about the mad man in the school itself, he might have been tempted to believe that all was indeed well in his home.

But it wasn't. He could not get the images of the corpses of his former fellow students out of his mind, nor could he stop himself from imagining what Jakuuth might be doing even now to the Magical Superior or his own mother. That thought alone propelled him up the steps to the next floor, and the next, and the next, moving as fast as he could, without hesitation or weakness.

Soon, he found himself running up the winding staircase leading up to the Superior's study. The pictures of past Superiors on the walls flashed by him as he ran. He fully expected to hear Jakuuth and the Magical Superior fighting each other, but he didn't hear anything. He briefly wondered if Jiku had been mistaken about seeing Jakuuth entering the Arcanium, but it was too late to go back now.

All of Darek's doubt were washed away, however, when he reached the top of the staircase and found the door—as purple as ever, its one eye torn out—to the Magical Superior's study ripped off its hinges and lying awkwardly in his path. He jumped over it without hesitation, landing on both feet in the Superior's study as he shouted, "Stop whatever you're doing, Jakuuth, or I'll—"

He stopped mid-sentence as soon as he got a good look at the situation he had jumped into.

The books in the Superior's bookshelves lay in scattered heaps on the floor, with many of them ripped or half-burned. The wooden table in the center of the room had been smashed in half, with the hundreds of statues of the different gods and goddesses from both Pantheons piled in a heap in the middle. Most of the statues had been smashed or broken in half, smoke rising from them, a sight that sent chills up Darek's spine.

At the back of the room, the Magical Superior and Mom

stood side by side facing Jakuuth. The sleeves of Mom's robes were burned and her hair smoked slightly, with sweat running down the sides of her face like water in a river. The Magical Superior looked a little better, though he was panting hard, as if he had just run a marathon. Both of them held their wands defensively.

As for Jakuuth, he didn't even looked scratched. He held his gavel before him like a shield, perhaps to deflect magical attacks from Mom and the Superior. If that wicked grin on his face meant anything, he looked like he could do this all day and still never get tired.

All three of them were now looking at Darek, Mom with joy, the Magical Superior with surprise, and Jakuuth with anger and annoyance.

"Darek," said Mom, her voice slightly shaky. "You're alive! I thought I wouldn't ever see you again."

"How did you escape?" Jakuuth demanded, sparks shooting from the head of his gavel. "No matter. I will kill you just the same, you and your whore of a mother and this old frog masquerading as the most powerful mage in the world. Then I will go back and kill Aorja for failing to keep you imprisoned."

Darek pointed his own wand at Jakuuth. "No, you won't. You may be powerful, but you're outnumbered three to one. If I were you, I'd suggest giving up. We might spare your life if you do."

"Darek is correct, Jakuuth," said the Magical Superior, returning his attention to the false Son of Grinf before him. "You already know that you can't beat us by yourself, no matter how 'Limitless' you might be. We will let you live if you put down your gavel and call off your Army."

"And then what, send me back to World's End?" said Jakuuth, shaking his head. "You fools. World's End is crumbling even as we speak. The gods are weakening and the katabans are scared and scattered. Soon only the Limitless will rule ... and the Limited will die."

"Weakening?" said Darek. "How are the gods weakening?"

"Their power is tied to World's End," said Jakuuth in a triumphant voice. "It's why the gods have always been careful to avoid bringing their conflicts to that island. If World's End is destroyed, then the gods—*all* of the gods—will fall with it."

That explains why Uron is attacking it, Darek thought. *If he makes the gods weaker, then it will be easier for him to kill them all.*

That thought only flickered through Darek's mind for a second; the next, his focus returned and he said, "The gods won't fall. I bet they are defending World's End even as we speak."

"That may be so," said Jakuuth. "But there is no way they can defend their city forever. Uron is there, aiding my Army with his own forces. You would have been wiser to go to World's End than here, Darek Takren, because even if you defeat me, Uron will still win."

"Then that's what we will do after we take you out," said Darek. "We'll go to World's End and help the gods defend it."

Jakuuth chuckled. "You think you can defeat me? I am the Son of Grinf. I am a Limitless. No mortal mage, not even other Limitless, can defeat me."

"We've been holding you off on our own pretty well so far," said Mom as she brushed some strands of stray hair out of her eyes. "Maybe you're not as powerful as you like to think you are."

Jakuuth grunted. "True, you two are much stronger than I expected. Nonetheless, you haven't seen me operating at my full power yet. I could smite you two from existence like the ants you are if I wished."

There was some truth to Jakuuth's boasts. Darek sensed that, while Jakuuth had indeed used much of his magical power already, he still had quite a bit more to go. By contrast, Mom felt almost out, like she had expended most of her power already, while the Magical Superior was maybe half empty at best.

"So you've been holding back," said Mom, sounding unimpressed, though her wand trembled. "Why?"

"Because I didn't think I would need to use my full power against you," said Jakuuth. Then he smiled. "It was good to see you again, Jenur, after so many years. Though you are much older than when I last saw you, I can see the beautiful young woman I initially fell in love with all those decades ago ... the beautiful young woman I should have killed the moment I saw her."

A sudden spike in Jakuuth's power was the only warning any of them got. A huge fire blast, hot enough to incinerate the scattered books and curtains lying on the floor between them, erupted from his gavel, so bright that it forced Darek to cover his eyes to avoid damaging them.

The fire blast was heading straight for Mom, but the Magical Superior intervened. He appeared between Mom and the fire blast and spun his staff in a circle like the arms of a windmill, creating a bright glow of energy that erupted into light when the fire blast hit it.

The fire blast deflected off the energy shield and hurtled toward the ceiling. Darek covered his head as the fire blast hit the ceiling with a loud *boom*, sending chunks of heatstone flying everywhere as the Magical Superior's study opened up into the bright blue sky above, though it was partially obscured by the smoke from the fire.

Without hesitation, Jakuuth teleported and reappeared behind Mom, but as soon as he did so, Mom whirled around and kicked him square in the jaw. Instead of sending Jakuuth staggering backwards, however, the Limitless just shook his head as if that had been a minor annoyance before pointing his gavel at Mom.

A loud *bang* followed, causing the spot where Mom and the Magical Superior stood to burst into flame, cutting off Darek's sight of them.

"Mom!" Darek screamed. "Magical Superior! No!"

But his screaming turned out to be premature, because a second later Mom and the Magical Superior reappeared next to him. Mom's robes were slightly burnt in the back and the Magical Superior's staff was blackened, but aside from that they appeared to be okay.

"We're fine, Darek," said the Magical Superior with a

cough. "Thank you for your concern, however. We appreciate it."

Before Darek could respond to that, Jakuuth yelled, "This works fine for me. I'd rather have all three of you in one spot anyway. Makes it easier to administer justice onto you!"

Once again, Jakuuth swung his gavel horizontally, only this time, he conjured a massive wall of flame that ate through the fallen books and curtains on the ground. The temperature in the room shot up a hundred degrees, causing Darek to break out into a sweat.

Nonetheless, he stepped forward and drew upon his own Limitless energy. Aiming his wand at the incoming wall of fire, Darek conjured an even thicker wall of ice that completely blocked off their view of Jakuuth and the fire wall coming toward them.

A moment later, the *hiss* of fire melting through ice met Darek's ears. He poured more energy into the ice wall to reinforce its thick coldness. He felt Jakuuth's flame pushing against his ice, but he wasn't going to give up yet.

Time to show Jakuuth what happens when you teach your worst enemy how to do everything that you can, Darek thought, squinting his eyes as he focused more and more on maintaining the wall.

Then without warning, something heavy and thick smashed through the ice wall, heading directly for Darek. The Magical Superior swung his staff, using his magic to divert the object's course and causing it to break through a nearby wall, revealing another portion of the sky outside.

"What was that?" said Darek, looking at the Magical Superior in surprise.

"A large rock that likely would have cracked your skull open if it had made contact with your head," said the Magical Superior, tapping his forehead. "But enough talking. Jakuuth is still active and we cannot afford to be distracted by anything."

As soon as the Magical Superior said that, Darek felt control of his ice wall leave him, as though someone had forcibly taken it from his hands. The minute he lost control of the wall, it evaporated into mist, showing the charred and burned remains of the Magical Superior's study, and Jakuuth, who kicked aside the ashes of what might have been a book at one point as he approached the three of them.

"Enough of this," said Jakuuth with a snarl. His hands were glowing now. "I wish I didn't have to do this, but it looks like I have no choice. If I am to get the revenge I deserve, then I will need to go all-out, as I should have done from the start."

He jerked his gavel up. His gavel glowed as brilliantly and brightly as the sun, but it wasn't just his gavel that glowed. His whole body glowed; no, not glowed, burned, like he was on fire. His skin rapidly burned away, revealing muscle and bone that glowed like his gavel. Heat radiated from his body, like that of a volcanic crater, making the air harder to breathe.

"What are you doing?" Darek asked, raising his voice to be heard over the flames that crackled around Jakuuth's skin. "Jakuuth!"

The Magical Superior, who sweat so profusely now that his auburn robes were as wet as if he had been dunked in the Crystal Sea, stepped back in horror. "Oh no. He's going to perform a full Divine Burst."

"A what?" said Darek, whipping his head to look at the Superior. "What is a Divine Burst?"

"It's when a mage uses all of their magical power at once in one big explosion," Mom explained quickly. "It usually results in the death of the mage who casts it."

"But Jakuuth is a Limitless mage," said Darek. "What will *his* Divine Burst look like?"

"I don't want to know," said Mom. She turned toward the exit. "We've got to get out of here before—"

"It's no use!" Jakuuth roared, his voice distorted by the flames that now enveloped him. "When I explode, I will destroy not only the Arcanium, but every building and being on North Academy! There's no way you can save everyone, not even yourselves!"

Darek almost said that that was a lie, but when he sensed Jakuuth's magical energy levels rapidly rising—rising far faster than even a Limitless's power should, going well past the Magical Superior's power level—he realized that there might be some truth to that claim. More truth than he'd like to admit.

"But you'll kill yourself, too!" Darek yelled. "How will you enjoy your revenge if you're dead?"

"I won't die," Jakuuth's voice rumbled like the flames that enveloped his form. "I am the Son of Grinf. Fire cannot kill me. Fire is my servant."

Darek looked at the Magical Superior and Mom. "What do we do? We can't evacuate the entire school in time, not when there's this huge battle going on below right now."

"We figure out how to stop him," said Mom. "That's the only option we have left."

"But how?" said Darek. He gestured at the blazing Jakuuth, who was now laughing like a maniac. "We can't even touch him. Even if all three of us combined our powers to summon a river of ice cold water, it won't be near enough to put out his flames."

Mom bit her lower lip. "Then what do you suggest we do? If we can't put out his fire, and we can't limit his magic, then are we all going to die?"

The Magical Superior had been rather quiet through the entire conversation. His old eyes were thoughtful, but hurried, as if he was thinking quickly and deeply about how to get out of this situation. Darek wasn't sure how useful that was, however, because he doubted even the Magical Superior could do anything about Jakuuth.

"We have to leave," said Mom, shaking her head as the ever-rising temperature caused more sweat to roll down her face. "We don't have much time left. We'll tell as many students and teachers about the evacuation plan as possible, but I doubt we'll save everyone. Better to save a few than to save no one at all, in my opinion."

"There is one option we could use," said the Magical Superior. "But I doubt either of you will like it."

"Really?" said Darek, looking at the Magical Superior

with hope in his eyes. "What is it?"

The light from Jakuuth's flames threw the age lines of the Magical Superior's face into sharp relief, making him look even older than he was. He stood as tall as he could in his old age, as if he was a soldier preparing to go to war.

"There are only a few minutes left," said the Magical Superior, "but I can tell you this: In order for me to save North Academy and everyone who lives within it, I must make the ultimate sacrifice."

"The ultimate—?" Mom gasped. "No, Magical Superior, don't."

"I have no choice," said the Magical Superior, shaking his head. "Jakuuth is right. With the speed at which his power is rapidly building, the explosion that will result will be beyond catastrophic. It will kill every man and woman here, no matter whether they're a student or one of his soldiers. It is the only way."

The Magical Superior stepped toward Jakuuth, but Mom grabbed his arm and jerked on it, causing him to look at her in surprise.

There were actually tears in Mom's eyes, which surprised Darek, as he had never seen Mom cry like this before. "Please, Magical Superior, don't. The teachers and students still need you. Even if it works, who will be the next Magical Superior? You don't have a pupil to turn the title over to."

"That is why I am granting you the temporary title of Magical Superior of North Academy, Jenur," said the Magical Superior "Out of all of the teachers at this school, I trust that you will know how best to lead it in my absence. At the very least, I know you will look toward the gods for guidance in determining who my official successor should be."

The tears were mixing with the sweat on Mom's face now, which made it impossible to tell where one began and where the other ended. But she didn't resist as the Magical Superior gently tugged his arm out of her grasp.

Then he looked at Darek and said, "Keep your mother and everyone else safe. And whatever else the future may bring, know this: As long as you trust in the gods—and yourself—you should be able to handle whatever comes, no matter how hard it may be."

Darek opened his mouth to say something (though what, he didn't know, as he was too grief-stricken to think rationally), but then the Magical Superior ran toward the flaming Jakuuth. Darek reached for the Superior, but his fingers only just brushed against the ends of the Superior's robes as they flowed out behind him.

Jakuuth was still laughing, laughing as loudly as a madman. He didn't even let up when the Magical Superior fired some kind of strange yellow energy chain at him, which wrapped around Jakuuth's flaming body like a cobra around a mouse.

"What are you going to do, O great Magical Superior?" Jakuuth asked, his mocking voice barely distinguishable from the roaring flames around him. "Hold me down? That will just make it so much easier for me to kill everyone and everything in the area! Even the mighty Walls will evaporate instantly upon being exposed to the heat of my Divine Burst."

The Magical Superior's clothes and even skin were starting to burn away from the sheer heat of Jakuuth's fire. Nonetheless, he stood proud and tall, almost like a god, and said, "Good bye, Jakuuth. May we both find peace in the beyond."

As soon as those words left his mouth, the Magical Superior and Jakuuth disappeared instantly. The temperature in the room abruptly dropped, allowing Darek to breathe normally again. A cold wind blew in from the hole in the wall from the boulder that the Magical Superior had redirected, causing Darek to shiver as it passed through the burned holes in his robes that he had not noticed until just now.

"Where did they go?" Mom asked, looking around the burned-out study in alarm. "They couldn't have possibly gone very—"

A loud explosion, like a volcano erupting, cut off Mom. Darek looked up through the hole in the ceiling from Jakuuth's earlier fire blast and saw, far up in the sky, a massive fire ball—much bigger than anything Darek had seen in his life—floating above the Arcanium. It was a perfect sphere, looking almost like a second sun in the sky, and it burned as hotly as any star, its heat noticeable even from where Darek stood, though it could also have been the heat from the burnt study that he felt instead.

"Why ..." Darek glanced at Mom. "Why is it so perfectly round like that?"

"The Magical Superior," said Mom. "He must have used the last of his magic to hold Jakuuth's explosion in one place. He probably didn't want the explosion to so much as touch the school."

"So that's why he sacrificed himself," said Darek, his eyes locked on the explosion that seemed to rage on forever against the transparent magical sphere holding it together. "He knew he couldn't teleport Jakuuth away before he exploded. The only way he could ensure the safety of the school was to contain the explosion as best as he could."

But even as Darek said that, grief rose in his heart unlike any he had felt before, worse than any mere sadness he had ever felt in his life. He now understood why Mom was crying ... because he was now, too.

Chapter Twenty-One

Durima sidled against the side of one of the many skyscrapers of World's End, doing her best not to look down, because she was currently over one hundred feet above the streets and knew that if she looked down even once, she would lose her cool and probably fall to her death.

Of course, I might just fall to my death anyway, Durima thought, wincing as the windows of a nearby building exploded outwards and rained glass onto her, though thankfully none of it stuck in her body. *Maybe it will be one of the gods fighting a half-god, or maybe one of those Limitless soldiers will spot me and try to kill me, or maybe I'll get caught in the middle of Skimif and Uron's conflict. I just hope I can survive long enough for my plan to work.*

Actually finding Skimif and Uron had not been difficult. After sending off Gujak and the Mysterious One to the ethereal to carry out their part of the plan, Durima had taken the ethereal herself to enter World's End quickly. When she landed, she simply followed the obvious trail of destruction and debris that led from the southern end of the city all the way to its center, near the Temple of the Gods, which as far as Durima could tell was one of the few buildings in the city not to be wrecked or damaged in some way.

Along the way, Durima had spotted more than a few disturbing sights. One street she walked along had been strewn with the corpses of her fellow katabans, along with a handful of humans who she assumed to be the Limitless soldiers that the Mysterious One had told her about. It had looked like a massacre, as if the Limitless had been murdering any katabans they could get their hands on. They had even killed the children. While Durima was not much of a fan of children herself, it had unsettled her deeply to see the corpses of so many young ones either burned black or torn to shreds by some unknown spell.

She had also spotted about a dozen Soldiers of the Gods trying to kill one of the half-gods, a monster that had vaguely resembled a giant dragon made out of water. She had left before seeing if they won, but based on the fact that the water dragon half-god had killed one half of the Soldiers in one blow, she didn't think they would succeed.

Then she almost got caught in a battle between the Tusked God and a boar-headed half-god with a poorly-chiseled stone body. Last Durima saw, the Tusked God ran his tusks straight through the half-god's body, although the half-god in question had been about to crush the Tusked God's skull in with a chunk of the street he had picked up.

Now Durima was here, having climbed the side of a skyscraper to get a better view of Skimif and Uron's battle. The two were standing on the rooftop of one of the lower buildings, close enough that Durima could jump onto it if she wanted to, but not close enough that she was in danger of being harmed or noticed by either of them. They circled each other like rival lightning tigers, which meant that soon they would be at each other's throats again.

My part of the plan is probably the easy part, Durima thought. *Just keep Uron in my sight, and when Gujak and the Mysterious One return, attack.*

The plan was simple. Gujak was supposed to enter the ethereal and tell all of the katabans traveling on it to exit the ethereal and stay on whatever islands they happened to find themselves on. If none of them listened to Gujak, the Mysterious One would order them to do it instead, seeing as he was a god, which meant that all katabans had to listen to him no matter what.

Once Gujak and the Mysterious One were sure that the ethereal was empty, they would return to World's End and inform Durima about that. Durima would then trap Uron in the ethereal, which he shouldn't be able to escape from, seeing as only the gods and katabans could enter or exit the ethereal on their own.

The plan relied on quite a few assumptions, such as that all of the katabans would evacuate the ethereal when the Mysterious One ordered them to, and that Uron would not have some way of escaping the ethereal. That second part in particular was hard to prove, as Durima still didn't know what the full extent of Uron's powers were.

For all I know, trapping Uron in the ethereal might just make him stronger, Durima thought. *But we don't have any other choice. Skimif can't beat Uron on his own, at least while Uron has the God-killer. At least banishing*

Uron into the ethereal might give us time to figure out a more permanent solution for dealing with him, anyway.

On the next building, Skimif fired a huge lava ball at Uron. Uron deflected it as easily as if it were a toy, and then stomped on the roof of the building, causing it to crack open like an egg. Skimif, however, jumped across the crack to avoid tripping over it, and the two ultimate beings stopped circling each other. They stood directly apart from each other now, which would have been the perfect opportunity for Durima to banish Uron into the ethereal, but with no sign of Gujak or the Mysterious One anywhere, she would just have to wait.

The sound of huge flapping wings nearby caused her head to whip to the right. She groaned when she recognized the Mican crystal claws and the pretty boy face of Commander Erich, Commander of the Soldiers of the Gods.

Only Erich didn't look quite like how Durima remembered him. His crystalline armor was cracked and burnt, one of his eyes was blackened, his nose was covered in blood, and one of his Mican crystal claws was missing a digit. His wings were missing at least a third of their feathers, with another third set in awkward-looking positions that looked painful.

"Durima the Demon," said Erich, his breathing hard as he leaned against the side of the building Durima clung to. "First a murderer, now a traitor. What will you be next, I wonder?"

Durima raised an eyebrow. "I don't know what you're babbling about, but can't we talk about this later? I am in the middle of something very, very important and I don't have the time to talk."

"Talk?" said Erich. He laughed like a maniac. "I don't want to talk. I want to kill you for what you did to World's End. Then I will find Gujak and kill him, too, unless he's already dead."

Durima braced herself against the building as it shook ominously. "What did *I* do to World's End? I haven't even been here for ... gods, I don't know how long because time doesn't make sense in the Void. I think you're losing it."

"This," said Erich, gesturing at the destroyed city all around them. "I know you are behind this somehow. I find it interesting how you and Gujak went beyond the Void; then, not too long after, Uron and his army of freaks emerge from within to destroy World's End. Without first killing you two."

Durima clung against the wall again as a window far above their heads exploded open, raining down glass on them. "You're not implying that Gujak and I are working for Uron, are you?"

"Working for or with, I don't care," said Erich, brushing some glass shards off his shoulders. He raised one of his Mican crystal claws. "The point is, you are still alive even though you should have died. My guess is that you allied with Uron to survive."

"You don't know what you're talking about," said Durima. She nodded toward Uron and Skimif below. "Right now, I am trying to defeat Uron, which I can't do if you try to kill me right now for doing something I would never even think of doing in a million years."

"I'm sure you are," said Erich. "Just as I am sure that Uron only wants to make Martir a better place. Not."

Erich's crystal claw tore through the air, forcing Durima to sidle along the wall as fast as she could to avoid it. Erich's claw slammed into the side of the building so hard that the digits became stuck in the rock, causing him to tug on them as hard as he could in an effort to free them.

"Shouldn't you be protecting the Council or something?" said Durima. "Or at least making sure that they are safe?"

"The Council evacuated World's End after the first attack," said Erich as he succeeded in tearing his claw from the building, sending chunks of stone falling to the streets below. "They're on their way north even as we speak. I stayed here in the city to stand along my Soldiers and to kill you."

"Right," said Durima. "Of course they would be the first ones out of the city. Why wouldn't they be? Not like they're fighters themselves."

Erich stepped closer to her, his eyes blazing with anger. "The Council are not cowards. They are simply too important to be put in harm's way. But what am I saying? Of course you think they should have been here. You wanted Uron or one of his cronies to kill them, didn't you?"

"When will you listen long enough to hear what I am saying?" said Durima. "Read my lips: I am *not* working with or for Uron. I am trying to stop him, same as everyone else. So either get out of my way or help me. I don't care what you choose to do."

"Lies," Erich snarled. "Lies, lies, lies. I will take you head and bring it before the Council as proof of your death."

"How will killing me stop Uron?" said Durima, sparing a glance at Skimif and Uron below, who still stood apart from each other without making any moves. "He's going to destroy World's End regardless, you know."

"I know that," said Erich. He raised his claw again. "But Lord Skimif already has him under control, so I thought I would be useful and take you out before you could complete whatever your evil plan is. Justice is justice, no matter how big or small you may be."

Once again, he swung his claw at Durima. She ducked to avoid getting her head taken off, but her foot slipped and she fell. In panic she reached out and grabbed onto the ledge she had been standing on, digging her own claws into the stone. The pressure on her claws hurt like hell, especially when Erich stepped on them, causing them to crack.

"Let go," said Erich as a strong gust of wind blow through, sending his hair flapping around his head. "There's nothing you can do now. Death is the only fitting reward for traitors like yourself."

Durima held on as tightly as she could, even as Erich pressed his foot down on her claws. Bits of stone fell off the ledge as her grip on it loosened. She still did not look down; if she did, she knew without a doubt that she would let go and fall to her death.

Her arms grew weaker, as they were unable to hold her weight like this for very long. Durima could not concentrate long enough to use her magic to help, either, largely due to the pressure Erich was putting on her claws. She probably had only a minute or two left before she was forced to let go and fall to her doom.

"Fall," Erich said, pressing down even more on Durima's claws. "Fall, damn it, and die like the pig you are."

Durima didn't listen to someone like Erich, but she felt her strength rapidly leaving her. Soon, she would have no choice but to fall, and when she did, she would have no strength to open a portal to the ethereal and save herself.

But then Durima heard a familiar *pop* of an ethereal portal opening. Then she saw Gujak appear beside Erich on the ledge, but instead of announcing his presence, Gujak shoved Erich forward.

Startled, Erich tipped over the side of the ledge and fell. He reached out with his claws for Durima's foot, but Durima lifted her legs out of his reach. She saw Erich's eyes widen in anger and hate as he fell screaming to the streets below; at least, until an ethereal portal opened beneath him and he fell into it.

"Durima, grab my hand," said Gujak, bending over slightly as he held out a hand toward her.

Once Durima was safely back on the ledge, which she now clung to as if it were her mother, she looked at Gujak in surprise. "You got here fast. Is the ethereal empty?"

"It should be," said Gujak, nodding. "No one listened to me, like you thought, but when the Mysterious One spoke, everyone obeyed him just like you thought. Everyone is in the Northern Isles now, living on human islands, so we're pretty sure that the ethereal is empty."

"Except for Erich," said Durima with a scowl. "Damn idiot has to go and mess things up."

"Maybe Erich went somewhere else," Gujak suggested. "I doubt he'll stay in there for long. He probably went to find the Council, I bet, and lick his wounds."

"You're probably right," said Durima. "We'll just have to risk putting Uron in there and hope it's as empty as you say. Not like we have any other plan, right?"

Gujak nodded.

"By the way, where is the Mysterious One?" said Durima, looking in both directions, but seeing no sign of that strange talking skeleton from earlier. "Wasn't he with you?"

"He vanished," said Gujak. "Literally. When all of the katabans left the ethereal, I turned and he was gone. I don't know where he went. I wish he was still here, though, because then I would thank him for his help."

"Doesn't matter," said Durima. "What matters is putting the next step of the plan into action, which is getting Uron into the ethereal. We'll have to move fast before he realizes what we're doing."

Gujak gulped and looked down at the building where Uron and Skimif were squaring off. "Uh, how do we do that?"

"Simple," said Durima. "You distract him, then I tackle him. When I tackle him, I'll open a portal into the ethereal. Once we're inside, I will leave immediately, before Uron realizes what happened, and Martir will once again be safe."

"That *is* simple," said Gujak. Then he cringed at the sound of some monster roaring somewhere nearby. "Almost too simple. Something *has* to go wrong."

"Knowing our luck, something probably will," said Durima. "But who knows? Maybe Rujan will smile on us today and everything will actually go right for once. Now come on. We don't have much time before Uron and Skimif begin trading blows again."

Chapter Twenty-Two

Darek wiped away the tears in his eyes as best as he could, but the grief in his heart continued to pound away like a blacksmith making a sword. Mom didn't even try to clean up her tears. She just continued to stare up at the blazing fire ball in the sky, which was actually starting to shrink, as if Jakuuth"s energy was running out.

"What do we do now?" Darek asked, looking at Mom—or, as he should probably more rightly think of her now, the Magical Superior—in confusion.

Mom looked at Darek through teary eyes. She sniffled and said, in a surprisingly matter-of-fact voice, "We have to help the other students and teachers beat back the rest of the Limitless Army. Jakuuth may be dead, but his men might not be aware of that yet. It shouldn't be as difficult now, though, because the Limitless are leaderless now."

"So are we," said Darek. "I mean, I know the Superior made you the temporary Superior for now, but—"

"We'll be fine," said Mom, though she certainly didn't look like she was fine herself. "We just need to go down and help however we can. With Jakuuth dead, I bet the Limitless Army will lose its morale, probably be easier to beat."

Mom took one step toward the exit and almost fell to her knees. She staggered against the door frame as Darek said, "Mom, are you all right?"

She sighed. "I'm fine, Darek, you don't need to worry about me."

Darek shook his head. "No, Mom, you're not. You used up too much of your power too quickly. You're not a Limitless like me. You should stay here. I'll go down and let the others know."

Mom stood up, but she still leaned against the charred door frame, clearly too weak to do much. She looked at Darek in disbelief. "You're a Limitless now?"

"Yes," said Darek. "Jakuuth taught me how to do it so I could 'help' the Army. We can talk about this later. The longer we stand here talking, the longer this useless war drags on."

"All right," said Mom. She slumped against the door frame. "You know, I think you have a point. I'll stay here and let my energy levels return to normal. No point in having a weak old woman by your side, eh?"

"Mom, you're not weak," said Darek as he helped her sit down on the floor. "Just tired. As soon as I deal with the Limitless, I'll return and get you back to your bed so you can rest, okay?"

Mom nodded, the tears in her eyes starting to dry up. "All right. But be careful. Those Limitless are absolutely ruthless."

"I know," said Darek. "Be back in a minute."

He straightened up and closed his eyes. A moment later,

Darek felt the cold wind of the outside blowing on his face and when he opened his eyes, he saw that he was standing outside on the steps of the Arcanium. The corpse of Raka still lay at the bottom of the steps, which he ignored as he looked out over the courtyard, surprised by what he saw.

It looked like every Limitless soldier and North Academy student and teacher were present here in the courtyard. The two sides looked as beaten and wounded as any fighters in a war, yet they were not battling each other. Instead, all eyes were on the massive fire ball in the sky, which had shrunk considerably in the seconds that Darek had teleported from the Magical Superior's study to the courtyard.

Why isn't everyone fighting? Darek thought. *Did they feel the deaths of Jakuuth and the Magical Superior? They must have. Those two were easily the strongest mages in the area; no way their deaths could have gone unnoticed for even a minute. Wonder how long this shock will last.*

Above, the fire ball soon dissipated entirely, leaving behind a charred black skeleton; the remains of Jakuuth. The skeleton immediately fell from the sky toward the earth, but rather than falling down into the Superior's study, it headed straight for the courtyard. Soldiers and students alike shrank back as the skeleton crashed into the center of the courtyard, leaving a trail of smoke and flame behind it as it did so.

Everyone stared at the small, smoking crater in silence, as if they expected the skeleton to get up and walk away. Of course, no such thing happened, but people on both sides continued to stare anyway.

The first to break the silence was a Limitless soldier, one who Darek didn't recognize. He said, in a low, confused voice, "What ...What *is* that? What happened? Where's Jakuuth?"

"And the Superior?" Jiku asked. "I can't sense the Magical Superior anymore."

Seeing an opportunity, Darek pointed at the skeleton and raised his voice, shouting, "That skeleton right there is what remains of Jakuuth, the so-called Son of Grinf and leader of the Limitless Army. He is dead."

The Limitless soldiers and Academy students and teachers looked at Darek as one. The students and teachers looked surprised, though pleased, to see Darek. Now that he got a better look at them, he saw that many of them were badly wounded, with burned skin, torn robes, bleeding arms and foreheads, and broken limbs, among other obvious injuries.

The Limitless soldiers, on the other hand, didn't look nearly as badly injured as the students and teachers, though it was pretty clear that they had just been fighting nonetheless. Aside from their torn clothes, many of the soldiers had cuts and bruises; one soldier appeared to have had his entire head of hair burned off, if his blackened scalp was a clue.

"No way," said one of the soldiers, her voice full of despair and disbelief. She pointed at the skeleton. "That can't be Jakuuth. He's the Son of Grinf. He can't die, not that easily."

"It's him, all right," said Darek. He gestured toward the

Magical Superior's study all the way at the top of the Arcanium. "Can you sense him anymore? If you can't, don't you wonder why?"

None of the soldiers answered. A handful shuffled their feet, while others looked away.

"That's because Jakuuth is indeed *dead*," Darek said, putting as much emphasis on that last word as he could. "Killed by the Magical Superior, who gave his own life to end Jakuuth's. The battle is *over*. We *won*."

The teachers and students all looked as shocked as the soldiers to hear that the Magical Superior was dead. Darek wished he could have revealed this to them at a better time, but at the moment, he wanted everyone to know the bare facts of the matter.

Darek lowered the finger he had been pointing at Jakuuth. "Now do you see? Without Jakuuth to lead you, what are you going to do? Do you really want to risk your lives and kill innocent people for no reason?"

His words seemed to have an effect on the Limitless. Half of them looked at their comrades as if searching for guidance, while the other half could not raise their eyes to meet Darek's. Darek was hoping that the Limitless would return to their original criminal instincts, now that they no longer had Jakuuth to bind them together.

What happens when you take away the main reason for the world's worst criminals to work together? Darek thought. *Hopefully, civil war.*

Darek's feelings of triumph—which even seemed to be encouraging the teachers and students, as most of them, even the badly injured ones, looked like they were ready to continue the fight now—evaporated as soon as he saw Jakuuth's bones twitch.

He blinked. *I didn't just see Jakuuth's bones move, did I? Of course not. It must be my eyes getting tired or something, making me see—*

Then one charred bone hand rose straight up. The sight of the moving bones caused soldiers, students and teachers alike to shrink back, widening the circle around the crater in the school's courtyard. A handful of the more frightened soldiers even teleported away, though Darek didn't try to stop them, as he was too focused on the surreal sight before him to act.

Like someone waking from a nap, the skeleton of Jakuuth Grinfborn sat up. Its left arm was detached, but it soon popped it back into its socket and swung it back and forth to test its stability. Then it slowly rose to its feet, ash falling off its shoulders as it did so.

"What in the name of the gods is going on here?" Jiku said as the skeleton rose to its full height. "This must be some kind of trick."

The skeleton then inclined its head upward to look at Darek on the steps. Rather than the empty eye sockets of a skeleton, fire burned within, like the flames of a furnace. Then it pointed at Darek.

"Darek ... Takren," said the skeleton. Its voice was harsh and bony, but there was no mistaking it for the voice of anyone other than Jakuuth. "Surprised?"

"No way," said Darek as he drew his wand from his belt

and aimed it at the skeleton. "No. This can't be. How—"

"I am the Son of Grinf," said the skeleton that was Jakuuth. "A Limitless, the greatest Limitless of all. How can you expect a simple Divine Burst to kill me? I am not a weakling like the Magical Superior. No mere mortal can kill a half-god like me."

The glimmer of hope that had shone in the eyes of all of the students and teachers quickly died away. As for the Limitless soldiers, they seemed to be gathering their courage back, because many of them raised their wands and began charging flames, crackling electricity, and light bursts, ready to begin the inevitable slaughter that was to follow.

"Try as you might, you cannot win," said Jakuuth. His skin was starting to re-grow on his skeleton, making him look more and more like a decaying corpse than a skeleton. "Now, my men, why don't we finish what we started? There is a whole world beyond these Walls that awaits my rule after this place is little more than a graveyard."

The Limitless soldiers shouted in joy and agreement. The students and teachers, on the other hand, were already retreating toward the sports field, though Darek didn't see what point there was in doing even that. The Limitless would hunt them down anyway.

With the Magical Superior dead, we might as well go down fighting, Darek thought. *Running away will only delay the inevitable.*

"Hunt down the mortals," Jakuuth snapped at his men. He nodded at Darek. "Kill every last one, teacher, student, or whatever. I will personally exact justice on this pathetic, lying excuse for a mage."

"Justice?" said another voice, this one seeming to come from everywhere at once. "I may not be Grinf, but even I can see that this is hardly just."

Jakuuth and the Limitless soldiers began wildly looking around for the source of the voice. So did Darek before feeling a thin, bony hand tap his shoulder, causing him to look to his right.

The Mysterious One walked past him without so much as glancing at Darek. Except rather than being a plain skeleton, the Mysterious One wore auburn robes, very similar to the ones worn by the Magical Superior prior to his death. He also carried a wand, but it was no normal wand. It appeared to be made out of gold and crystal, shining brilliantly in the sun, and it was at least as long as Darek's arm. A large ruby was attached to his upper arm, like the magic stones used by the aquarian mages, except twice as large as any Darek had seen before.

"What?" said Jakuuth. His face had almost entirely regenerated by now, but it was still only halfway complete. "Who are you?"

"A myth," said the Mysterious One. His voice was as deadly as a spiked mace. "A legend. A superstition believed by some and denied by others. An interesting topic of discussion for gods and mortal alike. I am many things, yet none of them describe me with one hundred percent accuracy."

"A legend, hmm?" said Jakuuth. He raised one of his

hands, which burst into flame. "Fitting, because once I am done with you, that's all anyone will remember you as."

Then Jakuuth looked at his men. "Men, raise your wands. We are going to blow this 'legend' into the Void, along with Darek Takren. Use everything you've got."

Although every Limitless soldier looked put off by the Mysterious One, they nonetheless aimed their wands at the God of Mystery and Magic. Despite that, the Mysterious One kept his pace as leisurely as ever, every step of his bony feet creating a clacking sound against the stone steps under him.

"On the count of three," said Jakuuth. "One ..."

The Limitless soldiers' wands began glowing with charging magical energy. Darek raised his own wand, despite knowing it was useless against so many enemies at once, while the Mysterious One did nothing except begin whistling a tune Darek didn't recognize.

The fire encircling Jakuuth's hand grew hotter and brighter. "Two ..."

The Mysterious One's wand glowed briefly, so brief that Darek wasn't even sure it had glowed at all or if it had been the reflection of the sun that he had seen. Whether the wand had activated or not, that didn't stop the Limitless soldiers' charged energy blasts from growing larger.

"Three!" Jakuuth roared.

As soon as that word left Jakuuth's mouth, the Mysterious One acted. He raised his wand and swung it once, the same simple motion a mortal mage used whenever casting a basic fire spell.

A second later, the Limitless soldiers' wands ceased glowing. The soldiers lowered their wands and stared at them in disbelief. One of the soldier shook his wand up and down vigorously, while another tapped his with one finger, and still another threw his to the ground and stomped on it in frustration.

As for Jakuuth, even his flame had died out. He looked at his outstretched hand in shock, saying as he did so, "What was ... why did my fire go out?"

Then the Mysterious One—still whistling that odd tune (though how he whistled without lips, Darek didn't know)— swung his wand and pointed it at Jakuuth.

Without warning, Jakuuth vanished into thin air like smoke. Only the burned grass on the courtyard indicated that he had been standing there in the first place.

"Lord Jakuuth!" the female soldier from before shouted. She glared at the Mysterious One, who had reached the bottom of the steps by now and was standing there looking as innocent as a kitten. "What did you do to him? What did you do to us?"

The Mysterious One tapped his chin, as if seriously considering that question. "Well, to answer your second question, I turned off your magic. You mortals may be incapable of killing me, but that doesn't mean I appreciate having your wands pointing at me like that. It makes me uncomfortable."

Then the Mysterious One gestured at the spot where Jakuuth had been standing. "As for your leader, Jakuuth is back in the Void, where his kind belong. I doubt you will ever see him again."

"You're lying," said the female soldier. She pointed her wand at him, even though it was now little more than a glorified piece of wood. "You hid Jakuuth somewhere on Martir."

"I have no reason to lie," said the Mysterious One. He shrugged. "But you don't have to believe me if you don't want to. You mortals have free will, so use it as freely as you will, even if in a silly way."

"I will kill you," said the female soldier, whose dark eyes reminded Darek of Aorja for some reason. "I will tear you apart bone by god-forsaken bone until you tell me where Jakuuth is."

"By yourself?" said the Mysterious One. "An impressive boast, but sadly one you won't get a chance to put into action. I think you 'soldiers,' as you fancy yourselves, have caused these innocent mages enough trouble for one day. Why don't you go back to the prison and complete the life sentences that your peoples gave you?"

With that, the Mysterious One waved his wand at them. Just like with Jakuuth, all of the Limitless soldiers vanished like mist in a gust of wind.

Then the Mysterious One lowered his wand and turned to look up at Darek. "There you go. North Academy is now safe, at least for the foreseeable future."

"But ..." Darek could hardly comprehend how easily Jakuuth and the Limitless soldiers had been beaten. "What was with Jakuuth?"

"What do you mean?" said the Mysterious One. "He was

nothing more than a power-hungry upstart who thought he was the son of a god."

"But what was he, *exactly*?" Darek asked, even though he wasn't sure if this was the most important question to ask right now. "You said you banished him beyond the Void, where his 'kind' belongs, but what is his kind? I thought he was human."

The Mysterious One shook his head. "Jakuuth was what you might call a 'half-god.' He wasn't half human and half divine. It simply means that he was one of the many, many failed creations of the Powers, a prototype, you might say, of Grinf, which is why he looked like Grinf so much."

Darek rubbed his forehead, trying to wrap his head around that idea. "I ... what?"

"You don't need to understand anything except that the half-gods have always lived beyond the Void," said the Mysterious One. "Well, until just recently, anyway, but that's where they belong and it is where Jakuuth will spend the rest of his days."

"Jakuuth told me about his mother, though," said Darek. "How can he have a mother if he wasn't actually human?"

"He was delusional," said the Mysterious One, spinning a finger at the side of his head. "He looks more human than most half-gods. I imagine he must have lost his memory of his true nature when he left the Void the first time all those years ago, perhaps was adopted by his 'mother,' if she ever really existed at all. Who knows?"

The explanation that Jakuuth had not been human made some sense to Darek, though he still found it hard to believe.

But how else can you explain him surviving a Divine Burst? Darek thought.

"We probably should have returned him to the Void after he was first defeated all those years ago," said the Mysterious One, stroking his chin. "I should have spoken up when the Katabans Council decided to imprison him beneath World's End, but I've never really been one to offer my opinion when it wasn't wanted ... or even known to exist, for that matter."

Decided he wanted to move on—the idea of Jakuuth being some kind of 'half-god' was too hard to understand, if it was true—Darek asked, "But why? Why did you—"

"Why did I help?" said the Mysterious One. "Is that what you're asking?"

Darek nodded. "Yes. I thought you were going to do something else."

"I've done what I need to do," said the Mysterious One, as vaguely as ever. "Besides, you might not realize it, but North Academy matters to me just as much as it does to you, maybe even more so. I couldn't stand to see Jakuuth and his cronies burn this place to the ground."

Now that actually made some sense to Darek. He smiled and said, "Because you're the God of Magic, right? Since this is one of the best magic schools in the world, it's only logical you would defend it."

The Mysterious One chuckled. "Oh, my connection to this school is far deeper than that, much more personal, you might say. But I won't, because that's not information you need to know right now."

"Personal?" said Darek. "What does that—"

He stopped himself mid-sentence when he realized that the Mysterious One was no longer present, leaving him all alone on the steps of the Arcanium, looking at the crater where Jakuuth had been standing mere moments ago.

Guess he's not called the Mysterious *One for nothing,* Darek thought. *Oh well. I should go tell the students and teachers that the school is safe. Then we can begin the long, hard work of putting everything back to the way it was ... or as close to the way it was as we can, anyway.*

Chapter Twenty-Three

The hardest part of any plan was the last step. As Durima climbed up the side of the building that Uron and Skimif currently stood upon, she had to tell herself that in order to get her in the right mindset to tackle Uron and trap him in the ethereal.

It will be hard because you will be scared, Durima thought, her eyes on the roof's edge, which she drew closer and closer to with each reach of her arms. *Scared of dying, scared of getting trapped in there with Uron, but don't worry because Gujak will distract him for you. And Skimif is there, too, so all you need to focus on is your part of the plan.*

Durima found herself wishing she could have spoken about this with Skimif first. But there was just no time to do that, even if she wanted to. She would just have to trust that Skimif would trust her and Gujak to do what they were trying to do, even if he didn't know what it was.

Finally, Durima reached the edge of the roof. She carefully peeked over to get a good look at the current situation.

Just like earlier, Skimif and Uron were at a standstill. Skimif's fists glowed with the light of the sun, while the fingers of Uron's ungloved hand looked as sleek and slimy as a snake. Neither of them seemed to notice her yet, which was fine by Durima. That would make her job so much easier to do.

The only problem was that Gujak did not seem to have reached the roof yet. As some strange eagle-like creature with tentacles went soaring by overhead, a Soldier of the Gods standing on it and stabbing it wherever he could, Durima began to worry that something might have happened to Gujak.

Unless he forgot, Durima thought. *And if he forgot, then I will personally come back from the Heavenly Paradise as a ghost and haunt him for the rest of his days.*

"Why do you insist on fighting me, Skimif?" said Uron. He gestured at the chaos all around them. "Do you not see your precious city falling apart all around you? I can already sense that you're getting weaker, just like the handful of other gods who are too stupid to run away. Sooner or later, I will find an opening and your reign over Martir will end."

"I fight you because I am the God of Martir," said Skimif. He coughed, an alarming sound to Durima. "And it's my duty to protect Martir from all threats, no matter how powerful or scary."

"I forgot how duty-bound and arrogant you are," said Uron in annoyance. "I suppose that is what I get for spending a year inside the Void. Thankfully, I will be able to spend the next year, and the next, and the next, rebuilding my home on the ruins of this one, just as I am destined to do."

"Destined?" said Skimif. He wiped away a trickle of what

looked like blood from his mouth. "What kind of destiny could someone like *you* have? The Powers didn't create you."

"Nor did they create destiny," said Uron. He clinched the God-killer around his hand. "Destiny is a force much larger than even the Powers. No one can escape its grasp, not even you gods."

"I'm not in the mood to debate philosophy with you, to be honest," said Skimif, shaking his head. He held out one fist before him while raising the other above his head. "Let's finish this once and for all."

"Of course," said Uron, raising his clinched God-killer in front of him.

At that moment, Gujak's head popped over the opposite side of the roof. Hope rose in Durima's heart as Gujak waved at her briefly before climbing onto the roof itself, though he crouched low so as to not draw attention to himself just yet.

All right, Gujak, Durima thought. *Shouldn't be long now. Just yell or jump or insult Uron or anything. I just need a split second opening—just one opening is all—and I can banish Uron to the ethereal for good.*

While Skimif and Uron looked ready to jump at each other, Gujak stood up and dusted his arms off. He then took a deep breath, but before he could say anything, an ethereal portal opened up right next to him.

Faster than Durima's eyes could follow, Erich jumped out of the portal. Gujak turned to look at him in surprise, but before he could say anything, Erich stabbed both of his

Mican crystal claws into Gujak's chest.

The sound of crystal cutting through wood was marred by Gujak's screams of pain, which were so loud that Durima could hear them even over the sounds of battle raging in the city below. His screams were so loud that Skimif and Uron both looked in his direction as if wondering what was going on.

Then Erich yanked his claws out of Gujak's chest, sending even more chunks of wood flying off his body onto the stone roof underneath. Without hesitation, Erich kicked Gujak, sending him falling off the roof, still screaming and yelling.

"Gujak!" Durima yelled, her shout causing Skimif and Uron to turn their attention toward her instead. "No! Gujak!"

Soon Gujak's screaming was lost over a nearby explosion, but she heard Erich, who laughed and said, "That is for trying to kill me, you murderer of the gods! I, Commander Erich, Commander of the Soldiers of the Gods, have avenged the Spider Goddess! Justice has been served!"

He raised his claws above his head and then looked at Skimif with a huge smile on his face. "Lord Skimif, did you see that? Did you see what I did? Did you? I just made Martir a safer place for everyone, including you. I am a hero, deserving of the highest honors that that title implies."

Skimif stared at Erich uncertainly. "Who are you again?"

Erich's triumphant smile vanished as quickly as the receding waves of the sea. "Lord Skimif—"

Durima didn't let him finish. She leaped over the edge of

the roof, opening an ethereal portal that briefly took her out of World's End. She rolled across the white, silvery road of the ethereal before opening another portal and emerging back onto World's End, close enough to Erich to get him.

She flew at Erich, who noticed her coming at him only a second before she slammed into him with her bulk. Durima pinned Erich to the roof underneath them, keeping his arms pinned to his sides with her short yet powerful legs.

"Get ... get off me, you murderer," Erich said, though she barely felt his struggling underneath her. "I am a hero, you idiot. I deserve to be treated as such."

Though Durima heard him, she didn't care. She just raised her massive fists above her head and then began smashing Erich's pretty human-like face in as hard as she could. Erich's screams of pain were quickly cut off when she smashed his lower jaw, yet she still attacked him even then. She didn't let up, not even after she no longer felt him struggling to get free underneath her.

She wouldn't let up, not after what Erich had done to Gujak. All reason had left her. The Demon within had arisen, as it usually did in times like this, and she gladly allowed it to control her every movement if it meant avenging Gujak's death. She was only vaguely aware of the sounds of Skimif and Uron resuming their fight behind her, all thought of her original plan forgotten in her rage.

Durima kept smashing and bashing, breaking Erich's skull, his teeth, and his neck. Blood splattered over her fists and chest and face, but all it did was enrage her further. The Demon kept urging her on, urging her to kill and smash

336

until the katabans known as Erich was no more.

But the events of the day had taken their toll on Durima's body. Fatigue began to settle over her arms, making her blows not nearly as swift or devastating as they once were. As she slowed down, awareness and reason returned to her mind, like inhabitants returning to a town they had been forced to evacuate.

Then Durima stopped, her shoulders slumped, her breathing hard, as she looked down on the bloody mess that had once been Erich's head and face. She became aware of the sticky blood on her body, which smelled like mud and salt.

Ow, was the only thought she could think, because all of the pain she had suffered over the last several hours had finally caught up with her. *Need to sleep. But can't. Not yet.*

Durima had only two choices: Recover Gujak's body, or see if she could possibly salvage the 'trap-Uron-in-the-ethereal' plan. Both sounded like too much work for her tired old body, though she figured she only had enough energy left to do one.

First things first, Durima thought. *As ... as important as retrieving Gujak's body is, Uron is the more immediate problem. Better deal with him first. Then get Gujak's body.*

Gathering what little strength she had left, Durima stood up. She turned around to see Uron and Skimif's fight.

Thankfully, the two almighty beings had not gone anywhere. They were both a flurry of fists and feet, punching and kicking at each other with the kind of strength that would probably demolish a mountain. Durima doubted they were landing any of their blows; at least, Uron apparently hadn't succeeded in touching Skimif with the God-killer yet, which was a good thing, of course.

Need to find an opening, Durima thought. *Can't do anything until there's a break in the fighting. Otherwise, I'll get pulverized like Erich.*

Just as that thought passed through her mind, Skimif and Uron leaped back from each other, skidding across the rooftop of the building. As they did so, the two thrust their arms forward, Skimif unleashing a blast of golden energy, Uron a blast of black energy.

The twin energy beams met in the middle, creating an earsplitting *kaboom* that forced Durima to slam her hands over her ears to save her hearing. The explosion created a large hole in the roof in between Skimif and Uron, which separated the two by a fairly wide margin. As before, they were staring each other down, no doubt looking for a weakness they could exploit in order to end this battle quickly.

Durima stood up, even though she was almost too tired to do even that. Neither Uron nor Skimif seemed to be paying her any attention, which made sense, seeing as they were busy fighting each other. Yet Durima wasn't sure if she was fast enough to reach Uron before he noticed her or resumed his fight with Skimif.

No time to waste worrying, Durima thought. *I'll have to do my best, no matter what Uron might do.*

Ignoring the tiredness in her bones, Durima dashed toward Uron as fast as she could, willing her body to move faster than it normally could under the circumstances. She felt maddeningly slow, like a slug, but she pushed herself anyway, even when her legs burned with pain and her arms felt like they were about to fall off any minute.

Then Uron glanced in her direction. Without missing a beat, he raised one hand and fired a burst of darkness at her. Durima, however, forced open an ethereal portal and vanished into it before the burst of darkness could get her.

For a brief moment, she was back in the ethereal, but then she opened another portal and ended up back in World's End, only a few feet from Uron. Uron's yellow eyes widened in shock as Durima slammed into his gut with her shoulder, hitting him with enough force to send him staggering back.

As soon as Durima made contact with Uron, she opened another portal directly behind him. Both Durima and Uron fell into the ethereal and the portal closed with a loud *pop* behind them as they did so.

Durima rolled off of Uron and landed on the ethereal road beneath her. She lay there, breathing hard, too weak to move, as Uron jumped to his feet and looked around the ethereal in confusion.

"Where am I?" Uron demanded, whipping his head back and forth as he looked at the stars in the sky and the shining white road that stretched on forever in both directions. "What is this place?"

Durima knew she should have opened another ethereal portal and returned to Martir immediately, but just the thought of doing a task as simple as that drained her. She could barely even lift her eyes to look at Uron, who had his hands on his head and was pacing back and forth as if everything was going wrong.

"No, no, no," said Uron. "Why can't I leave this place?"

"The ethereal," Durima said. "Not easy to get out of unless you're a god or a katabans."

Uron stopped and looked down at her. "The ethereal? Ah, yes, now that you mention it, I have indeed heard of that place. I did not think I would ever visit it, but it doesn't matter. I will force you to let me out of here. A temporary setback, that's all this is."

Durima watched as Uron reached for her with the God-killer, a smirk on his face, as if he was so smart for figuring out that he could use Durima to escape. She wanted to get up and leave, but she was too tired to even think about doing so.

Then an arm burst through the ethereal, its appearance so sudden and unexpected that Uron actually jumped. The arm grabbed Durima's fur and yanked her through the portal even as Uron, quickly recovering from his shock, lunged for Durima.

The tips of Uron's uncovered fingers brushed against Durima's feet, sending a shiver up her spine but only for a moment. Then Durima went through the portal, which snapped closed behind her, although she did catch one last look of Uron's smirking face, even though she had no idea what Uron had to be happy about.

As soon as the portal closed, the arm that had grabbed Durima gently put her on the remains of the roof that

Skimif and Uron had been battling on mere moments ago. Even with the sun in her eyes, Durima recognized the being standing over her as Skimif, though with the sun behind him, his face was covered in shadow.

"Are you all right?" said Skimif, his tone genuinely concerned. "Did Uron hurt you?"

Durima shook her head slightly. "No. Barely even touched me."

Skimif sighed. "Thank the gods. I was worried that a brave katabans like you might have been killed by him. Your death would have been a terrible loss to the world, for sure."

Durima blinked. "Lord Skimif ... do you even know who I am? What I did?"

"I am aware of your accident," said Skimif. He scowled. "And I am aware that there has been a very severe case of injustice committed against you and your friend Gujak. I will have to speak with Grinf about this later."

Durima did not get to hear what else Skimif had to say, however, because the last of her adrenaline had left her and fatigue drifted over her mind and body like a thick fog. She slipped into blissful unconsciousness, marred only by a deep laugh she heard in the back of her mind that she dismissed as nothing more than her mind making her hear things.

Chapter Twenty-Four

One week later ...

Darek Takren didn't feel comfortable following Mom down the steps to the 'Godly Chamber,' as she had said it was called. Aside from the fact that it was dark and narrow, Darek was pretty sure that tradition dictated that only the Magical Superior of North Academy—which in this case was Mom, even if only temporarily—was allowed to go down here. Darek hated going against tradition, even if it was for a good reason.

But Mom had insisted that Darek join her. She said that she trusted Darek with the conversation she was going to have with Skimif, and if Skimif had a problem with that, then he could bring it up with her later.

That's Mom, all right, Darek thought, looking at the back of her head as they walked down the staircase. *She's not even afraid to speak up against Skimif if she has to. If she stays as the Magical Superior, she'll lead the school very differently from the last one, that's for sure.*

Of course, thinking about the old Magical Superior caused Darek to choke and wipe away tears that had suddenly appeared in his eyes. As much as he understood the Superior's sacrifice, he could not help but wish that it hadn't had to happen. Even though the funeral for the Magical Superior had been a week ago—one of the very first things that the school did after Jakuuth and the Limitless Army were defeated—Darek still didn't feel like he had gotten the closure he needed.

I wish I hadn't tried to break through the ceiling while the Superior was alive, Darek thought with a sniff. *I should have listened to him. He only had my best interests at heart, just like everyone else in the school here. I was too stupid to realize that.*

Darek was still a Limitless. He had worried that the Mysterious One might have restored his magical energy to its original strength, but every time Darek sensed his own magical power, he felt as strong as ever. He wondered if the Mysterious One actually trusted Darek with that power or if the God of Mystery and Magic was simply too busy to take the time to take Darek's power away from him.

Either way, Darek didn't really want to lose it, even though he regretted it. He liked feeling Limitless, as if there was no peak too high for him to reach. It made the world seem a little less scary and uncertain, even though he knew that having limitless power did not necessarily mean you had no problems.

Finally, they reached the stone door at the bottom of the steps, only to discover that someone had apparently left it open. Mom and Darek looked at each other for a moment, but as neither of them sensed any malevolent forces beyond it, they entered through the open door into the Chamber.

As it turned out, Mom didn't need to bring the Skimif

statue—the only statue to survive Jakuuth's attack in one piece—in the first place. Skimif himself was already there, leaning against the stone podium as if he had been waiting in this Chamber for quite a while. When he saw Mom and Darek enter, he pushed himself off the podium and stood up straight.

"Jenur, Darek," said Skimif, folding his arms. "Good to see you two. I see that North Academy is already back on its feet."

"The damage that the Limitless Army inflicted on the campus buildings and grounds was easy enough to fix," said Mom with a shrug. "The worst damage was the lives lost in the conflict. We lost two teachers and about thirty students, not counting ... well, not counting the Magical Superior himself."

Skimif nodded. "I am sorry for your losses. We at World's End also suffered casualties. Fifty dead Soldiers of the Gods, plus a still unknown amount of katabans citizens who died in the initial assault. Most of the katabans citizens survived, thankfully, by escaping via the ethereal, although now they're stranded all over the Northern Isles with no way to get back to World's End."

"Couldn't you just teleport them back?" Darek suggested.

"That's what I've been doing," said Skimif. "Everyone is helping rebuild World's End, so I think that will be fine after a while. Also, I've been busy helping the other gods to find and destroy the rest of the half-gods."

"How's that going, by the way?" said Mom. "Are they

back in the Void yet with Jakuuth?"

She said Jakuuth's name as casually as any, but Darek caught a tinge of anger bubbling under the surface of her words. He chose not to mention it.

"No," said Skimif, shaking his head. "The half-gods were numerous, at least two hundred of them, and when Uron was banished into the ethereal, they scattered everywhere. Some are in the southern seas, some are in the Northern Isles, and a handful returned to the Void, but most of them are still unaccounted for. Ghatmos, the God of Hunting, has been leading the hunt, though I think it will take a while to find them all."

"What about the Limitless soldiers who allied with them?" Darek asked. "And Rema and Gonar?"

"Most of the Limitless soldiers lost the ability to use their magic soon after Uron vanished," said Skimif. "None of us know why, but it worked out well for us. The Soldiers of the Gods rounded up all of the Limitless and sent them back to Rock Isle. As for Rema and Gonar, they are currently being tried before the Katabans Council and will probably be executed for their crimes before the end of the month."

"Good," said Darek. "That's what those idiots deserve for all the trouble they caused us."

"Also, the Northern nations have reasserted control of Rock Isle," Skimif continued. "Though they're now considering shutting it down and putting the criminals in several different prisons scattered around the Northern Isles. Quite a few people seem to think that putting all of the world's worst criminals in one place is not the wisest move, to be frank."

"Aorja?" said Darek. "Is she still there?"

Skimif frowned. "She's missing. Last I heard, when the Carnagian and Shikan Navies arrived to reclaim control over Rock Isle, they found Aorja's chains empty. Even I don't know where she is, though I doubt she'll stay hidden for long."

Darek grimaced. He had been hoping that Aorja would be thrown back behind bars, but if Skimif's report was accurate, then Aorja was free again, no doubt planning to kill him in the most gruesome way possible.

"Besides that, peace seems to have returned to Martir at last," said Skimif. "Well, for now, anyway. Uron can't get out of the ethereal and no one can enter it, as I locked it from the inside and outside."

"Will he escape?" said Darek.

"Not any time soon," said Skimif. "As powerful as Uron is, he has no way of entering or exiting the ethereal on his own. Of course, Uron is dangerously clever, so his imprisonment is a temporary delay at best."

"How did he get in the ethereal, anyway?" Darek, scratching the back of his head. "Did you banish him there?"

"No," said Skimif, looking a little embarrassed. "Wish I'd thought of it first, though. It was actually a katabans named Durima who did it. You know, the one who used to serve the Ghostly God?"

"Her?" said Darek. "How—"

"I don't know," said Skimif, shaking his head. "She and her partner, Gujak, were supposed to be banished beyond the Void for their accidental killing of the Spider Goddess. I don't know how they got out, but I'm glad they did. Otherwise, I think World's End would be little more than pretty rubble by now."

"Where is Durima?" said Mom, tilting her head to the side. "And the other one you mentioned, Gujak. They sound like heroes to me."

"Gujak ... was killed in the Battle of World's End," said Skimif. "He was given a funeral yesterday, though one I did not attend. Nonetheless, Gujak helped save the katabans and our world, which is what makes him a hero in my eyes, even though he died before Uron was stopped."

"I'm sorry to hear that," said Darek. "How is Durima holding up?"

"As well as anyone who loses a close friend holds up," said Skimif. "She's currently back on World's End, helping rebuild the city. I've pardoned her, so she doesn't have to worry about being banished beyond the Void again. Though," he added with a scowl, "I will still need to speak with the Katabans Council about dishing out such harsh punishments to 'criminals' who aren't even criminals."

Skimif's angry tone made Darek feel unsafe, especially in such a cramped space. Darek may have been a Limitless, but he was still nothing in comparison to Skimif's power.

"Changing the subject," Skimif continued, his tone returning to a gentler one, "Darek, I wanted to thank you for a job well done."

"Me?" said Darek, putting a hand on his chest. "Why me? Both North Academy and World's End suffered serious damage and plenty of casualties from Jakuuth and Uron's forces. All of which could have been avoided if I had killed Jakuuth earlier."

"No doubt," said Skimif. "But it would have been much worse if you hadn't infiltrated the Limitless Army and learned about Jakuuth's true plans. I have informed the Ghostly God of your hard work, though he didn't seem interested."

"Yeah," said Darek, nodding. "He hasn't talked to me at all since Jakuuth and Uron were defeated. Did he tell you to tell me anything?"

"Not really," said Skimif. "I suspect that the Ghostly God was actually pleased with your work, though he's a hard one to read. He did say that he might have another job for you in the future, although he didn't elaborate on what that might be."

Darek's shoulders slumped. "Right. I still owe nine years of service to him, don't I?"

"See, Darek, that is why I always, always told you to be careful about the promises you make to gods," Mom said, jabbing him in the shoulder. "Because if you don't, then you might find yourself becoming the servant of a southern god for ten years."

Skimif shrugged. "Not much I can do about that one, to be honest. I usually try to stay out of the dealings between individual gods and individual mortals, mostly because the gods don't like it when I get too nosy about their dealings."

348

"It's fine," said Darek. "As horrible as it is, I'll live. Unless the Ghostly God gets hungry and decides to invite me over for dinner, that is."

"I'll make sure the Ghostly God doesn't eat you," said Skimif. Then he leaned forward slightly, his eyes locked on Darek. "Now, Darek, I heard that Jakuuth and his soldiers here at North Academy were defeated by a walking, talking skeleton wearing auburn robes and carrying a gold-and-crystal wand."

Darek started. "How did you know that?"

"I stopped by Rock Isle briefly to speak with some of the re-captured prisoners," said Skimif. "They were rather angry, but they told me more than enough. Now, who was that being?"

"The Mysterious One," said Darek. "You know, the God of Mystery and Magic?"

"Him?" said Skimif. He sounded genuinely surprised. "Are you sure?"

"Of course I am," said Darek, folding his arms over his chest. "None of the other gods can shut off magical power or banish half-gods beyond the Void, can they?"

Skimif stroked his chin. "No, they can't. Still, I never thought that the Mysterious One would ever directly intervene like that. Did he say where he's been for the past thirty years?"

"No, he didn't," said Darek. "I didn't even think to ask him. And before you ask, I don't know where he is right now, either."

"Very well," said Skimif. "I was hoping to speak with

him, but I can see that I won't be getting that opportunity any time soon. Anyway ... I am sorry about Chen's death. I didn't know him very long, but he was a great mage and an even greater man."

Darek felt the tears in his eyes returning, which he wiped away as casually as he could. "It's fine. The Magical Superior gave his own life willingly to save us. It's nothing to cry about."

"I just wish I could have spoken to him one last time before he died," said Skimif. "As the God of Martir, I can do a lot of things, but one of the few things I can't do is bring mortals back to life. Once their souls are resting in the Heavenly Paradise, there's nothing any of us can do about them."

"He was getting old anyway," said Mom, who was not crying at all. "I'm sure he thought he'd lived a long enough life. I don't even know how old he was exactly. Old enough, I guess."

Though Mom's words were somewhat blunt, the sadness in them was obvious to Darek. He didn't bring it up, however, because he didn't want Mom bursting into tears on him again, which she had gotten into the habit of doing even after the Superior's funeral.

"I'm glad to see you've both received some closure," said Skimif with a smile. "But we will need to appoint a new permanent Magical Superior of North Academy, and soon. Jenur, how are you holding up?"

"Fine," said Jenur. "There's a lot more work and responsibility, even more than I had as a teacher, but so far

I've been able to handle it."

"Very well," said Skimif. "Since Chen died without a pupil, I will be coming back sometime within the next few months to determine the new Superior. I will talk with you about possible candidates, Jenur, so I expect you to have a list of students or teachers who you think would make a good permanent Magical Superior."

Jenur nodded. "Yes, sir. I will work on that list right away."

"Excellent," said Skimif. "Now, I must go. I am calling a meeting of the gods on World's End in order to discuss ways how we can permanently deal with Uron. The meeting is in a few weeks, as World's End is still under construction, but I have some things to do in the meantime that require my immediate attention. I'll be in touch."

Darek blinked and Skimif was gone, leaving Darek and Mom all by themselves in the Godly Chamber. What little warmth Skimif had brought with him also left, leaving the room feeling as cold as a freezer.

"So, Darek," said Mom, turning to face her son, "what are you going to do now?"

Darek scratched the top of his head. "What do you mean?"

"You're a graduate now, remember?" said Mom, a smile on her face as she playfully slapped his shoulder. "You don't have any schoolwork to do, and the Limitless Army has been disbanded. Don't tell me you forgot about your new freedom, did you?"

"Uh, I guess I did," said Darek. "There has just been so

much happening over the last month or so that it completely slipped my mind."

"I'll give you time to think about it," said Mom. "But you should figure out soon, because you should have started your new life a long time ago. You can go anywhere, do anything, and be whatever you want now."

Darek nodded. "Yeah. I know I was thinking of visiting those Xocionian Ice Monks, the ones who live on the edge of the Great Berg, and training with them to become an even better pagomancer."

"Sounds great," said Mom. "You should send them a letter first asking for permission to stay with them, though. Trust me, they don't like uninvited guests, even if you're a pagomancer like them."

"Yeah," said Darek. "I'll do that later, after I figure out what I want to do. It shouldn't be that difficult, especially since I am a pagomancer myself and all."

"I know it'll work out for you," said Mom. "But no matter where you go, I will make sure to let you know about whatever developments happen here. At the very least, I will let you know who the next Magical Superior will be."

"Of course," said Darek. "Now, why don't we go back up and tell the rest of the teachers about what Skimif told us? No reason to be down here anymore, after all."

"Sure," said Mom.

She turned and headed out the open door. Darek followed, but stopped when he thought he heard something behind him. He looked over his shoulder, but did not see anything except for the stone podium in the center of the

Chamber.

Must be hearing things, Darek thought, shaking his head as he resumed following Mom out of the Chamber. *I'm just tired after all of the excitement over the last week. What I need more than anything is a good night's rest.*

So Darek made sure to close the door behind them as they left the Chamber, though as he did, he thought he caught a glimpse of something glowing green inside. He didn't focus on it, however, and it was soon lost from sight as he shut the door firmly closed.

Chapter Twenty-Five

Durima lay on the tiny, ill-fitting bed in the small apartment she had taken as her own since the end of the Battle of World's End. Every now and then her eyes were drawn to the empty paint buckets and blank canvases scattered around the room, the remains of whoever had lived here before she had moved in.

She closed her eyes to try to sleep, but it was impossible. She kept thinking about Gujak. It had been a long time since she had lost a friend in combat like that. She could still recall seeing how broken his body had looked at the funeral, more closely resembling a hacked-apart tree than a dead katabans.

His death ... for the first time in Durima's life, she thought death was unfair. It was never a thought that she had seriously considered before. Having seen many katabans die during the War, Durima had not thought that death could be 'fair' or 'unfair.' Death just was, and if you wanted to continue to be, you had to avoid it no matter what.

She dug her claws into the pillow under her head, causing some feathers to poke out. *Gujak didn't deserve to die. He was a good katabans. Not a smart or wise one, maybe, but he was always helpful and kind. Much kinder than I was, at any rate.*

That was why she had had such a hard time sleeping over the past week. In her mind's eyes, she saw herself at Gujak's 'funeral'—which consisted solely of Durima, as Gujak didn't have any other friends that she knew of, aside from the female he had liked but whose name Durima still didn't know—taking Gujak's remains and asking Diog, the God of the Grave, to keep them safe in the ground. She had buried Gujak's remains just outside of World's End, under a tree that had resembled Gujak before his death, albeit vaguely.

She hadn't bothered to put Gujak inside a coffin, as humans were known to do to their departed ones. A katabans's body wasn't as important to them as a human's body was to a human. To the average katabans, their physical body was merely a tool used for interacting with the physical realm.

It's obviously an ineffective tool, though, if we have to die with it, Durima thought, pulling her blankets as tightly around her body as she could. *Someone should do something about that.*

"Maybe you should do something about that," said a voice from a dark corner of the room, near one of the blank canvases. "At least, that's what I'd suggest if I was an idiot."

Durima froze. She had heard that voice many, many times over the past week, always at night, when she was alone, trying to sleep. She never heard it while working with the other katabans to rebuild World's End. It reminded her of the Void, even though she knew that the owner of this voice wasn't a product of the Void.

"Go away," Durima said into her pillow. "I'm not in the mood to talk."

"You never are," the voice jeered. "But if we are going to tear down this whole world together, then I think we will need to talk, whether you are 'in the mood' or not."

Still talking into her pillow, Durima said, "What if I talk to the gods and tell them about you? What if I do that?"

"Of course you won't," said the voice, as if her suggestion had been a dumb idea. "You are Durima the Demon, hero of the Battle of World's End. In a single day, you went from being despised by all to being the envy of katabans everywhere. You were pardoned by Skimif himself. You wouldn't risk throwing all of that away, not even to get rid of me."

For the first time, Durima heard footsteps coming from that corner. She still kept her face in the pillow. She hoped that this was nothing more than a nightmare, a horrible, awful nightmare brought on by something in her subconscious that she wasn't aware of. It was the stress of everything, she told herself, just making her see and hear things that weren't even really there.

Durima almost believed it ... until she felt the cold, metallic fingers brush her fur, causing her to whip her head out of her pillow and look up at the figure standing above her.

His smile revealing snake-like fangs, his yellow eyes glowing as malevolently as ever, Uron said, "Now, Durima, why don't we have that nice, long talk you've been avoiding for the last week? There is so much to do if you are going to help me escape the ethereal and destroy Martir, after all, that I hardly know where to start."

Coming May 2015:

The Mages of Martir, Book #3:
The Mage's Sea

A month after the events of *The Mage's Limits*, Darek Takren receives an urgent notice from the Undersea Institute, the second most prestigious magical school in the world, asking him to come help protect the school from a mysterious new threat.

Thinking he is strong enough to handle it, Darek travels to the school to aid his friends there. Yet he soon finds himself hundreds of miles beneath the ocean's surface, separated from the gods, facing a darkness no mage has ever fought before, while Uron's servants operate in the background to free their master from his prison.

Worse yet, at the end of his quest beneath the sea lies a terrible fate for Darek ... a fate he cannot avoid.

Available May 2015 in ebook and trade paperback wherever books are sold!

About the Author

Timothy L. Cerepaka writes fantasy and science-fiction stories as an indie author. He is the author of the Prince Malock World series of fantasy novels, the Mages of Martir series of fantasy novels, and the science-fantasy standalone *The Last Legend: Glitch Apocalypse*. He lives in Texas.

You can read more and find links to the rest of his books at his website at http://www.timothylcerepaka.com.

The Mages of Martir, Book #1:

The Mage's Grave

Thirty-five-year-old Darek Takren always did his best to keep up with the demands of the prestigious North Academy, a magical school where only those with the drive to succeed are allowed to learn. Having lived in the school for his whole life, Darek Takren sees North Academy as his home, a sanctuary safe from the troubles that plague the outside world.

But when his best friend is injured in an unexpected attack on the school, Darek Takren struggle to uncover the attacker's identity leads him into a much deeper scheme that, if successful, will spell the end not only for the school, but for the whole world and the gods themselves.

And he may not have what it takes to stop it.

Buy *The Mage's Grave* in ebook and trade paperback wherever books are sold!